MOTIVE X

STEFAN AHNHEM grew up in Helsingborg, Sweden, and now lives in Denmark. He began his career as a screenwriter, and among his credits is the adaptation of Henning Mankell's Wallander series for TV. His first novel, *Victim Without a Face*, won Crimetime's Novel of the Year in Sweden, and became a top-ten bestseller in Germany, Sweden and Ireland. *Eighteen Below* was a top-three bestseller in Germany, Sweden and Norway. Stefan Ahnhem has been named Swedish Crime Writer of the Year and been published in twenty-seven countries to date.

AGNES BROOMÉ is a translator of Swedish literature. She holds a PhD in Translation Studies, and her translations include August Prize winner *The Expedition* by Bea Uusma.

THE FABIAN RISK THRILLERS

The Ninth Grave (Prequel)

Victim Without a Face

Eighteen Below

Motive X

MOTIVE X

STEFAN AHNHEM

Translated from the Swedish
by Agnes Broomé

First published in Sweden as *Motiv X* in 2018 by Forum
First published in the UK in 2019 by Head of Zeus Ltd

9 7 5 3 1 2 4 6 8

A catalogue record for this book is available from the British Library.

ISBN (HB): 9781786694607
ISBN (XTPB): 9781786694614
ISBN (E): 9781786694591

Typeset by Divaddict Publishing Solutions Ltd.

Printed and bound in Great Britain by
CPI Group (UK) Ltd, Croydon CRO 4YY

Head of Zeus Ltd
First Floor East
5–8 Hardwick Street
London EC1R 4RG

WWW.HEADOFZEUS.COM

MOTIVE X

PROLOGUE

24 August 2007

INGA DAHLBERG TRIED TO push her thoughts in a different direction. If only for a few minutes. Towards the cloudless August sky or the music in her headphones. Towards the fact that she didn't feel tired at all, even though she was on her third lap around the blue trail. Or towards Ramlösa Brunn Park, which was so lush and verdant it was impossible to see more than a few feet in any direction.

But like ants that inevitably find their way into the kitchen, her thoughts stubbornly kept returning to the plan she'd spent most of her waking time rehearsing these past few weeks. The plan that in less than three hours would be put into motion and change her whole life.

This time, nothing could be allowed to go wrong. The tiniest glint of uncertainty in her eyes or quiver in her voice and the game would be over. After all these years, she knew Reidar all too well. He would instantly exploit any crack in her façade, reclaim control and subjugate her until she obeyed him like a well-trained dog once more.

But whatever happened and no matter how he reacted, she knew how to act to make him pick up a pen and sign.

And as soon as that was done, she would grab her prepacked bag and head for the door.

She almost didn't dare to believe that in just a few hours, they would have left. And be on their way to Paris, of all places. The most romantic of cities. Finally, it was goodbye to all the sneaking and hiding. To all the coded text messages, to worrying about being caught red-handed any moment. Not to mention the stress of having to go to bed with the wrong man every night.

Tonight, they would be able to move about freely in public. If they felt like it, they would be able to sit down on a bench and just hold each other. She would be able to put her head in his lap and see both him and the stars at once.

She and her lover.

She tasted the word. *Lover*. She liked it. It sounded both tender and sinful. And how they had sinned. Both at his house and hers, in the shower and in the car. Not to mention on the secluded strip of beach by the Rå River, where they'd done things she hadn't even thought possible.

And now, that chapter was coming to an end. Soon, he would go from being her lover to her beloved. They were going to leave Copenhagen Airport behind, drink champagne toasts and enjoy that their dream had finally become reality.

But it hadn't come easy. At first, he'd been reluctant and refused to listen, and she had felt a bit like a whiny child. It was only after she presented him with an ultimatum, threatening to reveal their little affair to any and all interested parties, that he had come to his senses.

Threats and hysterics were not normally her style, but she couldn't go on living a lie indefinitely. And now, in hindsight, it was clear he was in exactly the same boat. Suddenly, he stepped in and took charge, making plans for how they were to proceed.

She'd picked Paris as their destination, but he had bought the tickets, splurging on business class even, and when she thought about how in just a few hours they would be sitting there, holding hands, enjoying their extra legroom, she had to pinch herself to make sure she was awake.

But there were still things left to be done. As soon as she got back, she would shower and tidy up. She'd already cleaned the windows and watered the plants. The sheets were freshly laundered; they just needed to be pressed, then she could make the bed. The boeuf bourguignon, Reidar's favourite stew, was simmering on the hob, awaiting final tasting and seasoning.

Since it was Friday, he would be having a pint after work and just before seven he would come home in his stinking work clothes, which she would put in the hamper for the last time while he took a shower. Then she would serve dinner and wait for him to join her at the table.

And somewhere around there, he would, if all went to plan, react to something being different and ask her why she wasn't sitting down and eating with him. Sooner or later, he would taunt her about her failed diets and how they only ever made her bigger, when the truth was that she had in fact lost twenty-six pounds since she'd started running.

But this time, she wasn't going to let him rant uninterrupted. In her calmest and most controlled voice, she was going to tell him that she was leaving him.

True, it would have been easier to simply leave a handwritten note on the table for him to find when he got home. But if she wanted him to sign the papers, she had no choice but to look him in the eyes and make him understand that her mind was made up and that they were never going to have dinner together again.

Depending on how his day had been, there was a risk that he might jump up from his chair and become physical. He wouldn't hurt her. Not then and there. But he was not above throwing his plate and maybe even overturning the table. A more likely outcome, however, was that he would let his fury pump into the outermost arteries of his face while he asked her, calm as a pressure cooker, where the hell she was planning to go. How she could be naïve enough to think for even a second that she could get by without him.

Then he would paint himself into a corner even more by reminding her of their prenuptial agreement and asking her if her dippy little brain had managed to forget that the house, the car and most of the furniture de facto belonged to him.

Reidar loved saying *de facto*. It was as if he felt it made him two feet taller and his statement unequivocally true and irrevocable. It was at that point, when he was at his most cocksure and adrenaline-filled, she would put the divorce papers down on the table.

At first, she couldn't understand why her earphones, which were connected to her tiny iPod, were suddenly yanked out of her ears. Even less what it was that pushed, almost cut, into both her breasts and in the next moment her collarbones and throat. It was only when she fell helplessly backwards that she saw the fishing line glint in the sunshine.

*

The sky was beautiful, as blue and cloudless as it had been all summer. Apart from her own pulse, she could hear the tweeting of all the thousands of birds hiding somewhere just out of sight. But wait, hadn't she been listening to music? And why was she lying flat on her back in the middle of the trail?

She grabbed her aching throat and sat up. The back of her head was pounding. She probably hadn't been out for more than a minute or two, so she should still have plenty of time to get everything done before Reidar got home.

She was mustering the strength to stand up when she heard twigs snapping behind her. She turned around and saw the dense foliage next to the trail swaying.

'Hello? Is someone there?' she called out, even though there could be no doubt of that. 'Did you put up this fishing line? Hello!' She was angry now and was not going to just let it slide, even though she didn't really have time for this.

But when a man materialized from the wall of leaves, her anger vanished and she realized she should get on her feet right now and run. But she couldn't. It was as though gravity was extra strong where she lay. The same thing seemed to be true of her gaze, which was inexorably drawn to him as he stepped out on to the trail, a shovel in his hand.

Despite the cloudless summer sky, he was dressed in a dark grey raincoat and wellies so high they went well past his knees, blending with his trousers. Under the pulled-up hood of his raincoat, he wore a ski mask that hid every part of his face except his staring eyes.

She filled her lungs to scream for help, but never got that far because she spotted the wristwatch on his arm as he raised the shovel above his head. It was an Omega Speedmaster, just like the one that had cost her almost a whole month's salary.

She could see nothing except darkness. The tape covering her mouth was so tight she was afraid her lips would be torn off if she tried to scream, while the rest of her face felt battered and swollen. Oh God, he must have hit her with the shovel.

She still couldn't believe he was the one who had put up those tripwires, knocked her unconscious and now stripped her naked. If not for the Omega watch. Or had she been mistaken? Maybe the salesperson had lied about how rare that particular Apollo edition was, to push up the price? Yes, that was clearly it. It had to be.

What difference did it make anyway? Whoever he was, she was lying here, curled up, naked, her eyes and mouth taped shut, with no idea what was coming. Or was it already over? Had he had his way with her and left her here?

She was still outside, that much she could tell. But she wasn't by the jogging trail in Ramlösa Brunn Park; through the tape covering her ears, she could hear the sound of running water.

She wasn't really lying down, but rather sitting slumped over on her knees with her feet behind her as if in some yoga pose, with both arms stretched out in front of her. It was an awkward position, especially given the hard, uneven ground.

She tried to understand what it all meant. Why he had left her naked in this particular position.

She felt almost no pain. In her face or her body. It was as though every part of her was numb. As though her body no longer belonged to her. He must have drugged her; there was no other explanation. Did that mean she had been unconscious for a long time? Maybe hours.

Regardless, she now had to get away and get home as quickly as she could and shower so she could have everything in order before Reidar got back. Hopefully, she wasn't too far from home, and with luck her facial injuries might not look too bad.

He would obviously want to know what had happened. But it made no difference. Under no circumstances was she going to allow this to derail the plan. The first step was to try to take off the tape without making her injuries worse.

But when she tried to lift her arm, pain immediately jolted through her. A pain so overwhelming she screamed straight into the tape. It radiated out from the back of her hand, spreading like lightning through her fingers and wrist and up her arm. Also, her hand seemed to be stuck. What had he done? She tried to move her other hand, but it was the same there. It hurt so badly her stomach turned inside out. She tried to move her legs, but the pain emanating from her calves was possibly even worse.

She was stuck. How had he... She couldn't even take it in. What kind of monster was this?

'Well, well, well. She's awake,' a voice said suddenly. 'About time.'

He was back. Or had he been there all along? And didn't it sound just like him?

'Come on. Get up. Up on all fours.'

She braved the pain and did as she was told.

'Excellent. See, you can do it if you put your mind to it.'

It sounded like him, it did. But it couldn't be him. Maybe it was just the tape over her ears that made it hard to distinguish details.

She could feel his gloved hand patting her on the hip, as though she were a horse being inspected. Then it started caressing her lower back and in between her legs.

'Now just make sure you don't collapse again. If you do, you're done, for real.'

It was him. There was no longer any doubt.

It was Ingvar. Ingvar Molander, the man she loved more than anything, who had finally agreed to take her to Paris in just a few hours.

Pain shot up from her hands and calves when whatever it was she was stuck to started to move. She screamed as loudly as she could, but all that came out was inarticulate mumbling.

A moment later, she started tilting this way and that and suddenly had to strain every muscle in her body to stay on all fours. Then she felt the cold water wash over her hands and her fate slowly began to dawn on her.

PART I

13–16 June 2012

Wherever you dig, it doesn't matter.
Get deep enough and eventually, it'll smell bad.

1

At first, Molly Wessman could only just make out the faint melody. But as the volume increased, she became ever more aware of the dulcet harp tones that meant she had five minutes to wake up and switch her brain on before it was time to get out of bed. Five minutes during which she could still keep her eyes closed and stretch.

She felt rested and hadn't woken up once during the night, which was incredible, considering the presentation she was giving to the board this afternoon. Normally, she would have tossed and turned all night and come to work a wreck. Now, by contrast, she was convinced the board was going to approve her proposal and give her permission to implement the last round of absolutely crucial cost-cutting measures needed to turn things around.

And she had her new sleep app to thank for it. Before, she had never slept more than four hours a night. She had been constantly exhausted and taken sick leave so often even those of her colleagues who had young children had started to wonder what she was up to.

In the end, her then manager had called her into his office and told her what she herself had been unable to see. That she was heading straight for burnout. Then he'd given her the number of a therapist and told her about an app that used sounds and different kinds of white noise to help the human brain to relax, thus improving sleep.

It had made all the difference and, what's more, only cost a fraction of what the therapist charged for a handful of pointless conversations. It had even given her enough energy to go back to the gym.

She took a deep breath, filling her lungs like she'd learned in yoga class, and reached out for the phone on her bedside table. But when she turned the alarm off, she noticed something strange the second before the screen went black.

She didn't actually allow herself to check her phone in bed. Turning her alarm on and off was the only exception to the rule. In her new life, her bed was a screen-free zone, along with the bathroom and the dinner table. And yet she couldn't stop herself from tapping in her PIN and unlocking it.

She looked at the screen again, uncomprehending.

To someone who didn't know what it normally looked like, it would probably have seemed neither odd nor unsettling. But she did know, and as she looked at it, she felt panic starting to build. Before long, the pressure around her chest was so tight she couldn't breathe.

Her first thought was that it wasn't her phone. But the chip in the top left corner from when she dropped it was there, and the home button glitched just like it had been doing over the past few weeks.

Everything was right.

Everything except the background picture.

It should have been a picture of Smilla, her brown and white Boston terrier who had died three years ago from hypertrophic cardiomyopathy. But it wasn't a picture of Smilla.

Instead, it was a picture of her.

A picture of her, sleeping in her own bed, wearing the exact same T-shirt she was wearing right now. Even the toothpaste stain from last night was there, which meant the picture had been taken in the past eight hours. So someone had broken into her flat.

Maybe it was just a technical malfunction. Or some new camera function she had accidentally activated when she went to bed. But no, the picture was taken from above. Someone must have been in her bedroom.

Was someone having her on? One of the many nocturnal guests she'd brought home over the past few years, who had made a copy of her keys? Though she had no idea how that could have happened without her noticing. Or was it a warning from someone at work that she'd been too ruthless there?

The questions bounced around like ping-pong balls. Granted, there were likely disgruntled people among the staff, but hard as she tried, she couldn't think of anyone who'd be twisted enough to do something like this.

Then it struck her.

What if he was still in the flat. What if he was standing right outside her bedroom door, waiting for her. Or what if he was inside the...

She tried to regain her composure and convince herself she was just overreacting. But she couldn't. Before she could dare to leave the bed, she would need something to defend herself with. Something other than her pillows and duvet. Maybe her bedside lamp. Though it was far from ideal, it was the only thing she could think of that was within reach.

As though she stood a chance of fending off some strange man. Who was she trying to fool? She, who froze when she saw a spider. Running over people in a meeting using factual arguments was one thing. Physical violence was something else entirely.

But what choice did she have? Did she have a choice at all?

She turned over as carefully and quietly as she could, grabbed the lamp with both hands and tugged. The two screws were ripped from their holes, pulling out white plaster dust that fell on to her black pillowcase. Then she unplugged it from the outlet, wrapped the cord around her left hand and grabbed the wall mount with her right before putting her feet down on the floor.

To the beat of her own pulse, she squatted down and peered under the bed. Apart from her scales and the box of sex toys on castors, there was nothing there, nor had she expected there to be. On the other hand, she still found it hard to believe someone had really taken a picture of her with her own phone.

She stood up, walked over to the cleaning cupboard on the left and threw the door open. But there was no one in there either. She swapped the lamp for the metal tube from the vacuum cleaner, then searched the wardrobes.

Whoever it was, he was not in her bedroom, which for some unknown reason felt like a relief. As though everything would be okay, so long as she stayed in there.

She did, in fact, have her phone and could call someone. Whoever that would be. Gittan, who used to be her best friend, hadn't talked to her since the Christmas before last, when Molly had had enough of her nagging her about getting herself together and finding a man to move in with. She had no one to confide in at work either. That would be taken as a sign of weakness, and right now, weakness was the last thing she could afford to show.

Granted, she could call the police. But they were probably going to start by asking if the perpetrator was still in the flat. So she gave the bedroom door a little kick, and it opened without a sound.

In fact, the whole flat was very quiet. Unusually quiet, now she thought about it. It was as though the traffic on Järnvägsgatan a few blocks away had stopped, and the old man in the flat below hers had turned off his TV for the first time ever. All to underline the seriousness of the situation and set her even more on edge.

She stepped into the living room and looked around. The corner sofa by the window didn't seem to have been moved. Nor the armchair, the bookcase or the dining table in the other corner. There wasn't really anywhere for a person to hide, which was why she managed to muster the courage to move into the hallway and from there into the kitchen.

It, too, looked exactly like it had when she left it the previous evening. The dishes from her dinner were in the drying rack and the bag with rinsed-out plastic containers lay tied up on the floor, waiting for her to carry it down to the bins on her way to the car. She only really opened the pantry door to be thorough.

Then she turned on the lights in the bathroom and saw that yesterday's knickers lay discarded in the middle of the floor and that the shower curtain around the bath was pulled closed. Had she left it that way or was someone lurking behind it?

She raised the vacuum tube, walked over and tore the curtain aside.

There was no one there.

Maybe she had accidentally snapped a selfie in her sleep after all. Somehow, that would be just like her. Since she got her new phone, which had a front-facing camera, she had taken so many selfies she had started receiving warnings about her memory running low. There must be a logical explanation, and she had probably blown everything out of proportion because she was nervous about her presentation to the board.

Her pulse was finally slowing down, and she could at last breathe a sigh of relief and put the vacuum tube down, pull off her T-shirt and step into the bath. Then she closed the shower curtain again, turned on the tap and waited until it had turned from freezing cold to a little bit too hot before switching the tap from bath to shower.

She loved that burning feeling on her skin and turned the heat up even higher. She could stand under that jet forever, and this morning she needed it more than she ever had. She felt her fear being rinsed away with each drop of water.

She turned the shower off and dried herself quickly before stepping out of the bath. The mirror had fogged up as usual, and even though she knew she shouldn't, she wiped the condensation off with her towel.

Suddenly, there was screaming, so loud it hurt her ears. It took her a moment to realize the scream was coming from her. It was instinctive and seemed never to want to end. At the same time, the fog was returning, making her reflection increasingly indistinct.

Even so, she could still clearly see that a large chunk of her fringe had been cut off.

2

IT'S YOUR *FAULT*...

The sound of the bullet, like an arrow whizzing through the air. A rushing sound preceded not by a bang but rather a vacuum that had been equalized. An innocuous, barely noticeable whoosh, like when you open a new tube of tennis balls.

All of this...

Matilda, his own daughter, only thirteen years old, who had clapped her hands to her stomach and stared at the dark red stain growing bigger and bigger on her top. Her uncomprehending eyes and ever stickier hands as she collapsed on the white rug.

Yours and no one else's...

Everything had happened so horribly fast, yet Fabian Risk could still play the entire course of events frame by frame.

His hands, which had finally been able to hold the gun, aim and pull the trigger. The blood that had pumped out through the hole in the perpetrator's forehead, along with the realization that it was all over. Too late. And finally, the words from his own son, which would haunt him forever.

That it was all his fault. His and no one else's.

Nothing could have been more true.

The bullet that had taken Matilda's life had come as a complete surprise, despite all the warnings. He had managed to miss them all and pushed on with his investigation into the identify-theft killers.

Now he was sitting here, in the first row, with Theodor on one side and Sonja on the other, dressed in the dark suit he hadn't worn since a young Danish murder victim, Mette Louise Risgaard, was buried in Lellinge Church two years earlier. This time, it was his own daughter trapped under all the flowers in the coffin that looked too short.

But the guilt was the same.

His.

Next to him, Sonja was crying, and on the other side he could hear Theodor fighting back tears. He, for his part, felt nothing. It was as though the roller coaster of hope and despair he had been on over the past four weeks, sitting by Matilda's bedside with Sonja, had used up all his feelings.

His daughter had been murdered right in front of him, but the only thing he could feel was the stress of not feeling anything. He couldn't even hear what the priest was saying. The words stubbornly bounced around, blending together despite microphone and speakers.

'You do know this is your fault, don't you?'

The voice was so quiet it was impossible to pinpoint its origin. He turned to Theodor. 'I'm sorry, what was that?'

'Are you deaf? I said this is your fault!' Theodor was speaking so loudly the priest faltered.

'Theodor, not now,' he finally managed. 'We can talk about it later.'

'What do you mean, later?' That was Sonja, and now the whole congregation was listening. 'It's already too late. Don't you get it? Our daughter doesn't exist any more.' She burst into tears.

'Sonja, please…' Fabian put his arms around her, but she slapped them away.

'Theo's right. This is all your fault!'

'Exactly. So don't try to blame us,' a third voice piped up behind him.

He turned around and saw it was his boss, Astrid Tuvesson, who was sitting together with his colleagues Ingvar Molander, Klippan and Irene Lilja. He was just about to ask her why she was sticking her nose in, but was interrupted by the sound of the organ launching into the next hymn, which made the rest of the congregation stand up and start singing.

He didn't have the energy to do anything but slump in his seat, letting his eyes rove across the people singing around him. Everyone except Molander, who, though he was standing up and moving his lips, was not singing. Rather, he looked like he was talking. Was he saying something to him?

Fabian pointed to himself. Molander nodded, leaned forward and whispered in his ear, 'Drop it.'

'Drop what?' Fabian didn't understand.

'You're never going to prove it anyway.' Molander stuck his tongue out and pretended to hang himself, then he let out a raucous laugh that was drowned out by the howling feedback of the priest's microphone.

The alarm penetrated deeper and deeper into Fabian's subconscious. A beeping tinnitus note that eventually coaxed him into opening his eyes and realizing he wasn't in a church at all, but in the hospital, in the room where he and Sonja had taken turns sitting with Matilda for the past month. The only thing he didn't recognize was the dirty white curtain hiding the bed where she lay.

He could hear voices from the other side and got up out of the armchair, tore back the curtain and saw one of the three nurses pushing and turning the howling machine's buttons. The other two stood on either side of the bed, checking Matilda's pulse and eyes.

'What happened?' he said, but there was no reply. 'Excuse me, could someone please tell me what the fuck's going on?'

The shrill beeping stopped, leaving an oppressive silence in its wake. The three nurses exchanged looks; Fabian tried to gauge whether they had the situation under control.

Then Matilda coughed and opened her eyes. His darling daughter, who had been gone for an eternity, finally looked around the room with enquiring eyes. And then tears started trickling down his cheeks. It was as though they had been waiting for this, longing to burst forth.

'Hi, Matilda. How are you feeling?' one of the nurses said with a warm smile.

Matilda looked at them without speaking.

'Matilda, you're awake.' Fabian pushed his way to the bed and took her hand. 'You're back. Do you understand? You survived.' He turned to one of the nurses. 'Right? She's going to be fine, isn't she?'

'Absolutely,' she said, to the nodded agreement of the other two. 'All her stats look good.'

'Did you hear that, Matilda? Everything looks good.' He stroked her cheek, but she turned her face away. 'Matilda, what's the matter? Didn't you hear? You're going to be all right.'

Matilda shook her head and looked ready to burst into tears at any moment.

3

Police detective Irene Lilja could still feel her nether regions throbbing when she pulled on her helmet, straddled her newly serviced Ducati and roared away over the speed bumps of the suburban street. The make-up sex was the only reason she hadn't left Hampus a long time ago. He was never more passionate and fiery, while at the same time tender and thoughtful, as after a fight.

But they fought too often. Whatever the subject, an argument was always simmering just beneath the surface. It made no difference that they were generally on the same page deep down; they always ended up each other's polar opposites, though this particular fight had been about something she'd been mulling over for some time.

It wasn't that Hampus was an alcoholic, but he had definitely dialled up his weekend drinking and those bloody cans of lager were well on their way to becoming a natural extension of his right arm whenever he wasn't at work.

It went without saying that her bringing it up had triggered him instantly and, before long, she had been seeing red too. But it was only after she started emptying beer cans into the sink, one by one, that he had let his true colours show.

He had never hit her, but last night, for the first time, she had been afraid. The rage in his eyes when she had defied

him and opened yet another can had made her give serious thought to leaving him once and for all.

The phone call had come just as she passed Kvidinge on her way to the Helsingborg police station. She had been looking forward to ten uninterrupted minutes with the wind and the Ducati as her only company. But when an eleven-year-old Syrian boy in Bjuv turned out to have disappeared without a trace on his way to school, she had no choice.

If only it had been a Swedish boy instead, she thought to herself as she passed a Prius that was insisting on staying just below the speed limit. Then she could have let the uniforms deal with it, certain the boy was simply cutting class to smoke cigarettes behind the bushes with a friend.

But ever since the brutal murder in their neighbouring municipality, Klippan, almost twenty years ago, racism and xenophobia had been on the rise. That time, neo-Nazi Pierre Ljunggren, sporting a swastika armband and carrying a butterfly knife, had spotted dark-skinned Gerard Gbeyo by chance, hunted him down and stabbed him to death in the middle of the street, completely unprovoked.

Obviously, neo-Nazis and right-wing extremists could be found in just about any part of the country, but the south was definitely the most afflicted. Local politicians could try as they might to gloss over the region's racist reputation and talk it up as the greenest part of Sweden. The general sense was that it was more like Sweden's brownest.

She couldn't agree more, and when Hampus had surprised her on her birthday with a signed purchase agreement for a house, she had flown off the handle. Granted, the house was in Perstorp, not Klippan, but to her, the difference was negligible. The mere thought of moving to a small town where people walked around in knee socks, flew the local Scanian flag and felt growing immigration was the biggest single threat to national security set her on edge.

Besides, she had never wanted to buy a house, and the fact that Hampus tried to pass off the down payment as a present for her only made her more pissed off. He had gone behind her back and shoved his own dream of a house with a garden down her throat.

Now, a year later, she was less negative about it, even though the red bungalow was still one of the ugliest houses she had ever seen. Hampus going berserk with the garden shears, making every last juniper bush look like a ball, a dash or, in a few badly botched cases, male sex organs, had done nothing to improve its appearance.

But the neighbours on their street were actually really nice, from her limited experience, and she had neither spotted any knee socks nor been forced to listen to any xenophobic nonsense. Perstorp was apparently one of the few municipalities that had seen a decrease in right-wing extremist activity in recent years. She didn't know what the situation was in Bjuv, though it was likely no worse there than in Sjöbo, Trelleborg or Landskrona.

Even so, it was with a knot of worry in her stomach that she turned on to Gunnarstorpsvägen and parked the Ducati on the corner of Vintergatan, across the street from the white three-storey building.

Everything was quiet, apart from a man in tracksuit bottoms and a black hoodie who was standing by a lamp post, speaking Arabic into his phone while waiting for the dog he was holding by the lead to do its business. Further down the street, a gangly man who had pulled up his trousers far too high crossed at the pedestrian crossing and hurried past a young mother pushing a pram, probably on his way to Bjuv Mall, which would win first place in a competition to find Sweden's most depressing place, hands down.

The stairwell was painted white and stippled in different colours, as though the painter had walked around flicking his brush at the walls. Probably to make it look just a little bit grimy even when it was freshly painted. There were about as many Swedish as foreign names on the board.

Moonif Ganem, as the boy was called, lived on the third floor with Aimar, Adena, Bassel, Jodee, Ranim, Rosarita and Nizar. At least, that's what the multicoloured fuse beads on the door said.

After a few attempts at ringing the doorbell went unanswered, she opened the door and stepped into a hallway full of a chaotic jumble of shoes and clothes. The sound of agitated voices mixed with sobbing was coming from a room further in.

The boy's parents were sitting by the table in the crowded kitchen. His mother, who was wearing a long dark dress and a purple headscarf that covered everything except her face, was crying, despite her husband doing his best to console her. On the table, among the cheese, butter, juice and other breakfast things, lay a number of tarot cards, and a baby was playing with a collection of measuring cups on a blanket on the floor.

'Hi. You must be from the police.'

Lilja turned around to see a woman in her sixties with short grey hair and energetic eyes enter the kitchen.

'Ingrid Samuelsson.' The woman held out her hand. 'I was the one who called it in. I live in the flat across the hall.'

'Then maybe you can tell me what happened.'

The woman exchanged a glance with the mother, who nodded. 'Adena came over to me at half eight, beside herself with worry. Moonif's teacher had just called to ask why he wasn't in school.'

'And why are you so sure something bad has happened? Is there a reason to believe he's not just playing hooky?'

'Hooky? I no understand,' the boy's mother said, trying to collect herself.

'She means to say Moonif might have not bothered going to school.'

The mother looked nonplussed. 'My Moonif would never... He is very good in school. It's his favourite.'

The woman nodded and turned back to Lilja. 'Adena's right. I know, because I used to be a teacher and I help him with his homework sometimes.'

'I understand. But it's only just gone eleven. Maybe he's with a friend and lost track of time?'

'The cards say different,' the boy's mother said.

'What cards?'

'The cards on the table.' His mother pointed to the card that showed a skeleton dressed in a tattered black monk's robe. 'They say something really bad happened.' She clapped her hand to her mouth in an attempt to suppress her sobs.

'Just so I'm sure I've got this right. You've called the police because those cards—'

'I'm sorry, but could I say something?' the older woman broke in, stepping in between Lilja and the boy's mother.

'Between you and me, I don't think anything serious has happened either. Just like you were suggesting, he often walks to school with Samira from next door. I've nothing bad to say about her, but she's full of ideas that have nothing to do with school, put it that way.'

'And yet you called the police. As though we have nothing better to do.'

'What was I supposed to do? She was beside herself. I mean, look at her.' The woman turned to the boy's mother, who was still crying softly. 'We give them a roof over their heads and money so they can get by. But how are we ever going to make them feel at home if we don't also give them some empathy? That was all I was hoping for. That someone from the police would come by and show that we actually care.'

Lilja felt embarrassed. Not by the woman, but by herself. Because she walked around thinking she was better than everyone else because she voted for the left-wing party and gave money to charity whenever there was something particularly terrible on the news. When it came down to it, she was just like everyone else, too jaded to care. 'You're right,' she said and nodded. 'I'm sorry.'

Then she took out her notepad, walked up to the parents and sank into a squat. 'My name's Irene Lilja. I work for the Helsingborg police and I will do everything I can to make sure Moonif comes home safe and sound.'

'Thank you so much,' the boy's mother said, wiping away her tears. 'Aimar is not so good at Swedish, but he is also very happy you are here.'

She exchanged a look with the boy's father and gave him a smile.

'First, I need a picture of your son.'

'I can get you one,' their neighbour said and left the kitchen.

'Can you describe what he was wearing when he left the flat?'

'He had red trouser and blue jacket with Spiderman buttons.'

'Did you notice anything different about him this morning when he was leaving?'

'No, everything was the same. He was so very good.' His mother shook her head.

His father said something in Arabic.

'Moonif didn't want to take the glass recycling. But everyone has to help, I told him. All Swedish people recycle and we should too. So he took them even though he didn't want to.'

'And this Samira, where does she live?'

'House across the street, first floor.' The boy's mother pointed.

'Did Moonif's teacher say whether she was in school or not?'

'I don't know. I was so very worried and didn't know to ask.'

Lilja nodded and put a comforting hand on the boy's mother's arm just as their neighbour returned with a school picture in which the neatly combed boy was dressed up in a nice white shirt, waistcoat and bow tie.

'He told me he picked out the clothes himself and dressed up so Samira would like him,' the woman confided quietly while the boy's mother lit incense sticks and started shuffling the tarot cards. 'I do think they're a bit infatuated.'

*

Lilja hurried down the stairs. She needed to get out and get some fresh air. Something about incense made her feel sick and when the boy's mother had started asking the cards about how she should proceed with the investigation, she'd decided to wrap things up.

All statistics suggested the boy would turn up of his own accord in the near future and that there would be an innocuous explanation for his disappearance. But she had promised to contact the school and Samira and her parents, and if that didn't turn up anything, she was going to contact the local Bjuv police and ask them to put out a missing person alert.

It was the sign that changed her mind. Instead of stepping outside and filling her lungs with fresh air, she opened the metal door that was standing ajar next to the stairs to the basement.

Recycling Room.

According to the boy's mother, Moonif had taken the glass recycling down there, so there might be some clue as to where he'd got to.

A fluorescent ceiling light turned on automatically when she stepped into the room and looked around. Apart from a number of big bins on wheels lined up against the grimy concrete wall, the room was as empty as it was silent. There was no one there. Even so, she decided to open the bins one by one and root around the cardboard, newspapers and sticky plastic containers.

But she could see no sign of a missing boy. Not until she turned on the flashlight on her phone and peered in under one of the bins. In that moment, it became clear she had made a grave error and that the boy's mother and her tarot cards had been right all along.

The tiny button with the blue and red superhero was lying on the floor only inches in from the edge of the clear-glass bin. Had it just come loose or had someone grabbed the boy violently? Someone who had happened to come in and see their chance. Someone who lived in the building.

She went back into the stairwell and walked over to the blue felt board with the names of the residents, while pulling out her phone and finding the number of Sverker 'Klippan' Holm.

'*Hi there. How are you doing? I heard you stopped by my lovely hometown.*'

'The jury's still out on whether it's really all that lovely. And while we wait for it to return its judgement, I need your help with doing a quick check of the people who live in this building.'

'*No problem. What's the address?*'

'Vintergatan 2A.'

'*Wow, that really is my old 'hood. Did you know I took my first trembling steps in a garden on Trumpetgatan 8, just a few minutes from there? It's obviously changed quite a bit, but—*'

'Klippan, not now,' Lilja broke in, realizing she should have called Astrid Tuvesson or Ingvar Molander instead.

'*All right, but just say the word if you need a suggestion for a good place to go for lunch. If you ask me, that would have to be schnitzel and—*'

'Klippan, for fuck's sake!' Her voice echoed all the way up the stairwell; it was an effort for her to lower it again.

'I think he might still be in the building, with one of the neighbours, and I don't know about you, but for my part, the last thing I want is to get there too late.'

'*Well, there's no convicted paedophile living there,*' Klippan said in a tone that did nothing to hide that he was insulted.

'Right now, a suspected one would be plenty,' Lilja said in a tone that did nothing to hide that she didn't give a flying fuck.

'*None of that description either. But there's someone on the second floor who works as a nursery teacher at the Sunflower not too far—*'

'Do you have a name? I need a name.'

'*Yes, if you would let me finish, his name's Björn Richter, he's thirty-two years old and lives, as far as I can see, alone with all his—*'

'With all his what?' Lilja's eyes were caught by a small rust-red stain on the wall by the stairs leading down to the basement.

'*Wait, I just have to check if it's him.*'

It wasn't that she'd failed to notice it before. She had just assumed it was one of the hideous stipples.

'*Yes, that checks out. Talk about creepy—*'

'Klippan, would you mind telling me what you're up to?'

But this particular spot was slightly bigger than the rest and smeared on one side, which indicated it had been made later.

'*Yeah, I just have to—*'

She couldn't be sure, of course. For that, she would need to take a sample and let Molander run an analysis. But it certainly looked like blood. If it came from the boy, the location of the stain suggested that they hadn't left through the front door, but rather walked down the basement stairs, which is why she continued down the steps and realized Klippan's silence was due to the fact that the call had cut out.

Just like the door to the recycling room, the basement door was ajar, and here too her mere presence was enough for the fluorescents to flicker to life.

Storage, a sign on the grey metal door on her left said. *Electrical Service Room*, read the one straight ahead. Both were closed and locked. To the right were two more doors, one of which was open.

On her way to it, she passed a board on which the residents could book laundry times by moving a personal lock around the available slots. Of course it was a laundry room, and judging from the sound, the machines were running.

The fluorescent lights turned on, and it was instantly clear to Lilja that the laundry room had the exact same layout as the one she and Hampus had had in Helsingborg before they moved to the house in Perstorp. Three washers in a row, a dryer, a drying cabinet and an old mangle no one used.

It was the furthest of the three washers that was running. It was significantly larger than the other two and would easily accommodate a large rug or three sets of bedclothes in one go. They'd had one just like it in Helsingborg and that in itself was a good reason to move back.

But she couldn't see any bloodstains or other signs of the boy. So she went back out into the hallway and continued up the stairs after deciding to have another go at the door leading to the storage units. Both the boy's parents and the lady next door should have keys to it.

But when she heard the washing machine rev up and start the spin cycle, she realized something wasn't right, so she stopped and turned to the booking board. It was Wednesday the thirteenth of June, but there was no lock in any of the slots under the number thirteen.

In other words, no one had booked the laundry room that day.

4

THE SILENCES BETWEEN THE signals in his headset were so drawn out, it felt like someone had deliberately reprogrammed the tempo just to make him stressed. On his first try two minutes earlier, they had eventually been replaced by the much more frequent beeping of the busy signal. But not this time. This time the silences seemed endless, and Fabian had to pace back and forth in the hospital corridor outside Matilda's room to stay calm.

'*Hi.*'

It took him a moment to realize it was actually Sonja answering and not just another beep. 'Sonja, guess what's happened.'

'*Uh, what?*'

'Just sit down and listen, because this is—'

'*Fabian, I'm sorry, but I'm in the middle of something here. Is it important?*'

'You might say. You see—'

'*So, are we done here or what? I actually really do have to get going,*' he heard Theodor sighing in the background.

'*The only thing you have to do is stay right here.*'

'*What the fuck for? If you and Dad are just going to—*'

'*Theo, you're staying here!*'

'Sonja, what happened?'

There was a long, tired sigh. '*Okay, so I went into his room to collect dirty laundry and change the sheets, my God, you should see the state of it. Anyway, I found two...*' She broke off. '*Look, I think it might be better to talk about this later... Just tell me what's so important.*'

Fabian's mind went blank, but he remembered why he had called as soon as he turned to look into Matilda's room, where the staff were busy running tests and noting down stats. 'She woke up. Matilda finally woke up.'

'*What, she did? But... Really? How is she?*'

'Good. I think. At least, considering the circumstances. That's what they're telling me. That her stats look good. But if you ask me...' He faltered, trying to find the right words.

'*What, is she not okay? Fabian, what are you talking about?*'

'Maybe it's just me, but—'

'*I'll be right there.*'

Before Fabian had realized that Sonja had hung up, one of the three nurses came up to him.

'We're going to leave the two of you alone now. If you need us, just call.'

Fabian nodded and waited until everyone had left before shoving the phone in his pocket and going back into the room to see Matilda, who was lying in her hospital bed, staring into space. He cleared his throat but got no reaction. He tried again, but it was as though she was oblivious to his presence. If not for the fact that she blinked from time to time, he would have been convinced something had gone terribly wrong.

He pulled one of the chairs up to the edge of the bed and sat down. 'Hi Matilda,' he said, taking her hand as cautiously as he could so as not to disturb the canula taped to the back of it. 'How are you feeling?'

After a while she turned her head, as though it required a great effort, and looked at him exactly the way she had when she first woke up. Her eyes were as calm as they were serious and in every way completely different from the lively, inquisitive Matilda he knew. And that was what worried him.

There was no doubt it was Matilda lying there in the bed. The problem was that it didn't feel like it was her looking back at him.

'I don't know if you have any idea what happened to you,' he said, with no real plan of how to go on.

'I remember,' she said, and he instantly understood that her memories of that night were as detailed as his own.

The perpetrator must have broken in and surprised them, her and her friend Esmaralda. Maybe they had been down in the basement, performing one of their séances. Then he had forced them up into the living room and placed them on the sofa next to Sonja to wait for him to come home.

He, her own father, who should have been her rock, but who was so often absent, even when he was home. He, who once he did show up hadn't reacted to the first warning, but only realized it was serious when it was too late. When the bullet had already ripped through her stomach, causing her to collapse, bleeding, on the rug.

'I'm sorry,' he said, instantly regretting it. How could she ever forgive him?

'You did your best,' she said faintly. 'How can anyone do more than that?'

Had he heard that right? Was this really Matilda?

'That's not the problem,' she continued, seemingly about to drift off.

'No? Then what is? Matilda, tell me so I can help you.'

'There's nothing you can do. Like so many other things, it's not up to you.'

'I don't understand. What's the matter? You're alive, and according to the doctors, you're going to make a complete recovery.' He took her other hand, too. 'The fact that you're lying here, talking to me, is amazing.'

'That's exactly it.' She heaved a sigh and closed her eyes. 'I survived.'

'Matilda, listen to me. You don't think that I... Me and Mum, who's on her way over here right now, by the way, we love you more than anything. I hope you know that. Nothing can make us happier than that you're all right and still with us.'

Matilda shook her head. 'It's not that.'

'Okay.' He tried to catch her eye, but this time she was too weak. 'Can you tell me what it is?'

'You wouldn't understand.'

'At least give me a chance.' No matter how much he wanted her to confide in him, he could understand her silence. He was the one who had let that monster over their threshold.

'Greta.' The word was whispered so quietly, Fabian was unsure he had heard it right.

'Greta?'

Matilda swallowed. 'Water... Is there water?'

Fabian hurried over to the sink, filled a plastic cup with water from the tap and helped her drink it. 'Just so I'm definitely getting this right. This Greta. Is that the ghost you and Esmaralda were talking to in the basement?'

'Not a ghost.' Matilda shook her head. 'A spirit. She said someone in our family's going to die.'

Fabian had thought those Ouija board games had been a bad idea from the start, but now the whole thing had become such a fixation it was the first thing she thought about when she woke up. 'But, sweetie, you survived.'

'But if it's not me… Then one of you—'

'Matilda, listen to me. What happened to you should never have happened. It should never even have come close to happening. But it did, and neither you nor some spirit calling itself Greta is to blame for that. I am. I'm the one who—'

'It's no one's fault,' Matilda breathed. 'She just knows what's going to happen, that's all.' A single tear trickled down her cheek.

Fabian hugged her. 'Matilda, it's not that I don't understand that you're worried. Quite the opposite. You clearly believe in these things. But try to think of it as a dream.'

'Dream? It's not a dream.'

'In a way, that's exactly what it is. The problem is you can't see it. And how could you? How could you know you're actually just asleep?'

Her eyelids were growing heavier. But her lips were moving; to hear what she was saying, he leaned in closer.

'What if you're the one who's asleep.'

5

Even with the fluorescent lighting, the flash of the camera lit up the room enough for Lilja's shadow to be sharply drawn on the white concrete wall behind her. During her six years as a violent crime investigator, she'd seen quite a few things that would have given the most hardened person insomnia. Everything from bodies that had lain undiscovered for so long the coroner had to scrape them off the floor to bodies that had been so badly tortured it hurt just to think about what they'd been put through.

Bodies.

That was how she had always thought of them when she was in the coroner's office or, like now, at the scene of a new murder. *Bodies*. Not people with real lives, dreams and hopes, but lifeless bodies. A conglomeration of atoms that together formed a mass. All to push down her feelings, keep a clear head and think logically.

But she couldn't any more. The shock had sunk its claws deep enough into her that the only thing she could manage was to sit on a stool, staring at the wall. Granted, the wall wasn't completely uninteresting; apart from her own shadow, which reappeared every time one of Molander's assistants snapped a picture, there were a few scratched-in swastikas and racist slogans, though they seemed too time-worn to have anything to do with the murder.

This was the first time she had ever found herself unable to look at a murder victim. Even for a moment.

Because it wasn't just a body. It was an eleven-year-old boy with a beautiful name, a jacket with Spiderman buttons, friends and a life just waiting to be lived. A boy who had been asked to carry a bag of empty bottles to the recycling room on his way to school. But he had never made it there. Instead, someone had attacked him and dragged him down to the laundry room.

She was still having a hard time taking in the details of the course of events, although the words coming from Molander and his two assistants were clear enough.

'Ingvar, listen, I don't know. I have a bad feeling about this.'

'Fredrik, if you want to talk about your feelings, call your therapist or your girlfriend,' Molander said, sounding as dry and matter-of-fact as ever. 'We have to focus on getting this body out. Or are you saying we should leave him here and just let the residents go about their business?'

'No, but I honestly don't know how we're going to do it. Not without damaging the body even more.'

'All right.' Molander sighed; his knees cracked when he squatted down. 'My suggestion is that we simply disconnect the whole drum and open it up with an angle grinder. What kind of feelings do you have about that?'

'So this is where you're hiding.'

Lilja turned around to see Klippan in the doorway, and everything suddenly felt a little better.

'How are you getting on?' he continued as Molander's assistants removed the back of the washer and went to work with screw guns.

'For obvious reasons, getting him out is a bit tricky.' Molander got back up and stretched out his back. 'But it's dogged as does it.'

'What do you mean? Is there more than one reason?' Lilja said, primarily to show that she had snapped back in.

'You can say that again. To be exact, about fifteen hundred rpms.'

'Bloody hell...' Klippan shook his head. 'It's enough to make you start wondering where this world's heading.'

'*Start* wondering? I've been wondering that for years,' Molander said as he helped to lift out the cylindrical drum and place it on a blanket. 'I suggest you cut this, and then it should be fairly straightforward to break it into two halves. Okay?' His assistants nodded and Molander turned back to Klippan and Lilja. 'This is going to be loud, so if you have anything else to say, you'd better spit it out now.'

'Have you found anything of interest?'

'Not really. A few specks of blood, probably from the boy. And fingerprints from at least fifty people, some in peculiar locations if all you're doing here is laundry.'

'Two uniformed officers from the local station are going door to door, collecting prints from the residents,' Lilja said. 'We'll have to wait and see if there's a match.'

'So you suspect one of the residents,' Klippan said.

Lilja shrugged. 'I just figure it would be easier for someone who knows the common spaces, knows there's a washing machine of that size here and has a key to get around.'

'He might just as easily have used the victim's key,' Molander said. 'It would be more interesting if we found fingerprints that didn't match any of the residents'.'

'And that swastika.' Klippan pointed to the wall behind Lilja. 'It's several years old.'

'That doesn't necessarily mean the motive has changed,' Lilja said.

'Well, maybe we should refrain from rushing to conclusions.' Klippan looked around.

'True, and we should keep all investigative avenues open and blah blah blah. But forcing a little boy who has fled from Syria into a washing machine, what is that about if not racism and—'

The sharp sound drowned out everything else as the angle grinder cut through the metal of the washing machine drum in a shower of sparks; the only thing Lilja and the others could do was cover their ears and wait until the assistants had finished and were carefully prising the drum open.

Having been unable to make herself look at all, Lilja was now unable to tear her eyes away from the boy. Judging from the face alone, it almost looked like nothing had happened to him. The closed eyes visible behind his matted black hair made it look more like he was asleep.

But Moonif wasn't asleep.

Like an oversized foetus, he was curved from the neck down, his spine describing an almost perfect circle. His legs were bent too, but the wrong way, stretching out on either side of his head, down past his shoulders where his feet were pressed against his body.

The sight cut through every layer of experience and made everyone in the room pause. Even Molander seemed taken aback. No one said anything. Klippan, who up until now had stayed calm, stood gaping, making it look like the heart-rending scream was coming from him.

But it wasn't Klippan's voice, it was a woman's.

Lilja was the first to react. She rushed over to stop the boy's mother from throwing herself on top of her son. But the woman fought her like it was a matter of life or death; it was only when Klippan stepped in that they managed to overpower her and usher her out of the laundry room.

'Calm down,' Lilja bellowed.

But the boy's mother continued to kick and flail her arms about in her attempts to get free of Klippan and refused to give up until several minutes later.

'There now,' Lilja said as Klippan slowly relaxed his hold on her.

The woman collapsed in tears, which after a while morphed into a kind of wailing lament.

'There now,' Lilja said again, and gently put her arms around her.

'She's in shock, she needs something to calm her down,' Klippan said, breathing heavily and wiping sweat off his brow. 'I suggest Helsingborg Hospital. Then we can interview her later this afternoon after the meeting.'

Lilja nodded and started leading the woman down the basement corridor.

What had made them crawl out of their lairs? Was it the sweet smell of death that had drawn them? Or was the blue-and-white police tape fluttering in the wind enough to make people crowd in and gawk at them curiously?

It had only been an hour and twenty-five minutes since Lilja arrived. At that point, the area had been virtually deserted. Now she estimated the crowd to be at least forty people, who followed every step she and Klippan took as they guided the boy's mother to the car.

Luckily, she could see no telephoto lenses, which indicated the media hadn't yet joined the fray.

'This is the victim's mother, Adena Ganem,' Lilja told one of the two uniformed officers, and she was about to instruct them to take the woman to Helsingborg Hospital when she spotted a gangly man in the crowd on the other side of the police cordon.

He was watching them, but that wasn't what made her react and have Klippan take over. Everyone was watching them. Nor was it that she'd seen him crossing the street when she first arrived, nor his slightly unusual appearance with jeans pulled up high, blindingly white trainers and a beige jacket with the Sweden Democrats logo on the chest.

It was his smile.

A smile that made him, unlike everyone else, positively beam with glee. Could it be the perpetrator was still here? It wouldn't be the first time. Contrary to what people might think, it was not at all unusual for a perpetrator to stay near the scene of his or her crime to keep an eye on the police's work and, first and foremost, other people's reactions.

She took a few steps towards the man and noted an instant shift in his expression. The smile was still there, but the worry in his eyes was new, as was the nervous twitching below his left nostril. A second later, he had melted into the crowd.

He wasn't going to get away. Under no circumstances was she going to let him disappear, she repeated to herself as she stepped over the police tape and pushed her way through the gaggle of curious onlookers.

And there he was. Two hundred feet further on, she saw him dash across the car park next to the mall, looking back over his shoulder to check if she was following him. She was. But only to see him run straight out into Norra Storgatan.

The old orange Volvo coming from the left didn't have a chance to stop in time.

The collision itself was no more than two dull thuds when the man landed on the bonnet and then hit the windscreen before disappearing on the other side of the car, which skidded to an abrupt stop.

Lilja raced across the car park and saw the door on the driver's side open and an older man climb out, take a few steps and then bend down over the body, which was likely lying right next to the car. She could only hope he had survived. There was almost nothing worse than criminals who chickened out and went off and died before they could be made to explain their motives.

That didn't seem to be the case here, though, since she could see him getting to his feet on the other side of the car's grimy windows. She was almost there now and would have no trouble catching him.

But instead of pressing on across the street on foot, the man got in the driver's seat and started the car, leaving a foiled Lilja and a bleeding car owner in his wake.

6

TWENTY-FIVE DAYS, FOURTEEN HOURS and forty-two minutes.

Astrid Tuvesson, chief of the Helsingborg crime squad, tore her eyes from her wristwatch and left her office. Another eighteen minutes and she was going to break her old record. Granted, she wasn't actually sure about the exact minutes. But according to the doctor, it was good to fix on a concrete time at this early stage, so you could count the hours. He'd also claimed things would get easier with each passing day, and that eventually it wouldn't even occur to her to count. But in that, he had been wrong so far.

The truth was, she thought about it all the time. Every day, every hour and every minute was a struggle. The thirst, that damn thirst. How she loathed never being allowed to quench it. And the doubt that had just grown stronger with each passing day. Was it really worth it? But that wasn't something she told anyone, not even her sponsor.

When she got to the kitchen, she poured the freshly made coffee into a thermos, took the milk out of the fridge and continued towards the conference room. This was her third day back at work since she nearly died of hypothermia a month ago, locked in a chest freezer by the same terrifying pair who shot Matilda. She actually had another six weeks of sick leave to take and could have stayed home, reading one of the many books awaiting their turn, or finally getting into *The Wire* that everyone was always going on about.

But the thirst, in combination with the loneliness, had left her climbing the walls and she was convinced she would have fallen off the wagon if she'd stayed home any longer.

Here, she had colleagues to distract and keep an eye on her. She had a role to fill and things to do, even though she was not above admitting she'd been looking forward to a few relatively quiet work weeks, especially since they were still recovering from their latest case, by far the most difficult murder investigation she had ever been in charge of.

But apparently, that was too much to hope for.

They hadn't even had time to take down and archive the pictures from the various murder scenes – the victims lined up as though it had been a case of crimes against humanity – before it was time to put up new pictures. This time from a laundry room in Bjuv, where the perpetrator had forced his victim into an oversized washing machine and set it to rinse and spin.

As if that wasn't enough, Fabian's desk was glaringly empty and would not be filled again until after the summer when he came back from his sabbatical. It was a long time, and she could already sense they were going to miss his ability to think outside the box.

At the moment, there was no indication this was anything but a stand-alone act of madness. Besides, serial killers were very rare in Sweden. But in light of the fact that the country had been rocked by not one but two cases involving serial killers in the past two years, she was not about to jump to conclusions. That both investigations had ultimately ended up on her desk made her even less likely to make a snap judgement.

She gathered up the pictures from the previous murder investigation, put them in a folder and had started erasing the notes on the whiteboard when Klippan arrived with his laptop.

'Molander says we're going to have to start without him. He's still in Bjuv.'

'Has he found anything?'

Klippan shrugged. 'You know how taciturn he can be when he's in that mood.' He poured himself a cup of coffee and sat down. 'Hey, where's Lilja?'

'I'm sure she'll be here any minute. How have you got on? How's the mother doing?'

'Probably as well as you or I would be if our children had just been centrifuged to death in a washing machine.' He shook his head. 'I spoke to the hospital. They've given her a tranquillizer, and if you ask me, we're not going to be able to interview her any time soon.' He fell silent and sipped his coffee. 'I don't usually have any trouble understanding why some people act the way they do. I find it's usually possible to understand even the most heinous crimes if you really put your mind to it. But this. This is not just sick. It's fucking incomprehensible.'

'That attitude is hardly helpful. You know that as well as I do,' Tuvesson replied just as Lilja entered, carrying a folder.

'Sorry I'm late. What did I miss?'

'Nothing. We've only just started, but I think we're trying to understand the motive.'

Klippan nodded mutely.

'What do you mean, trying? If this is not an open and shut case of racism and xenophobia, then what?' Lilja poured herself a cup of coffee.

'And what are you basing that on, other than that the victim was from Syria?'

'We're talking about Bjuv. Isn't that enough said?'

'It really isn't.' Klippan turned to Lilja. 'Bjuv is not particularly racist compared to some other municipalities.'

'Klippan, I didn't mean to offend you. I know you grew up there and I'm sure things were different back then. People watched *Roots* and *The Onedin Line*, and an ice cream cost no more than two kronor. Today, they're carving swastikas into the walls and spit on other people on the bus if they are of a different skin colour.'

'That was actually in Staffanstorp, not Bjuv.'

'Fine, but I'll give you one guess where that old git was from.'

'Listen, I don't think we're going to get much further on this right now.' Tuvesson walked over to the whiteboard wall. 'Let's instead agree that xenophobia and right-wing extremism is one of several possible motives.' She wrote it on the whiteboard wall. 'What others could there be?'

'Irene, didn't you say something about him dating someone called Samira, or whatever?' Klippan said.

'No, I said he had a bit of a crush.'

'What are you getting at?' Tuvesson said.

'I was just wondering if it could be honour-related.'

Lilja was about to sip her coffee but instead she put her cup back down and turned to Klippan. 'Are you saying Samira's family forced an eleven-year-old boy with a pre-adolescent crush down to the laundry room and shoved him into a washing machine?'

'Irene, I find this every bit as horrible as you do. But why not?' Klippan shrugged. 'I'm no expert when it comes to honour-related violence.'

'No, but you're walking on very thin ice, just so you know.' Lilja shook her head and drank her coffee.

'Better than being blind.'

'I'm sorry, who's blind?'

'Irene…' Tuvesson tried to intervene, but she couldn't get a word in.

'No, I want to know what he means. Because if it turns out we have a closet racist on the team, I want him as far away from this investigation as possible.'

'You're certainly not shy about throwing the word racist around. If it's not the perpetrator, it's me,' Klippan said, pointing to himself. 'But since you're asking, I'm neither racist nor xenophobic. I'm just not as hysterically politically correct as you, which means I can see things for what they are. Which may not be such a terrible thing, considering the work we do.'

'Like what? What is it you see so much more clearly than I do?'

'Facts. Facts that even though they hurt are still bloody facts. Like how, these days, it takes refugees an eternity to break into the job market. That foreign-born individuals are over-represented when it comes to both assault and lethal violence, not to mention rape and robbery. That most of the organized crime networks in this country are based primarily on ethnicity. I could go on, but if I know you, you've already stopped listening.'

'Oh no, I'm all ears, I'm just still waiting for a connection to Moonif Ganem and his family.'

'To see it, all you have to do is a quick search of the criminal records and decide not to close your eyes.' Klippan turned to his laptop. 'Take the son, Bassel Ganem, for example. He's been reported for assault on three separate occasions and most recently sexual assault as well. Or his older brother Nizar, who has been convicted of both a mugging and criminal possession of a gun. Granted, their father, Aimar, has never been reported or charged with anything, but on two occasions the neighbours have called the police, citing loud fighting and screaming. That's the boy's family. What Samira's family looks like, I have no idea. And no, none of it is proof that we're dealing with honour-related violence. I just don't think we can disregard it before we've even looked into it.'

'Of course we'll look into it.' Tuvesson wrote down *honour-related* next to *xenophobia*. 'Klippan, can you handle that?'

'Absolutely,' Klippan said, avoiding Lilja's eyes.

'Listen.' Tuvesson put down the marker and turned to them. 'Given what's happened, it's no wonder our reactions are slightly different. But in order to work together, we have to be civil and think of our different perspectives as an asset.'

'Absolutely. I'm sorry,' Lilja said and turned to Klippan, who nodded.

'And now for something completely different,' Tuvesson continued. 'How's our stabbing victim doing?'

'Ralf Hjos. Well, from what I'm told, he's doing okay given the circumstances. No vital organs were damaged. Apparently, the wound was not too deep.'

'And the car? Any trace of it?'

'Not yet,' Klippan said. 'But I've put out an internal alert for both the model and the plates, so if he's still driving around, it shouldn't be long before we nab him.'

'I think we should ask the public for help, too.'

'All right,' Klippan made a note.

'Oh, right, I completely forgot.' Lilja took out a police sketch of the man she had been chasing. 'Here he is.'

'When did you have time to have that done?' Tuvesson looked at the sketch.

'Just now. That's why I was a bit late. I figured it was best to get it over with before I forgot that creepy smile.'

'Is it Gudrun Scheele?'

'Of course it's Gudrun Scheele,' Klippan said, studying the drawing.

Gudrun Scheele was a half-blind former art teacher in a wheelchair who had retired almost twenty years earlier and happened to live in the same nursing home as Klippan's mother. He had noticed her collection of portraits on one of his visits and asked if she would consider helping the police out, and the rest was history.

As usual, she had used coal, and with the help of deft shadowing and more or less strongly marked lines managed to draw a face that leaped off the page. It was miraculous every time.

'I was in the hospital anyway, so I just had to swing by Bergalid on my way back here,' explained Lilja, who seemed to have calmed down. 'And your mother says hello. She was bitter, to put it mildly. Apparently, you promised to stop by and set the channels on her TV over two weeks ago.'

Klippan shook his head. 'I was there yesterday.'

'What, does she have Alzheimer's? Why haven't you said something?' Tuvesson exclaimed.

'Because that's not what's wrong with her. What she does suffer from is selective memory lapses. Whenever it suits her.'

'What do you reckon? Should we make this available to the public along with the car?' Lilja asked.

'No, let's hold off, keep it internal for now. And see what the prosecutor has to say.'

'Is it Stina Högsell?'

Tuvesson nodded just as her phone started ringing. 'Speak of the devil... Hi, Stina. Give me two seconds, I'm just wrapping things up here. Klippan, you know what to do, and Irene, I suggest you start mapping the racist elements of Bjuv.'

'Absolutely. I was going to pay a visit to the Sweden Democrats.' Lilja downed the rest of her coffee and stood up as Tuvesson left.

'Why the Sweden Democrats?' Klippan said.

'Because they're both xenophobic and racist. And because the guy wore a jacket with their logo. Any other questions I can answer for you?'

7

LILJA TURNED ON TO Blekingegatan and thought to herself that it, and the adjacent Hallandsgatan and Smålandsgatan, must have been planned with a view to creating a whole new suburb on the edge of Bjuv. Yet another grand political vision that had, apart from a few scattered houses, amounted to nothing more than a sea of vacant lots where the grass now had free rein to grow.

Yeah, right, we don't have the space to accommodate more immigrants, she thought and put the Ducati's kickstand down outside the Sweden Democrats' office, which was located in one of the detached houses.

Sievert Landertz, the party's chairperson in Bjuv, represented everything she hated about the Sweden Democrats. A polished surface concealing an odious inside. His neat tie, which gave him the air of a dependable banker. His perfectly trimmed stubble, not to mention his deceivingly friendly smile.

Landertz was one of the so-called reformers the national leader, Jimmie Åkesson, had roped in in his attempt to normalize and build public confidence in the party. He had also purged the most rabid racists and severed the party's ties to Nazism, by pretending they had never existed.

The strategy had unquestionably been successful. Despite

one scandal after another, the Sweden Democrats were on their way to becoming the country's third-largest party.

The door opened before her fingertip had even left the doorbell. And by Landertz himself, no less.

'Hello. Irene Lilja from the Helsingborg police.' She held out her ID.

'Yes?' Landertz inspected the ID. 'What is this regarding?'

'As you may have heard on the news, we're in the middle of a murder investigation.'

'Yes, I heard about that Syrian boy. Just terrible.' Landertz shook his head, and she had to suppress an urge to slap him and let him know she wasn't fooled by his dissembling. 'But I don't see how I can be of help.'

'I'm sure I can explain that to you. But I think it would be better if we discussed this inside.'

'Could it possibly wait? I'm in a bit of a rush and I'm afraid I don't have—'

'Should I take that as you trying to obstruct a murder investigation?'

'No, not at all. Not at all. I'm just—' He broke off with a sigh. 'Could we make it quick? As I said, I don't have—'

'How long it takes is up to you,' said Lilja, who was already pushing her way in.

It looked exactly as she had expected. A number of offices and a kitchen to the right, the latter with a table on which a half-eaten kebab was sitting next to a Coke Zero.

'Why don't we go to the kitchen,' Landertz called to her as he locked the front door.

But Lilja had no interest in seeing the kitchen. She wanted to get into his office and therefore walked off in the opposite direction until she spotted his name on a sign next to one of the doors on her left.

'Or we could head into the conference room on your right!'

Lilja opened the door and looked into Landertz's office, which faced the street. The walls were white, the office furniture beige, and plastic potted plants were scattered around the room. 'This will do fine,' she said as she continued to look around.

The walls were covered in posters of Jimmie Åkesson and Swedish landscape photos with blue-and-yellow flags waving against a clear blue sky; the books were neatly organized by size in the bookcase. Among them were the *Law of Sweden*, a few books about integration and ten or so historical titles about the First and Second World Wars.

The two Ikea armchairs by the window looked so new she had to wonder whether anyone had ever sat in them. The same was true of the tidy desk. A computer screen in the middle. A desk topper and a leather pen holder, a letter knife and a document folder, also in matching leather.

In other words, not a swastika as far as the eye could see. Not even a few doodled Nazi symbols on the underside of the desk for her to find.

Nor had she expected any, though she had to admit she was a bit disappointed. The Sweden Democrats was a party founded by Nazis, there was no question about it. But Åkesson and his friends had been so effective at rooting out the extremists, only polished populists like Landertz remained. In a way, that was almost worse. At least before, it was clear where they stood. Now, people suddenly thought they were voting for a mainstream party.

'Okay then, what can I do for you?' said Landertz, who had entered the room.

'As I mentioned, it's about the murder of Moonif Ganem.'

'Yes, that much I've gathered. I hope you're not insinuating that I or one of my colleagues had anything whatsoever to do with it.'

'Not at all. Insinuations are not my thing. So just to be clear, no one suspects you of personally shoving him in the washing machine.'

'Good.' Landertz glanced at his watch. 'You see, both I and the party feel it's fundamentally important to recognize that all people are equal, regardless of their skin colour or ethnic background.'

'Oh, really? Well, I guess you learn something new every day.' Lilja emphasized that with an exaggerated smile. 'That must mean, then, that you are as eager to see the murderer caught as I am.'

'Of course I'm eager. I just don't understand what I can—'

Lilja cut him off. 'You can start by having a seat.' She waited until he had obeyed. 'Let me tell you where things stand. We suspect the perpetrator is one of your party members.'

'Okay.' Landertz checked his watch again and then folded his hands and started twiddling his thumbs. 'I'm not sure what to say to that. I obviously hope you're wrong.'

'Does any particular member spring to mind, off the top of your head?'

'No, who would that be?'

'I don't know. But there's always bad eggs whose views make them stand out and who might even resort to violence to make themselves heard.'

'I'm sure there are. But unfortunately, that's not something I would know anything about. And I have to say it's a bit rich that the first thing you do when the victim turns out to be of foreign extraction is to come here and cast aspersions on our members. I can tell you that our membership base consists primarily of ordinary, upstanding citizens who pay their taxes, recycle and stay home at night watching TV.'

'Proper model citizens, in other words. Not a xenophobic racist among them.'

'No, just people who are concerned because the country they helped build is buckling under the weight of mass immigration, which is only going to get worse. That I can promise you. This is nothing compared to what lies ahead.'

'Since you're apparently so pressed for time, maybe we should try to stick to the subject. Which is to say, your members. And to save even more time, I suggest you just give me access to your membership lists, so I can go through them at my leisure.'

Landertz looked uncomprehending. 'But that's impossible.'

'Where there's a will, there's a way.' She allowed herself another smile.

'But you have to understand. It would be political suicide to give you details about our members.'

'Assuming that it gets out, which is entirely up to you. Either you give it to me now, and it stays between us. Or I go to the prosecutor and come back with a warrant and a press gaggle who will see to it that there are really big headlines about how the supposed law and order party is in fact obstructing a police investigation and protecting a murderer.'

Landertz nodded and took a deep breath before meeting her gaze. 'All right, then go talk to your prosecutor.' The smile spreading across his face revealed that he had not only called her bluff, but that he was relishing it.

And he was right. The membership lists of political parties were among the hardest things to get access to, and in this case they didn't have close to the evidence required.

Landertz stood up, looking at his watch. 'As I mentioned, I'm short on time and I have to ask you to—'

'Do you recognize this man?' Lilja showed him the police sketch and noted an instant reaction. His eyes stared fixedly a little too long before proceeding to scan the rest of the drawing. 'You know who this is, don't you?' It was only then she realized that in her wildest dreams, she hadn't imagined he would.

'No, sorry. I've never seen him before.'

'Are you sure? Look again.'

Landertz sighed and pretended to have another look. 'No.' He shook his head and handed the sketch back. 'I'm sorry, but I have no idea who that is.'

'Something made you react, though, didn't it?' If he denied it again and shook his head, she could be completely certain he was lying and then she was going to make damn sure there were headlines.

She almost didn't notice the sound when the window behind her broke. It was only when Landertz screamed and threw himself to the floor that she realized something serious had happened. When she turned around, one of the Ikea armchairs and part of the rug and curtain were on fire.

Fuck, fuck, fuck, she had time to think as she jumped over

Landertz on her way out of the office. 'Get that fire under control,' she called as she ran towards the door.

'No, wait! The fire extinguisher! You have to get the fire extinguisher!'

'And where is it?'

'In the kitchen! Hurry, before it's too late!'

Lilja turned back to the kitchen and immediately spotted the red fire extinguisher sitting in the middle of the room, still in its packaging. She quickly unwrapped it and hurried back to the office, where Landertz was busy trying to smother the flames by stomping on the rug and beating his suit jacket against the armchair and the wall, to which the flames had spread.

'Step aside,' Lilja shouted and started spraying foam at the fire, which went out in seconds, leaving behind an acrid, sooty smoke.

She put the fire extinguisher down on the floor and quickly established that there was only very limited material damage. Some new glazing, a lick of paint and a new rug and armchair and it would look just like before. And yet there was no limit to how dire the consequences might be.

The flames had died, buried under foam.

The fire, on the other hand, was likely to spread.

8

For the first time in a month, Fabian went over to his record collection at the far end of the living room and let his eyes rove across the rows of CDs. He owned more than four thousand albums, and that was after weeding out a quarter when he'd left Stockholm over two years ago.

For a whole month, silence had been the only sound he could bear. It was the longest he had gone without music in his whole adult life. A month ago, a madman posing as an art collector had nearly destroyed their family. He had manipulated Sonja, becoming her muse and lover, and inserting himself into all their lives. Then he shot Matilda right here, in Fabian's own living room. Fabian couldn't bear to think about what might have happened next if he hadn't been able to get to a gun himself. And now, with those events playing on a loop in his mind, it was as though his brain was unable to take anything else in. Not even Brian Eno's soaring escapism had worked. The smallest note had given him an instant headache.

But now, his spirits had finally returned. He felt like doing things again. Getting up in the morning and defying the rain with a jog through Pålsjö Forest. Cooking a nice meal and gathering the family around the dinner table.

What with Matilda's waking up and her doctors' assurances that she would be able to go home by the end of the week, he could finally feel firm ground under his feet again. True, she had been acting a bit strange and they were far from done discussing what had really happened to Theodor that night. But somehow, he felt sure everything would be all right. That at the end of the day, there was nothing to prevent them from becoming a proper family once more.

The only X in the equation was Sonja.

Until now, there had been no room or time for her or him. Much less for them. If there even still was a *them*. Not too long ago, Sonja had informed him she wanted a divorce. A concept he had kicked around himself on and off for the past few years, which she had now appropriated.

The warning signs had been there all along. Flashing red, blaring like klaxons at the end of a bad disaster film. And yet he had been caught off guard by her suddenly being ready to move on without him, declaring in the same breath that there was nothing he could do about it.

But where Sonja stood now, after her lover had revealed himself to be an impostor, he had no clue. He didn't even really have a clear idea of what had been done to her in the hours before those horrifying events in their living room.

He did suspect the worst, based on what little he knew. For instance, her expensive art piece 'The Hanging Box' had, for some reason, been confiscated by the police as evidence. Then there were the bruises all over her body, which he had caught a glimpse of at one point, when he forgot to knock before entering their bedroom. And it wasn't just the bruises. What he saw was a broken woman who seemed to have lost all faith in herself.

At least when it came to her art, if she was to be believed, she was done with it. She was nothing but a talentless bluff anyway. It wasn't something they'd talked about, just something that had trickled out in throw-away subclauses; whenever he brought it up, she shut him down. Just like she had every time he'd broached the subject of their future.

The past few weeks had, granted, been one long crisis, and all their energy had been spent sitting by Matilda's bedside; maybe everything would change now that she was coming home. Maybe things would finally return to normal.

He pulled out *Gone to Earth* with David Sylvian and studied the cover. It was the second CD he'd bought, after *Sign o' the Times* with Prince, and he could still remember playing it for Sonja in the flat they'd just moved into together.

She had liked it so much she had improvised a dance, and he had turned it up so loud their neighbour had eventually rung their doorbell. But they had simply stuffed the bell with cotton wool and opened another bottle of wine. As though no problems would ever find them, so long as they stood united.

He connected the speakers in the kitchen, turned the volume up and started making dinner to the sound of old Japan members Steve Jansen and Mick Karn's sophisticated groove in 'Taking the Veil'.

Since Sonja was spending the night with Matilda, it was just him and Theodor. Which meant last night's leftover pasta, fried crispy in olive oil with some finely sliced garlic, a few chopped tomatoes and olives, would have to do.

The door to his son's room was closed, as usual, so he tapped it gently before opening it, only to see Theodor startle violently in his desk chair and quickly turn on the screensaver on his laptop.

'Dinner's ready.'

'All right, I'll be right there.'

Fabian nodded and turned to leave but stopped mid-motion. 'Actually, what are you up to?'

'Nothing. I said I'll be right there.'

Fabian remembered his own teenage years all too well. Like Theodor, he had been prone to shutting himself up in his room, driven by an overwhelming need to be left alone, always worried about the door being thrown open at any moment by a curious parent.

Now he was the annoying parent who put his foot in the door and asked endless questions. The difference was that in this case, it wasn't about a packet of cigarettes or a few well-thumbed porn rags, but the gun Theodor had brought home. About his broken nose, which even though the surgery was weeks ago, was still swollen and a yellowish blue colour. About what had really happened before he came home that night almost four weeks ago.

He had tried, but his attempts had amounted to nothing more than a few awkward enquiries met with an explanation that, in short, Theodor had been walking, completely innocently, through Slottshagen Park on his way to meet up with some friends when he was attacked and robbed at gunpoint. A man had walked by with his pit bull, and that had made the perpetrators drop the gun and run. Theodor had decided to bring the gun home to give to Fabian, the only part of the story that wasn't clearly a bald-faced lie.

'It sounded like you and Mum were fighting today,' he said halfway through dinner. 'She said something about finding two—'

'Yes, she found two packets of cigarettes.' Theodor sighed. 'Like that's worth making such a fuss about.'

'No, I suppose it's not, though you're well aware of how your mother and I feel about you smoking. But there's something else you and I need to talk a bit more about, and that's that gun of yours.'

'Why? I've already told you everything.'

'You have, have you?'

'Um... yes. You've asked me, like, a thousand times.'

'Then how come I feel I've had no answers?'

'How should I know? Don't ask me.' Theodor shrugged and helped himself to seconds.

'As a matter of fact, that's exactly what I'm doing, and just so you know, I'm not going to give up until you tell me exactly what happened that night.'

'But I already did. What is it you want to hear?'

'The truth. How about giving that a go? Like who those robbers were, and why they went for you of all people. If there even were robbers. What friends you were going to meet, you who always claim you don't have any friends. And this man with the pit bull, who you can't give a description of either. Was he masked, too? And why didn't he react when you ran off with a gun in your hand? The truth, Theodor. It's all I ask.'

'The truth?' Theodor got up from his chair, bright red in the face. 'You want the truth? Huh? Do you?' His voice was breaking. 'The truth is you should thank your lucky fucking stars I brought the gun home that particular night. If not for the gun, you would have had to watch your family get executed, one after the other. But maybe that would have been better, because then I wouldn't have had to put up with this shit.'

Fabian had to agree. Even though Theodor's words stabbed like knives, every last one of them was unequivocally true.

9

THE LOCKSMITH CHECKED THE new locks were working properly, handed the keys over to Molly Wessman and packed up his tools. After he disappeared down the stairs, she entered, closed the door behind her and stood waiting in the dark for a minute before turning the lock and latching the chain she normally never used.

It didn't make her feel safer in the slightest. Her beloved flat down in Norra Hamnen, which had cost a fortune, had turned into a place that made her feel nothing but pure, unadulterated fear. But what was she supposed to do, she thought to herself, and continued in through the hallway without turning on the lights.

The living room looked the same, and yet not.

Nothing felt like hers any more. The TV, the sofa, the shelf with all her things. The whole flat. It was as though she had entered a strange country, having ignored every sign asking her to turn around and go somewhere else.

The problem was that she had nowhere else to go.

Pretending to be working late and sleeping on the sofa in the office would never work. Her colleagues would instantly know something was amiss.

Staying over with friends was not an option either. Having gone through her entire contact list, she had been forced to conclude it didn't contain a single person she was close enough with to just turn up on their doorstep.

Friends had never been her thing. She had always preferred to be alone. Especially to being in a couple. She couldn't see the point of chafing against the same old person every day, while the sex grew more and more uninspired. Especially when she had a sex life most people would cut off their little finger for.

At least, that's what she'd had, in that previous life that had ended the moment she woke up this morning, a previous life that was increasingly feeling like a dream. Like a before and an after, in which loneliness was breaking her down like an injected poison.

She went into the room that had been her bedroom and saw that it looked exactly like when she left it to go to the office. She'd tried to act normally there. She'd hidden her shorn fringe under a wide headband and after a few minutes' practice in front of the bathroom mirror, she'd been able to squeeze out a tolerably natural-looking smile.

But it had been like walking around in a bubble in which her paranoid thoughts bounced back and forth, drowning out all other sounds.

She had seen guilty people everywhere. Janne in IT, who undoubtedly knew how to hack into a phone. Anders who had been fired, but who still had a month left of his notice period. Not to mention all the people who had already been let go. At every turn, she had been greeted by false smiles, searching eyes and insinuating questions about how she was feeling.

Panic had crept nearer and nearer and peaked in the middle of her presentation to the board. Suddenly, she'd been unable to get a word out, had just stood there in silence, watching everyone's confused looks. In that moment, she'd felt convinced the perpetrator was there among the sea of suits and ties. Someone who despite all the cutbacks was unhappy with the numbers and wanted her gone at any cost.

You could have cut the silence with a knife before she finally regained her ability to speak and finished her presentation. After that, she had cancelled the rest of her meetings, left the office and gone straight to the police to file a report.

Unfortunately, they hadn't taken her seriously. Instead, they had forced her to give a urine sample and implied that she must have been under the influence of alcohol or drugs and had simply forgotten bringing a visitor home.

But she had insisted and told them about the people at her work who might hold a grudge on account of the restructure. About how certain members of the board had always been against her. About the old man working the tills at her local supermarket who always undressed her with his eyes and insisted on rolling out his mat right next to hers at yoga practice.

They hadn't listened, though, and in the end, she had got up and left the police station without another word. She hadn't even got to telling them about all the people she met at the clubs she liked to frequent.

And somewhere on her way out of the police station, it had dawned on her that checking in to a hotel, staying over at the office or forcing herself on some distant acquaintance wouldn't make any difference. Because no matter how much she wished to, this wasn't something she could run away from, since the perpetrator could be just about anyone.

10

ACCOMPANIED BY SYLVIAN'S SOARING 'Sunlight Seen through Towering Trees', Fabian grabbed the handle of the Pavoni portafilter while simultaneously raising the lever to release the hot steam. Then he lowered it again in a slow, smooth motion and soon the coveted drops of espresso began dripping into his cup.

His conversation with Theodor was far from over. The whole thing was so inflamed it was impossible to bring it up without it leading to a big row. At the same time, he had to admit that Theodor was right. If he hadn't had a gun tucked into the waistband of his trousers on the night Matilda was shot, they would all likely have been killed.

He added foamed milk to his coffee and took the cup with him to the basement, where he continued past the washing machine, the drying rack and the storage shelves behind the curtains he had hung up as a partition.

On the other side a completely different, cosier vibe prevailed. The lighting was warmer and rag rugs made from fabric scraps covered the floor. A threadbare armchair stood next to a floor lamp and an end table in one corner and along the outer wall stood his old desk with the avocado-green drawers, which for some reason he just couldn't part with. A larger screen was connected to his laptop; in the pool of light from the floor lamp lay an unused notepad,

Post-it notes of various hues and a clutch of newly purchased pens.

Sonja had offered him her studio in the attic. But he was convinced she would eventually find her way back to her art and had instead set up his study at the back of the basement. Not to pay bills, surf the web and order takeaway. No, this was a space dedicated to one single purpose. The investigation of his own colleague, Crime Scene Technician Ingvar Molander. It was an investigation their late colleague, Hugo Elvin, had initiated and secretly worked on for years. Now the responsibility was Fabian's.

Had Elvin's unexpected death just over a month ago not in fact been suicide but rather the inevitable consequence of having come too close to the truth about Molander? If so, Molander had not only killed his best friend and colleague, he had also arranged a detailed staging of it as a tragic suicide prompted by Elvin's supposed long-standing gender dysphoria and secret desire to become a woman. He had not only strung him up by a swag hook, he'd put him in a dress and made his face up with lipstick, powder and eye shadow.

But that was far from all. If Elvin was to be believed, two years ago, in the middle of an ongoing investigation of several murders among a group of old classmates from Helsingborg's Fredriksdal School, Molander had drugged Ingela Ploghed from that same school class, surgically removed her uterus to mimic the perpetrator's signature method and left her to bleed to death in Ramlösa Brunn Park. She survived, only to jump from a building a few weeks later.

And even that wasn't the end of it. Three years before that, Molander had supposedly also been behind the so-called Ven Murder, in which a certain Inga Dahlberg was attacked while out running, also in Ramlösa Brunn Park, and subsequently raped and sent naked down the Rå River with both hands and feet screwed to a wooden freight pallet.

These crimes, and potentially more, Molander had allegedly committed while they were all working together. While they were having each other over for dinner, visiting crime scenes and at times working such long hours they spent more time with the team than with their own families.

And yet no one but Elvin had suspected him, and since the methods used had drawn inspiration from their ongoing investigations, suspicion had naturally fallen on other perpetrators instead of the real serial killer, who was sitting at the same lunch table and sipping coffee from the same thermos as them.

It was almost too much to take in, and the most convenient explanation was that Elvin had simply been wrong. Somehow, the whole thing just seemed too far-fetched. At the same time, he couldn't think of anyone who'd be better placed to produce a crime scene with misleading clues than Molander.

He had considered involving Tuvesson so there would be someone for him to bandy ideas around with, but had in the end decided that her alcohol problems constituted too big a risk. True, she had managed to stay sober for a month now, but it was anyone's guess how long it would last. If she were to fall off the wagon, it would only be a matter of time before Molander found out. Besides, he was the one who had found the key to the desk drawer where Elvin had kept his secret investigation.

It had already been two years since the day he borrowed Elvin's desk during the investigation of the Fredriksdal Murders. A spilled cup of coffee had made him peer under the desk, where he spotted a key taped to the underside. A key that turned out to unlock the biggest of the three desk drawers. He had opened it out of sheer curiosity and realized it was full to the brim with folders and thick envelopes.

He had closed the drawer again without examining the contents and not given it a second thought until he bumped into his old colleague from Stockholm, Crime Scene Technician Hillevi Stubbs. As it happened, she knew both Elvin and Molander because the three of them had done their police training together. She had laughingly dismissed the claims that Elvin had wanted to undergo gender reassignment, which put the entire suicide theory in a new light.

Fabian put his coffee cup down and went over to the whiteboard, which was completely empty, waiting to be filled with pictures, hunches, clues and theories. He didn't want to put any of Elvin's conjectures and clues up; he was going to fill the board with his own conclusions and facts he had verified himself.

From now on, this was his investigation. Not Elvin's. And as though to underline that, he put up one of the pictures he'd taken of his former colleague after finding him hanging from his own swag hook, wearing a floral dress, earrings and bright red lipstick.

The first step was to examine every last detail relating to Elvin's death to determine whether there was the slightest possibility Molander was behind it. He pulled out his phone, found Stubbs's number and waited while it rang.

In the best of worlds, he would come to the conclusion that Elvin really had taken his own life and that everything was a big misunderstanding. That way, no one ever had to find out what he had been up to in his basement, and they could all continue working together like the close-knit, efficient team they were.

'*Well, well, if it isn't Fabian Risk.*' To Fabian's great relief, Stubbs sounded almost happy.

'I hope this isn't a bad time.' He knew no one who disliked being called up more than Stubbs. During their years together at the Stockholm Police, she'd always been the one to call if she wanted something. For him, and everyone else for that matter, contacting her had always been out of the question.

'*Of course it's a bad time. What other kind is there?*' she said without any trace of irony in her voice. '*But I'd be lying if I said I was surprised, though I had expected your call straight after the funeral. And speaking of which, what happened to you? You just disappeared.*'

'I don't know if I had time to tell you, but my daughter, Matilda, was seriously injured. It was actually so bad we didn't know if she was going to pull through.'

'*That's right, you did mention something like that. How is she now, then?*'

'She's getting there, and she's actually being discharged this weekend.'

'*Thank goodness. It must have been awful.*'

'You can say that again. And you? Enjoying Malmö? Or do you miss fast-paced Stockholm?'

'*As you know, they're pretty trigger-happy down here, so we keep ourselves busy. But correct me if I'm wrong. You didn't call to catch up, did you?*'

'Maybe you remember talking to me about Hugo Elvin at the funeral?'

'*Yes, you mentioned something about him being depressed and wanting a sex change.*'

'That's the official explanation, though I have to admit I feel more and more doubtful, personally.'

'*It sounds insane, if you ask me. I don't understand where they got that from. Did he leave a suicide note?*'

'No, but there was quite a bit of women's clothing in his flat. Knickers, bras, all sorts. And he was wearing make-up and a dress when we found him. His browsing history was full of various sites with information about gender reassignment and—'

'*Okay, that's enough,*' Stubbs broke in. '*That Hugo was a woman trapped in a man's body is nonsense. Suicide, maybe. He was in his head a lot even back when we knew each other, and if I'm not mistaken, it's not something that eased with time. But that stuff about his gender identity doesn't hold water. It's as likely as me going vegetarian.*'

'But how can you be so sure?'

'*Let me make myself absolutely clear. Both during and after our student days, Elvin and I were more than just friends, and without going into salacious detail, let me simply assure you that the last thing he doubted in this life was his manhood.*'

11

SEEN FROM ABOVE, THE area between Klippan and Kvidinge was nothing but an open wound in an otherwise beautiful landscape. Instead of a harmonious jigsaw puzzle of fertile fields in various shades of green and rapeseed yellow, the area looked like someone had deliberately attempted to destroy that idyll.

Since Kvidinge Stone Crushers first broke ground there in 1963, the company had continued to dig deeper and deeper into what was now an area the size of fifty football fields. Voices had been raised to stop the devastation and replace the quarry with something else. But so far, none of the suggested fairgrounds, music festivals or shopping malls had been given the green light.

For that reason, Kvidinge Municipality had, while waiting for a proposal everyone could get behind, opened a temporary refugee reception facility in one of the many pits the diggers had left in their wake.

The facility, which consisted of a number of interlinked two-storey barracks whose first floors were served by external staircases, occupied only a fraction of the pit. Even so, it housed one hundred and eighteen asylum seekers, most of whom were on their way to bed when the four-wheel pickup slowly rolled down into the pit with its lights off.

The three men wore dark clothes and their soft trainers made practically no sound in the gravel. They clearly knew exactly what they were doing; they fanned out and surrounded the facility, each carrying a jerry can.

As though psychically linked, the three of them undid the caps of their cans almost simultaneously and started dousing the wooden façade, which had only received a simple primer coat. The glistening petrol ran down the wooden cladding and either dripped on to the gravel or was absorbed by the concrete plinths.

The window sills were given an extra dousing, and with the help of nail guns equipped with silencers, the front door was bolted to the frame with seven-inch nails. Then the three men each took out a lighter.

The entire operation took no more than three minutes.

The rest was chemistry.

12

It was over two hundred years old, made of white marble in the shape of an icosahedron with a surface consisting of twenty equilateral triangles. Twenty sides, each with an engraved number, apart from the number ten, which had been inscribed with an X.

Since the gilding of the numbers had long since worn off, a stranger would have to touch the grooves or hold the dice up to the light to see the result. He, by contrast, had long since learned to recognize the different sides from the patterns in the marble.

It was by far his most valuable dice and as always when he picked it up from its bed of cotton wool, he was struck by how heavy it felt in his hand. But then, that seemed fitting for the dice he used for the first roll, which set everything else in motion. Without it, nothing.

He cupped his hands around it and began to shake it.

Two or higher. That was all he needed to be allowed to take on a new mission. Which of the nineteen sides ended up face-up determined the number of days, counting from today.

The only number he mustn't roll was one. If, against all odds, that side faced up, he would have to abort the whole thing and none of what he had prepared and looked forward to would happen. The fun would be over before it had really begun.

The police hadn't even found the body from his mission in Klippan yet, the first in what he hoped would be a long, beautiful string of missions.

It had been several weeks already, and so far there had been no reports of the dead old man. Apparently, no one missed him. And then there was the fact that the body was in a long, hermetically sealed plastic tent and therefore didn't emit the foul reek of death.

The cocoon-like tent had been his response to the dice's chosen *cause of death: asphyxiation*, and it had proved to be a trickier endeavour than he'd originally thought. After a number of failed attempts, he had settled on a construction consisting of two bicycle wheels fastened to either end of a six-and-a-half-foot-long steel pipe.

The unconscious man lying on the living room floor hadn't measured more than five feet ten inches, so he had fitted nicely between the wheels, and he had secured the man's neck, arms and legs to the steel pipe with various straps.

Then he had put a big, transparent plastic bag over one wheel and the man's head and another one over his feet and lower half. He had taped the openings of the two bags together with duct tape. The bicycle wheels at either end had kept the plastic reasonably taut and after three layers, he felt satisfied it was airtight.

Pleased, he'd sat down on the floor and waited. It wasn't something the dice had ordered him to do. He had fulfilled its requirements and was mostly just curious how the man would react when he woke up from the blow to the back of his head, and how long it would take for the carbon dioxide to make him pass out again.

The old man had woken up much sooner than he had expected and as soon as the first shock wore off, he'd tried to free himself, until he realized that was impossible. Then he had proceeded to writhe around instead, in a desperate attempt to punch a hole in the plastic cocoon.

Luckily, he'd had the foresight to tape up the man's mouth, so he wasn't able to bite, though in all honesty the original purpose of the tape had simply been to spare him from having to listen to his screaming. Because scream is what he'd done, almost continuously, until he had passed out again, three and a half hours later.

The whole thing had been a tremendous success. He'd been so fired up, he'd needed a twenty-kilometre run before being able to relax in a hot bath.

The day after, he'd taken out his icosahedron, champing at the bit to get started on his next mission as soon as possible. But for some unfathomable reason, he had rolled an eighteen. It was the third highest number and meant he had to sit back for eighteen full days before striking again.

But now, it was finally time again, and he had been shaking the icosahedron for so long the cold marble had warmed to the same temperature as his hands. This was a step he didn't mind drawing out. It was like the seconds before an orgasm, and once the die was cast, there was no turning back.

He closed his eyes, opened his hands and heard the dice land on the felt table cover with a light thud, roll a few inches and come to a stop.

A two.

He exhaled and immediately felt his pulse slowing. Once again, he had avoided rolling a one and being forced to abort the whole thing. Instead, he now had a new mission as early as Saturday and had to shake his head at the way the dice insisted on challenging him. But this was exactly what he wanted, and if he could just focus on the present and ignore everything else, he would probably be able to pull it off, even with such a tight deadline.

The next roll was to determine the unlucky victim. For this, he brought out his collection of six-sided, anodized aluminium dice and shook one of them in his hands.

This was a so-called pre-roll to determine how many dice he was going to use. In this particular case, the option was one or two, which meant one, two and three represented using one dice and four, five and six represented two.

A five.

He picked up another dice and shook both for a good long while before releasing them on to the felt.

Two twos.

He stood up and walked over to the map of western Skåne that was pinned to the wall. The map formed a perfect square, which in turn was divided into 144 equal, numbered smaller squares. Twelve along the horizontal axis and twelve along the vertical. In the top left corner was Mölle, where he used to take the bus as a child to swim in the sea.

In the top right corner was Bjärnum, which he felt sure was as unexciting as it sounded. The bottom left corner was Copenhagen, which despite its peripheral position constituted the natural centre of the region. In the bottom right corner was Sjöbo; without knowing why, there was something inside him that wished the dice would take him there.

But not this time, since column four lay much further west. He picked up one of the dice to perform another pre-roll.

A three.

In other words, the number of squares going down was going to be decided by one dice. He picked the dice back up, shook it again and eventually rolled.

A four.

He put his finger on the square and instantly saw it was Hyllinge; when he zoomed in on the area in question on Google Maps, he realized the dice had chosen Hyllinge Mall. It was a location completely devoid of residential buildings, which meant he would have to go there and let the dice choose its victim at the scene.

That was going to be a new experience; he would have liked to have had a bit more time. But he wasn't worried. On the contrary, he was looking forward to it. Besides, he already had an idea for how to make his selection.

13

TWENTY-SIX DAYS, EIGHT HOURS and twelve minutes.

Tuvesson scratched underneath her watch strap and waited for Lilja, Klippan and Molander to take their seats around the conference table. 'All right, let's get cracking,' she said, even though the coffee thermos was only just being passed around. 'Since we all have our hands full and are one man short to boot, I figured we'd try to keep it to thirty minutes. So let's keep it brief. Okay?'

Lilja and Molander both nodded and shot Klippan a glance.

'Why is everybody looking at me?' Klippan exclaimed. 'And speaking of one man short, shouldn't we call Mr Risk and ask him to come in? After all, he's been home for over a month now.'

'I would really prefer not to.'

'And given what he and his family have been through, he surely needs his time off more than ever,' Lilja said, shaking her head.

'So when's he supposed to be coming back?' Klippan sipped his coffee.

'Sometime after the summer, end of August,' Tuvesson said. 'We're just going to have to get by without him. And since we're on the subject, I'd like to remind you that I'm checking into Tolvmannagården to start my twelve-step programme this afternoon. I'll be gone for five weeks.'

'Five weeks?' Molander exchanged looks with the others.

'I know, it's an awfully long time, but what choice do I have?'

'And if we need to get in touch with you?'

'I'm sorry, you can't.'

'Hold on just one minute,' Lilja said. 'What do you mean, we can't? We're in the middle of a—'

'Look!' Tuvesson held up her hands defensively. 'I know the timing couldn't be much worse. Believe me, I want nothing more than to stay here and work with you. But I have to take this seriously and put my health first. I hope you can understand that.'

'Of course,' Lilja said, nodding along with the others.

'Good. Then I think we should get going with—'

'Just one more thing,' Lilja broke in. 'Who's in charge of the investigation while you're gone?'

'Me, of course,' Klippan said. 'Who else?'

'I don't know.' Lilja shrugged. 'Maybe someone who's a bit more—'

'Klippan's right,' Tuvesson cut in. 'He's going to lead the investigation, and I assume you will all make sure there is as little friction as possible.'

'A bit more what?' Klippan turned to Lilja.

'Nothing. Forget it. It's going to be great.'

'All right, let's start with the missing Volvo. Any sign of it?'

'Nothing yet, unfortunately,' Lilja said.

'My money's on it being dumped somewhere outside

Bjuv,' Klippan said. 'If he'd been driving around in it, we'd have nabbed him already.'

'And the CCTV footage? Have you started going through it?'

'Not yet. We're still waiting for some of the tapes, but as soon as we're done here, it's next on the list. Hopefully one of them caught the Volvo.'

Tuvesson nodded and reached for one of the coffee thermoses.

'It's empty. Try this one.' Klippan handed her one of the others. 'By the way, is there any new information about the fire at the refugee reception facility outside Kvidinge?'

Tuvesson shook her head as she filled her cup. 'Still only three dead. Which, regardless of how absurd it sounds, has to count as good news, considering how bad it could have been. The question is whether it's safe to assume this is a direct response to the fire at the Sweden Democrats' offices. Irene, what do you reckon? You were there when it happened.'

'It has to be retaliation by a right-wing extremist.'

'Which doesn't necessarily mean the Sweden Democrats were involved,' Klippan put in, one finger in the air.

'That depends on how you define involved. They were definitely the ones who published the addresses of all the refugee reception facilities on their Facebook page. And either way, I'm not sure I'd call the fire at their offices a proper fire. The alarm didn't even have time to go off.'

'A fire's still a fire, no matter who holds the match.'

'Pardon me, but what the fuck's that supposed to mean?'

'Just because you don't agree with the Sweden Democrats politically and the arsonist potentially belongs to a Muslim minority doesn't mean you get to pretend like nothing happened.'

'Of course not, and I don't.'

'It's exactly what you're doing. You're trying to make light, making flippant comments about alarms not going off and whatever. But a fire is a fire regardless of your political affiliation.'

'Of course it is. My point is simply that the attention given to the fire in the media is not even close to being in proportion to its size. That bloke Landertz has been on every front page and commanded a lot more column inches than the fire at the reception facility.'

Klippan shrugged. 'Whatever that has to do with our investigation.'

'I'm sorry, I can't stand for this any longer.' Lilja got up as though she were too upset to stay seated. 'You almost sound like you're a Sweden Democrat yourself, which of course you have every right to be. But if we're going to work together on this case, I need to know where the hell you stand.'

'My political views have nothing to do with this. Yours, on the other hand, seem to both hobble you and blind you to how you approach the investigation.'

'Who's blind here? Do you seriously still think this has nothing to do with racism?'

'Irene, you're going to have to get a hold of yourself,' Tuvesson said. 'Klippan is right. Our political opinions have no place in this room. If you have a problem with that, I'm going to have to ask you to leave.'

Lilja said nothing, just looked at each of them in turn as though she were in fact considering leaving the meeting. But then she gave a curt nod and sat back down.

'All right,' Tuvesson continued. 'Back to the subject at hand: the fire at the Sweden Democrats' offices. Do we have any suspects at all?'

'The case is being handled by the Bjuv Police,' Lilja replied.

'Fine, would you mind getting in touch with them and checking what they have so far? A lot of signs point to it being a direct response to the murder of Moonif Ganem.'

Lilja nodded almost imperceptibly and made a note in her papers.

'Then I suggest we move on to the laundry room. Ingvar, how are you getting on? Have you found anything?'

'So far nothing more than a bunch of fingerprints, bloodstains and lots of hair. Not entirely unexpected in a laundry room. But ask me again after lunch, we should be done by then.'

'All right, then let's move on. Klippan, have you had time to have a closer look at Samira and her family to see if this could be honour-related?'

'I have, and there's nothing in the criminal records. On the contrary, they seem to be model citizens. Both the mother and the father work in health care and speak fluent Swedish even though they've only been here for three years.'

'What do you know,' Lilja said, topping up her coffee. 'There's that kind of immigrant too.'

'That said, I'm still far from convinced the motive has to be racism.' Klippan held up his hand pre-emptively to silence Lilja. 'And before you throw your coffee in my face, I would appreciate it if you'd hear me out.'

'No need to worry. I prefer to drink it.'

'Klippan, tell us. What motive are you considering?' Tuvesson said.

'Paedophilia.'

Tuvesson nodded thoughtfully. 'How old was he?'

'Eleven.' Lilja turned to Klippan. 'Why paedophilia? As far as I know, there were no signs of sexual assault.'

'Have we heard from Flätan yet?' Molander asked.

'Yes, I actually saw him yesterday. Which reminds me, I forgot to show you these.' Tuvesson handed out a number of pictures showing Moonif lying on a gleaming morgue gurney. 'I have to say I've never seen Flätan so shaken.'

'That's hardly a surprise.' Lilja picked up and studied one of the pictures. The slender body had been straightened out as much as possible but still lay in a kind of reverse foetal position with his legs bent the wrong way. 'I can't even imagine how painful it must have been.'

'Has he determined a cause of death?' Molander asked.

Tuvesson nodded. 'Internal bleeding. Apparently too many instances to count. Which makes things worse.'

'How?'

'It means it was the spinning that killed him, not the water from the rinse cycle, as one might have assumed. Though there was quite a lot of that in his lungs, too.'

'Oh my God...' Lilja dropped the picture and put her head in her hands.

'I'm sorry, but I don't get it,' Klippan said. 'Granted, it's horrible. But why would it be so much worse?'

'Ingvar.' Tuvesson turned to Molander. 'The programme the murderer used. Approximately how long would it take before the spin cycle started?'

'I'm not entirely sure, but I'd guess after about fifteen or eighteen minutes.' Molander shrugged and sipped his coffee.

'Are you saying it was a full fifteen minutes before he...' Klippan faltered and seemed to disappear into himself.

'Okay. But did he find anything of interest?' Molander said eventually. 'Such as signs of sexual violence?'

'Not that I know. But you know how tight-lipped Flätan is before he's completely done. So paedophilia could absolutely be a motive. It's kind of odd we haven't thought of it until now.'

'Do you have a suspect?' Lilja asked.

'I do, this bloke.' Klippan started up the overhead projector and connected his laptop, displaying a picture on the wall of a pear-shaped man with slicked-back hair, a moustache and glasses. 'I found these pictures on his Facebook page.'

'Cool cat. Who is he?'

'Björn Richter. You know, the one I told you about on the phone. The one who lives on the second floor in the same building and works as a nursery nurse at the Sunflower Nursery.'

'Right. The one you thought was creepy but you couldn't say why.'

'Are you seriously telling us he works in a nursery?' Tuvesson exclaimed.

'There's always a shortage of male teachers. I assume people like him can get a job anywhere,' Lilja said.

'Well, we shouldn't judge people on appearance alone,' Tuvesson said. 'But I'm not sure I'd be comfortable with my children being in his care.'

'You haven't seen the worst of it.' Klippan clicked to the next picture.

It showed the man in what appeared to be his living room, sitting on a plastic-covered sofa, surrounded by hundreds of china dolls. He was posing with a lot of dolls in the next picture as well, but in that one he was in his bedroom, under the pink duvet of his king-sized bed.

14

THE SMELL OF STAGNANT air hit Fabian when he opened the door to Hugo Elvin's flat, switched on the much-too-dim ceiling light and let Hillevi Stubbs in.

It was one day short of a month since he'd been there with Molander and found Elvin dead, hanging from a swag hook in full drag. There hadn't really been a proper investigation because Flätan, the coroner, had concluded that nothing suggested it being anything other than suicide.

This was the first time he'd set foot in the flat since then; to make sure no one could get in and contaminate the scene, he had made sure the locks were changed and paid the rent out of his own pocket through to August.

'I can see why he might have been depressed.' Stubbs looked around the dreary hallway with its beige string wallpaper and framed pictures of Elvin's home town, Simrishamn. And just as Fabian had the first time he visited the flat, she stopped in front of one of the black-and-white photographs, in which a boy in a dress was helping his mother hang laundry. 'I would be too, if I had to live like this.'

The only thing he'd told her was that she should have a look around as an experienced crime scene technician and see if anything jumped out at her. Nothing about Molander being a suspect and not a word about them flying completely under the radar.

After some coaxing, she had agreed to come, but only after making it very clear that she was taking a half-day off work to visit a friend in Harlösa and that she therefore had no more than half an hour to give him.

'But to be honest, I still don't understand what you think I could add when Molander's already been over this place,' she continued as she walked through the hallway. 'Say what you will about that man, but he's undoubtedly one of Sweden's best.'

'As I said on the phone, this hasn't been a priority.' Fabian closed the front door behind him and followed her inside.

'No, sure, if no crime's suspected, that's just how it goes.'

'I would say it had more to do with the other investigation we were busy with at the time. It was complex enough to use up all the oxygen. And surely even the best can miss things?'

'I said *one* of the best.' Stubbs turned her back on Fabian, walked into the living room and looked around in silence. At the blue decorative plates hanging in a row above the door lintel and continuing down on either side. At the String shelf with all its little knick-knacks, the plush sofa facing the old television set and the coffee table with its dark green tiles and a lace tablecloth.

'So it wasn't in here,' he said, but got no reaction. 'He was hanging in the other room. If you follow me, I could—'

'Please, shut up, will you?'

Fabian knew Stubbs far too well to be offended. Her brusque manner was simply a sign of her being focused. *Become one with the scene*, as she had said to him once in Stockholm.

A few minutes later, she turned to him and nodded, and he showed her further down the hallway, into the bedroom, where the bed was as neatly made as the last time he'd been there. The laptop was still sitting on the little desk by the window that looked out at Hälsovägen, which despite its healthful name was Helsingborg's most carcinogenic street.

'Here's some of the clothes I told you about.' Fabian opened one of the wardrobes, which was filled with women's underwear, wigs, dresses and pumps. 'And over by the window you'll find his computer with the search history. Do you want me to start it up?'

'No.' Stubbs continued in past the heavy maroon drapery, which had been pushed aside.

Fabian followed her into the innermost room, where a divan stood in a corner, facing a wall of books. Other than Elvin no longer hanging from the ceiling, it looked the same as when he and Molander had last been there.

He studied Stubbs as she walked around, absorbing the atmosphere. Sometimes with open eyes, studying some small detail, but just as often with her eyes closed. This time, he wasn't going to break the silence; he walked over to the bookshelf and squatted down in front of the row of photo albums on the lowest shelf.

He had already flipped through the albums once without finding anything of interest. Even so, he was drawn to them.

The albums had years written on them. He pulled out the first, which had '62–'68 written on its spine. Just as he remembered, page after page was filled with photographs from Elvin's childhood. Most showed him as a seven-year-old, doing everything from using a bow and arrow, playing football and fishing to dressing up as a cowboy and playing with Meccano.

In some of the photos he was with his parents and in others his sister, who now lived in Switzerland. If Molander was to be believed, Elvin had fallen out with her over conducting the estate inventory for their parents, and since she hadn't even bothered to come for his funeral, there may well be some truth in that.

There was a photo missing on one of the pages, and another on a different page. He remembered from his own parents' old albums that the photos tended to come unstuck and lie around loose here and there. But there were no loose photos here, not in the album and not at the back of the shelf. Suddenly, he realized what he was really looking for.

'Right, so what is it you want me to say?' Stubbs asked. He decided his search would have to wait until they were done and put the album back on the shelf.

'Anything,' he said, standing back up. 'Whatever jumps out at you.'

'Fabian, if you're expecting me to find something that points to it being either suicide or murder, I'm afraid I'm going to have to disappoint you.' She looked at her watch. 'And besides, time's almost up.'

'But surely there's something here that gives you pause—'

'I'm not blind,' Stubbs broke in. 'I see any number of things. But nothing that would help you launch a big investigation. Which is what this is about, isn't it?'

'Or not.' Fabian walked up to her. 'Let's just for a few minutes entertain the notion that this wasn't suicide.'

Stubbs sighed and checked her watch again. 'Fine... But make it quick. We can start with the pictures of him you emailed over. As far as I can tell, he looked like he weighed well over 15 stone. Straight away, you have a problem. Just lifting him would have been difficult, not to say impossible. And then you have to string him up from the swag hook to boot. Add to that that he would likely put up a fair bit of resistance and fight for his life, unless he was unconscious. Speaking of which, was there an autopsy?'

Fabian nodded.

'Any cranial damage indicating violence?'

'No.'

'And the toxicology report?'

'Nothing out of the ordinary.'

'So he was neither drugged nor knocked senseless. Come on, you can hear what it sounds like, can't you?'

'The only thing we know for sure is that he wasn't drugged at the time of his death,' Fabian said. 'But that doesn't necessarily mean he couldn't have been drugged when he was winched up, only to be kept alive until he—'

'Hold on, what do you mean, winched?'

'Well, or hoisted up using some kind of pulley system, assuming we're dealing with a lone perpetrator.'

Stubbs laughed and shook her head. 'This is starting to sound like some kind of bloody science fiction fantasy.'

'But certainly possible, right?'

'I suppose everything's possible these days. But that's not the same as saying it's likely.'

'Granted, but how about this for a scenario. First he's drugged and his arms are tied behind his back. Then he's hoisted up. Maybe in some kind of harness, to make sure he doesn't suffocate straight away. Then the killer could take his time with the noose while waiting for him to wake up.'

'Right, and then what? Once he wakes up?'

'Well, then he just lets him dangle there, potentially giving him water to drink until the tranquillizer has passed out of his system. Once it has, he cuts the ropes to the harness and leaves it to gravity.'

Stubbs shrugged. 'It still sounds like a bad three a.m. film to me. But all right, I can play along. Sure, it's possible. About as possible as winning the lottery.'

'And yet, someone does win every week.'

'Sure, but that's not my point.'

'I get that, and I hear what you're saying. But just to follow it through to the end. You said you can see any number of things – I would love to hear what they are. Besides, I actually still have six minutes before you have to go.'

'Were you always this stubborn?' Stubbs heaved a sigh but did scan the room again. 'All right, fine, take the books on the shelf. Why are all the titles in alphabetical order except *Man Alive*, *Redefining Realness* and *Beyond Magenta*?'

'What? You mean—'

'I don't mean anything. But wouldn't it make more sense to have all your trans literature on one shelf, or, alternatively, placed alphabetically with the other books and not scattered randomly like this? It doesn't prove anything one way or another. I just find it peculiar. And since we're on the subject. Those dresses in the wardrobe out there. They're at least four or five sizes too small, if the idea was for Elvin to wear them.'

'You're thinking they didn't belong to him. That someone else put them there.'

'That would be the conspiracy theory. Another explanation could be that they did belong to Elvin, and that he was planning to lose weight before potentially having surgery, though I have a hard time picturing that. And there's one more thing. Come look at this.'

Fabian followed Stubbs, who walked over to the divan at the far end of the room, squatted down and used a small flashlight to illuminate the floor.

'See the marks?' She aimed the light at one of the marks on the floor.

'Sure, I would guess it's from a sofa or something.'

'Exactly. Over the years, it's what happens. Especially if there's nothing to prevent it.'

Fabian nodded, though he had no idea where she was going with it.

'But strangely enough, there are neither marks nor pads under the divan.' She carefully lifted it up to demonstrate.

'Maybe he got new furniture just before he killed himself so the place would look extra nice for when we came.'

'Sure, maybe he did. The problem is that the marks on the floor don't match the divan or any other piece of furniture in this flat. Which would indicate that he relatively recently replaced a different piece of furniture with this one to add to the trans look. Which might not be what I would spend energy on if I were about to kill myself.' Stubbs and Fabian both stood back up. 'So yeah, there's some strange things here. I hardly think, though, that they would be enough to start a whole investigation. Besides, you're missing the most crucial component: the motive.' She spread her hands. 'Also, I think your watch is slow, because according to mine, I'm two minutes late and really do have to go.'

If there was one thing he did have, it was a motive. But he couldn't tell her about it. At least not yet. Instead, he walked Stubbs to the front door, thanked her for her input and promised to visit and bring pastries the next time he was in Malmö.

As soon as he was alone again, he went back into the hallway to look at the framed photograph of that boy in a dress helping his mother hang laundry. And of course it was Elvin as a boy, and his mother. He even recognized the dress from the pictures of his sister.

And yet he was convinced that was far from the whole truth when he took the picture off its hook, fetched the album with the two missing photos and left the flat.

15

LILJA WAS SITTING BY one of the illuminated islands in Molander's lab in the basement, eyes glued to the four screens on which harassed-looking passengers were scurrying up and down the platform of Bjuv Station.

Four CCTV tapes running simultaneously, showing that even a small town like Bjuv had a rush hour full of backs and faces, prams and rollators struggling to alight or board before the doors shut again and the trains pulled out.

Staying focused watching one tape was challenge enough. Watching all four at once without missing anything important was virtually impossible, but it would take too long to scrutinize each one in turn.

At least she knew what she was looking for.

Because somewhere in the crowd of passengers, she should be able to spot the man in the beige Sweden Democrats jacket. If not on this particular train, then on the next one or the one after that.

He had managed to slip away in a stolen orange Volvo 240 right in front of her. Eleven minutes later, which was to say at 11.46, that same orange car had been caught on CCTV by a camera belonging to an OKQ8 petrol station in Åstorp, just north of Bjuv, which in turn had led to the assumption that the perpetrator wasn't a Bjuv local but had either arrived in his own car, which for obvious reasons he'd been forced to leave behind, or by train.

They had been able to rule out the car alternative with the help of one of Molander's assistants, who had still been at the scene. He had been tasked with walking around, noting down the licence plates of all the cars parked in the vicinity. Then Molander had found the address of each and every owner, who had all, without exception, turned out to be registered in Bjuv and to look nothing like the smiling man in the composite sketch.

The door was opened and Klippan entered. 'I've talked to the Sunflower Nursery and they confirm Björn Richter was at work at seven in the morning the day Moonif died.'

'Is that the neighbour with the dolls?' Molander asked.

'Exactly. I've also been in touch with some of the parents, and they all say he was there when they dropped off. They are also unanimous in the opinion that he is the best thing to have happened to the Sunflower in years. According to them, no one has a better way with the children than Björn.'

'Does that mean we're dismissing the paedophilia theory?' Molander said.

'At least for now. And how are you getting on?'

Lilja was hoping Molander would answer, so she could carry on undisturbed. But he said nothing, and Klippan came over to stand behind her like an old schoolmaster making sure her handwriting was correct. Granted, on paper he was temporarily in charge of the investigation while Tuvesson was away. But the way he'd been trying to boss her around all morning was nothing short of pathetic.

'Irene? Hello? I asked you a question.'

Was he actually tapping her shoulder right now, or was she imagining it? Jesus, he really was. What was next? Patting her on the head and asking her to fetch him coffee? It took some effort to suppress the urge to turn around and slap him.

'Don't you worry,' she said instead, without looking away from the screen, even though there was nothing much to see just then. 'I promise I'll let you know if I find him.'

It was best not to care, to just shrug it off and keep her head down. Whatever he said and no matter how much he relished playing the big man, she wasn't going to give up until she'd found the man with the taunting smile.

She had just finished with the 7.16 train from Åstorp and was now focusing on the passengers disembarking from the 7.33 from Helsingborg.

'Because it's getting late.'

'Yes, I know how to tell the time, in case you were wondering.' Clearly, he wasn't going to go away.

'There's no need to be so prickly. Whether you like it or not, I'm in charge. And I think it's time for you to start focusing on some other things, too.'

'What do you mean, other things?' Damn it, now she actually had to hit pause and turn to him. 'I happen to be looking for him and not "some other things". Why don't you do that yourself?'

'What do you think I'm doing? And Ingvar.' Klippan nodded to Molander, who was also watching a screen showing CCTV footage. 'But given how much video there is, I need you to help out too.'

Tuvesson had only been gone a few hours, and she already missed her. And Fabian, why couldn't he be here?

At least that would have given Klippan someone else to pick on. 'Klippan,' she said, feeling frustration undermining her attempt at a smile. 'I'm going to help you as soon as I've found him, found the train he arrived on, requested the CCTV footage from that particular train, established where he got on, found out what the surveillance situation is at that station and, if it all works out, homed in on him sufficiently to make an arrest. When that's done, I promise I'll help you look for "some other things".'

Klippan sighed so heavily she could smell the coffee he'd just drunk and the egg he'd probably had for breakfast. 'Irene, I'm sure that's all fine and good. But he's not our only lead.'

'As a matter of fact, that's exactly what he is. Right now, he's by far our most solid lead.'

'Maybe. But that doesn't mean he's guilty.'

'I'm sorry, who are you saying is guilty of both the carjacking and the attempted murder of Ralf Hjos?'

'Okay, fine. But I was talking about—'

'Secondly,' Lilja cut him off. 'His behaviour reeks of guilt. Consider his running away. If he's so innocent, why take off at all?'

'I don't know.' Klippan shrugged. 'A lot of people do weird things when the police are around. Take my neighbours, for instance. If they're chatting out on the street and I come out to get the paper or whatever, they—'

'They what? They make a break for it and stab people up and steal their cars?'

'No, but—'

'Exactly. Thirdly, there's his sickeningly smug smile.'

'And since when do we equate a smug smile with a solid

lead?' Klippan looked over at Molander. 'Ingvar, help me out here, will you?'

'No thanks, you sort out whatever that is between yourselves,' Molander said, his eyes glued to the screen.

'I'm aware we can't build our entire case on a smile,' Lilja said. 'But walking around grinning, given what had just happened...' She shook her head.

'Maybe he didn't know what had happened.'

'Klippan, come take a look at this,' Molander said.

Klippan went over to Molander, giving Lilja a chance to press play and return to the sea of people on her screens. And almost immediately, the bottom left screen caught her attention. It was not unusual for her to spot something now and then that made her rewind and review the tape frame by frame. But this time, it felt different.

'See that red Seat?' Molander continued, pointing to the red car whose rear end was just visible at the left edge of his screen.

'Yes, what about it?'

'For one, it's not parked within the lines, but look at this.'

Suddenly, the rear lights came on and then the car indicated and disappeared out of shot.

'As you can see, it's 8.20, which tallies with the time of the murder.'

'Where's the camera?'

'It's by a cashpoint on Norra Stationsgatan, just over fifty feet away.'

Lilja couldn't see the man's face, because he'd got off the train with his eyes lowered. And the camera was shooting from above. But the blindingly white trainers, the pulled-up jeans and the beige jacket were enough to make her sure.

'Try backing up and see if you can zoom in on the plates,' Klippan said.

'No need,' Molander said. 'I already did.'

'And?'

'HUT 786. It's a rental from Hertz on Gustav Adolfsgatan in Helsingborg.'

Klippan turned to Lilja. 'I don't know about you, but to my mind, this is exactly the kind of thing that's worth looking into. I myself have a long list already, so if you wouldn't mind handling this one, I'd be ever so grateful.'

'Sure,' Lilja replied. 'But in case you're interested, I've found him.'

'You have?' Klippan came over to her and leaned in closer to the screen where the picture was paused to show a man with blue jeans and a beige jacket from behind. 'You can't even see his face.'

'It's him, okay. I know it's him. Just look at this.' With a few quick commands, she clicked over to another clip on the next screen. 'This is from the mall when I was chasing him.' She dragged the clip's time marker to 13.06.2012 11.42.53 and pressed play.

The sequence playing out in front of them showed the man she had chased yesterday running into the shot from the right and continuing straight into the street where he was hit by the orange Volvo, which slammed on its brakes and came to a stop as the man landed on the bonnet and then hit the windscreen before tumbling to the ground.

'See? Exactly the same clothes.'

Klippan nodded while the driver, Ralf Hjos, climbed out of the car and bent down over the man who was lying motionless on the asphalt.

'And the time fits perfectly. He arrives on the 7.33 train from Helsingborg and Moonif leaves his flat twenty-five minutes later.'

The stabbing happened so quickly it was easy to miss if you didn't know it was coming. The prone man's arm that suddenly jerked up and Ralf Hjos, who immediately collapsed as the other man got to his feet, wiped his small knife on his victim's clothes, got into the car and drove away. Seconds later, Lilja could be seen rushing over to the bleeding man.

'You're right, it's probably him,' Klippan conceded at length. 'And like you said, now we can request the CCTV footage from the train in question and see where he got on. But, as I said, that needn't stop us from looking for other things as well.'

'No, I hear you, and I promise to go over all the material again and see if I can find anything else.'

'You will?' Klippan looked genuinely surprised.

'Yes, now that we're on to him, I feel a lot calmer. Besides, I agree with you that it's too early to close a lot of doors.'

Klippan exhaled, though the look he gave her was full of insecurity.

'It's fine. So long as we don't abandon the other lead altogether.'

'Maybe when you're done you could drag yourselves over here and take a look at this instead?' Molander said, waving them over.

The clip he played them was from the same petrol station in Åstorp that had caught the orange Volvo passing by. According to the time stamp, it was from the day before as well, but much later in the day, specifically, 15.54.43. This time, a dark blue Mercedes was visible in the shot, and it didn't just drive by, it turned in to fill up.

Two men in dark jackets with pulled-up hoods and Palestinian keffiyehs concealing their faces climbed out of it. One inserted a credit card into the machine and punched in his code while the other got a jerry can out of the boot.

'What does it say on their jackets?' Lilja asked while the two men filled the can with petrol.

'KMY,' Molander replied.

'Klippan's Muslim Youth.' Klippan shook his head. 'Really smart wearing those particular jackets when you're buying petrol to firebomb the Sweden Democrats in Bjuv.'

'Maybe they wanted their allegiance known without revealing their identities.'

'I wouldn't put too much store in the jackets,' Molander said. 'The car's registration number is far more interesting.'

'I was just thinking that,' Klippan said. 'Did you look it up?'

Molander gave Klippan a withering look, but couldn't even be bothered to add a sigh to it.

'Fine, sorry.'

'And here's the owner.' Molander clicked up a picture that filled the entire screen and turned to the others.

Even though Lilja recognized him and had met him only yesterday, it took her several seconds to realize she was staring at the local Sweden Democrats chairman, Sievert Landertz.

16

SIEVERT LANDERTZ'S REGISTERED RESIDENCE was Åkervägen 10 in Söndraby, just east of Klippan. It was an area that reminded Lilja so much of her own neighbourhood in Perstorp it immediately put her in a bad mood. Of course this was the kind of place a Sweden Democrat would live. It was as obvious as the fact that she and Hampus had to move as soon as it could be arranged. It didn't matter where to, so long as it got her away from all the Scanian flags.

Not to mention all the trampolines. Practically every garden around here was home to a blue monstrosity. But there was no sign of bouncing children. They were probably tucked into their beds, having *Mein Kampf* read to them for story time.

'Here it is.' Klippan nodded to the house on the corner ahead of them and pulled over, killed the engine and unbuckled.

While he did that, Lilja pulled out binoculars and studied the white wooden house built in the middle of the plot, which also had room for a trampoline. There were two flagpoles, flying the Scanian and Swedish flags respectively.

'Irene? Are you coming?'

'Slow your roll. It looks like the front door's about to open.'

Indeed, moments later, two figures exited and walked towards the garage.

'See who it is?'

'The tall one is Landertz himself, in all his glory. I don't recognize the other one, but my guess would be it's his son.'

'Okay. Then we might as well bring them in now, before it's too late.' Klippan opened the door on the driver's side.

'Or should we maybe follow them and see where they're going?'

Klippan stopped and pondered that for a few seconds, then gritted his teeth, closed the door and buckled back up. He waited until the dark blue Mercedes had reversed out of the garage and turned east down Vedbyvägen before turning the key in the ignition and following. All without a word, which was highly unusual for him.

Lilja had no problem understanding if he was cross with her. She would likely have been, too, had the situation been reversed. But the truth was that she had no faith in him as a boss. As an officer of the law and a detective, yes. She knew no one more meticulous and determined than Klippan. But he wasn't a leader, and everyone, with the possible exception of Klippan himself, knew as much. In an attempt to break the sullen silence, she turned on the radio.

'*Three dead and around twenty injured, of which several are women and children, makes the fire at a refugee reception facility outside Kvidinge one of the deadliest in Skåne in recent years,*' the news anchor was saying. '*According to the Bjuv Police, there are several leads but at present no suspects. One of the theories is that this may be retaliation for the firebombing of the local Sweden Democrats' offices. What follows is an excerpt from this afternoon's interview with local party chairman Sievert Landertz.*'

'*You have published the addresses of several refugee reception facilities on your Facebook page. Isn't that aiding and abetting Nazis and xenophobic organizations, particularly in the light of the most recent fire?*'

'*Absolutely not,*' Landertz replied. '*That's just typical headline-grabbing, left-wing nonsense.*'

'*But the Kvidinge reception facility is one of the facilities whose addresses you published.*'

'*All we've done is to inform citizens of what is going on. That's what you're supposed to do in a democracy. The municipalities, on the other hand, constantly circumvent their duty of providing information to local residents. And do you know why? So the local residents won't have time to protest.*'

'*But aren't you even slightly worried about possible consequences?*'

'*We condemn all forms of violence. And I can promise you that if someone has their mind set on committing violence against people or property, they would have no trouble finding the addresses for themselves. It's not rocket science.*'

'No, this isn't working any more,' Klippan exclaimed, breaking his record-long silence and turning off the radio. 'It's getting dark. I have to move closer if we want to have a chance of seeing whether they turn west or east on road 21.'

'Sure. You're in charge.'

'I know.' Klippan sped up. 'I just wanted to inform you and head off any unnecessary bickering at the pass.'

Lilja was about to ask who was bickering, but instead managed to squeeze out a smile and a nod just as Klippan came to a stop behind Landertz's car, which was idling at the junction with road 21, waiting for a gap and indicating to turn left.

'By the way, have you heard anything from Fabian?' Klippan said after a while.

'No. Have you?'

'No.'

An awkward minute of silence later, the car in front of them turned out on to the motorway. Klippan followed it towards Perstorp, where it turned right on to the much smaller Gustavsborgsvägen. Having been surrounded by quite a bit of evening traffic, the Mercedes in front of them and their own car were now the only two vehicles in sight.

They were so deep into the countryside, they didn't pass a single house in the five minutes before the brake lights in front of them came on.

'What do you reckon?' Klippan slowed down to watch the Mercedes, which had turned left and continued down a narrow, tree-lined road. 'Doesn't that road look awfully private?'

Lilja nodded. For the first time, she agreed with her colleague. The road unquestionably led to a private farm, and if they turned too, it would be obvious they were tailing the Mercedes.

Klippan slowed down further, apparently waiting for her to take charge. She was just about to tell him to carry on straight ahead when she noticed in the wing mirror the lights of two more cars indicating left.

'Follow it.'

'Are you sure?'

'No, but apparently the two cars behind us and that one there are heading up there as well, so we don't have a lot to lose.' She nodded at a car coming towards them, indicating right.

Klippan turned on to the gravel road and continued down it a few hundred yards. It ended in a large area where around forty cars and motorcycles were already parked.

Sievert Landertz and his son were already walking towards a clutch of torches burning further off in the gloom.

'All right. Now what?' Klippan said as soon as he'd found a free spot.

'Now we find out where we are.' Lilja was already climbing out of the car. 'But if you want, you can wait here.' She closed the door before he could answer and set her course for the torches. Being alone was never a good idea. But right now, she preferred almost anything to being with Klippan.

Unfortunately, she heard a car door open and shortly after close again behind her, and seconds later she picked up the sound of panting as Klippan hurried across the grass.

'What are you doing? Have you lost your mind?'

She stopped and turned to him with a sigh.

'Fine, go on, sigh. But surely you don't for a second think I would let you go on by yourself. What if something happened to you? How would that look, and how—'

'Enough. I get it,' she hissed. She watched two men in long leather coats getting out of a car together with a woman with blonde hair.

'Good. And from now on, I want you to keep a low profile and let me do the talking.' Klippan strode on ahead towards the flickering light by the entrance.

She was about to object, but it was too late. Klippan was already thirty feet ahead of her, walking towards the man standing by the entrance, who was so well-built it looked over the top even from a distance. Instead, she decided to do as she was told and slowed down to avoid drawing attention.

'Good evening. So, what's going on here?' Klippan said to the bouncer.

'And who are you?'

Klippan showed him his police ID. 'Sverker Holm from the Helsingborg Police.'

The bouncer chuckled and shook his head. 'Then you've got the wrong address. This is a private event.'

'Pardon?'

'I said that if I were you, I'd crawl back down whatever hole I came from as fast as I could.'

Klippan turned round to look for Lilja but couldn't see her anywhere in the dark.

Meanwhile, the bouncer greeted another group and let them in, unaware that one of the two women didn't belong.

17

The garden behind Fabian's semi-detached house was really much too small to be called a *garden*. It was more of an outdoor area with a patio, a small patch of lawn, a few shrubs and a storage shed. And even though it was late, the whole scene was illuminated by a pale light. It was almost midsummer, and at this time of year the night was never truly dark.

On the other side of the double curtains covering the grimy basement window, Fabian pulled on a pair of powdered latex gloves and took out the framed black-and-white photograph of a young Hugo Elvin wearing a dress, helping his mother hang laundry. Then he carefully put the photograph down on the desk in the light of the desk lamp, picked up his squirrel-hair brush and applied a powder consisting of equal parts soot and potato starch.

The visit to Elvin's flat with Stubbs that afternoon had given him reasons to be both more and less suspicious of Molander. It was unquestionably far-fetched to think he had staged an entire gender identity crisis. Not to mention the nearly impossible method that would have been required to make the hanging itself look self-inflicted. And yet not even Stubbs had been able to ignore all the things that pointed to something being amiss.

Like he had suspected, the powder refused to stick to the frame, the glass or the backing. So there were no fingerprints. That in itself was odd. The glass was one thing, but the frame and the backing? Why wipe those clean of prints unless you had something to hide?

He turned the frame over, bent up the four little metal points and lifted out the backing. The photograph had no marks and no stamps on the back; it was pure white, which made it hard to say whether the paper was new or not.

He went over to the printer in the bookcase, lifted the lid of the built-in scanner and placed the photograph face down on the glass. As soon as the printer cable was plugged into the laptop, some driver or other sprang into action, asking if he wanted to scan a document.

Surprised at how easy it was, he clicked yes, named the file *Young Elvin in dress* and chose the highest resolution. A few minutes later, the picture appeared on his screen.

This was his first time analysing a photograph, and he had imagined needing to use Photoshop and having to run the picture through various filters and contrast enhancers to get answers. But it only took a few commands, zooming in on Elvin's head, to establish what he had been suspecting for the past few hours.

The picture had been manipulated.

It was undeniably Elvin's head, but the light on his face came from the left, not the right as in the rest of the picture. Furthermore, there was something about the sharpness that was out of line with the sharpness of the dress, which in turn made the contrast around the hair and by the neck more noticeable, despite obvious attempts to even them out.

Elvin had been inserted, in all likeliness scanned from one of the photographs missing from the album. The other was probably of Elvin's sister, wearing a white dress, helping her mother hang laundry.

In other words, Elvin's gender dysphoria was a fabrication. Probably intended to provide a motive that was shocking and complex enough to overshadow everything else, to make sure no one would even begin to suspect that he had been murdered.

He felt his pulse start to race and a rush of adrenaline. All of a sudden, it was as though he could see into the future, all the repercussions that would follow if it really did turn out to be Molander, a member of their own team, who was behind Elvin's death. He had no idea how adept Molander was at photo editing, but given his general technical know-how, it wouldn't surprise him if he was at least proficient.

Granted, the perpetrator could be anyone from an old convict who had done his time and come back seeking revenge to just about anybody. But if Elvin's suspicions had turned out to be true and Molander had realized he was on to him, he had not only a motive but also the expertise needed to commit a murder so convincing that no one other than Elvin himself would know to be suspicious.

What he didn't have was any solid evidence.

But as Stubbs liked to say, it didn't matter how meticulously you cleaned up after yourself – somewhere, there was always a speck of dust.

18

Was this some kind of concert?

That was Lilja's first thought as she slipped away from the group she had pretended to be part of and continued on her own. The adrenaline-fuelled metal music from Sabaton's latest album, *Carolus Rex,* blared out of the speakers, filling every nook and cranny of the barn, which felt like a gig venue with spotlights nestled among the wooden beams in the ceiling and a raised stage at the far end.

It was one of Hampus's absolute favourite bands, and even though he was fully aware of her feelings about their music, he insisted on constantly putting them on and turning the volume up as if he was trying to subject the entire street to Guantãnamo-style torture.

She estimated the number of people to be around a hundred and fifty, including members of some of the worst criminal motorcycle gangs ravaging Skåne at the moment. But this wasn't a motorcycle club get-together. That much was clear from the elegant suits and the long leather coats, not to mention the swastika armbands.

She pulled out her phone and called Klippan, only to be redirected to his voicemail, where she left a message telling him she was inside.

'I would like to start by welcoming you all,' a voice said over the speakers, moments after the music had faded out, and the audience moved towards the stage where a short man dressed in something resembling a brown scout uniform was standing behind a podium. 'It's good to see so many people here, and this is just the beginning! Because as I'm sure you've noticed, people are finally starting to realize that unified resistance and violence is the only way forward!'

Several people in the audience clapped and whistled.

She'd heard rumours about these kinds of events. Secret Nazi meetings arranged by the Party of the Swedes, the National Democrats or the Nordic Resistance Movement Third Nest, as they called themselves in Skåne. They often rented a venue under a false name, such as a school auditorium, or, like tonight, gathered in a barn in the middle of nowhere.

In order not to draw attention to herself, she carefully shifted towards the edge of the crowd, where she could slip into the shadows, climb up on a chair and film the whole event on her phone.

'This is something the Muslims have already realized,' the man behind the podium continued. 'They declared war on us a long time ago, and I promise you that unless we do something, we'll soon have sharia laws and burka requirements in this country.' Scattered booing could be heard. 'Exactly! Many of us have been too blue-eyed, but then there's nothing wrong with being blue-eyed, if you know what I mean.' The booing turned into laughter. 'We have to fight back now! Soon, it'll be too late!'

Applause and shouting took over; soon, the whole venue was filled with raised right arms.

'Let's give tonight's first speaker a round of applause. The man who never ducks the debate. Who like no one else knows how to make his voice heard and open doors for our policies! The one and only Sievert Landertz!'

Landertz stepped out on to the stage dressed in a dark leather jacket, shirt and tie, and, to the sound of applause and cheers, shook hands with the man in the scout outfit and stepped up to the podium.

'People tell me all the time that you can't judge all Muslims by what some Muslims do,' he said as soon as the audience had settled down. 'That only the most fundamentalist Muslims and Islamists are a problem. If you ask me, that's semantics, and if semantics is the name of the game, we might as well call them by their real name. Which is to say "rats", or why not "cockroaches"?' There was more scattered laughter and clapping. 'They're certainly not people!' He shook his head and smiled as if that was self-evident. 'I don't know about you, but I call them vermin!' The shouting and cheering grew louder. 'And what do we normally do with vermin? That's right! We exterminate it!' He mimed spraying pesticide in the air, and the venue exploded with cheering and raised right arms when he upped the ante by pulling on a swastika armband.

Lilja was not surprised in the slightest. Landertz was far from the first Sweden Democrat to have come out of the Nazi closet. Even so, it made her feel sick; she wanted to march up on to the stage, snatch the microphone from him and ask what in God's name they thought they were doing.

'At one end of the scale are people who are one hundred per cent human, like everyone in here,' Landertz continued. 'At the other end, they're one hundred per cent Mohammadan, and right now they're pouring in across our borders! Parasites out to rape our women, defecate in our churches and leech our country of all its riches. Just look at the numbers, it's undeniable. We build. We produce and create. And what do they do? They take! They take our money. Our jobs. Our university places. Our homes. The bloody swine even have the gall to take our seats at the front of the bus!'

The audience was virtually roaring out its frustration at this point. Landertz eventually had to signal to them to simmer down before he could carry on.

'But of course, we don't hear about that on the news or read about it in the papers, which makes me wonder if it isn't time to call the media by their real name too, which is to say "Lügenpresse".' Several people in the audience laughed. 'But the "terrible" fire at the refugee centre outside Kvidinge, *that* they report on. What a sob story. I have no idea who was behind it, but whoever they are, I think they deserve a round of applause!' People whistled and clapped and those right arms shot up again in unison. 'We got rid of three rats! Three disgusting black cockroaches who can no longer breed and multiply. If we're lucky, we'll get rid of some more parasites before this is over!' Applause erupted once more.

It was hardly unthinkable that one or several of the arsonists were present. But there were too many of them for her to consider trying to take down everyone's details. Nor could she call for backup and surround the place, since the gathering, no matter how repellent, was not illegal in itself.

On the other hand, they had all arrived by car or motorcycle, and even if they weren't the registered owners, there should be enough connections.

She had paused her filming to write a message to Klippan, asking him to walk around and take pictures of all the licence plates, when suddenly the chair disappeared from under her. It happened so quickly she hit the floor without being able to catch herself. The phone slipped from her hand and slid out of her reach.

'And what do we have here?' A man dressed in leather with a denim waistcoat took a few steps closer, squatted down next to her and leaned in so close she could see every last detail of the Terminator tattoo that covered his neck and parts of his face.

'Is this yours?' said another voice, and her phone was held out to her by a hand that was missing its middle finger.

She nodded and watched her phone hit the ground and get crushed by a heavy boot.

The room was completely still now, apart from the groans she emitted as she defied the pain in her hip and got back on her feet. Her insides were in uproar and her heart was beating so fast and hard her chest hurt.

To conceal how she was really feeling, however, she made a show of brushing the dirt off her jacket, slowly and calmly, with one hand. Only when she was done did she turn to the man in the scout uniform who had stepped forward along with the bouncer.

'My name is Irene Lilja,' she said, ensuring she made eye contact with all three of them. 'I work for the Helsingborg Police and am currently investigating the murder of Moonif Ganem.' She paused and looked at all the people who had now turned to her. 'We have a suspect and I want to know if anyone in here recognizes him.' She pulled the zip of her jacket down halfway and moved her hand towards her inside pocket.

The reaction was instantaneous; three guns were suddenly aimed at her.

'You don't seriously think I'm going to shoot you, do you?' she finally managed to get out, and to her own surprise, her voice was steady. She added a little laugh and underlined it by shaking her head as she pulled out the police sketch from her inside pocket.

Her theatrics seemed to have worked. True, the guns were still aimed at her, but none of the men were able to conceal the uncertainty in their eyes when they looked at her, and that uncertainty disarmed all the tattoos, studs and muscles. This wasn't what they had expected and, weapons or no weapons, it was now her hand on the tiller.

'This is what he looks like,' she continued and held out the picture to the short man in the scout outfit.

But the bastard didn't even glance at the picture; he was staring at her hand holding it. Her trembling fucking hand.

And just like that, the tiller slipped out of her grasp; she was powerless to act when he tore up the sketch and smilingly let the pieces fall to the floor.

'You want to know who that is? You really want to know?' He took a step closer. 'He's a true hero. A man who did what was necessary for our country. Unfortunately, I don't know who he is, so I can't thank him personally. But I can make sure the news of his deed, which hopefully wasn't his last, spreads all the way down to the rats' nest that washing machine boy came from. Then maybe they'll think twice before coming here. Besides, the kid should be grateful. Not everyone is washed that clean before they go.'

He turned to the man with the Terminator tattoo. 'Make sure you escort our guest all the way out.'

The man nodded and turned to the two others, who grabbed her arms and hustled her towards a door next to the stage.

All the way out.

She wanted to resist but had no choice but to follow them backstage. She wanted to wrench free and use any ensuing confusion to pull out the gun they had forgotten to frisk her for.

All the way out.

Did that mean what she thought it meant?

Yet another door was opened and she was led out into a yard where a car was parked.

Not just *out*, but *all the way out.*

Were they going to drive her into the woods and put a bullet in her head? Or were they going to lock her in the boot while the car was crushed into a small cube at the nearest junk yard? She wouldn't be the first police officer to disappear without a trace.

'Help!' she heard herself scream. 'Klippan, I'm here. On the other side!'

The reply came in the form of a fist against her cheekbone. An inch or two lower and her jaw would have been knocked out of joint. Instead, she passed out and had no way of knowing that she was put into the boot of the parked car and driven away.

19

Fabian emptied the brown evidence bag and the clutch of keys clattered on to the desk in the basement. There were seven keys in all. Seven keys, each different, and each one marked with coloured gaffer tape around their heads. Of the two blue ones, one was marked with a four-digit code, and on one of the two white keys, a longer code of six digits was printed. The other had a drawing of a fish. The three green keys all looked completely different and had question marks on them.

He used his phone to take pictures of each of the keys in turn. He had no idea what the different markings meant, but they all fitted in a lock somewhere and he wasn't going to give up until he knew the purpose of each one.

The discovery that the photograph of the young Elvin wearing a dress had been doctored had prompted him to delve into the Molander investigation in earnest. He had spent all evening and soon half the night in the basement, going over and photographing some of the contents of Elvin's locked desk drawer.

He had already flipped through some of the calendars. With a few exceptions, virtually every day had been marked with the initials I.M., presumably for Ingvar Molander, followed by two times of day. One in the morning when he arrived at the station and one later in the afternoon or evening when he left.

Sometimes, Elvin had drawn a face that was either happy, grumpy or simply had a dash for a mouth, and on some pages there was further information, which could be anything from Molander changing his phone number and which investigations he was working on to whether he had been on leave or just happened to make an odd comment during a meeting. On certain pages there was also a third time noted, which as far as Fabian could make out indicated when Molander got home, which suggested Elvin had at times gone so far as to stalk him.

One of the envelopes contained a collection of black-and-white photographs showing a woman getting into the passenger seat of a car. Or coming out – it was impossible to tell. Unfortunately, none of the pictures showed her face. When she wasn't turned away from the camera, her hair was in the way, and as for the driver, it was too dark to see much more than that it was a man.

The car looked like a grey five-door Saab 9-3. But the registration plates weren't visible in any of the pictures.

And then there were copies of various investigations. It wasn't the first time he'd been through them, but it was the first time he'd taken the time to really dig into the details. He had decided to start with the oldest. It was by far the one he knew the least about.

The victim, Einar Stenson, was seventy-three years old when, on Saturday 21 April 2007, he passed away in his summer house by Ringsjöstrand in Hörby. Hörby was in the middle of Skåne, in the Southwestern Götaland Police District. Consequently, the investigation hadn't been handled by Tuvesson and her team, but by a certain Ragnar Söderström in Eslöv, who had concluded it was a tragic accident that for a number of reasons had proved fatal.

According to the investigation, Einar Stenson had been alone in his summer house when he slipped on the newly waxed kitchen floor. He had fallen forward across the cutlery basket of his open dishwasher. The basket had contained, among other things, a kitchen knife pointing up, which had penetrated Stenson's abdomen. A nose fracture and a laceration on his forehead suggested he had hit his head and passed out, which explained why he had bled to death.

It was undeniably a highly unusual accident, but at the same time completely plausible. A quick internet search revealed that Stenson was the only Swedish victim of such an accident. But in the UK, both a thirty-one-year-old woman and a six-year-old boy had died under what could be described as virtually identical circumstances.

The notes in the margin, however, indicated that Elvin had been very sceptical. He had, for example, highlighted the entire paragraph describing the kitchen floor as newly waxed and therefore very slippery, particularly since the victim had supposedly been wearing wooden clogs. The words *newly waxed* and *clogs* were circled and had question marks next to them.

But if the technical investigation was to be believed, the floor had, in fact, been waxed and in one of the pictures showing the victim slumped face down across the open dishwasher door, the left clog was still on his foot, while the right had fallen into the pool of blood on the floor.

It was an unsettling picture in more ways than one. Not because of all the blood that had spread out across the dishwasher and the floor, or the point of the knife sticking out through the victim's checked shirt like a tiny silver shark fin. No, the truly frightening thing was just how little it took to end everything. As though it were enough for chance to suddenly decide to mess with you, just for a laugh.

One of the other pictures was taken from the ground up and from that angle was in some ways even more disconcerting, even though the victim had been removed. It showed the bloody knife sticking straight up out of the cutlery basket. It hurt just to look at it, as though he himself, Sonja and, above all, the children had really just been lucky every time they'd placed a knife exactly like that and not ended up dead.

But Elvin had had questions about this, too. He had marked the length of the blade with a question mark. It was not clear why. Instead, the red felt-tip symbol looked more like something had occurred to him and then he had simply moved on. Maybe he had followed up at a later date. Maybe the thought had been forgotten.

A search for Einar Stenson informed Fabian that he had spent most of his professional life working as a sports photographer for several newspapers. One of his most famous images was of a young Zlatan Ibrahimović in a header duel during one of his first years of playing for Malmö FF. In 1952, Stenson had married his wife, Flora, and soon after they'd had two daughters, a few years apart, Ulla and Gertrud Stenson.

Gertrud...

Fabian read the name again to make sure he'd got it right.

Yes, it did say Gertrud. But could that really be her or was it just chance having him on?

He typed in her personal identity number and as soon as her information appeared on the screen, he understood why Elvin had been so interested.

Gertrud Stenson had been born in 1956 at Ystad Hospital. At twenty-two, she had changed her surname when she got married in Hörby Church and since then, she had gone by the name Gertrud Molander.

That made Einar Stenson Ingvar Molander's father-in-law.

There was no way that was a coincidence.

20

Early summer mornings, there really was nothing more beautiful, Lilja mused as she got the go signal over the radio and climbed out of the car, crossed the road and stepped into Landertz's garden. Wisps of mist swirled a few feet above the ground like whipped cream, obscuring all the ugly cars, garden furniture and trampolines.

But she wasn't able to appreciate any of it. Not even the way the first faint light of the rising sun set everything sparkling, though the day had barely begun. There was a darkness in her mind that overshadowed everything, and deep down, underneath the imposed calm, she was seething with fury.

A few hours earlier, she had woken up on the lawn in her own garden with one cheek pounding with pain. Her clothes had been soaked through and she was so cold she felt she might never warm up again.

She'd gone inside to find Hampus passed out on the sofa with the TV on and one hand in his sweat shorts, and judging from the remnants on the coffee table, he had ordered pizza and knocked back far too many beers. But she hadn't even had it in her to be irritated; she had simply continued to the bathroom to have a hot bath.

And there, shrouded in hot steam, reality had slowly returned. Dumping her in her own garden had been a clear warning. A signal so she wouldn't trick herself into feeling safe.

We know where you live.

After putting on some clean clothes, she had called Klippan from her home phone, convinced he was both awake and beside himself with worry. But the signals had rung out unanswered so she'd left an account of events on his voicemail and assured him she was okay and that she was planning to haul Landertz in for questioning as soon as she got the chill out of her bones.

Fifty minutes later, she had woken up and listened to his terse reply on her answering machine. A reply she had no intention of heeding, responding to or even admitting she'd heard.

No time to talk. Good to hear you're okay. Landertz can wait. Better for you to rest. Talk later.

The doorbell sounded like one of those annoying brightly coloured plastic toys you can't turn the sound down on and whose batteries refuse to die. A minute later, the door was opened by a woman with tousled hair, wearing panda slippers and a dressing gown.

'Good morning,' Lilja said, noting that the hallway looked like any other hallway. 'My name's Irene Lilja. I'm looking for your husband.'

'Eh... what?'

'Your husband. Is he home?'

'Yes, but...' The woman looked her up and down. 'What's this about? It's only just gone half six.'

'6.33, to be exact.'

'Hello there, what's going on?'

She couldn't see him, though there could be no doubt

who that nasal voice belonged to. When, moments later, he stepped outside with wet hair, dressed only in an unbuttoned shirt, underwear and socks, she felt like she'd stepped right into their bedroom.

'So, we meet again.' She fired off a smile, pretending not to notice the pain from the blow to her cheekbone.

'Hold on a minute. You two know each other?' The woman stared from Lilja to Landertz and back. 'Sievert. Can you explain what this is—'

'Why don't you go back inside and get breakfast ready instead?'

'Sure, but—'

'I'll have a double espresso and a glass of freshly squeezed juice with my yoghurt. And don't forget to keep an eye on how much chocolate milk William drinks.'

The woman gritted her teeth and went back inside without so much as another glance at Lilja.

'What's this about?' Landertz said as he buttoned his shirt. 'I thought we were done with each other.'

'Sorry to disappoint.'

'If you think I've changed my mind about our membership list, you're mistaken. I've actually looked up what the law has to say about it. It classifies our membership list as "sensitive information", which means, to put it plainly, that you can forget about extracting so much as a syllable from me.'

'I can't argue with that, so I can understand if you haven't changed your mind. But you will, and soon. By the way, did you have a good time yesterday?'

'Yesterday?' Landertz looked nonplussed. 'If you're referring to the fire in our offices, all I can say is that it was yet another clear sign of how incapable our country is of receiving more refugees. This is exactly what happens when you crowd too many ethnicities into one place. Increased conflicts breed violence that in turn breeds even more violence. So no, why would I have thought that was a good time?'

'Wow.' Lilja gave him a slow clap. 'Impressive. That was a more or less verbatim excerpt from yesterday's interview in *Kvällsposten*, and it's not even quarter to seven yet. But I wasn't actually referring to the fire the day before yesterday. I was talking about your little performance last night.'

'Performance.'

'How did you put it again? The refugees are nothing but vermin that need to be exterminated with poison?'

'I don't know what you're talking about.'

'No? Well, you looked to be on fine form. And in case you've forgotten, I have it all on film. All the heiling, the swastika armband and every word of your lovely speech about rats and cockroaches.'

Landertz's face changed as the severity of the situation dawned on him. 'So that was you.'

Lilja nodded. 'And now the ball's in your court. Either I send the video to the newspapers, or the "Lügenpresse" as you like to call them. Or you give me a copy of your membership list, and the papers will have to miss out on this particular scoop.'

'Well, that does sound tempting, but as far as I understand it, that mobile phone broke.'

'Never heard of iCloud?'

Landertz met Lilja's eyes in an attempt to gauge whether she was bluffing.

'We can stand around glaring at each other all morning. But if you don't trot back inside and fetch what I want pretty soon, Jimmie's going to be calling. And I can promise you he won't be happy when he finds out what you get up to at night.'

Without another word, Landertz turned his back on her and disappeared into the house, returning minutes later with a USB stick in his hand. 'I hope you're aware that this is pure, unadulterated blackmail.'

Lilja countered with a smile, took the USB stick from him, slipped it in her pocket and pulled out her radio: 'I'm done here.'

'*Roger*,' said a male voice on the other end, and soon after, three men in police uniforms materialized out of the morning mist.

'What the fuck is this? We had a deal.'

'We do, and you don't have to worry. The video will stay in my possession, at least until further notice.' She nodded for the officers to arrest him.

'But, hey, no, hold on, calm the fuck down,' Landertz said as he was manhandled and pressed up against the wall. 'I haven't done anything illegal! I've done fuck all to give you the right to just march in here!'

'Personally, I would probably categorize your lovely little diatribe as hate speech, which can net you a maximum of two years behind bars. But you're right. It wouldn't really get you anything worse than a fine in reality. Inciting arson, on the other hand – that is, oddly enough, more generally frowned upon, even if it's just your own office.'

Landertz, who had just had his hands cuffed, looked completely uncomprehending.

'You don't have to act surprised. You know as well as I do it was your son and one of his mates.' She turned to one of the officers. 'By the way, you should probably head inside and get him, too, before he drinks too much chocolate milk.'

21

GAZING OUT THROUGH THE bus window towards Hyllinge Mall with the ICA Maxi supermarket in the foreground, he noted that the sky had become overcast and there was rain in the air. But it didn't matter. Given everything that lay ahead, this day would turn out amazing regardless.

He couldn't remember when he'd last had such high expectations of an individual day. Not even the time he ran away from home with all his money burning a hole in his pocket could hold a candle to today. Just seven years old at the time, he'd made it all the way to Påarp, across the sound and down to Copenhagen to go to the Tivoli amusement park.

The feeling of being completely free to do whatever he pleased had filled him with such a sense of power he'd been walking on air and had stayed until his last coins were spent and the sun had long since set.

All the things he'd done since then had been attempts at recapturing that same intoxicating exhilaration. Even if just one last time. He'd tried going to Tivoli again, more than once. He'd tried alcohol and drugs. He'd travelled around the world and experienced more than most people could ever dream of. But he'd never come close to that feeling of effervescent ecstasy that had almost made him fly.

Not until now.

Hyllinge Mall was not just his first stop, it was an amusement park that was more exciting than all the world's amusement parks put together. The stakes were much higher and, consequently, the potential consequences more dire. Anything could happen and nothing was up to him. Thanks to the dice, he knew no more about what was going to happen over the course of the next hour than the first time he got on a roller coaster and pulled the cold metal bar down over his legs.

The dice.

He had the dice to thank for everything. For some inexplicable reason, it had brought him out here to Hyllinge Mall, of all places, and now it was going to lead him straight into the unknown and select his victim.

The bus pulled over and stopped on Åstorpsvägen. After getting off himself, he helped a mother get her buggy off and then watched it for her until she had managed to collect a protesting three-year-old who was doing everything he could to scratch her eyes out. She had got on two stops after him and the brat had howled more or less constantly since then. Every one of her increasingly desperate attempts to calm him down, taking the form of colourful smoothies, had either ended up on the bus floor or all over her.

To make matters worse, he'd also been forced to sit next to an obese woman in gym clothes who had terrible breath. He had never understood why people who clearly never worked out insisted on walking around in ill-fitting synthetic clothes in garish colours.

But he was in too fine a mood to let it bring him down, even though he would have preferred the dice to have chosen car, Vespa or even bike instead of bus. The mall was built for motorists. They hadn't bothered to put in a proper pedestrian path across the car park, where two-thirds of the spots were already taken even though it was only twenty past ten.

He waited until the mother with the buggy had walked away before sitting down on the graffiti-covered wooden bench in the bus shelter and taking his six-sided precision dice out of its cloth bag. He weighed it in his hand and rubbed each of the sides with his fingers to warm it up.

Hyllinge Mall consisted of three separate buildings. ICA Maxi and the home improvement store Bauhaus occupied one each and the rest of the shops jostled for space in the third. The first question was which of the three he should choose. ICA was represented by a one or a two, Bauhaus by a three or a four and the last building by a five or a six.

He cupped his hands to make a space for the dice between them and shook it until he felt sure the dice had had enough time to make its decision.

A two.

It had started spitting, so he pulled his hood up, left the bus shelter, crossed the car park, slunk in through the automatic doors of the ICA Maxi supermarket and grabbed one of the red wheeled baskets.

There were no customers in the first section, which contained kitchen things and meaningless plastic rubbish that no one ever bought. So he continued on to the vegetable section, which was his least favourite by some margin. In fact, he disliked it so much he'd started to avoid fresh vegetables altogether.

Not only did you have to pick your own vegetables and put them in bags, it was also becoming increasingly common for customers to be required to weigh their wares themselves and put price tags on them. Like being suddenly press-ganged into unsalaried employment. Just finding the right kind of lettuce among all the options took forever.

Then it was the other customers. Like the old lady squeezing and picking up mangos to sniff them, like some kind of dog.

He went over to the new potatoes and put one after another in a bag while studying the old lady from afar. She was dressed all in blue. Blue raincoat, blue shorts and blue wellies. Even the frames of her glasses, which were dangling on her chest, were bright blue.

In other words, the odds were on her side.

Five out of six possible outcomes were in her favour. The only thing she wouldn't survive was a five, since five represented blue.

The order of the colours and which number should represent which one was something he'd had to ponder for quite a while before deciding that the only logical choice was to follow the order of the rainbow.

That meant red was represented by a one. Then followed orange, yellow, green, blue and finally purple, represented by a six. White, black, brown and grey were neutral and therefore irrelevant.

But in this case, it was all about the number five.

He grabbed one more potato, tied up the bag and put it in his basket. Then he stuck his hand in his pocket, pulled out his dice and started shaking it in his cupped hand, while walking over to the crate of red onions. Once he reached it, he opened his hand and looked.

A three.

The dice had said yellow, and as far as he could see the old lady didn't have a speck of yellow anywhere, which meant she would live to eat her mango, provided she actually managed to pick one eventually.

A man who looked to be around forty was standing by the mountain of strawberries, rooting around and swapping out berries in a quest for the perfect punnet. He wore a purple polo shirt and white shorts. Unfortunately, his boat shoes were brown. But the sweater whose sleeves were tied around his neck had red and white stripes, which at least gave the dice two colours to play with. A one and a six. Compared to the mango lady his odds were, in other words, halved.

Maybe that was why he so abruptly wrapped up his strawberry selection and hurried off into the meat section. As if that would save him.

He went over to the herring fridge from where he had a good view of the man, who was evidently having a barbecue tonight. Once again, he shook his dice and felt that palpable, familiar shudder of pleasure when he opened his hand.

A five.

In some ways, it was a relief. This was actually a lot more fun than he had expected. It became even more fun when a boy of about ten walked up to the marina bloke and slipped a gaming magazine in a plastic sleeve into his basket.

'Dad, there's a mobile phone shop in the mall. Can we please go after we're done here?'

'No, I've already told you you're not getting a new phone.'

'Why not? How am I supposed to—'

'Because it's the third one you've lost in two months.'

'But please… I promise I'll be more careful.'

'Rutger, what have I told you about nagging?'

'I can pay for it myself, if you could just lend me—'

Rutger. The name alone was gold.

'If you don't stop pestering me, you'll have to go and wait in the car.'

Oh Dad, there's no need to get worked up. If the odds are anything to go by, that nagging will soon be a faint memory.

Rutger clearly liked colours. In addition to a green baseball cap, he wore a red raincoat with a blue hood and blue piping around the pockets. His grey trousers broke the pattern a little, but it was made up for by his gold-studded purple belt. Maybe the belt matched the shirt under his jacket, or maybe Rutger was just a little bit rebelliously queer and had topped his outfit off with a pink glitter top? Or maybe not even queer – after all, the upper classes had always had a soft spot for pink, which made about as much sense as their second favourite colour, mint green.

But whatever. With his yellow shoes with built-in wheels under the heels, five of the six colours were represented, and poor Rutger would likely never have a chance to let his sexual orientation blossom.

If not for the lack of orange, it would have been game over for Rutger already. Now he had a one in six chance. A two was what he needed to keep breathing. No more, no less. Was this it? Third time lucky.

He took out his dice and shook it in his hand, giving it extra time now, even though that obviously had no effect on the result. Contrary to popular belief, the dice had no memory; each individual throw was isolated from all previous throws and the result was simply the whim of the dice. Or, put differently, pure chance.

That said, chance was always constrained by the odds. No matter how badly chance wanted to roll ten sixes in a row, it wasn't particularly likely to succeed. And right now, neither chance nor the odds were on little Rutger's side.

'Are you getting something or what?'

He squeezed the dice and turned to the short but muscular man with a beard, dressed in a motorcycle outfit. 'Oh, I'm sorry—'

'No worries. But if you wouldn't mind moving.'

'Of course, absolutely.' He quickly stepped aside and felt his pulse begin to race. Soon, he would break into a sweat, too. Also, he hadn't picked up a single jar of pickled herring, even though he'd been standing there, blocking the fridge, for several minutes. Talk about making yourself conspicuous. Damn.

He turned away, only to discover that both the boy and his father were gone. Fuck. He looked around; it was all he could do not to start dashing wildly around the shop. The CCTV cameras had probably started zooming in on him already. The whole thing would be over before he'd even warmed up.

He made sure to keep putting things in his basket as he quickly moved towards the tills. At least stressed people in a hurry were a common enough sight.

It was all that bearded man's fault. If not for him, the dice would have given its verdict and he could have focused on following them to their car and noting down their registration number. Now the mood was ruined, and of course neither Rutger nor his dad were anywhere to be seen when he reached the tills.

Where the fuck were they? They couldn't have just disappeared. No one could escape the will of the dice. No one. And he was the one holding it, which meant the boy's fate was in his hands. Thus it was decided and thus it was going to be.

Then he realized where they were. Of course. How could he not have thought of it? The more a parent was annoyed by a child's nagging, the more likely he was to give in to it. Something young Rutger had clearly worked out long ago. And if one thing didn't work, apparently, another might.

Because there they were, in one of the aisles in the section for useless plastic things, getting a big box containing a plastic guitar off the shelf. He took out his dice, shook it, only for a moment this time, and opened his hand.

Maybe he had just seen it wrong.

Were those really two little diagonal dots and not three?

Maybe he hadn't shaken it for long enough.

No, it didn't matter. Or at least, it shouldn't. But what if he hadn't given chance a proper chance? On the other hand, he'd been shaking it when the bearded bloke interrupted him, so no matter how badly he wanted one, he had no excuse to start over. The dice had been given all the time it needed, and it had settled on the two little dots. He just had to take it and let those ungrateful pricks continue towards the tills.

Disappointment broke over him like a wave, even though he knew how utterly futile that was. After all, this was exactly the point. Not knowing who, when and where. His own will had nothing to do with it. He was nothing but a passenger who had climbed on to the roller coaster blindfolded, about to take the most amazing ride of his life.

So why didn't he feel exhilarated or excited? Had the bearded bloke ruined things for him or had it been the two aggravating dots on the dice? He didn't know. Either way, the mood was far from ideal, and all he wanted to do was to abandon his basket and go home. But he couldn't. Someone was supposed to lose their life tomorrow and he still didn't know who.

Maybe he was just hungry. It had been almost three hours since his last meal, and a small break wasn't against the rules, was it? If only to collect himself and get back in the mood. A rotisserie chicken leg, a tomato and a lemon-flavoured Ramlösa.

He could feel his spirits starting to return on his way over to the meat counter. When he took his queue number and noticed that the two people ahead of him in line were dressed in all grey and all black respectively, he felt his decision to take a break had been validated.

The girl behind the counter, who was dressed in white, called the next number and began to serve the man in black jeans, a black T-shirt and a dark jacket. His clothes were both neat and classy, so in some ways he deserved to live.

'And how can I help you?'

He hadn't realized the red digits were showing his number and that there was suddenly another person behind the counter. *Lennart Andersson*, according to the name tag pinned to his butcher's smock. He looked to be well over fifty, though he was clearly doing everything in his power to look at least ten years younger. He was unusually fit for his age, and that, combined with his low hairline and fake tan, conspired to trick the eye. It was better to look at a person's hands. That's where you could count the rings. No surgery in the world could change people's hands. Just like his colleague, Lennart was dressed in white, though with one small but significant difference.

His red tie.

Granted, only the knot was visible, but that was more than enough.

'One rotisserie chicken leg,' he said. He pulled out his dice and started shaking it while the man walked over to the heated display case.

A one.

One single dot in the middle.

It was what he needed to move on to the next phase.

The dice bounced on to the counter with a small bang and rolled over towards the basket of discarded queue numbers, where it finally came to a stop.

'Anything else?' Lennart put the price tag on the chicken bag.

A one.

Bloody hell, he really had rolled a goddamn one.

The decision had been slow in coming, but it was made now and in hindsight it seemed completely right.

'No, thank you, that's great, Lennart. Really great.' He allowed himself a smile, slipped his dice back into his pocket and picked up his chicken leg.

'All right then, have a good day.'

'And you, and you. You never know how long the good times last,' he said and walked towards the tills.

22

'ALL RIGHT, THAT'S ALL I wanted to ask you.' Lilja stood up.

'What, so we're done already?' said the woman who had been caught on CCTV, dashing across Norra Stationsgatan in Bjuv just minutes after someone turned on the rinse cycle in a laundry room a hundred yards away.

'Yes,' Lilja said, walking the woman to the door. 'But if we have more questions later, we will of course contact you again.' She couldn't see any reason not to believe the woman's story about going to the shops and not having enough credit on her card and therefore having to rush home to get cash. She'd even shown her the receipt saying *purchase cancelled*.

The woman was the third person she had been able to cross off the list of people who'd caught their attention in one way or another when they watched the CCTV tapes. To be honest, they had mostly caught Klippan's attention. For her part, she considered the whole thing a big waste of time. But she had promised, and being as firmly in his bad graces as she seemed to be after slipping into the Nazi rally without him, she wasn't going to pick a fight over this, too.

He certainly was cross. So cross, he'd posted a handwritten 'busy' sign on his door and was refusing to take her calls. Three times she had tried to call him after bringing Landertz and his son in, and each time he had declined.

One of the times, he'd sent a text saying he was busy and that they'd have to talk later. As though he were the only person in the world with things to get on with.

But she wasn't going to let him drag her down to his level and act cross back. That was his thing. Besides, she only had the man with the rental car left to check before she could actually make herself useful by sinking her teeth into the Sweden Democrats membership list.

That said, she hadn't been able to refrain from sneaking a quick peek between interviews. Mostly to reassure herself the USB stick wasn't empty. And it certainly hadn't been.

It turned out the party had about eight thousand members nationwide. Approximately two thousand five hundred of them lived in Skåne; narrowing the area down further to just Bjuv and its surrounding municipalities, that number went down to eight hundred and forty-seven people, of which two hundred and nine were women. Since the list included their personal identity numbers, she had been able to filter out anyone under twenty-five or over sixty and finally landed on a list of three hundred and eight names, any of which could turn out to be the man with the smile that appeared before her every time she closed her eyes.

There was no guarantee he was on this particular membership list, but research had shown that even people with more extreme right-wing and even Nazi views often voted for the increasingly mainstream Sweden Democrats in order to secure a first foothold in parliament.

Besides, she was convinced Sievert Landertz had recognized the man in the composite sketch, even though he'd continued strenuously to deny it during his preliminary interview that morning. He'd also threatened to sue them if they didn't release him immediately, and he would not only sue the police, but her personally for deliberately destroying his political career.

There could be no doubt Landertz had orchestrated the firebombing of his own office. But even though they had proof his car had been involved, that was not, according to Högsell, enough to press charges. And since the son denied everything as obstinately as his father, anyone could arguably have used the car because, if their information was to be believed, they routinely left the key in the ignition.

Hardly surprisingly, Högsell had advocated releasing them on their own recognizance. Lilja had agreed to let the son go, but not Landertz, not under any circumstances. In his case, she had referred to chapter 24 of the Code of Judicial Proceedings, which allowed them to hold him for up to three days if he was considered instrumental to the investigation.

So he was staying behind bars until twelve o'clock on Monday. That alone helped cheer her up a little. And it didn't hurt that the newspapers had already sniffed out the fact that he was under arrest.

She still had a few minutes before her interview with the rental car driver, Pontus Holmwik, so she gave her mouse a prod to wake up her computer screen, which was displaying the names of all the Sweden Democrats on her filtered list. For some reason, they were sorted in reverse alphabetical order with surnames like Östlund and Zachrisson at the top.

She was scrolling down through the list when her phone started ringing. Of course it was Klippan. Now he wanted to talk. But she was busy; he would have to wait. She declined the call and returned to the names on her screen.

Her first thought was that she'd seen it wrong.

Her second was that it was someone else with the same name.

The third, she was unable to follow through to the end.

Wallsson was not an uncommon name per se.

But there was only one *Hampus Zacharias Wallsson.*

Her Hampus was a member of the Sweden Democrats. Fuck. She wanted to throw up all over the screen.

'Hi, hello. Are you Irene Lilja?'

She looked up and in the doorway saw a man, dressed in a tight black leather jacket and equally black jeans, loosening the checked scarf tied around his neck. 'Yes, I am.' She got up to shake hands. 'And you must be Pontus Holmwik. Come in and take a seat. Can I get you anything to drink?' She couldn't tell whether she was shocked, angry or sad. She was probably all those things at once. According to the information on her screen, he had joined two years ago, in conjunction with the parliamentary election of 2010. And he hadn't breathed a word about it. Not one goddamn word.

'No, thank you, I just had a drink.' The man chuckled and sat down in the visitor's chair. 'I mean, water, or, actually, tea.' He laughed again. 'I'm sorry, I'm a bit nervous. I've never been called in for questioning by the police before.'

'There's no need to worry. We just need to clear up some things. Hopefully you can help us with that.' She and Hampus almost never discussed politics. But she remembered him saying during one of the election debates that he was going to cast his vote for the Social Democrats.

'Can I just ask how long it's going to take? Because I have an important—'

'Fifteen, twenty minutes, tops.' Lilja cut him off and flipped to a blank page in her notepad. 'Let's jump right in, shall we?' That prick had lied right to her face. 'According to our information, you rented a car from Hertz on Gustav Adolfsgatan here in Helsingborg last Wednesday. Is that correct?'

'Yes,' the man said with a nod.

'Then you drove to Bjuv that morning and parked the car on Norra Stationsgatan, next to the mall.'

'I don't know what the street's called, but I'm sure that's right.' The man smiled and nodded again.

It wasn't that you had to vote for the same party just because you were a couple. 'Were you visiting someone?' On the contrary, she felt vague contempt for couples who always voted for the same party and agreed with each other on everything just so they wouldn't have to think for themselves.

'No, I don't know anyone in Bjuv.'

'So what were you doing there?' But the Sweden Democrats, that was a different matter. That's where she drew the line. 'I assume you didn't rent the car just to go to Bjuv Mall and eat at the Amore Pizzeria.' If he voted for them, his world view had to be so fundamentally different from hers she simply couldn't see how they could stay together.

'Pizza? Oh no, I'd be the size of a whale.' The man chuckled. 'I was just scouting locations.'

'What do you mean, locations?' She had no choice but to leave him. As soon as she got home, she would have to pack her bag and go.

The man shrugged. 'Anything that might work as a backdrop for my dog pictures.'

'Dog pictures? I'm sorry, I'm not sure I understand,' Lilja said as she declined another call from Klippan. 'Is that your job?'

'Yes, people send in pictures of their dogs or cats. I edit them into different backgrounds. Like mountains, meadows or behind the wheel of a car. Completely up to the client. Then I filter the picture and tidy it up a bit before I print it and frame it.' He added a smile as though what he had just described was the most natural thing in the world.

'And this is something people pay you for?'

'Yes. It pays really well.'

'What's the name of your company?'

'PetFrame. Initially, I called it BeautyPet, but that made everyone think it was a beauty salon for pets, so I came up with PetFrame instead, which says exactly what it's about. Right?'

The door opened and before Lilja could react, Klippan was standing in the middle of the room. 'Högsell has just been on to me about not having enough to hold Landertz. Just so you're on board with us releasing him.'

'I'm not on board. We know he had something to do with the fire, and I'm fairly certain he knows who killed Moonif. So Landertz stays. Also, I'm in the middle of something.'

'Okay, we'll talk more about it later.' Klippan sighed. 'That's not why I'm here.'

'Fine. But whatever it is, it can wait until I'm done here.'

'Not really,' Klippan said and walked up to her desk.

She was aware that she was tired and had been running on fumes for the last few hours, and she was aware that she was about to completely overreact. But she'd had it up to here with his bullying. He'd been in charge for twenty-four measly hours, but was already walking around like he owned the whole fucking building.

'I'm sorry,' the man said. 'But are we done or did you have more questions?'

Lilja raised her hand apologetically to the man and stood up to give Klippan the kind of chewing out she normally reserved for Hampus. But seeing the photograph he'd just put down on her desk took the wind out of her sails.

'Assar Skanås, forty-eight years old, single, no children.' Klippan met her eyes. 'Isn't he the one you're looking for?'

How the hell had he managed this? She picked up the picture and studied the smiling man she'd spent the last two days trying to track down.

23

THE FIRST TRACK HAD consisted mainly of piano clinking and down-pitched voices. But as soon as the marching drums and angelic chorus of the second track came on, Fabian knew Apparatjik was the exception that proved the rule.

It was the first time he'd listened to the disc since buying it, and since the GPS informed him his destination in Ringsjöstrand was still nine minutes away, he turned the volume up.

He actually didn't have a lot of time for so-called supergroups. They seemed intrinsically unable to amount to anything other than a watered-down compromise. The Power Station with Robert Palmer and members of both Chic and Duran Duran was maybe one of the more embarrassing examples, though the Traveling Wilburys with giants like George Harrison and Bob Dylan weren't really much better.

But Apparatjik seemed to be bucking that trend. With members from Mew, A-ha and Coldplay, this constellation was considerably more interesting than its constituent parts.

He lowered the volume back down when he had to slow the car to avoid running over all the ice-cream-eating beach tourists who had braved the overcast sky and in many ways typical June weather. Fifty yards further on, he crossed a small bridge, parked by the side of the road and climbed out to walk the last bit.

Whether Hugo Elvin had ever come out here was impossible to say from the sparse notes in the margins of the investigation. He had reacted, that much was certain. To what exactly, other than a few minor details, was hard to say. Maybe he had simply been interested because the victim was Molander's father-in-law, and maybe he had eventually concluded that it really had been an accident, however unusual.

The whitewashed house was located in the middle of a hilly garden, less than a hundred feet from Ringsjö Lake. It was undeniably beautiful, a small, completely secluded piece of paradise.

This was where Molander's father-in-law, Einar Stenson, was impaled on his own kitchen knife, in the couple's summer house. His widow, Flora Stenson, lived in the house year-round now, and walking around the corner he spotted her on her knees, weeding, despite being eighty years old.

There was an old transistor radio next to her on the ground; Jessika Gedin was holding forth about the perfect breakfast and exactly how many millimetres wide the peels should be in orange marmalade to create optimal satisfaction.

'Excuse me, are you Flora?' he called out from afar so as not to scare her, but he still noticed her starting before turning the radio down.

'Hi, my name's John.' Fabian held out his hand to the woman, who stood up and wiped her hands on her apron before taking it.

It wasn't a lie. His name was John, or to be exact, it was John Fabian Gideon Risk. John was after his grandfather, who had changed his first name from Johan in 1963, after the American president was murdered. Where Gideon came from, he had no idea, and when he'd asked his parents once as a teenager, the mood had turned so uncomfortable he'd never mentioned the subject again.

'Yes?' the old woman said, looking him up and down with a sceptical air. Then she shook her head. 'I don't want to buy anything.'

Fabian let out a small laugh. 'No need to worry. I'm not here to sell you anything.'

'You people always are. If it's not a new well that needs to be drilled, it's the roof that needs replacing. But I don't want anything, and it doesn't matter what kind of tax deductions you try to tempt me with.' She waved her hand about as though chasing a fly and moved to turn back to her strawberries.

'I'm terribly sorry, but that's not at all why I'm here.'

He had thought long and hard about whether to drive out to Ringsjöstrand. The risk of her calling Gertrud afterwards and telling her about his visit was, perhaps, not great. Particularly since Gertrud had told him at one of their dinner parties that she'd lost touch with her mother after her father passed away.

But even so, he couldn't ignore the fact that his visit inevitably did involve a certain level of risk. If there had been another way of getting a clearer picture of the motive behind Flora's husband's death, he would have preferred it.

'Oh no? Then what's this about? I'm assuming you're not

here to fix the kitchen drain, which I've called Hjalmarsson's Pipes about at least a hundred times.'

'I am, actually,' he heard himself say and instantly noticed a shift in her attitude.

'I'm sorry, do you work for them or are you having me on?'

'Neither. But I'd be happy to give it a go.'

'And how much would that cost? Don't think I'll fall for just anything.'

'A cup of coffee would be nice.'

Fabian tightened the clamping ring around the plumbing trap under the sink and ran the tap to make sure there were no leaks. 'There. That should do it,' he said as he washed his hands, rolled down his shirt sleeves and went over to the small kitchen table where Flora Stenson was waiting with two cups of coffee and a plate of Finnish sticks.

'If I'd known it was that easy, I'd have done it myself,' she said, picking up one of the finger-shaped biscuits. 'But then you wouldn't have had a chance to get to your real reason for coming.' She met his eyes. 'I may be old. But I'm not stupid. At least not stupid enough to think all you're after is coffee.'

'I'm just here to ask some questions.' He sipped his coffee.

'Are you a reporter?'

Fabian shook his head. 'I'm with the police. If you want, I can show you my ID.'

'You have kind eyes. That's good enough for me. My husband always said I was too trusting. But what's the point of anything if we can't trust one another?'

'That's a very good question,' Fabian said, even though he couldn't tell her even close to the whole truth. 'I'm going over some of our old cases, and your husband's accident five years ago caught my eye.'

'I suspected as much.' Flora sighed and shook her head. 'All the detectives and officers who traipsed in and out here back then wasn't enough, I guess. Not to mention all the reporters. True, it was a strange, not to say spectacular, accident that did need to be investigated properly. But at the time, I really just wanted to be left alone.'

Fabian nodded and decided to allow himself one Finnish stick.

'And that wasn't the end of it. Just a year or so later, another detective came sniffing around here, asking a lot of questions, implying that maybe it hadn't been an accident after all, though he never said it in so many words. And now here you are, having coffee. You don't think it was an accident either?'

'Unfortunately, that's not something I can comment on at the moment. What do you think?'

'Nothing. And you know why? Because it doesn't matter what you or I or anyone else thinks. Einar's gone and no thinking in the world can bring him back. All right, out with your questions now. I have other things to get on with.'

'It happened here, in the kitchen, correct?'

Flora nodded.

'How often do you wax this floor?'

'Wax?' She chuckled. 'That was exactly what the other one asked, and the answer is still that I never waxed this floor once.'

'And Einar? Might he have?'

'I'd have been surprised if he had. On the other hand, Einar was a constant surprise. With him, there was always something unexpected around the corner. I think that's what I loved most about him. Are you married?'

Fabian nodded.

'Then you know how hard it can be.'

He nodded again.

'But it really only takes two things to make it work. Trust and secrets. Without both those things, a marriage will either be eroded from within by jealousy and fighting or it will become soul-destroyingly tedious.'

'And what secrets did Einar keep?'

'If I'd known, they wouldn't have been secrets.' She laughed a little and picked up another biscuit. 'It's like Ingvar, my son-in-law, always used to say. What you don't know won't hurt you.'

'Speaking of Ingvar, how were things between him and Einar?'

'Why would you ask about that?' Her eyes, the mood, her tone. Everything had changed in an instant.

Fabian shrugged. 'No reason. I'm just trying to form a better picture of Einar and his closest relationships.'

'You're not a very good liar, are you?' She fixed Fabian levelly. 'Of all his nearest and dearest, you start with Ingvar.'

'I'm sorry, that was just happenstance. I didn't mean anything by—'

'Happenstance? Are you sure? Because Einar never liked Ingvar. Nor did I, for that matter.'

'Why not?'

Flora paused before replying, as though she felt a need to weigh her words carefully before letting them out. She was just about to speak when a phone started ringing somewhere in the house. An old phone with a mechanical ringer. 'Excuse me. Have a refill and some biscuits while you wait.' She got up and disappeared into an adjoining room.

Fabian seized the opportunity to look around the kitchen and compare it to the pictures in the old investigation. From what he could see, nothing had changed since the accident. It was the same fridge and hob, the same yellow cupboards, and it even looked like the same kitchen towel hanging on its hook. The dishwasher was the same as well, an old avocado-green Husqvarna that looked like it had survived itself several times over.

He opened it. The smell that greeted him begged for someone to run a programme even though it was only half full. Several forks and spoons in the cutlery basket were placed handle down, but the knives were all put in handles up.

Afterwards, he couldn't recall whether it was that or something else that had triggered his epiphany. And it didn't matter. What mattered was that now he knew what Hugo Elvin's notes might have been referring to.

He pulled out both racks and checked to make sure the top one couldn't be lowered and raised. Then he started searching the drawers until he found what he was looking for.

The kitchen knife.

He checked that the length of the blade and the handle matched the information in the case file. Then he placed it in the cutlery basket point up and pushed both racks back in, and yes, the knife was in fact so tall it blocked the spinning spray arm. It was, in other words, highly unlikely that Einar Stenson would have put the knife in the basket himself.

Was that what Hugo Elvin had realized? That it had actually been Molander who had waxed the floor and placed the knife in the dishwasher? All to make it look like a tragic accident instead of murder. It was far-fetched in a number of ways, but by no means impossible.

The question was why? What had Einar Stenson done to deserve to die? What was the motive for taking the risk inevitably associated with ending the life of another human being? And of a close relative at that.

Einar had evidently never liked his son-in-law, and that feeling had likely been mutual. But *not liking* someone was very far from what could be counted as a motive. There must have been something else. Something that constituted a concrete threat and made Molander feel he had no choice.

'No, I don't need your help any more,' he heard Flora shouting into the telephone. 'Because someone already came by and fixed it.'

Fabian continued into the hallway.

'His name's John and he doesn't work for Hjalmarsson's Pipes.'

Framed photographs from various sporting events hung on the walls. He had never taken much of an interest in sports, but the pictures drew him in. They were all black-and-white and taken from a distance, though with impressive sharpness, and showed everything from a young Zlatan Ibrahimović when he was still playing for Malmö FF to Patrik Sjöberg when he cleared the bar at 2.42 and broke the world record at the Stockholm Stadium.

The pictures continued up the stairs, and it was only when he stopped to have a closer look at the iconic picture of Björn Borg on his knees, kissing the Wimbledon trophy, that he realized he was on the first floor.

At the other end of the landing was a balcony door, and to the left a bedroom with a double bed, a bedside table and built-in wardrobes. Immediately to the right was a bathroom with a bath, a toilet and a washbasin all in the same shade of green as the dishwasher.

Next to the bathroom was a room with a big desk on which sat, among other things, a sewing machine and a half-finished quilt. One corner was occupied by a reading chair filled with patterned fabrics; a bookcase that completely covered one of the walls was crammed full of photography books, old photography magazines and a large collection of camera flashes.

On the opposite wall was a breakfront filled with lenses of every conceivable size, from small wide-angle ones to three-feet-long telephoto ones. A collection of tripods jostled for space in front of the wallpapered door of a built-in cupboard.

Maybe it didn't mean anything. Maybe they were just somewhere else in the house. But the fact was that, so far, he hadn't come across any camera bodies. A professional photographer of Einar Stenson's calibre without a single camera body in his studio was much too improbable. He should have owned countless models.

He guessed it was Molander. That he'd got rid of them and that this was where the key to his motive was hidden. On a strip of film or a memory card.

To make sure he hadn't missed anything, he moved one of

the tripods and opened the cupboard door, only to discover it wasn't a cupboard at all but a staircase to the attic.

The attic was every bit as cluttered and chaotic as you would expect an attic to be after a long life. The ceiling was low; he could only stand upright under the roof ridge.

In the light from a grimy window on the short side of the house, he could see stacked moving boxes and woefully overloaded shelves vying for space between the trusses. Two free-standing cupboards flanked an old brown desk, which in turn was littered with enlargers, processing trays and bottles full of processing chemicals.

He pulled out the top desk drawers and realized he'd found what he was looking for.

24

Irene Lilja's hands shook so badly she had to hold her coffee cup in both to keep from spilling. Granted, she was tired and exhausted after last night's events. But that wasn't why her hands were trembling.

It was pure, unadulterated fury.

The thought of Hampus secretly joining the Sweden Democrats had made her so upset that for the first time in several years, she'd broken out in hives; her arms were itching so badly she wanted to scratch herself bloody. She hadn't even been able to absorb the fact that Klippan had actually managed to identify the man in the police sketch; she'd had to take a two-hour timeout just to calm down.

She had been moderately successful on that score. Once or twice, she'd come close to driving out to confront Hampus at the roadworks on road 111 outside Laröd where she knew he was working, but in the end she'd managed to restrain herself and had instead written a long email in which she explained why she was leaving him. In a postscript, she'd also advised him – for his own safety – to stay as far away from their home as he could for the coming days, so she could pack up her things.

But she hadn't sent the email. Just as she was about to press send, she'd realized the best punishment would be to leave him without a word of explanation. To secretly sort out somewhere to live and a new phone number and then suddenly just be gone one day, for good. Since he'd gone behind her back, she could go behind his.

Three rapid knocks on her door interrupted her thoughts. Klippan popped his head in. 'How about it? Ready to get back to it?'

'Absolutely.' She put her cup down. 'Why don't you start by telling me how you went about identifying him.' She held up the picture of the smiling Assar Skanås.

'Not much to tell. Routine investigative work seasoned with a pinch of luck.' Klippan closed the door behind him. 'After a while last night, I realized you must have managed to sneak into that event. So instead of twiddling my thumbs, I used the time to note down the numbers of all the cars and motorbikes outside.'

'So that's why you didn't pick up when I called?'

'No, that was because of something completely different, and without going into too much detail, I can only say there are better things to get up to when you don't have access to loo roll.' He shook his head and sat down across from her in the visitor's chair. 'Anyway, once I'd jotted down all the plates there wasn't much for me to do but to wait for you to come back. But you didn't. Everyone else came out and drove off, but not you, and in the end I was the only one left. I honestly didn't know what to do. I tried to call, I don't know how many times, but I kept being put through to your voicemail. I even went into that barn, but it was completely empty, not a trace of you.' Klippan shook his head and swallowed.

'And then what happened?'

'I drove back here, and when I saw that you were calling from your home phone, I knew you were okay.'

'But you couldn't be bothered to pick up or call back.'

'I was driving. Do you know how dangerous that is? *Don't tempt fate, that call can wait*, as I'm always telling Berit.'

'All right, and then Assar Skanås turned out to be the owner of one of the cars.'

'Exactly.' Klippan pulled a Snickers bar from his jacket pocket. 'It took some time, especially as it was harder than I thought it would be to find pictures good enough to compare with the sketch.' He unwrapped his chocolate bar and took a bite. 'After a few hours, all the noses, eyes and jawlines were parading in front of my eyes, even when I closed them. Oh hey, want a bite?' He held out his half-eaten Snickers bar.

'No, I'm good, thanks.'

'Sure?'

Lilja nodded.

'All right.' He shoved the rest of the bar into his mouth. 'Anyway, I finally found him, and what's even better, he's the owner of a well-maintained Renault 16. Remember those? I actually had one myself in the eighties. It was green and one of the best cars I've ever owned. You know, the engine was located behind the transaxle, and since each wheel had separate torsion bar suspension, you didn't even have to slow down on turns or care if the road was—'

'That's great, but do we have anything else on him?' Lilja cut him off after concluding that Klippan was feeling more like himself again and should therefore be okay with her directing the conversation. 'Like an address.'

'Yes, you were right, he's registered in Åstorp.' Klippan consulted his notes. 'Fjällvägen 29, to be precise.'

'Is it a house?'

Klippan nodded. 'It's in his name. He probably inherited it from his parents since he's been registered there his entire life.'

'What does he do for a living?'

'Nothing.'

'What do you mean, nothing?'

'Nothing,' Klippan repeated. 'And this is where it gets interesting. You see, he's claiming full disability and doesn't seem to have worked at all for the past twenty years.'

'What's wrong with him?'

'Who knows?' Klippan shrugged. 'We'd need access to his medical records, and to get that we'd need to get Högsell on board. And to be honest, I'm not sure we have enough for her to give the go-ahead. But I did find two convictions. One from 1977, when he was fined for sexual assault after going into the girls' changing rooms at Åstorp Swimming Pool to masturbate.'

Lilja shook her head, even though deep down she was happy that they were finally pulling in the same direction and knew where they were going. 'And the second one?'

'It's from 2007. I don't know if you remember, but it was in the papers.'

'What did he do?'

'He assaulted a clerk in a corner shop. Apparently, he came in with his older brother and bought a scratch card, and when they didn't win he went berserk and beat her up with the card reader.'

'And this clerk, was she of foreign extraction?'

Klippan nodded.

'How would you feel about heading out there together to bring him in?'

'I thought you'd never ask.'

25

'HELLO? EXCUSE ME,' THE yoga instructor called out when she noticed Molly Wessman starting to roll up her mat. 'I don't recommend leaving in the middle of a session. If you're not feeling well, it's better for you to just sit down and focus on your breathing.'

It was 40 degrees in the room and incredibly humid to boot, but that wasn't why Molly ignored the instructor and kept walking towards the door. She didn't feel unwell in the slightest. On the contrary, she enjoyed the heat, even though the main reason she had signed up for the Bikram session had been to clear her mind.

Unfortunately, the image of her sleeping face was always there, haunting her, and no matter how hard she tried to focus on her breathing, she was unable to stop thinking about who might have taken it, why, and what might be next. If anything was next?

It was now two and a half days since she'd woken up and seen the photograph of herself on her phone and then realized, soon after, that her fringe had been cut off. Since then, she had been unable to think about anything else. Even though nothing else had happened. Absolutely nothing. The only thing that had changed was her.

She had gone from being one of the high achievers in the office to feeling completely debilitated, reduced to a disorganized ninny who couldn't take three steps without anxiously looking over her shoulder.

She didn't just sleep poorly. She didn't sleep at all.

If she carried on like this, she would collapse. And over nothing worse than a shorn fringe and a measly picture on her phone. Was she really that feeble? Sure, someone had broken in to her flat and her phone. But the most likely scenario was, if she was being honest with herself, that that was the end of it. That it was over. That whoever it was had had their fun and was going to leave her alone from now on. And either way, the locks to her flat had been changed so they wouldn't be able to get in if they wanted to.

So why couldn't she just put it behind her and move on?

Like in boxercise class. Boxercise had actually worked significantly better than Bikram yoga, despite being insanely hard. She hadn't thought of that damn picture once, for a whole hour. It was only in the shower afterwards that anxiety had come creeping back in, making her feel like someone was watching her. Her, the woman who always showered at the gym and had no problem being naked in front of others.

Apparently, that wasn't possible any more, which is why she now pulled her coat on over her sweaty yoga clothes and hurried outside.

There were people everywhere. Just like every Friday afternoon, when people tried to sneak out of work early to get to the shops before the queues got too long. They were moving all over the place, cutting across the streets and bumping into one another. Everyone had longed for the weekend and now it was finally here. Now they were finally going to have those after-work drinks and throw those dinner parties. They were going to spend time together and solve the world's problems over yet another bottle.

She had never liked weekends. They were a waste of time, just one long wait for Monday to roll around again. If she wanted to go out and have fun, she could do that any day of the week, and the last thing she wanted was to have to share her dance floor with wasted out-of-towners.

But on this particular Friday, she wished for nothing more than to be part of the crowd. Those normal things she'd always despised and done everything to get away from. Now she was standing here alone, not knowing how to get through the claustrophobic eternity stretching out ahead of her.

She'd left the car at home that morning because she preferred being with the commuting public on the Öresund train to being alone. But instead of disappearing into anonymity on her way to work, it had felt as though everyone was staring at her. As though any one of them could be the perpetrator. A brief smile or a fleeting look had been enough to make her break out in a cold sweat.

In the light of that experience, she now decided to skip the bus to the station and instead hurried over to the other side of the street and got into the back of a taxi, even though the driver was busy reading about that awful laundry room murder in Bjuv in the evening paper.

'Are you free?'

'Absolutely.' The man shot her a smile in the rear-view mirror as he folded up his paper and turned the engine on.

'I'm going to Stuvaregatan 7 in Helsingborg. Do you know where that is?'

'No problem.' The man pulled out and once again met her eyes in the mirror and smiled.

Why was he smiling so much? Was it simply because he'd just scored a ride from Landskrona all the way to Helsingborg? But this could hardly be the first time he'd driven that way today. If that was even what it was about? If this was even a taxi? There had been a sign on the roof. Hadn't there? She'd been so stressed and had just wanted to get away from all the people. She couldn't see a taximeter. And then that damn smile again.

It was him. Of course it was him. Who else could it be? She had fallen straight into his trap. He had obviously tailed her and sat outside waiting for her to come out of the yoga studio. But she'd come out earlier than he'd expected, which was why he'd been unprepared, reading the paper, when she got into the back seat.

Why hadn't she just got on the bus like she'd planned? It was better to be surrounded by people, even if they did stare. She turned around and saw her bus pulling up to the stop. 'I'm sorry, could you pull over, please?'

'Pull over? Why? We're still in Landskrona.'

'I changed my mind. I want to get out.'

'You can't get out here,' he said, slowing down for a red light. 'Besides, the taximeter is already running, so it—'

'Taximeter? I don't see a taximeter.' She pushed the door open before the car had even come to a full stop.

'Hey, wait, you can't just— Hey,' the driver called out after her. But Molly was already narrowly escaping a collision with a Vespa that zipped by.

'Look where you're going,' the man in black on the Vespa yelled after her as she hurried on, gesticulating wildly to catch the bus driver's attention.

Out of the far corner of her eye, she caught a glimpse of

a car slamming its brakes to avoid her, tyres screeching. But she didn't care. The only thing she wanted was to get as far away from that taxi as possible.

Having climbed aboard the bus, she found a free seat next to a woman playing Murder Snails on her phone, one of the few passengers who wasn't staring at her. In a way, she could see where they were coming from. Her entrance had been anything but inconspicuous.

But enough was enough. She really wasn't all that interesting. The more she thought about it, the more it irked her. What gave them the right to stare at her like a monkey in a cage? Who the fuck did they think they were? Fucking pricks.

Fifteen minutes later, she got on the Öresund train to Helsingborg, and when that proved to be no better, she decided to give people a taste of their own medicine. Meet their eyes and stare back until she'd won each battle. One by one, she would make them look away. Make them crawl back into their holes until no one dared to so much as glance at her out of the corners of their eyes.

She started with the old lady sitting diagonally across from her, and it took only a second or two to make her look away. The same was true of the young man sitting next to her. He looked down at his phone before she could even get started.

Why had she never thought of this before? Why walk around all worried, acting like the world was coming to an end when it was likely nothing was going to happen at all? That man in the car was probably a completely normal taxi driver who was entirely justified in wondering what on earth she was doing, and all the people staring were just rude idiots who could be put in their place with a simple glare. No, from now on, she was going to stop feeling afraid and reclaim her life.

By the time the train approached Helsingborg, she had defeated them all, except for a man in a baseball cap and T-shirt sitting further back. Maybe he'd figured out what she was doing and decided to engage. Or maybe it was just a pathetic attempt at flirting. Either way, she wasn't going to give up.

Staring a complete stranger in the eyes was exhausting. It did more than make time slow to a crawl and each second last for a minor eternity. It made everything stop. Suddenly, she could see every detail of his face. The cluster of hairs on one cheek that he'd missed shaving. The dark brown *snus* stains on his front teeth when he smiled.

She didn't like the way he kept smiling at her. As though this wasn't hard for him in the slightest. As though he was in fact enjoying having her full attention. No, she didn't care for it one bit, and she wouldn't be surprised if he undid his fly and started masturbating.

Or maybe that was him.

She had been so busy trying to win, the thought hadn't occurred to her until now.

What if that was him. What if he was just sitting there, biding his time. Making sure he kept just the right amount of distance to avoid being noticed, but close enough to enjoy her descent into madness.

She looked out of the window. They were on their way into the tunnel, so they'd soon be arriving at Knutpunkten, where everyone would get off. The most important thing was to make sure she alighted before everyone else. So she got up and went over to the doors without succumbing to the urge to look over her shoulder.

The train slowed down. In a moment, the doors would open so she could dash across the platform, up through the departure hall and out the other side, then continue across Järnvägsgatan and in among the buildings, melting into the crowd.

She counted the seconds just to have something to do while she waited and heard someone come up right behind her. As the train came to a halt, she couldn't stop herself turning around and looking straight into that brown smile.

Then the doors opened and she could finally hurl herself out and run away. No looking over her shoulder now. Just follow the plan, get up the escalators, through the concourse and out the other side. But running proved impossible. There were people everywhere. Travellers were pouring in from every direction. But there was nothing for it. She had to press on, push and shove and not care about the people shouting after her.

It was the same on Järnvägsgatan. People everywhere, people whose one purpose in life was to get in her way. And once more, she yielded to the instinct to look behind her as she stepped right out into the street.

Suddenly, someone grabbed her arm and yanked her backwards, away from the bike lane, thereby saving her from being run over by a cyclist in bright Lycra. She felt a sudden sting in her right buttock.

'Careful, you'll get run over,' said a voice she thought she recognized. When she turned around, she saw a man in black she'd never seen before.

'They don't stop for anything around here.'

But how come she'd recognized his voice? They'd never met before. Or had they? Right, it was him, the man on the Vespa who had shouted at her when she crossed the street. He must have followed her all the way from Landskrona.

Without thinking, she kneed him in the crotch, wrenched free of his grasp and bolted across the bike lane and Järnvägsgatan. Cars were honking all around her, but she raced on up Präsgatan towards Bruksgatan, even though in her heart of hearts she knew it was pointless.

26

THE HOUSE WAS LOCATED at the end of the road, bordering on billowing rapeseed fields that eventually turned into the vast forests, meadows and deep ravines of the Söderåsen wildlife reserve. But idyllic was the last word Lilja would have used to describe it. The whole place made her so uneasy she wanted to tell Klippan to turn around and drive as far as he could in the opposite direction.

Instead, she got out of the car and signalled for the two uniformed officers in the car behind them to block the road with their car.

'I guess we really have to hope we've come to the right place now,' Klippan said, checking the magazine of his gun.

'This is the place.' Lilja started walking towards the house, pushed the squeaky wrought-iron gate open with her foot and continued into the garden, where she spotted a car, barely covered by a tarp.

'Are you thinking what I'm thinking?' Klippan walked over to the car and pulled off the tarp.

Inconceivably stupid as it seemed to park it in his own garden, that was clearly exactly what Assar Skanås had done. Because there it was. The orange Volvo he had escaped in after stabbing its driver.

Without a word, Lilja nodded for the two officers who

had just joined them to circle around to the back of the house while she and Klippan proceeded towards the front door.

Normally, they would have rung the bell, and if no one opened, they would have engaged the services of a locksmith. This time, she had brought her own lock pick, to save time. But it wouldn't be needed since she could see the door wasn't, in fact, completely closed.

The air was thick with damp and mould; she could feel how each breath pulled things into her lungs that had no place there. They continued into the yellowish-brown hallway, covering each other with their guns.

The hallway turned into a dark passage with stained, dirty grey carpet and walls covered in fake wood panelling, framed embroideries and a collection of old rifles. The two doors on either side were closed, as was the door on the far side.

The first door on the left opened into a tidy bedroom, furnished with a single bed, a desk with two barbells and a book from the Nordic Resistance Movement entitled *Handbook for Activists in the Resistance Movement*.

The door opposite led into a kitchen with a small table for two. On it sat, among other things, a plate of spaghetti drenched in ketchup and a glass of milk. She dipped her index finger in the milk; it was still cool.

They moved on to the next door in silence. This bedroom was a mess. Bedding, tattered Barbie and My Little Pony magazines, an unopened Lego City box that, ironically, contained a building set for a prisoner transport, a jar of pink slime and a collection of Star Wars figures, along with some child-sized underwear.

Lilja turned to Klippan, who was standing right behind her. 'You told me he doesn't have children,' she whispered and immediately realized what was going on.

'He doesn't.'

Klippan had clearly been correct in his assumption. Assar Skanås was not only a dyed-in-the-wool Nazi, he was a paedophile, too.

They returned to the corridor and continued to the next door, which had a sign on it depicting a peeing boy. Just like the other doors, this was closed but not locked. Unlike the other rooms, the light inside was clearly on.

On Lilja's signal, they tore open the door and pushed into the empty bathroom, which didn't look like it had been refurbished since the house was built.

But that was not what caught Lilja's attention.

Nor was it the three-foot swastika on the wall next to the bath.

It was the faint sound of voices.

It sounded like children's voices, two girls who had suddenly started talking to each other.

She turned to Klippan, who nodded for them to continue down the corridor. The further into the house they got, the more distinctly they could make out the voices. But they didn't sound sad and there was no crying to be heard. On the contrary, they seemed excited and playful.

The corridor ended in a closed door with smoked glass panes through which you could only dimly make out what was happening on the other side. Lilja pushed the handle down. This door was locked, or maybe just stiff. She didn't know and didn't care; she raised her foot and kicked it in.

The sight that greeted her as she stormed into the living room with her gun at the ready was shocking, but with each throbbing of her pulse, her shock gave way to confusion. What she saw was two very young children, both girls, sitting naked on the floor, their legs spread wide, trying to put socks on their feet.

She had seen the same scene many times before. So many she'd lost count. When she was little, it had been one of her absolute favourite TV shows, and this particular episode, in which Madicken and her younger sister Lisabet sit naked on the floor getting dressed, she remembered as if she'd seen it yesterday.

Back then, neither she nor anyone else had raised an eyebrow at the nudity or indeed reacted to it in any way at all. It had seemed perfectly natural and completely unrelated to sexuality. Today, it was impossible to watch it without feeling like a paedophile, and there was talk of censoring it along with other, similar scenes in the Astrid Lindgren oeuvre.

But no one was watching. The TV was playing the DVD in front of an old red sofa that was as stained as the carpet in the passage. The coffee table was littered with a pile of Astrid Lindgren DVDs: Pippi Longstocking, Lotta on Troublemaker Street and Emil of Lönneberga – all of which contained nude scenes that would never have been included if the films had been made today.

'Looks like you were right,' she said, as she scanned the room for other doors. 'The motive's paedophilia.'

'Given that swastika out there, I'd say we were both right,' replied Klippan, who was on his way over to an open bureau on which lay several document folders.

Had he seen them coming and made his escape? Was that why he'd left the house with the door unlocked and a film playing?

Through the glass back door, which was slightly ajar, she could see the two uniformed officers secure the garden behind the house.

'Come and take a look at this,' said Klippan, who had laid his gun down and put on his reading glasses. He handed her one of the documents from the folders, and as soon as she started reading, she realized why he found it so interesting.

... *After an initial examination, the patient is judged to be psychologically deficient... clear paedophiliac characteristics... closed ward... medication and therapy... Claims to hear voices.... Mental illness...*

It was excerpts from Assar Skanås's medical records, and they seemed to indicate that he had been in and out of the closed psychiatric ward of Malmö Hospital for years.

... *With his current medication and regular therapy, the patient's level of awareness about his own mental state is deemed sufficiently high for him to successfully maintain equilibrium in his home environment...*

The document was dated 8 June 2012, which suggested Assar Skanås had been discharged only five days before the events in Bjuv. Cutbacks and lack of beds and resources were likely the official explanation. Incompetence was the real one.

27

Apart from his first visit to Tivoli, this had without a doubt been the best day of his life. Even though it was several hours ago now, his adrenaline was still pumping. Not even in hindsight could he think of any way it could have gone better. Possibly it had taken the dice slightly longer than expected to pick its victim in the supermarket that morning. Other than that, everything had worked out beautifully.

Even so, he had felt unusually anxious and been scared to go straight home without making sure he wasn't followed. He simply couldn't believe it was this easy. That he could do practically anything without anyone suspecting, so long as he left all the decisions to the dice.

He was back in his building now. Since the lift door on his floor was still insisting on letting out a tiny squeal every time it was opened, even though he'd greased the hinges, he took the stairs.

At least the door to his flat didn't squeak, and as soon as he'd closed it behind him, he turned the lock, first the original lock and then the extra one he'd installed himself with espagnolettes that fastened the door to the floor, walls and ceiling. Then he put the chains on, pressed his face against the door and peered out through the peephole.

The stairwell outside was empty; a minute or two later, the lights went out. He continued further into his flat, stepped behind the curtain on the right side of the window and looked down at the street.

A taxi stopped and dropped passengers outside Sam's Bar, where the outdoor serving area was already as crowded as the patrons were drunk. In other words, it looked like a normal Friday night in June, and he should be able to take off his clothes, put them back in the wardrobe and take a bath without worrying.

With the floating pillow behind his neck and only his nose, forehead and chin above the steaming surface, he closed his eyes. He needed twenty minutes. Twenty minutes of complete relaxation before he could move on to the next phase of his current mission.

Because that was what he needed to focus on. His current mission. Without complete focus, he wouldn't stand a chance. All the other things would have to wait until the dice were more generous with the time frame.

As usual, he woke up without having been aware that he was falling asleep, and for the first few seconds he felt like he would never be able to shake the drowsiness. But then it rushed into him, the energy he needed so badly, and it made him almost fly out of the bath.

The dice had picked its victim and it was time to find out who he was.

He pulled on his robe, left the bathroom and continued through the living room into the bedroom, which was so small it only had room for a bed, a small desk by the window, a chair piled high with clothes in one corner and a wardrobe in the other.

The wardrobe door was already ajar, so all he had to do was push the clothes to one side and step inside. Then he pulled the door shut behind him until its three magnets connected with a click. With his right hand, he fumbled along the back of the wardrobe until he found the hole, which was only just big enough for him to stick his middle finger in and reach the rectangular metal plate on the back, just above the hole. He pushed the plate to one side.

The lock mechanism clicked and the back of the wardrobe sprang open. He continued into the dark, closed the back behind him and pushed the metal plate back into its holder. Not just the middle one he had just opened, but the top and bottom ones that could only be accessed from this side. Finally, he reached up for the blackout blind, pulled it down to cover the locked door and turned on the overhead light.

The windowless room he was now in didn't officially exist. Not even his landlord would find it, if he ever decided to pay a visit. The flat was still a one-bed, like his contract stated, just a slightly smaller one. And so long as no one was specifically looking for the missing square feet, they would never be noticed.

The extra wall dividing the bedroom down the middle had only taken a weekend to build, though he had both insulated it and used double plasterboards on each side. Even so, it had taken him more than three weeks to completely finish the project.

He'd had to put up new wallpaper, and to make sure it didn't look too new and modern, he'd chosen a greyish-blue kind typical of the 1960s. The light from inside had also stubbornly kept leaking out along the edges of the newly built wall, but that had only taken him three and a half days to fix.

The secret room was almost a hundred square feet and furnished with a narrow bed, a work table with an internet-connected laptop and a desk chair. A built-in bookshelf covered the entire back wall, except for where the bed stood. Most of the shelves were still empty. Unlike the chest of drawers, which was filled with clothes and did double duty as a bedside table. Next to the chest of drawers was his store of tinned ravioli and drinking water, which, according to his calculations, should last him two weeks if he had to go underground.

One of his biggest challenges had been to figure out how to avoid a sanitary disaster when answering the call of nature. To take care of his urine, he had purchased ten one-and-a-half-litre, sealable plastic bottles.

For his faeces, he had acquired a sturdy metal bucket with a lid and covered the rim with polyethylene foam pipe lining, thus constructing a seat that was in fact more comfortable than it looked. The bags in the bucket could be sealed and replaced, but it remained to be seen if that was enough to keep the stench at bay.

He sat down at the desk, opened his laptop and went to hitta.se. Of course, Lennart might not be listed in any publicly accessible database. But he didn't seem like a person who would be aware that he was in them by default unless he actively opted out. Much less that they could pose any kind of security risk.

A quick search told him there were over seven hundred people in Skåne named Lennart Andersson. After limiting his search to an area within moped distance of ICA Maxi in Hyllinge, he got that number down to fifteen, which was still too many.

Instead, he tried Facebook, typing in Lennart Andersson with the additional search term Skåne in the search field, which resulted in a list of eight people. Unfortunately, none of them was his Lennart Andersson. Then he tried ICA Maxi's website, clicking through to the Hyllinge supermarket.

Under the tab Meat Counter, he found Lennart Andersson and three of his colleagues, posing in front of the counter with big smiles on their faces and their arms around each other's shoulders.

The page also informed the reader that Lillemor Ridell, Fridolf Aronsson, Lennart 'Beefsteak' Andersson and Magnus Brittner always put cleanliness and quality first. And they urged customers not to be shy about asking whether the entrecôte was locally sourced or even just for a good Friday night chicken recipe.

Beefsteak, he repeated to himself.

He went back to Facebook and added the nickname to his search.

And there he was. The man with the fake tan who had sold him a chicken leg with a carefree smile and wished him a good day. He was wearing the same smile in his profile picture, though in that he was distastefully sweaty and wearing a headband and a sleeveless, neon-blue synthetic gym top. So what he was dealing with was a fitness fanatic who likely possessed both strength and stamina.

He pondered whether this might constitute a problem. But since he had no idea yet what the method was going to be, dwelling on it was a waste of time and energy, so he scrolled down the page instead.

Lennart 'Beefsteak' Andersson was a typical member of his generation as far as Facebook went. He didn't seem to see the point in hiding anything, since he had nothing to be ashamed of.

His profile used the 'friends' privacy setting, which meant anyone could see he had 137 friends, their names, and in some cases where they worked. He liked Smokey, Gasoline and Queen and, hardly surprisingly, Lasse Stefanz, Wisex and Robert Wells as well.

He must be into genealogy, too, since he'd liked pages such as The Federation of Swedish Genealogical Societies, Friends of Roots and the County Council Archive. Sportswise, he favoured body-building, though he also seemed to have his sights set on doing Iron Man in Kalmar at the end of the summer.

What he couldn't find, however, was a home address, nor any pictures, apart from the obnoxious profile picture. In order to access those things, he would have to get Lennart to accept a friendship request.

He couldn't see his colleague Lillemor Ridell among Lennart's friends, so he immediately set to work creating a profile for her, even though she probably already had one. A cropped picture from the ICA Maxi website would have to do for her profile picture. Five minutes later, he'd fired off a friendship request.

He only just had time to pull on underwear, a T-shirt and socks before Lennart accepted.

Shift doesn't start until noon tomorrow so plenty of time for an hour of rowing, a leg session and twenty minutes of sun! #beach201 #onlyasoldasyoufeel #ironmankalmar

Lennart's latest status update was only a few minutes old and accompanied by a bare-chested brag selfie taken in front of the bathroom mirror.

It was all he needed.

Who and *when* were set in stone. All that remained for the dice to decide was *how.*

The initial roll was to determine which category to settle first. Odd numbers represented *murder weapons* and even numbers *ways of dying.*

A three.

He pulled out his list of weapons numbered from one to twelve and did a pre-roll to decide whether to use one or two dice.

1. *Pistol*
2. *Rope*
3. *Crossbow*
4. *My body*
5. *Spear*
6. *Knife*
7. *Slingshot*
8. *Sword*
9. *Rifle*
10. *Item from crime scene*
11. *Machine of some kind*
12. *Baseball bat*

A four.

That meant he had to use two dice, so he took out another and shook both in his cupped hands before releasing them on to the green felt.

Two fives.

In other words, he was going to use something from the crime scene. It could be anything at all, so long as he hadn't brought it with him. In many cases, that and number eleven might be the most challenging options. But this time, it was definitely the best. Particularly given that he had less than twelve hours to prepare.

All he needed now was a final confirmation. One last roll of the twenty-sided marble dice to set his plan in motion.

All sides except the one marked with an X meant he could get started. He quickly picked up the dice, shook it and rolled.

An X.

He stared at the dice as though he couldn't believe it. But it really was an X. With odds of one in twenty, that side, like all the other sides, should be a highly unusual outcome. Now it was the second time in two weeks.

But it didn't matter. The die had been cast, and he had no choice but to head over to the bookshelf once more and take down the notebook with a big X on its cover.

In it were 120 neatly written pages, each with a unique side mission he had to complete. It could be an addendum to the main mission, like grabbing a trophy or hurting one of the victim's colleagues, too. But it could also be another full-on mission, with all that entailed.

He had designed them himself, with the help of the dice, and while some of the side missions were relatively straightforward and harmless, some were detailed and completely insane and could potentially end everything.

Here too, a pre-roll was needed to determine the number of dice. But since there were 120 missions, he might need as many as twenty dice, which was why the white icosahedron was going to decide again.

A seven.

He took out seven six-sided precision dice, shook them all together for more than a minute and then rolled.

A two, a five, another five, a six, a three, a one and one more six.

He added up the seven numbers, picked up the notebook and flipped to page 28.

The side mission was an addition to his main mission at ICA Maxi and had a description that was only two words long.

Eyewitnesses required.

28

Computer can't read camera memory card.

The Google search couldn't be described as anything other than a last-resort cry for help in Fabian's attempts to access the contents of the digital camera he'd found in Einar Stenson's attic. If you could even call them real attempts, given that he had no hope of succeeding.

He had not been surprised to find that the batteries were empty, had leaked and started to rust. After all, the camera had been left in a damp attic for at least five years. But even after cleaning it meticulously with cotton buds drenched in vinegar and changing the batteries, it had refused to come to life.

At that point, he'd taken the memory card out and cleaned it and the terminal it connected to, but to no avail. He'd then tried inserting the memory card into his computer's card reader, which had prompted a discouraging message to appear on the screen:

J:\DCIM\100CANON is not available.

The file or catalogue is damaged and can't be read.

Two reboots later, still with the same message, he'd been ready to throw in the towel and head upstairs to clean up and prepare for Matilda's homecoming the following day. He'd already wasted too much time on the plasticky little camera, which he had hoped would give him a clue as to why Molander might have wanted his father-in-law dead.

But he hadn't been able to tear himself away. He had stayed in the basement nursing what amounted to an obsession with accessing the contents of the memory card.

He had tried sticking it in Matilda's camera, which had been a Christmas present, only to be rewarded with the message *unknown format*. The only way forward at that point had been to take the camera apart and calmly and methodically go over its insides and make sure everything looked okay. Just to be safe, he had dried any potential moisture with Sonja's blow-dryer.

The whole thing had taken him over an hour and a half, and he had heard himself say a quiet prayer before reinserting the new batteries, carefully sliding the memory card back in and pushing the tiny 'on' button. He had even closed his eyes, hoping it would emit a little tune when it started.

Nothing.

If he'd had a hammer to hand, he would have smashed the camera. But he didn't, so now he was sitting at his computer, staring at the results of his Google search.

To his surprise, his question had generated over 133,000 hits. He clicked on the second one, which redirected him to www.thephotosite.se where a certain *Alfred_d* seemed to be getting the exact same message about the file or catalogue being damaged and unreadable.

He had already tried all the suggested solutions.

All except one.

PC Inspector was a piece of German freeware that claimed to be able to re-create and repair files on external memory cards. Even if you had accidentally reformatted a memory card, the programme could help. It sounded too good to be true, and given that it was completely free, there could be no doubt it contained a virus or something else you would never under any circumstances want on your computer.

And yet, he pressed download.

He regretted it immediately but couldn't help looking forward to what would happen when the growing bar reached one hundred per cent, and against all better judgement, he followed every instruction, approved the user licence and even put in his VISA number and CVC code.

It was only after the laborious installation process was completed that he realized he had purchased the full version of the software with free updates for years to come.

It looked like a proper programme at least, and from what he could see it was already scanning for external memory units. Unless it was in fact encrypting his entire computer so it could threaten to erase it all unless he transferred a lot of money to some Russian bank account.

Found 8GB Sandisk memory card in slot J.

Do you want to recover deleted and broken files?

He pressed YES, which started the process; whatever it was the programme was doing, it apparently wasn't going to be quick. The percentage counter remained stubbornly stuck on three per cent for several minutes before switching to four. It was only when he heard the ding signalling an incoming email that he realized he must have nodded off.

From: 7hcx3h+fbpyhpq8xakfo@sharklasers.com
To: fabian.risk@gmail.com
Subject: Theodor
I assume you realize your son is one of them.
/D
http://politiken.dk/indland/art4925602/Anklageren-forventer-høje-straffe-for-medlemmer-af-den-såkaldte-smileyliga-når-retssagen-starter-næste-uge

The link redirected him to an article in the Danish daily *Politiken*. It was about the impending trial of four Swedish teenagers who, wearing yellow smiley masks, had killed three homeless people in Helsingør in the most elaborate and brutal ways conceivable. And they had filmed each deadly assault and posted them online.

Fabian was very familiar with the case. For obvious reasons, it had made a splash on the Swedish side of the sound, too, and people had argued for holding the trial in Sweden on the grounds that two of the defendants were minors. But since the crimes had been committed in Denmark, that was apparently where the trial was going to take place. Specifically, in Helsingør.

He did a search on the Smiley Gang and read several articles written about the spectacular case. But nowhere was there any mention of there being a fifth member. All the sources mentioned three boys and one girl, all of whom were currently in detention in Denmark.

What did any of that have to do with Theodor? He hadn't been to Denmark, and he definitely wasn't detained and awaiting trial. Right now, he was at the cinema watching *The Avengers* and soon he should be on his way home. Could this be a mistake?

The message was written in Danish and signed D.

It could have been sent by just about anyone, but if he had to guess, he would have said it was Dunja Hougaard. A Danish colleague of his, who two years earlier had sacrificed her entire career by going against her boss, Kim Sleizner, to help him with an investigation. Dunja had even ended up saving Theodor's life when he had been kidnapped by a terrifying serial killer who wanted to punish Fabian for the crimes of his past. Since then, they'd only been in touch sporadically, if at all.

Except for about a month ago, when he had run into her in the lobby of the police station. She had needed his help to get the names of the residents at various addresses. That's right, hadn't she said something about it being near where he lived?

But not once had he seen her name mentioned in connection with the smiley case. Kim Sleizner, on the other hand, figured prominently, together with a certain Ib Sveistrup from the Helsingør Police. Had she been secretly working on the investigation? Was that why she'd asked him for help and not Tuvesson? That wouldn't be entirely unlike her. Especially if Sleizner was involved. Did that mean she knew something no one else did?

He pulled out the middle drawer on the left-hand side and took out a cloth bundle, placed it on the desk in front of him and unfolded it. There it was, the gun Theodor had come home with on that fateful night when the earth had shattered beneath their feet.

Since then, Matilda's hospital stay had demanded all his attention; he hadn't given the gun so much as a thought and had almost managed to forget it even existed. But here it was, waiting to be handed in, registered and examined, and of course he would do that, as soon as he'd found out exactly where Theodor had got it from.

It was a Heckler & Koch USP Compact 9 mm, a model designed for close-range combat, common among the Danish police. That much he knew, but since the serial number had been scratched out, there was no way of doing a search on it.

Was this the connection to Denmark? Could it really be true that his own son was mixed up with those heinous crimes? He had not been well, that was for sure. But that unwell... It had to be a misunderstanding.

He had tried to bring it up with Theodor more than once. But when he hadn't run away and withdrawn into his shell, he had, like the other night, reacted with rage. And Fabian's guilt had made him tiptoe around any potential conflict, no matter how small. But the time for that was over. He didn't care what Theodor's reaction was. As soon as he got home from the cinema, the truth was going to come out.

He found Dunja's number on his phone and dialled it to ask if it was really her. It took a few seconds for the technology to connect, but instead of ringing, he heard an automated woman's voice.

'*The number you have dialled is no longer in use. The number you have dialled doesn't exist. The number you have dialled is no longer in use. The number...*'

He hung up and tried again, but this time he put the number in manually, only to be greeted by the same automated voice.

Maybe there was a technical error. Maybe she'd changed providers. There could be any number of reasons why the number wasn't working. But this was Dunja, and if he knew her right, it was a very deliberate choice.

From: fabian.risk.privat@gmail.com

To: 7hcx3h+fbpyhpq8xakfo@sharklasers.com

Subject: Re: Theodor

Hi Dunja.

It seems you have a new number. Please call me so we can talk about it over the phone instead. I assume it's you. If not, please tell me who you are and why you are contacting me regarding my son.

Kind regards,

Fabian Risk

He sent the email and had an almost instantaneous reply.

Final-Recipient: 7hcx3h+fbpyhpq8xakfo@sharklasers.com

Action: failed

Status: 5.1.1

Remote-MTA: dns; gmail-smtp-in.l.google.com.

(2a00:1450:4010:c0d::1b, the

server for the domain gmail.com.)

Diagnostic-Code: smtp; 550-5.1.1 The email account you tried to reach does not exist. Try double-checking the recipient's email address for typos or unnecessary spaces.

Fabian didn't know what to think. Her number didn't work and she sent cryptic emails from an address you couldn't reply to. What was she up to?

He picked up his phone, found Kim Sleizner's mobile number and was about to dial it when a window suddenly popped up in the middle of his computer screen.

Recovery of 8GB Sandisk memory card completed.

Do you want to view the files?

Right. The pictures on the memory card. That's what he'd been doing. He clicked YES, which opened a new window.

A window full of pictures.

He double-clicked the first one, which showed Flora Stenson waving to the camera from her vegetable patch. It was taken on 13 September 2005. Two years before Einar Stenson died. The next picture was a selfie taken only six minutes later, standing on a jetty by Ringsjö Lake. The next picture showed two steaks on the grill alongside jacket potatoes wrapped in aluminium foil and topped with big dollops of Béarnaise sauce.

For a professional photographer, the pictures were surprisingly mediocre. The small digital device clearly hadn't been Einar's forte, and given that there were only about twenty pictures, he had likely grown tired of it quickly and stuck it in the attic.

The rest of the pictures were private, too, and from Fabian's perspective completely uninteresting. Most looked to be from Christmas 2005, and even though he had only been to Molander's house three or four times, he felt he recognized the beige sofa and the rectangular dinner table set for a Christmas feast. Molander and his wife, Gertrud, were in some of the pictures; she was wearing a red skirt, he a button-down shirt and a lambswool jumper.

The only picture he couldn't make head or tail of had been taken in the days after Christmas and showed a group of about ten men seated around a set table in a basement room. Every one of them was laughing uproariously, holding full *Snaps* glasses and looking merrily straight into the camera.

On the back wall was a sign; when he zoomed in on it, he could see it said *PC Celluloid* under a logo depicting an old-fashioned box camera. Of course, it was a photography club. A club that, if the name was anything to go by, only concerned itself with analogue film, which explained the hilarity when Einar pulled out his little digital marvel.

He couldn't be sure. But something told him he was finally breaking new ground. Hugo Elvin had undeniably sniffed out a lot. But chances were he hadn't been here. That didn't mean there was anything of interest to find. But if there was, he was finally a step ahead of both Elvin and Molander.

29

'THERE IS STILL NO *statement from the Helsingborg Police regarding the arrest of Sievert Landertz early this morning,*' the newscaster said. '*But according to unconfirmed sources, the arrest relates to the fire in the Sweden Democrats' offices in Bjuv. And in today's interpellation debate, leader of the Sweden Democrats Jimmie Åkesson seized the opportunity to comment on events.*'

'*This is what I call a threat against democracy,*' Åkesson said. Lilja could feel her mood souring just from hearing the sound of his voice. '*Can anyone here seriously believe that our justice system would ever contemplate detaining a Social Democrat like this, without any concrete—*'

Lilja turned the radio off. She'd had enough. If it wasn't a threat to democracy, it was a threat to freedom of speech. As though there was no concrete evidence against Landertz. He had the word *guilty* practically tattooed on his forehead, for God's sake.

She had backed her car in between two shrubs that grew at exactly the right angle to hide her from anyone coming down the gravel road. From there, she also had a perfect view of Assar Skanås's house just twenty yards away and would be able to call for backup the moment anyone set foot near it.

Having made sure he was neither in the house nor lurking somewhere in the garden, she and Klippan had decided to hold off on calling in Molander and his team and instead to keep the house under surveillance overnight, in case he returned.

But she had been staked out in her car for over four hours now and hadn't done anything other than stare at an abandoned house through a zoomed-in camera lens while the news went on and on about Landertz and that damn party of his, which would probably be able to recruit even more members off the back of this debacle.

Besides, the dashboard showed an outside temperature of just twelve degrees, which meant she had to turn the heat on in her seat and wrap herself in a thick blanket to stay warm. Something that in turn meant she had to start the engine every fifteen minutes and let it run for at least three.

She lost a fight to suppress a yawn at the exact moment the blue numbers on the dashboard changed to 00:00. She had two more hours before Klippan was coming back to relieve her, and unless something happened pretty soon, she was going to fall asleep and drift so far away a Third World War could start without her noticing.

She stepped out of her car, stretched and filled her lungs with the damp night air. They had agreed not to enter the house alone. Partly to leave it as untouched as possible for Molander, but also in case Skanås did come home. Then they would be at a significant disadvantage. Skanås had proven himself to be very dangerous and completely unpredictable, and in the house he would also have home court advantage.

But the house was one thing, the garden something else entirely. When she was well inside it, she stopped and looked around. At the Volvo sitting there, only partially covered by the tarp, and at the lawn, which she'd only just noticed was freshly mowed, much like the flowerbeds were completely devoid of weeds.

Something wasn't right, but she couldn't put her finger on what; and then her phone started playing 'Sommartid' by Magnus Uggla. Which meant it wasn't Klippan calling. That would have elicited the old Bakelite ringtone. No, this ringtone was one of her absolute favourite songs and especially chosen just for Hampus. A relic of a time when she'd been so head over heels in love, her whole body had ached.

It was his third attempt at calling her that night. He was probably wondering where she was and why she didn't pick up. Nothing weird about that. But just as she couldn't stand the rest of Magnus Uggla's terrible mainstream discography, she couldn't bear the thought that she was living with a Sweden Democrat.

So she let the call go to voicemail and continued around to the back of the house, to the back door that led into the living room. It was still ajar, as it had been when they first got there.

Everything pointed to Skanås having spotted them through a window and fled through this very door. But where had he gone after that? And the Renault, his own car, where was that? As far as she could see, there was nowhere to park it in the back and nowhere to drive off to. There wasn't even a road, just fields.

Suddenly, she heard the sound of a doorbell inside the house, an electronic melody spreading through the dark. But there was no one on the other side of the house, ringing the bell. Instead, she noticed that the cordless phone in its dock was lighting up in the gloom just inside the glass door.

She pulled the door open wide enough to squeeze through and leaned in over the display that showed the number 072-684 43 82. While the melody kept ringing out as though it was never going to give up, she did a search for the number on her mobile but got no hits, which suggested it belonged to an anonymous prepaid SIM card.

Careful not to contaminate the receiver with her own prints, she pulled her shirt sleeve down over her hand before picking up the phone and pressing the green button, silencing the ringing.

'Yes, hello…' she said, but there was no answer. The only sound she could hear was someone breathing heavily on the other end, sounding almost winded. 'I'm sorry, who am I speaking to?' It was a man. That much she could make out. A man who had just wrapped up a workout or finished some other physically demanding activity.

'*What are you doing in my house?*'

It was him. It was really him. 'My name's—' she heard herself say before she was cut off by a click.

30

Fabian had just clicked into the photography club Celluloid's website when a sudden draught gusting through the basement announced that the front door had been opened and closed again.

Theodor was home.

That was why he was now standing on the first-floor landing outside the closed teenage door, gathering the strength to knock. This was the time. No matter how Theodor reacted, this was it. But there was no reaction, so he knocked again, harder this time, and was rewarded by a tired sigh from the other side.

'Yes... what is it?'

He opened the door, stepped into the gloom and saw Theodor lying on his bed, squinting against the light coming from the hallway behind him. Granted, it was half past midnight, but it was also mere minutes since he came home. Had he even gone to the bathroom and brushed his teeth? What's more, the room reeked of both smoke and alcohol.

'Have you been drinking?' he heard himself say, noting that Theodor's clothes lay in a pile on the floor.

'Um, what?' Theodor tried to focus his eyes on him.

'I asked if you've been drinking. This place reeks of alcohol,' he said, realizing it was probably the absolute worst way of initiating an intimate father – son conversation.

Theodor sighed. 'Yes, two beers. Happy? Or was there something else you wanted to talk about?'

'Happy? Why would I be happy?' Regret was pointless. It was already too late, even though he'd been in his son's room for less than thirty seconds. 'You know what Mum and I have said about drinking before you're eighteen.' Apparently, this was all his son had to do to throw him completely off balance.

In an attempt to steer the conversation in a gentler direction, he took a deep breath, walked over and sat down on the edge of the bed. 'Look, I wasn't exactly teetotal at your age either.' He met Theodor's eyes. 'It's not that I don't understand that people your age need to break rules and try forbidden things. And between you and me, I have no problem looking the other way if it's two beers. But two beers is nowhere close to what you've had tonight. Can we agree on that?'

Theodor pondered that for a while before nodding.

'Good. Because that actually wasn't what I wanted to talk to you about.' He broke off again.

'What? Did something happen?'

'I don't know. That's what I'm trying to find out.' He simply had no idea how to go on. 'We all make mistakes from time to time, don't we? Take me, for instance. I've done my best, but I would also be the first to admit that I've hardly been the world's best or most involved dad. And in the light of everything that's happened, it's clear I've made more mistakes than most. Mistakes that in some cases are so serious that we're going to have to live with them for the rest of our—'

'All right, stop, what are you on about?' Theodor cut in.

'It's the middle of the night and I'm exhausted. Could we maybe talk about this some other time?'

'I'm sorry.' Fabian shook his head. 'This is already some other time, or the time after that. Much as we might like to, we can't put it off any more. I need to know, right now, what really happened that night you came home, beaten black and blue and with a gun down your trousers.'

Finally, a reaction. In the form of an eye-roll, sure, but it was better than nothing.

'We've already talked about that. I don't even know how many times.' Theodor shook his head. 'I was walking through Slottshagen on my way to meet up with some friends and these blokes appeared and—'

'You're right,' Fabian interrupted. 'That particular story I've heard enough to last me a lifetime. But that's not what really happened, is it?'

'Of course it fucking is.' Theodor glared at him from bloodshot eyes.

Fabian shook his head. 'No, you weren't walking through Slottshagen, and there were no "blokes" who held you at gunpoint until a third "bloke" appeared with a pit bull and scared them off.'

'Fine, believe whatever you want.' Theodor snorted derisively. 'Like I care...'

'Theo, I can see it. It's clear from a mile away that—'

'What do you mean, see it? You never see anything before it's too late,' Theodor hissed. 'What the fuck is it you imagine you can tell from looking at me?'

'That you're not okay.'

Theodor faltered, as though that had been the last response he'd expected.

'I can see you've got something on your mind. Something heavy, that's eating at you, and if you think it's going to just go away on its own, you're wrong. It's going to get worse and worse, and if you don't do something about it, eventually you'll rot inside.'

For the first time, his son actually seemed to be listening without protest. 'You said I never see anything before it's too late,' he continued. 'Painful as it is, I have to admit that that's been true too many times. But I'm trying to change that, and that's why I'm here now and not some other time. Because it's not too late. There's always a path leading forward, and yours starts with the truth. No matter how difficult and terrible it may be, that's where we have to start. Otherwise everything's going to fall apart. So I'm asking you again. What happened that night?'

Theodor was quiet, his eyes looking for something to rest on as he took in what had been said. But when they couldn't find a safe point, his chin started to tremble instead.

Almost an entire minute passed before he met Fabian's eyes again. 'Okay,' he said in a voice as fragile as a butterfly wing. 'You're right. I wasn't on my way to meet up with friends. I was standing by the cashpoint down on Stortorget Square when they appeared. Suddenly, they were just there, waving the gun around, telling me to get all my money out.'

One lie replaced with another.

He could see it in his eyes and felt disappointment rush through him. 'Theodor… Dunja's been in touch. You know, Dunja Hougaard, who saved your life two years ago.' Suddenly, there was panic in Theodor's eyes. 'She tells a very different story. One that takes place in Denmark and in which you are one of—'

'It wasn't me! I promise it wasn't me! They forced me. I never wanted to, but they forced me to be their lookout while they—' Theodor broke off and scrunched up his face to fight back the tears.

'While they what? Pushed a big firecracker down the victim's throat and lit it?'

'But I was never part of it. I promise, I didn't do anything. I had no idea. I just accidentally watched one of their videos where they pushed this guy in a shopping trolley. It was horrible. You could see him struggling to get out, but he couldn't, because they'd tied him to it and... Fuck, it's the worst thing I've ever seen... Straight out on to the motorway, and then there was a lorry and—' Theodor broke off again as silent sobs took over, racking his whole body.

Fabian wanted to comfort him and say it was all going to be all right. That time would heal all wounds. But he couldn't get a word out. It was as though everything had short-circuited – his ability to speak, to think, everything.

'They said that I was done for if I told anyone. Dad, I promise. I never wanted to be in on it, but I had to help them, I had no choice. She'd dropped the necklace with my name on it and probably my fingerprints, too.'

'Who? Who had your necklace?' His brain was finally snapping back in.

'Alexandra. She was in on that crap, and when I realized that, I just wanted to get out of there. Leave and never come back. But Henrik, this mate of hers, refused. Said I was one of them whether I wanted to be or not.'

'And Dunja? Where does she fit into this?'

'No idea. She just knocked on Alexandra's door one day. I'd just seen the video and didn't know what to do.'

'So what did you do?'

'We hid until she gave up. We must have sat behind that sofa for at least an hour.'

In some ways, his son was so big now; in just another year or two, he would be taller than him. And yet he was also still a little boy hiding behind sofas.

'And the gun?'

'Henrik gave it to me when I was on lookout in Helsingør. That's when she showed up again. I don't know how she knew we were there.'

'So it was Dunja you got in a fight with?'

Theodor nodded.

She must have been working on the investigation. That's why she'd asked for his help finding the names of a number of residents in his own neighbourhood of Tågaborg.

'But hey…' Theodor met his eyes. 'We don't have to tell Mum about this, do we? We can keep this between us, right?'

'Theodor, you have to know that's not possible.' Fabian made an effort to sound calmer than he felt. 'Of course we have to tell her. And you also have to report to the Danish police as soon as possible.'

'What do you mean, report? Why?' Theodor was blanching.

'To give a statement and tell them about your involvement and about—'

'No, listen! I didn't do anything! The only thing I did was stand there and—'

'Exactly, Theodor. You were there. How you got there, whether anyone forced you or not, doesn't matter right now. The only thing that matters is that you were there.'

Theodor stared at him, but it wasn't anxiety or worry

Fabian could see in his eyes, nor was it distress or nerves. No, his eyes shone with pure, unadulterated terror. Which was exactly what Fabian felt, too. At what lay ahead and what was going to happen to his son.

'If you want to put this behind you, the only way is to give a statement telling the police exactly what happened.'

Theodor's face turned even whiter.

'I will go with you and make sure you have a good lawyer. But it's going to be up to you to—'

The warning signs had been there. The fear in his eyes, his breathing and his deathly pale face. He should have known. Even so, Theodor's vomit seemed to come out of nowhere.

31

Even though it was still early and the sun had only just peeked over the treetops, Lilja was sweating like she'd hit menopause. And that was after taking off both her windcheater and her fleece; apart from the jeans that clung to her legs, she now wore nothing but an old T-shirt, which was also sopping wet.

She turned off the trail and sat down on a tree stump about thirty feet into the woods, pulled one of her water bottles out of her backpack and downed it, despite the water being lukewarm and tasting faintly of plastic.

Looking at her phone, she noticed that the marked area on the map had changed again. Having been cheese-puff shaped just over an hour ago, it was now more evocative of a balloon someone had sat on.

Molander, who was running the triangulation from the station, had explained that the shape depended on the number and types of masts the phone in question was connected to at any given moment. And whether the antennas were omnidirectional or unidirectional; and if the latter, what angle they covered.

Either way, the area was much too large, covering about a square mile. Which didn't sound overly large in itself, but the inaccessible terrain of Söderåsen, coupled with the fact that she and Klippan had only been able to commandeer two uniformed officers on account of the football games that weekend, made the task considerably harder than finding a needle in a haystack.

With ten men, they could have positioned themselves along the edge of the area and moved in towards the middle in a coordinated fashion. Now, they had no choice but to try to encircle him by covering one cardinal direction each, which left vast areas completely unmonitored, making it easy to slip through the net. In fact, that had already happened twice, and if nothing changed soon, they would have to abort the mission and wait until after the weekend, when they would have more manpower.

Once something did change, she assumed the app she was using to receive information from Molander was acting up or had frozen somehow, so she shut it down and restarted it. But it made no difference. The marked area on the map still looked wrong.

Round like a tennis ball and, compared to before, tiny.

So tiny it only covered about twenty thousand square feet.

And if that wasn't enough, she was only a few hundred yards from the centre of the area. If the map was correct, that had to mean he had suddenly come into contact with several masts at once, which also meant he could disappear again at any moment.

Looks like you're heading right for him, Klippan texted. *We'll be there as soon as we can.*

She got up, took out her gun, shoved two extra magazines into her back pockets and hurried off. Back out in the sunshine, she crossed the path and continued across a small clearing with dried-up branches and roots that did their best to ensnare her feet and sprain her ankles. But she managed to avoid any disasters and was soon entering the woods on the other side.

She gave her phone another glance as she passed a large boulder; the area on the map was still small and their paths would soon cross, unless he suddenly changed direction.

She stayed absolutely still, but couldn't hear anything other than the flies buzzing around her sweaty neck. Maybe he'd already heard her and stopped, too.

At length, she left her hiding place behind the rock, looked around and pushed on deeper into the trees, whose foliage dappled the sunlight. At first, she jogged on light feet, jumping over the mossy rocks and fallen trees, but after a while, she slowed down to a walk, almost a crawl, checking her location on her phone from time to time.

After a while, the trees began to thin out and the forest opened up into a clearing where the sunlight was so strong it took her eyes a moment to get used to it. But as soon as they had, it became clear they were not out here chasing a shadow.

The charred rocks had been dispersed, true, but it didn't take her long to find the spot where they had presumably ringed a fire as recently as the night before. Some little way off, the grass was flattened in a near perfect rectangle of about six by three feet.

Something glinted in the grass. She squatted down and realized on closer inspection that it was a shell casing, and just as she had pulled on a latex glove and was about to pick it up, she froze at the sound right behind her.

It was no branch snapping. And no twig. It wasn't even leaves rustling in a way the wind could never make them do. What it was, she didn't know. Maybe it was just her imagination. Even so, she put her hands in the air and turned around slowly to stare straight into his black eyes.

The stag was standing only a few feet away from her and seemed at least as surprised as she was. She was struck by how majestic he was with his big antlers and jet-black eyes, which stared at her as though he could read her mind.

The bang was loud, but the accompanying echo made it impossible to pinpoint its origin. It was the whooshing sound, cutting through the air right in front of her face, that made her realize someone had shot at her. The bullet hit the grass a few feet to her left as she dived right. The stag was already gone, as though it had never existed.

She crawled through the grass, trying to collect herself. A normal rifle bullet travelled about eight hundred yards per second, more than twice the speed of sound. But the bang, the whooshing sound and the impact had happened more or less simultaneously, which meant the shooter couldn't be more than about fifty yards away.

She'd been lucky. As that realization sunk in, shock took over. But there was no time for shock now. Now, she had to get away as quickly as possible. If only she could have spotted him through the tall grass. But she didn't dare get to her feet, so she kept crawling at a perpendicular angle from the bullet's trajectory.

She could only hope he could see neither her nor the grass around her move. If she could just get out of the open clearing and back into the forest, the trees would hide her and she could go around and come at him from behind.

Then one more shot rang out, and another.

She froze and was holding her breath while doing a mental inventory of her body to make sure she hadn't been hit when she heard a dull thud. A sound that scared her a lot more than the gunfire.

Was that him, jumping down from his hiding place? If he'd been up a tree or in a hunter's blind, he would definitely have seen her. Wasn't that footsteps she could hear now? Yes, she could even hear a twig snapping.

Should she get up and try to run away? No, that would just make her an easier target. Better to keep her gun at the ready and... The sound made her stop thinking and start acting. The sound of something metal being pulled out of its sheath.

With her gun in both hands, she rolled around and saw his outline against the blinding sun, with a butcher's knife in his hand and a rifle slung over his shoulder.

The seconds were dragged out as if to give her more time to aim at his leg and squeeze her right index finger harder and harder around the trigger. But something made her hold off.

Even though his eyes, nose and mouth looked the way she remembered from the police cordon in Bjuv, she felt increasingly sure something wasn't right. The smile wasn't there, for example, and when a cloud finally hid the sun and she could see his face more clearly, she instantly realized what the problem was.

It wasn't him.

32

He took up position a few feet from the stone wall down at the Parapet Pier in Helsingborg's Northern Harbour. It was just over three feet tall and curved almost exactly like Lennart Andersson's meat counter at ICA Maxi in Hyllinge. There was no point going for a longer run-up now since he wouldn't get one when it actually came to doing it for real.

His first attempt had gone so-so. He'd hesitated and not managed to gather enough momentum to get over the wall. His second attempt had gone better and on his third, he'd made it across the entire road, landing on one of the big rocks on the other side. On his fourth try, he hadn't even needed his hands for support.

Like with so many things, it was about believing it would work. Like when he was a little boy and learned how to break a pencil with his index finger. He'd worked at it a whole weekend straight without succeeding; it had felt like his index finger was about to snap, not the pencil. It was only when he'd made his mind up to go all in without hesitation that he finally did it, and from then on, it hadn't even been hard.

He did a fifth jump; now it felt like the easiest thing in the world. It was just like with the extra mission. When he first saw the X, he was anxious, and when he rolled his way to page 28 of the notebook, he'd been convinced this was most likely going to be his last mission. Now, on the other hand, he was convinced it was going to come off brilliantly.

He'd even almost forgotten he was wearing the mask. If not for the sweat trickling down the inside of it, he wouldn't have given it a thought. That's how well it fitted him.

He'd ordered it from the US the moment he'd finished writing his 120 additional missions. Almost a thousand dollars it had cost him, and even though he'd splurged on express delivery, it had taken five weeks to get to him.

But it was a perfect fit, and as best he could tell, it seemed to work just fine out in public. This was his first time wearing it outside his flat.

Most people had passed him without reacting. As if they hadn't noticed him at all. A few had looked twice, as though they couldn't quite put their finger on what was off. Others had gone so far as to turn and look. Then he'd tempted fate by strolling down the pedestrianized stretch of Kullagatan on a late Saturday morning.

The mask was hot, though. He took it off, wiped the inside clean with a towel and put it in his backpack before jumping on his bike and pedalling off towards Hyllinge.

33

It was a completely electronics-free process. No ones and zeros. No driver routines, cables or memory cards. Just the pure chemistry of the hydroquinone spreading through the cassette and coming into contact with the film roll's layer of gelatine, where it began to convert the silver halides that had been exposed to light to metallic silver. A process that rendered a darker negative the longer it was allowed to go on.

Developing analogue film required both skill and experience. The developer had to be able to perform steps such as pulling the film out of its cassette and loading it on to the reel blindfold, from muscle memory, since those things had to be done either inside a changing bag or in complete darkness.

He had found the rolls of film in a locked compartment in one of the lockers at the Celluloid photography club. Once upon a time, the locker had belonged to Einar Stenson; he had managed to open the compartment with one of the keys from Hugo Elvin's drawer. It was the smallest of the three marked with green tape and a question mark.

Six rolls of film, each with twenty-four pictures that had to be developed. All black-and-white but of varying graininess and ISO values, which required different developing times and developer concentration.

Four of the photography club's members had offered their services. They'd hung up the developed films to dry, then cut them into strips of four and placed them in a holder in the enlarger, where the negatives filtered the light of the incandescent bulb, projecting their images on to the emulsion side of the photopaper for a few short seconds.

It was only once the exposed photopaper was placed in a tray of developer that Fabian could finally see the pictures as they took shape, seemingly out of thin air.

Since Einar Stenson had been a professional sports photographer, there were a lot of sports pictures, showing everything from handball to curling, but there were also beautiful nature shots with mirror-like lakes, billowing fields of grain and trees emerging from morning mist. There was also a handful of truly gorgeous portraits of Einar's wife, Flora Stenson, and a picture series of a couple of magpies building a nest. What Fabian wasn't finding, however, was anything that might explain why Molander would have taken Einar's life.

After the first few hundred pictures, everyone's enthusiasm started to wane. Fabian was less affected than his four volunteers, who had naturally been hoping to discover something juicy to gossip about around the dinner table.

One had already bowed out and the remaining three were so despondent they didn't react when Fabian lingered over the developing tray.

At first, the fields that were slowly darkening looked like hundreds of dots growing into larger patches. Little lakes of darkness that eventually came together in the shape of a car. A grey sedan with its driver's door open and with someone…

Or wait... Fabian watched the developing process for a few more seconds to get more details.

Yes, someone had just opened the driver's door to climb in behind the wheel. Someone with glasses, dressed in what looked like a checked shirt under a sports jacket.

The man's face was turned away from the camera, but Fabian recognized both the driveway and the house. He still remembered taking Sonja and the children there for the first time two years ago for a team barbecue, thrown in the middle of a complex murder investigation.

Of course it was Ingvar Molander. He wasn't even surprised.

By now, he could also see that the car was a grey Saab 9-3 with registration number HOT 378. In other words, the same model and colour as the one in the pictures Hugo Elvin had found. He felt justified in assuming this was the same car that an as-yet-unidentified woman had been climbing into in those pictures.

Einar Stenson had apparently been tailing Molander, and on this particular night he had followed him to his rendezvous with the unknown woman. Had Molander had an affair? Was that what all this was about? Had Einar discovered that Molander was cheating on his daughter Gertrud?

The picture was moved to the stop bath on its way to a tray of fixer before being hung up to dry, but Fabian was already staring intently at the next picture, whose dark fields were becoming more clearly delineated.

Once again, the same Saab, but this picture was taken from behind and in a completely different location, with trees and shrubs in the background. Molander was only a dark silhouette. The woman was more visible, wearing the same dress as in the pictures from Hugo Elvin's drawer and walking towards the car with a big smile on her face.

But it was when Fabian saw the next picture, the last one before Einar must have run out of film, that he started getting a strong feeling. A feeling of recognition. He couldn't say where he had seen her before, but the longer he studied her zoomed-in face, the more convinced he became that he had seen that woman not too long ago.

34

The man who had shot at Lilja out on Söderåsen was waiting for her in the interview room when she finally entered and slowly pulled the door shut behind her. She had left him to stew for a few extra hours on purpose, with nothing but a small plastic cup of water to keep him company. All to help him realize who was in charge.

But the moment she turned around and met his gaze, she knew the hours of quarantine had not been enough. The cup sat untouched, and the way he looked at her as she walked up and took a seat across from him was so intense that her own eyes dropped to the floor out of sheer self-preservation.

And as if that wasn't bad enough, she involuntarily shot him a conciliatory smile once she had mustered enough strength to look up again. The whole thing was so ridiculous she wanted to slap herself so she could snap out of it and start over.

'Are you Igor Skanås, Assar Skanås's younger brother?' She looked him straight in the eye, determined not to look away before he did.

Igor Skanås nodded, seemingly completely unperturbed by her attempt to dominate him.

'I would prefer if you answered audibly since this is a police interview and not a pantomime,' she continued, her eyes already burning from not allowing herself to blink. 'Nodding has a tendency not to be picked up by the audio recorder.'

'I bet, but maybe by one of the many CCTV cameras?' Now he was smiling, but since he still hadn't blinked even once, it only served as another reminder of who had the upper hand.

'Good. Then at least we've established that you have the ability to speak.' He studied her. But not in a sexual way. There was no lust in his eyes. No flirting. Not a trace of the lewdness she so often had to deal with. No, this was something else entirely and much more meticulous, which for some reason made her feel even more exposed. 'Let's start with why you shot at me.'

'If I'd been shooting at you, you wouldn't be sitting here now.' His smile had vanished, and for a split second he looked away towards her right side before fixing her again.

'So you claim you were aiming at the stag, even though the start of hunting season is over four months away?' Her eyes couldn't take it any more; she pretended to cough so she could close them for a few seconds without making her defeat too obvious.

'That's correct.' He smiled as though he could see straight through her pathetic charade.

'So, to put it differently, you admit to an offence against wildlife?' Had he been looking at her ear? Both of her ears protruded slightly, as she was well aware. But not enough to cause a reaction. 'Wonderful. Then let's put that aside for now and talk about the reason we're here, which is your brother, Assar Skanås.'

'What about him?'

'He's a suspect in the murder of eleven-year-old Moonif Ganem. You may have read about it in the papers.'

Igor Skanås showed no reaction, apart from possibly lowering his eyes a fraction.

'Or perhaps you haven't been keeping up with the news since you've been out in the woods, hunting?' What was he looking at now? Her nose? What the fuck was he up to?

'You should try it sometime. A few hours in, you can even hear your own thoughts.'

'And what are your thoughts? Regarding the allegations against your brother.'

Igor Skanås crossed his arms and leaned back in his chair with a smile. 'I assume this is about the little brown boy who went for a spin in the washing machine?'

'Excuse me?' She had assumed he was joking, testing her boundaries. But his smile wasn't the smile of someone joking around. It was simply an outward expression of his delight. 'A spin in a washing machine. Is that how you see it? That it was what he needed to wash his dirty brown skin clean. Maybe you would have preferred it if he'd poured in a bottle of bleach to make the boy even paler?'

'Sure, why not?' Igor Skanås opened a tin of *snus*, unfazed by her outburst.

Things were starting to make sense now. The swastika, the tidy room and the Renault Klippan had seen at the Nazi gathering. Those were all Assar's brother's doing.

'If we're lucky, it serves as an example and thins out the hordes of people who think they can just come here and take over,' he continued. 'So yeah, sure.' He gathered *snus* between his thumb, index and middle finger and pushed it up loose under his top lip. 'Given how many little gingerbread men die of starvation every day, it seems a fairly low price to pay for saving this country from complete meltdown.'

She was about to argue with him. Her arguments were lined up like the gun belt of an automatic weapon. But she remained silent because she'd just realized why he was studying her.

She would have given a lot to be able to stand up, leave the room and let someone else take over. But there was no one else, and no matter how heinous Igor Skanås was, he wasn't who she was after.

'Your brother. Is he as big a racist as you?'

'You should ask him.'

'Fine, I just have to find him first. When did you last see him?' she said, doing everything in her power to keep her feelings from showing.

'Wow, okay, I guess we're changing the subject again.'

'We're here to discuss your brother. Not your twisted world view.' Giving him short shrift was all she could do. 'So if you wouldn't mind focusing on answering, I promise I'll ask questions. Like this one: When did you last see Assar Skanås?'

'Last Wednesday when he got back, at around three or four in the afternoon.'

'Did anything seem strange to you? Anything out of the ordinary that stood out?'

'Everything about Assar is strange.'

'But there was nothing to make you suspect that he had just committed a murder.'

'No.'

'You didn't ask where he'd been or what he'd been doing? Or why he came home in an orange Volvo 240?'

'He wouldn't have told me anyway, since he was in a mood.'

'What kind of mood was that?'

'Closed. Shut up inside himself. When he's like that, it's best to just leave him to his own devices.'

'And what did he get up to?'

'The usual.' Igor Skanås shrugged. 'Put on some Astrid Lindgren films.'

'So he's the paedo and you're the Nazi. Wow, your parents really did a great job.'

'I have no problem articulating and defending my political views. But as you said, we're not here to discuss me. As far as my brother's concerned, he's always liked children, and in a way he's still a child himself. He has an imagination like no one else and for as long as I've known him, he's lived in his own bubble.'

'But if everything's just the same old, and you didn't react to anything, why did you call him last night?'

'So that was you in our house. I figured.'

'Would you mind answering the question?'

'I wanted to make sure he was still at home, watching films.'

'But he wasn't home.'

'Apparently not.'

'And not even that made you at all worried that something may have been amiss?'

'Worried? My brother is sick and needs help. He's been sick for as long as I can remember.'

'Would you describe him as mentally deficient?'

'No, I would describe him as a bleeding crackpot, and if you ask me, he shouldn't be allowed out in public.' Igor

Skanås chuckled and shook his head. 'Not only does he hear voices, he usually obeys them, too. If he's cold, he might decide to make a fire in the middle of the floor, and just a few years ago he was convinced he was a French winemaker. For six months he walked around with a red neckerchief and spoke pretend French, even in his sleep.'

'Fine, but if he's that bad, why is he living at home?'

'Good question. Beats me.'

'It does? I mean, it seems pretty convenient for you to have the house, your car and whatever else registered to your brother. I haven't checked, but I wouldn't be surprised if there were quite a few unpaid parking tickets.'

'Look, I've tried to get my brother committed a thousand times. But every time, they keep him for a few days, clean him up and do their little studies that more or less give him the medical all-clear, so long as he takes his medication.' Igor Skanås snorted derisively and shook his head. 'And you know why? Because they can't afford to do anything else. Because even though we have some of the highest taxes in the world, we can't even find the money to look after someone like Assar. That might strike you as a bit odd, until you realize all the money is going to the rainbow of people pouring in across our borders. Apparently, those are the people we should worry about. Not our own.'

'You almost sounded like you had a point somewhere in that racist rant.' She stood up, pleased to have hit a nerve. 'I take it, then, you haven't been in touch with him since you took to the woods. So if you have nothing more to add, I think we should—'

'I have. I talked to him last night.'

Lilja stopped mid-step and turned around. 'Last night? But he wasn't home last night.'

'No, so I tried his mobile instead. You might have heard of them.'

'What, he has a mobile phone? And you're only telling me now.'

'You didn't ask. Besides, you could have just looked him up in the phone book.'

He was right. How could she have missed something so basic. 'How did he sound?'

'Agitated. Stressed. Just like he usually does when he hasn't taken his medication in a while and is about to have a breakdown.'

'Did he say where he was?'

'No, I didn't ask. I just told him to go to the nearest hospital, but that pissed him off and he hung up.'

Lilja nodded and opened her notepad to an empty page. 'Would you mind writing down his number here.'

Igor Skanås gave her a look.

'Yes, I know he's in the phone book. But I would still like you to humour me. Then you can leave.'

'So we're done?'

'For the moment. But I want you to call me if you think of anything else.'

Igor Skanås scribbled down the number, stood up and walked towards the door. But before he reached it, he turned back to her. 'There's one thing I've been wondering.'

'Yes?'

'You have Jewish blood in you, right? You do, don't you?'

35

It took Molly Wessman a moment after she regained consciousness to realize she must have passed out. She had no idea what time it was, if it was early in the morning or the middle of the night. She didn't even know where she was, other than that she was lying on something hard and cold.

The hours before she had drifted off had been pure torture. She actually felt a little better now; maybe whatever was wrong with her was passing.

Her body still ached, though, especially her stomach and innards. Or was it her kidneys? Apparently, kidney stones could be fiendishly painful. But she wasn't that old, and fatty foods had never been her thing. No, a stomach ulcer was more likely. Given how stressed she'd been lately, it was actually remarkable she hadn't developed one sooner.

The shower curtain with the red dots. She recognized it now. It was her own. At least she was in her own bathroom.

She tried to get up, but the pain in her stomach returned with such force it felt like someone was grating her innards. Everything went dark and she didn't even dare to scream for fear that would make it worse.

As the pain subsided, she decided she would need to have another go at shoving her fingers down her throat. It was her only option if she wanted to survive. At this rate, she was going to pass out again before long and this time she might never wake up again.

That said, she always felt that way when she was ill. She'd never been good at being sick. The slightest temperature and she started preparing for the end. Especially when she had food poisoning or a stomach flu. There was nothing worse than feeling nauseous, and now she was both sick and in a hellish amount of pain.

She took a deep breath to summon her strength, grabbed the edge of the toilet bowl and heaved herself up so she could lean over it and stick her fingers down her throat.

The problem was that no matter how far down she shoved her fingers, the only result was a series of gagging convulsions that made her feel like she was about to snap in half. Not even poking at her uvula brought up anything other than a small amount of searing bile.

And blood. Black lumps of clotted blood.

That was what scared her the most. A bleeding ulcer meant her stomach might be perforated, which was serious enough in itself. But when she thought about it, she hadn't had any symptoms until yesterday, which meant this was probably something else entirely.

For the first time in her life, she felt a clear, unequivocal fear of death. What she had once looked down on as a weakness suddenly yawned before her like an abyss.

She wasn't ready to die, not by a long shot. She, who had just got started and had so many things left to experience. Others might lie down and give up, but not her. It would take more than this to break her.

Her phone… She had to find her phone and call someone. Anyone. If she waited much longer, she wouldn't be able to. Where had she put it? She tried to stand up but was too weak, so she crawled into the hallway on all fours.

The sun was streaming in through the living room window, hitting the hallway floor, which it only did in the afternoon. So she had been sick for somewhere between ten and fifteen hours, since coming home the night before. She had noticed the nausea going up the stairs, and she had only just managed to get her coat off before having to run to the toilet.

Her boots were still sprawled on the floor by the front door, and apparently she had balled up her coat and tossed it on the shelf above the hooks. Of course, that's where her phone was, as high up as possible and, given her condition, practically impossible to reach.

Gritting her teeth against the pain, she started crawling towards the front door. But after no more than a few feet, she had to lie down on her stomach and drag herself the last bit.

When she reached the door, she coughed up a few more lumps of coagulated blood before summoning her last ounce of strength and pulling herself up via the door handle and her raincoat, which was hanging on its hook.

But as she grabbed the shelf to heave herself upright, it came loose from the wall, ramming into her shoulder as she hit the back of her head on the floor. She ignored the pain. It was nothing compared to what was happening in her stomach. The only thing she could bring herself to care about was that her phone really was in her coat pocket and that it had a thirty-three per cent charge.

She just about managed to dial 112 and turn on the speakerphone before she dropped the phone in yet another blood-filled coughing fit.

'*This is Emergency Services,*' a woman's voice said on the other end.

'You have to come here. I'm really poorly.'

'*I'm sorry, could you repeat? I can't hear you very well.*'

'Come here. You have to come here.'

'*We can't come until you tell us what happened and where you are.*'

'Blood... I'm vomiting blood and can't take it for much longer—'

'*Have you been shot or injured in some other way?*'

'No...'

'*And you've not been in a car accident?*'

'No, I'm just poorly... Really, really poorly...'

'*Okay, then I would recommend that you call your doctor or go to the nearest A&E... Hello, are you still there? ... Can you hear me? ... Hello? ...*'

An annoyed sigh was followed by a click.

Then silence.

36

From the 144 developed pictures, Fabian had picked out sixteen and placed them in chronological order on his work table in the basement. They all belonged to the same series of events. Sixteen frozen moments in time that together outlined an occurrence, a rendezvous between a man and a woman.

Fabian studied the pictures one by one, first with the naked eye and then under the light with a loupe to make sure he hadn't missed any details. They were all taken from a considerable distance with a powerful telephoto lens, and there was no doubt a professional photographer had been holding the camera. Even though the pictures had been taken late at night in difficult lighting conditions, most were razor sharp.

The black contour behind the wheel couldn't be anyone but Ingvar Molander, and the first pictures had clearly been taken outside his house as he reversed out of his driveway in the grey Saab 9-3, which according to the *Swedish Road Traffic Registry* had been registered to him from 6 January 2003 to 21 September 2007.

Judging from the verdant greenery in the garden and Molander's unbuttoned sports jacket, which hid parts of his checked shirt, it was sometime between June and August, and with the aid of the loupe he could make out the tax sticker in the middle of the licence plate.

The big 3 told him that March was the last month before a new MOT and tax payment was due, and the two smaller numbers – 07 – in the top right corner next to the three crowns revealed that the last year it was valid for was 2007. Which in turn meant Einar Stenson had taken the pictures sometime during the summer of 2006, just over nine months before he died.

The rest of the pictures were from a completely different location and showed Molander waiting in the car, which was parked in front of a backdrop of green leaves. The twilight was more or less unchanged from the previous pictures, which suggested no more than twenty minutes or so had passed. On the other hand, you can get pretty far in a car in twenty minutes.

But thanks to the signs on the black signpost in the top right corner of the picture, Fabian was able to identify the location, even though he couldn't recall when he'd last been there.

The signs pointed to, among other things, *The Springs* and *The Water Pavilion*, names that could only refer to Helsingborg's three-hundred-year-old spring, to be found in Ramlösa Brunn Park, which happened to be just a few minutes' drive from Molander's home on Lindhultsgatan.

The smiling woman in the summer dress who was walking towards the car and climbing into the passenger seat was harder to identify. He'd had the feeling he'd seen her before when he first saw the picture at the Celluloid photography club, and now that he was able to study her more closely, he felt exactly the same.

If Molander had had an affair, it should, statistically speaking, have been with a colleague. But after going through the staff register of the police department, he concluded that she didn't work for the police in Helsingborg, Malmö or any of the smaller municipalities. Nor for the regional detention facility nor the Prosecution Authority. Nor was she one of the many assistants he had gone through over the years.

When the work angle failed, Fabian had turned to more outlandish ideas, such as searching for pictures of the staff at the hairdresser out in Väla Mall where he knew Molander usually went for his haircuts. But she had been nowhere to be found, and after spending more than two hours on the search, the whole project began to seem futile, so he sat down in his armchair to rest his eyes and think about how to proceed.

He was convinced he'd seen her not too long ago. If not for that, he might have been able to let it go and start working on some other lead. As it was, he was completely blocked and felt compelled to keep banging his head against the same wall. Not even the fact that Sonja and Matilda were coming home any minute...

How daft could he be not to have thought of that?

Gertrud Molander's girlfriends.

They were much rarer than workplace liaisons. But friends, both one's own and one's partner's, were still a solid second when it came to affairs, and it went without saying that Molander might have found his lover among them.

Molander didn't have a Facebook profile. According to him, social networks were the beginning of the end for humanity and a much greater threat than climate change. Fabian did have a profile but was never on it. And if he was, it was to read other people's posts, never to write his own. But unless he was mistaken, Gertrud Molander had sent him a friend request a few months ago.

He got up and walked over to his computer, but before he could even type in the password, he realized where he'd seen the woman.

She'd been there all along, right in front of him, so close it hadn't crossed his mind. The realization broke over him like an icy wave when he turned to his whiteboard and looked at the picture of her lying naked on a beach, entangled in seaweed, washed up like driftwood by the wind and waves. Her eyes were wide open and half-filled with sand, and one arm and one leg were still screwed to the wooden pallet.

The woman's name was Inga Dahlberg, and she had been attacked on 24 August five years ago while out running in Ramlösa Brunn Park, then raped and sent down the Rå River with her arms and legs nailed to a wooden pallet. She had been washed ashore over twenty-four hours later on the island of Ven in the middle of Öresund, between Sweden and Denmark.

The method used had been similar to Danish serial rapist Benny Willumsen's MO, and since everything had pointed to him having crossed the sound to the Swedish side, all the material had been incorporated into that case file.

But during the trial, which had dealt with a string of torture-like rape murders, Willumsen had eventually been declared not guilty on account of insufficient evidence in the so-called Ven Murder, which had remained unsolved.

But Hugo Elvin had secretly suspected Molander and when Fabian typed in Inga Dahlberg in the search bar and saw her address, he could see why.

Ingvar Molander had had an affair with his next-door neighbour.

That must have been what Gertrud's father, Einar, had discovered. A discovery that had cost him his life.

37

Lilja looked at the number Igor Skanås had written in her notepad. He'd been right; the number had been listed in the phone book online under Assar Skanås's name and address. It was just plain embarrassing that she hadn't thought to check. Normally, that was part of the routine checks that were run as soon as a suspect was identified. A task that had fallen to her this time and that she had completely overlooked.

Sure, she could blame the fact that they were severely short-handed and that Klippan's muddled leadership had undermined any kind of logical thinking and made it virtually impossible to deal with the most straightforward of routines. But the truth was that she was to blame.

That said, it was very unusual for a suspect on the run from the law to not even bother buying a pay-as-you-go SIM card. Though she supposed it tallied somehow with his remarkable decision to drive the Volvo all the way to his home and do nothing more to conceal it than to throw a tattered tarpaulin over it. It was as though he hadn't given the consequences a moment's thought.

At least she had now belatedly talked to Molander about doing a triangulation for the number, but since he had spent the whole morning triangulating Igor Skanås's phone, he'd made it clear she would have to wait until he was done processing the brothers' house. It went without saying that was an important task, too, but she was far from convinced it was the right way to prioritize.

Not an hour passed without a reminder of how badly understaffed they were. In less than six weeks, their team had been halved. She would never see Elvin again and Risk would, if she'd understood it right, not be back until sometime in late summer.

Normally, his way of keeping everything to himself would irk her. Now, she missed him and his unexpected ideas, which though not always accurate were invariably interesting.

Not to mention Tuvesson. God, she missed her so badly. No one could direct their work or put their foot down without causing offence like she could. Now they were drifting, each on his or her own, almost as unstructured as Assar Skanås. It was in large part her own fault. She hadn't been able to take Klippan's leadership seriously. His theories about the underlying motive even less so. And yet, he'd been right and she'd been wrong.

He could have rubbed her nose in it, but he was apparently so cowed he hadn't even said I told you so, let alone demanded that she follow his instructions from now on. It was as though he'd completely given up on being in charge.

The best she could do was to apologize. Hopefully that would give him enough confidence to take the tiller again. Maybe he would even dare to grab Molander by the scruff of the neck and order him to start the search for Assar Skanås's phone before it was too late.

She left her office and walked down the corridor past the kitchen. That's as far as she got before her phone rang, and at more or less the same moment that she saw it was Klippan calling, the man himself burst out of his office.

'There you are.'

'Yes, I was coming to talk to you. What happened?'

'Another murder.'

38

Sonja had always been the one who organized the children's birthday parties. He had at most helped run the games or hand out goody bags and, when the children got older, he'd put together playlists for them. If he'd been there at all and not buried in some investigation or other.

This time, he was in charge. The apple pie still had twenty minutes left in the oven and the burgers were resting under their plastic wrap, waiting to be fried. The table was laid and the kitchen cleaned.

The only thing left to do while Sonja and Matilda were hanging up their coats was to turn off Yello's 'To the Sea' from *Pocket Universe*, an album that always put him in a good mood, and instead turn on a mix CD he'd made with a few of Matilda's favourite artists, like Justin Bieber, Beyoncé and Rihanna.

'Welcome home,' he said as he went to meet them. 'You're finally here.'

'We are, and the house looks so lovely.' Sonja shot him a smile that would normally have eased the weight on his shoulders, but now was neither here nor there, since Matilda didn't even bother to turn around.

'Thanks, sweetheart,' he said and gave her a hug.

Maybe that was crossing a line, given that they hadn't had any physical contact whatsoever recently. But the way she flinched and almost shied away showed just how far apart they had really drifted, even though she quickly pulled herself together and returned the hug for the sake of appearances.

'Matilda.' He turned to her, arms outstretched. 'Can I have a hug from you too?'

'I'd rather not. I'm still sore from all the surgeries.'

'All right, but you let me know the minute you feel better. You've no idea how much I've missed you.'

Matilda nodded with a smile that signalled nothing more than tolerance.

'Imagine, back home again,' he went on, feeling as though he was trying to accelerate with the clutch engaged. 'It's almost hard to believe you're really here and we're all together again.'

'Yes, isn't it incredible,' Sonja agreed. 'And speaking of which – where's Theodor?'

'In his room. I'll go get him. Sonja, would you mind toasting the bread? It's all set up. And, right, Matilda, guess what we're having for starters?'

He'd been hoping it had been something temporary connected to her waking up in the hospital. But apparently it hadn't been, because there it was again. That strange, distant look. As though it wasn't his own daughter standing there, looking up at him with a stony expression.

'Toast Skagen!' He squeezed out a smile and wished the ground would swallow him up. 'You know. Your favourite, with hand-peeled prawns, mayonnaise and the whole shebang.'

'My goodness, that sounds delicious,' Sonja said. 'You've gone to so much trouble.'

'It's only right. It's not every day your daughter comes home after a month in the hospital. And to wash it down, I thought we might have some...' He opened the fridge and pulled out a bottle of champagne. 'Ta-da!'

'Oh, Fabian, you shouldn't have. Not on my account.'

If not for the voice, he would have been sure that was Sonja. But odd as it may sound, the words came from Matilda.

'No need to worry,' he said, as he felt himself getting even more worried. 'Of course there's non-alcoholic bubbly for you and Theo. Also, you should feel free to call me Dad.' He added another half-inch to his smile before turning to face her, only to be met by those eyes that seemed to be looking straight through him, making him ever more uncomfortable.

'I've stopped drinking sugary drinks. I think I'm going to go upstairs and rest for a bit instead.' Matilda turned and started walking towards the stairs.

'No, okay, wait, hold on a second. Why?' He put the bottle down and hurried after her, looking for a trace of his daughter somewhere deep inside. 'Are you not feeling well?'

'I'm fine, just a bit tired. But it's okay. The real question is how you're feeling.'

'Me? I'm not sure I'm following... Do you understand any of this?' He looked over at Sonja, who looked like she was miles away. 'Sonja?'

Sonja jumped and turned to him. 'I'm sorry, I didn't hear you.'

'I'm talking about all of this. The champagne, the balloons, the music. All the food.'

'Well, what's wrong with it?'

'It's so incredibly over the top.'

'Over the top? How can it be over the top? It's for you. All of this is to celebrate that you're finally—'

'Fabian, I don't know who you think you're fooling. But this...'

'Would you please stop calling me Fabian!' He could feel something break inside him. 'I'm still your father, you know, even though you seem to think that—'

'Fabian.' Sonja cut him off, putting a hand on his arm. 'Try to listen to what she has to say instead.'

'All right, fine, fine.' He jerked his arm away from her hand, which was little more than a condescending pat on the head anyway. Listen? Who was she to talk about listening? 'I just wanted to do something nice to show how happy I am that Matilda's finally home again. But you know what. Forget it.'

'Oh, Fabian...' Sonja said in that same condescending tone.

'No, I mean it. Let's just forget it. If she doesn't want to, she doesn't want to.' He grabbed the champagne and threw open the fridge so violently the things in the door fell over.

'As if any of this is for me.'

'Excuse me?' He turned to Matilda, and this time he didn't give a fuck about the look in her eyes.

'Okay, I'm going to head upstairs and see where Theo's got to,' Sonja announced suddenly, and she walked off towards the stairs to the first floor.

'I said, none of this is for me,' Matilda repeated, preventing him from calling after Sonja to thank her for her tremendous support.

'That's interesting. Who's it for, then?'

'You. Who else?' The answer came without a moment's hesitation and, unlike him, she hadn't raised her voice at all so far. 'This is about you feeling guilty. Nothing else.'

He was about to object and launch into a rant. The thing was, though, that she was right. His thirteen-year-old daughter had hit the nail on the head. 'Of course I feel guilty,' he managed at length, and he clapped his hand to his cheek as though he'd just been slapped. 'You were this close to dying because of me and my job.' He illustrated his words with his thumb and forefinger. 'How could I not feel guilty? If not for Theodor coming home just then with that gun... I don't know. I can't even—' He broke off and realized he was crying.

A whole month had passed without him being able to squeeze out so much as one tear and now, suddenly, the tears were streaming down his face, even though the only thing he could feel was anger.

'But you shouldn't. None of what happened was your fault.'

'Matilda, listen to me.' He dried his tears as best he could. 'If not for my investigation, none of this would have happened. Okay? If I hadn't prioritized everything else over the most important thing in my—'

'If, if, if,' Matilda cut him off. 'You can list as many *ifs* as you like. It doesn't change anything. What happened, happened and no matter how badly you wish there was something you could do to change it, there isn't anything.'

And so it came back to this. All her talk about Ouija boards and how nothing really meant anything because everything was predestined anyway. 'And what does Mum say about all of this? Or have you not told her you're convinced that she, Theo or I will die soon because you survived?'

'Fabian, it's not something I think. I know it,' Matilda said with a serenity that indicated she had made her peace with it.

'Matilda, you're thirteen years old. That might feel really mature. But I've lived a bit longer than you, and—'

'How can you be so sure of that?'

'Oh, we're going to get into reincarnation now, too?' He didn't know whether to laugh or cry. 'All right, you can be as old as you like. But that doesn't change the fact that no one can see the future. Believe me, it's impossible. No matter how much you want to, no one can predict what's going to happen.'

'But some people can, and Greta happens to be one of them.' Matilda crossed her arms. 'But you don't even think she exists, so why would you believe she has gifts?'

'So you're telling me, in all seriousness, that everything in life is predetermined?'

'Not everything, but the important things. The big moments that really mean something are almost always written in stone.'

'Like a member of your family dying in the near future?'

Matilda nodded.

'So all our choices and actions are in fact meaningless?'

'They have meaning, but only on a small scale. We can shape our path, choose whether to go left or right or backwards, but the goal we eventually reach is never up to us. No matter what we do, that's where we'll end up.' She took his hand in hers, and he was surprised to feel how warm she was. 'You did your best. Who can do more than that?' She got up on tiptoe, kissed him on the cheek and turned towards the stairs.

Fabian watched her walk away and felt powerless to silence the nagging notion that it wasn't his daughter disappearing up the stairs.

'Everything looks lovely.'

He opened his eyes and saw that Sonja had returned to the kitchen. 'Nice to hear someone appreciates it,' he said and rubbed the gritty remains of the tears from his eyes.

'Hey…' She walked up to him. 'Don't take it too much to heart.'

'Sonja, she's walking around believing in the supernatural and is convinced one of us is going to die just because she survived. How am I supposed to not take that to heart?'

'I'm sure it's just a phase.'

'No, it's her friend, that Esmaralda, who's put ideas in her head.'

'At the hospital, they told me it might be weeks before she's her old self again. So just let her play pretend with the occult for a while. No, I think this thing with Theodor is a lot more serious.'

Fabian could only nod. 'Then at least he told you. At least that's something.' He pulled out the bar stools from the kitchen island and got out two wineglasses. 'We have to talk about what to do. He's refusing to listen to me.'

'What do you mean, do? We don't even know if it's true. The important thing is for him to start seeing a therapist so he can get some professional help. Maybe even medication.'

Fabian opened one of the wine bottles he'd bought for the main course and filled their glasses. 'Of course he needs help. But the trial in Helsingør starts next week, and I see no other option than to—'

He'd turned the sound off so he wouldn't be bothered during dinner. But since the phone was sitting next to the cutting board at the edge of his vision, he couldn't help but notice when the screen lit up. It was Astrid Tuvesson, and if there was one thing he was sure of, it was that she would never call unless she absolutely had to.

Something had happened.

39

THIS WAS JUST TOO much. That was Klippan's only thought as he turned into ICA Maxi's car park. *Too much, too much, too much*. Until two months ago, nothing had happened in absolute years. Now it was all happening at once.

They weren't just in the middle of an urgent manhunt for Assar Skanås. The arrest of Sievert Landertz was a problem that had snowballed out of their control. Over the past few hours, the discontent among the Sweden Democrats sympathizers had grown exponentially; it was only a matter of time before their mail server crashed.

It made no difference that it was glaringly obvious Landertz had helped plan the fire in his own party offices; if they couldn't produce solid evidence soon, they would have to release him.

It was best not to even think about the fire at the refugee reception facility in Kvidinge. Technically, the Bjuv Police were in charge of that. So far, though, they hadn't made any real headway and he could already hear the critics on the left accusing the police of racism.

He backed into a free spot and looked over at the entrance, where people were crowding around with their empty trollies, trying to catch a glimpse of what was going on inside. At least that meant the cordon was up and the shop evacuated. That was something, though not nearly enough. The whole car park should have been closed to give the ambulance and police vehicles room to manoeuvre. The way things stood, the press photographers, who were no doubt on their way already, would have no difficulty zooming in straight through the glass doors to snap pictures of the ongoing police work.

Responsibility rested with him now. It was his job to climb out of his car, push through the crowd, duck under the police tape and take over the investigation. Make sure everyone was doing what they were supposed to and that nothing was missed. But he couldn't. He couldn't even bring himself to unbuckle his seat belt.

It just wasn't him. This whole *I'm the one in charge and you'd better do as I say* role was a bad fit for him, and to be honest, he'd never been particularly interested in it. But the hierarchy was what it was and he hadn't had any choice but to grit his teeth and try to do his best until Tuvesson came back.

A few deep breaths later, he got out of the car and walked towards the crowd outside the entrance; once there, he heard himself order everyone to remove their cars from the car park then give the uniformed officers clear instructions on how to expand the police cordon.

When he entered ICA Maxi, he only had to walk through the automatic barriers and the plastic toys section before he spotted two of Molander's assistants putting on protective clothing in the fruit and veg section. And over by the bread aisle, a few members of the staff were comforting a colleague who had gone to pieces.

'There you are,' Molander called out as he emerged from the Tex-Mex and spice aisle, wearing his white work coat. 'Where have you been? We've been here for over an hour already.'

'As you know, we have a number of other cases that need seeing to as well, and speaking of which, we're going to need another triangulation now we have Assar Skanås's number.'

'Yes, yes, Lilja's already been on to me about that.' Molander snorted derisively. 'If only she'd thought to check the phone book before we spent the entire morning locating his brother.'

'I know, but the worst thing we can do now is to turn on each other. Tell me how you're getting on instead.'

Molander shook his head. 'So far, we've only really been able to do your job. We've talked to the staff and a handful of customers who witnessed the event.'

'Why haven't you got started on the technical investigation?'

'The answer to your question starts with F and ends with lätan.' Molander snorted again. 'Don't ask me why, but he seems to think the coroner has first dibs on the scene. He has categorically refused to let us in for almost half an hour now. Bloody crank. Thinks he's so special with his striped trousers and long hair.'

'All right, I'll take care of it,' Klippan said, even though conflicts were not his forte.

'If anyone should have first dibs, it should be me and my team.'

'Ingvar, I said I'll take care of it.' There was nothing unexpected about Flätan and Molander rubbing each other up the wrong way. They were both extremely competent in their fields. Their egos and posturing were the problem. They had never been able to fit into the same room and likely never would. 'Tell me about the witness statements instead.'

'All right.' Molander started walking him towards the scene. 'Some of the information is contradictory, but then isn't that always the way when something out of the ordinary happens? But the aggregate picture of the course of events is that the perpetrator, a dark-skinned man with an odd appearance and his hood pulled up over—'

'Odd appearance?'

'Yes, several of the witnesses put it exactly that way without being able to specify what was so odd about it. Either way, the man was supposedly queueing, waiting for his turn by the meat counter, when all of a sudden he jumped over to the other side, snatched up one of the knives and stuck it into the victim's throat.' Molander pulled the string that opened the door marked *No Unauthorized Access* and continued into a short hallway with shabby walls and glaring fluorescent lights.

'So it wasn't premeditated at all?'

'Let's put a pin in that for now, because the altercation didn't end there,' Molander continued as he showed Klippan into a room where a row of carefully placed stepping pads led to one of the assistants who was squatting down, taking pictures of something on the floor. 'Apparently, the victim was in remarkably good physical shape and—'

'Well, well, well, the prodigal son returns,' Einar 'Flätan' Greide exclaimed on his way through the swing door leading to the area behind the meat counter. 'Exquisite timing, I have to say. I just finished.' He pulled off his bloodstained silicone gloves, turning them inside out in the process. He pushed them into his tattered suede briefcase, decorated with hippy fringe and embroidered peace signs, and pulled out a glass bottle filled with something green and viscous, which he knocked back without ceremony. 'Where was I?'

'You had just finished,' said Klippan, who, though he was very familiar with Flätan's unique sartorial sensibilities, couldn't tear his eyes away from the red-and-white striped trousers poking out from beneath his blood-spattered lab coat, which made his legs look like candy canes. 'And I'm given to understand that the crime scene technicians have been kept waiting a bit too long.'

'Oh, that's okay, I'm sure they'll live.' Flätan turned back to the swing door, pushing it open with his elbow and inviting Klippan and Molander into the space behind the meat counter.

'I will, of course, conduct a more thorough examination once I get the body back to home base. But as you can see, it doesn't take a genius to determine that the victim experienced hypovolemia and bled out soon after.'

The pool of blood was about three feet across; when Klippan squatted down, he could see the coagulated surface layer ripple in the barely noticeable draught from the swing door.

'Is that it?' Molander said.

'Pardon me?' Flätan, who was about to leave, stopped in the middle of a stepping pad and turned to face Molander with a look on his face that made it abundantly clear what he thought of him.

The main puddle was far from the only blood. Large areas of the floor were stained. The same was true of the white-tiled back wall and several of the work surfaces. Even the buttons on the scale and the roll of wrapping paper were stippled with blood.

'Well. Don't you have a scenario in mind? Even a hypothetical one?' Molander said, seemingly unfazed by Flätan's look.

The victim, who according to his name tag was called Lennart Andersson, was of middle age with hair growing in a semi-circle around his bald pate. He was lying on his back in the middle of the pool of blood. His right arm was outstretched, his left bent with its hand over a bloody gash in his throat.

'Like I said, you've been able to work undisturbed for quite a while now, and as far as I can make out, quite a few things happened here before the hypovolemia set in.'

'Of course. A blind chicken could see that. But I'm not in the habit of discussing my personal theories with all and sundry. I prefer to wait until I've conducted a full autopsy and can present facts.'

The victim's work coat, which had once been white, was now so covered in blood the white patches that were left looked like stains. The handle was the only visible part of the knife lodged in his chest.

'If you're interested in baseless suppositions and theories, you should contact my colleague Arne Gruvesson instead,' Flätan continued. 'He's something of a specialist when it comes to rash conclusions and sloppy work.'

There was a meat fork in the victim's face as well, rammed in so deep next to his nose that the two tines poked out below his jaw.

'I daresay there's more here than "baseless suppositions". You only have to look at the blood spatter to see a pretty clear scenario, if you ask me.' Molander met Flätan's eyes.

'I had no idea you were a blood spatter expert.'

'Expert might be pushing it. But at least I know what I'm talking about. That crack, for instance, suggests the perpetrator jumped over the counter somewhere around here.' Molander pointed to a crack in the curved glass of the counter. 'Then he probably snatched up one of the knives from this cutting board.'

'Not *one* of the knives. That one.' Flätan pointed to the corner where a long, thin knife lay on the floor. 'It matches the wound in his throat, and the powerful blood spatter indicates that he had a blood pressure of somewhere between 120 and 180, which must be considered completely normal, considering the situation he was in. Ergo, that must have been the first cut.'

'I feel like you're skipping a few steps and oversimplifying when you just assume that a powerful spatter means normal blood pressure.'

'Well, I apologize. I summarized it in slightly simplified terms so you could understand.' Flätan allowed himself a smile. 'The thing is that if you cut the carotid artery of an otherwise uninjured man, the spurt can easily reach six feet with each contraction of the heart. And if you take a closer look at the footprints in the blood, you'll also notice that the victim stayed in the same spot rather than dash about bleeding all over the place.'

'Surely you're not implying the carotid artery was completely severed?' Molander shook his head. 'He would have collapsed in a matter of seconds, and it would have been game over.'

'True. It was partially severed, though definitely enough to create the fountain of blood we see the effects of here. It was only when he pulled the knife out with his right hand to defend himself that he had some success in stopping the bleeding with his left.'

'Well,' Molander said, doing a weighing motion in the air. 'That assumes the perpetrator took or knocked the knife out of his hand, or that he dropped it himself. Either way, it should have ended up somewhere near where he stood and not all the way over there. I'd bet anything he threw it as far away as he could.'

'You know how I feel about gamblers. He could just as easily have dropped it. The perpetrator could have kicked it.'

'Not according to the blood on the floor. Even you would be able to see that if you had a closer look,' Molander said. 'That knife flew through the air and hit the wall exactly here.' He walked over, sank into a squat and pointed to a small notch in the wall diagonally above where the knife lay. 'That also explains some of the witness statements about the victim screaming at the perpetrator to calm down. Which in turn suggests there's no link whatsoever between the victim and the perpetrator.'

'Agreed, it was probably just a crazy person who went berserk when he couldn't wait for his turn any longer.'

'Sure, maybe. Either way, it seems to have been completely unplanned. Because once the knife is out of the picture and the victim is standing there with his hand on his carotid artery, trying to get the perpetrator to calm down, I'm guessing he picks up that cleaver and strikes a blow full in the—'

'No, the cleaver comes later, when the victim is on the floor. The wounds are so deep the perpetrator must have used both hands. At that point, he used this.' Flätan pointed to the knife still buried in the victim's chest. 'And this time, he doesn't make the mistake of leaving it in. Instead, he keeps a firm grip on it and stabs him again and again, five times, until he manages to get it in between the ribs and sever the aorta. Only then does the victim stop resisting and collapse, at which point the perpetrator can switch to the cleaver.'

'And the meat fork?' Molander nodded to the twin-pronged fork in the victim's face.

'The cherry on top, I guess. How should I know?' Flätan shrugged. 'At that point, it was already over.'

'Already, that's one way of putting it. I would say—'

'Fabian?' Klippan exclaimed with his eyes on the swing door through which Fabian was entering. 'What are you doing here?'

'Tuvesson called.'

'What? What do you mean, Tuvesson? She's in rehab and seclusion. And you? Aren't you on sabbatical?'

'Apparently not any more. Because there's been another murder.'

'We know. We're kind of up to our ankles in it,' Molander said.

'Her name was Molly Wessman,' Fabian continued, ignoring Molander. 'Her neighbour, who happens to be good friends with Tuvesson, found her about an hour ago.'

PART II

17–24 June 2012

'Everything you know is wrong.'
G. PARLDYNSKI

40

Kim Sleizner turned over in bed. He could feel the sheet had come off the mattress and was bunched up underneath him. As if that wasn't bad enough, light was persistently seeping in through the gap between his bespoke blackout blinds.

A glance at his phone informed him it was only twenty-three minutes past five in the morning. He had hoped it would at least be gone half six, considering the eternity he'd already spent twisting and turning, increasingly sweaty and entangled in the damn sheets that had cost him a fortune and which, according to the salesperson, would breathe and give him a wonderfully restful sleep.

Restful. The word felt like being spat at in the face. He hadn't slept all night. In fact, he'd barely shut his eyes since Friday afternoon.

And once again, it was all Dunja Hougaard's fault.

Ever since she leaked a story to the media about him entertaining a whore in the back seat of his car, it's been his own little mission to crush her.

That little cunt was worse than a fucking cockroach. It didn't matter how much he stomped, gassed and put out traps. One way or another, she always managed to scuttle away.

Just a month ago, he'd used his position as head of the Copenhagen Homicide Unit to demonstrate his authority and show her, once and for all, that she was never going to be able to get out from under him, not even if she schlepped all the way up to the Helsingør Police to beg for a job.

And yet, that is exactly what she'd done.

He couldn't say exactly what had triggered his anxiety, but for the past week he'd felt increasingly sure something was amiss. Things had been too quiet. Especially considering what he'd done to her.

For some bizarre reason, she hadn't retaliated. He almost felt disappointed, even though part of him was relieved at the easy victory. At finally having managed to break her so comprehensively she would never get up again.

But just a week later, worry had started gnawing at him again.

It had simply been too quiet.

It was at that point he'd requisitioned the computer files. The ones he shouldn't really be able to get without a warrant, which would only ever be granted under very special circumstances directly related to national security. The ones that drilled into her life, describing every last detail in the form of long columns of numbers.

Since last Friday, he'd been able to see everything, from her emails to her text and call lists. He'd been able to study the traffic from her IP address and see every website she'd visited. If she'd bought a pair of knickers, he would be able to tell how much they cost and where she got them. If he wanted to, he could probably find out the colour and size as well.

The problem was that every fucking list and table was empty. Not one row, not one goddamn number for him to look at. No timestamps or any kind of information whatsoever.

At first, he'd been convinced something was wrong. Furious, he'd called up Mikael Rønning in IT, only to find out everything was exactly as it should be. That the files genuinely didn't have anything to offer but empty tables and columns full of zeros.

Unlikely as it seemed, Dunja The Cunt Hougaard had not shopped, emailed, called, got cash out or travelled abroad in the last month. There was no trace of her.

She had done nothing, as in zero.

Nothing as in gone underground.

As in licking her wounds and planning her revenge.

He could sense it, and it left him sleepless.

For the first time in his life, he was worried for real.

41

He'd tried to sleep, but hadn't been able to keep his eyes closed for more than thirty seconds at a time. And that was after wolfing down a big steak with French fries and Béarnaise sauce and two large glasses of Coke across the street at Sam's Bar. After that, he'd completed a gruelling workout session in his flat and followed it up with an hour's meditation in the bath.

But nothing had helped. Even though it would soon be twenty-four hours since his little trip to ICA Maxi in Hyllinge, he was still so wired he couldn't sit still.

But then again, he had never experienced anything like it. Nothing else compared. That feeling of knowing no one else had any idea, of just standing there, holding his queue number and waiting for the right moment. My God, they must have been so shocked. They hadn't even screamed. Or maybe he'd been so focused he hadn't heard them. Either way, no one had even tried to intervene.

Lennart 'Beefsteak' Andersson, on the other hand, had been exactly as physically fit as he'd feared and had, consequently, offered a good deal of resistance. But in hindsight, he counted that as a plus. Instead of the whole thing being over in seconds, he'd been forced to go at it for well over a minute before the old man gave up and he could escape through the staff entrance and cycle home.

In a few minutes, the day would be six hours old and even though he'd originally intended to wait for a few more hours, his fingers were itching for it already. He needed his next fix, and he needed it now.

He took out the icosahedron, which with its twenty sides would decide when his next assignment would take place, unless he rolled a one. If that happened, he would simply have to give it up for good. Or maybe not so simply. The risk of there not being a next time made his stomach knot.

He shook the dice, released it on to the felt and didn't know if he could believe what he was seeing.

A two.

He'd only had two days to prepare last time. And now it was a two again. On the other hand, this was what he wanted, and he preferred being pressed for time to being forced to twiddle his thumbs for twenty days.

He took out the tin with the six-sided precision dice, which were going to decide where his next victim would be found and who they were going to be. After a number of throws, chance had homed in on Helsingborg, specifically Kärngränd 4, second floor, whoever lived behind the far-left window.

Then he moved on to how it would happen, this time selecting from the category *Ways to die.*

He pulled out his list of twelve possible outcomes and did a pre-roll as usual to determine the number of dice, in this case one or two.

A three.

Thus directed to use one dice, he picked up the same one again, shook it and let it fall.

1. *Dehydration*
2. *Beheading*
3. *Starvation*
4. *Asphyxiation*
5. *Drowning*
6. *Electrocution*
7. *Decompression*
8. *Poisoning*
9. *Fire*
10. *Exsanguination*
11. *Disease*
12. *Traffic accident*

A five.

So the person in question was going to be drowned on Tuesday. He was already looking forward to it and almost felt two days was too long.

Now he just needed the final confirmation. The final roll of the icosahedron to verify that this was what he was supposed to do. The green light he needed to get started on the preparations.

The ten, represented by an X, was the only thing he didn't need right now. The time frame was too tight for a complicated side mission. But he wasn't worried. He'd already rolled X twice in a row, so the risk of it turning up again had to be considered minimal.

He sent the dice tumbling across the felt and didn't know whether to laugh or cry when he saw the X for the third time.

It was as if the dice was stuck in a glitch, he mused as he went to fetch the notebook with the 120 numbered side missions and rolled the twenty-sided dice once more.

A twelve.

He took out twelve six-sided dice; it was so many he could barely shake them in his cupped hands without dropping some.

Three threes, two fives, four sixes, two fours, one two.

He flipped to side mission fifty-three and felt an abyss open up at his feet as soon as he started reading.

He was intensely disappointed.

He read it again, slower this time. But he'd read it right the first time, and no matter how badly he wanted to pick the dice back up to give them another chance, he had no choice but to follow the rules and start his preparations, regardless of how impossible the task might be.

42

Matilda hadn't even been home twenty-four hours. And yet there he was, on the top floor of the police station on a Sunday, so early the morning mist hadn't dissipated, waiting for everyone to pour themselves coffee so the meeting could start.

The phone call from Tuvesson was entirely to blame. It had put him at a crossroads where the curious part of him immediately wanted to push the green accept button to find out what was going on. The other part had already realized it was almost certainly serious enough that, coupled with his own private Molander investigation, it would occupy his every waking hour.

'These croissants are several days old,' announced Lilja, who didn't look like she'd had nearly enough sleep. 'Look.' She picked one up and snapped it in half.

In the end, Sonja had told him to pick up and, as he'd suspected, there had been another murder, which meant his colleagues now had not one but three complex murder investigations on their hands.

'Dunk it,' Klippan suggested. 'That's what I do.'

But even knowing that, and despite Tuvesson's assurances that she would never have called unless it was absolutely necessary, he'd declined to end his leave early.

'Or you could throw it away and save the calories until

there are fresh ones,' Molander countered as he entered the room.

Too many times, he'd put his job before his family. Too many times, the perpetrator had come first, and every time he'd failed to realize the price he and his family paid.

'Waste of food, I say.' Klippan dunked his croissant in his coffee, making the cup overflow.

There was always going to be another case. They would never stop coming. The same was true of perpetrators and victims. But he only had one family, and he'd struggled through the past few weeks sleepless, worrying that soon it would only exist in the pictures in their photo albums, as a reminder of his failures.

Tuvesson had respected his position and not let even a hint of disappointment shine through when she'd wished him a lovely rest of the summer and asked him to send the family her love.

Instead, Sonja was the one who had reacted. Not with a happily surprised smile and maybe even a hug. No, she'd just shaken her head and asked him what he was doing. Why he didn't do the obvious thing and help his colleagues.

Matilda was home and in one piece, and she, Sonja, was more than able to run the house. *Who do you think you're fooling? This is what you want*, she'd said, and he'd replied that the only thing he wanted was not to lose his family.

She'd taken the phone from him without a word and dialled Tuvesson's number, and while it rang, he'd wondered to himself if this meant his family was already lost. That it didn't matter how much he tried. That the split was inevitable no matter which path he chose.

At the same time, he couldn't deny that Sonja was right.

This was what he wanted. Molly Wessman's strange death had all the ingredients required to trigger his curiosity. And he'd only just scratched the surface.

Then there was Molander. It remained to be seen whether he'd be able to work side by side with him while simultaneously conducting his basement investigation.

'All right, if everyone's done making a mess, we should get started.' Klippan got to his feet.

'Not a lot of mess to be made when everything's rock hard,' Lilja commented.

Klippan walked over to the whiteboard wall, which was already full of pictures and notes from the three investigations. 'As you already know, we have—'

'Hey, wait for me.'

Klippan and the others turned towards the door to see Tuvesson enter, carrying a tray piled high with fresh chocolate croissants, almond pastries and fancy lattes from Café Bar Skåne.

'Astrid? I thought you were supposed to be in rehab for several weeks and—'

'That was the plan.' She put the tray down on the table and started handing out lattes. 'But that's simply going to have to wait until things calm down.'

'In all seriousness, Astrid. Is it really a good idea for you to leave in the middle of your programme?'

'No, but to be honest, I don't see that I have much choice. These are exceptional circumstances, and to have even a chance of solving these cases, we're going to have to use all available resources. Which is why Fabian's here, too.'

'But Astrid, this is your health we're talking about,' Lilja said. 'Wouldn't it be better to ask Malmö for help?'

'Exactly what I was going to suggest.' Klippan pulled out his phone. 'I'm calling them right now.'

'You bloody well aren't!' Tuvesson banged her fist on the table. 'Enough already. Astrid this and Astrid that. Me coming back to work is not the same as me falling off the wagon. If you're so damn worried, I guess you can test me regularly, see if I can close my eyes and put my fingertips together or whatever. As far as Malmö's concerned, I've already been in touch with Thomas Winkel, who told me he can't lend us so much as an eraser because they, too, have their hands full with an investigation that requires all their resources. Was there anything else?' Tuvesson fixed Lilja, Klippan and Molander in turn, but was met with silence. 'Wonderful. Then I suggest we get started. Because in less than forty minutes, I have a meeting with Stina Högsell about that Sweden Democrat.'

'If you're referring to Sievert Landertz, she's been hounding me too,' Klippan said.

'Right.' Tuvesson walked over to the pictures of Landertz posted on the whiteboard wall, diagonally below the pictures of the laundry room, the victim Moonif Ganem and the suspect Assar Skanås. 'According to Högsell, we brought him in for questioning Friday morning, and he's been detained since. Is that correct?'

'Ask Irene.' Klippan nodded to Lilja. 'She's refusing to listen, even though it's clear as day we don't have nearly enough to hold him.'

'What's with the accusations?' Lilja put down her coffee, which she had been about to sip. 'I'm not refusing to listen. I just don't share your opinion. I think we do have more than enough to keep him until noon tomorrow.'

'So, what is it we have, concretely?' Tuvesson asked as she studied the pictures of the washing machine drum inside which Moonif's slender body appeared glued to the sides.

'Firstly, he's suspected of planning the fire in his own party offices.'

'But we still don't have any proof,' Klippan put in and picked up one of the fresh chocolate croissants.

'The arsonists used his car. And I happened to be there when it happened. All he wanted was for me to leave. He was so nervous, sweat was literally dripping from his forehead. He had even just purchased a new fire extinguisher. It was still in its packaging.'

'And secondly?' Tuvesson said.

'He lied to my face about not knowing Igor Skanås. I know I showed him a picture of his brother, but they look the same don't they? And I'm convinced he's lying about quite a few other things that could have helped our investigation. Thirdly, his Sweden Democrat gig's just a façade. In reality, he's a dyed-in-the-wool Nazi who would jump for joy if he saw those pictures of Moonif in the washing machine.'

'Sadly, that's not a crime, though.'

'Sure, but setting fire to a refugee centre is.'

'You're not seriously saying he did that?' Klippan said.

'No, but I think he knows who did. What would be the point of setting fire to his own offices and posting the list of refugee centre addresses online, if he didn't?'

'What's happening with that investigation anyway?' Tuvesson asked. 'It's my understanding it's being handled locally, but have we heard anything from the Bjuv Police?'

'All I know is they've secured tyre tracks from the scene. If you ask me, they should be checked against the car I was put in when they dumped me in my own front garden.'

'Right, I heard. It must have been awful.'

'That's putting it mildly. But that's how they operate. They try to scare you into silence.' Lilja let out a snort of derision and sipped her coffee.

'So you're saying they might be the same people who set fire to the refugee centre?' Klippan said.

'Why not?'

'Either way, it sounds like something we should look into,' Tuvesson said. 'But that doesn't change the fact that we have to let Landertz go. Much as we may want to nail him and everything he stands for, I see no other option as things stand.'

'Fine,' Lilja said, so curtly it was almost inaudible.

'Let's move on to this Assar Skanås fellow. I've been told an internal alert has been put out about his disappearance.' Tuvesson walked over to the whiteboard and took down the picture Klippan had found of him. 'Tell me what you have on him.'

'We have quite a lot,' Lilja replied. 'But maybe it would be better if I sent you a report later in the day, so we don't take up everyone's time.'

'One thing might be worth mentioning,' said Molander, who looked like he was having a hard time suppressing a smile. 'Me and my little team have had a match, or rather several matches.'

'What kind of matches?'

'Fingerprints. Three of the prints on the glass part of the washing machine door match several of the ones we found at Skanås's home, on the toys and children's films.'

'And we're sure they're not his brother Igor's prints?'

'Positive.'

Lilja exchanged looks with Klippan and the others. 'Wow, that's great. So we have solid proof. Then maybe you would even consider prioritizing that mobile triangulation as soon as we're done here?'

'Absolutely, so long as you promise to keep your fingers crossed it's really his number this time.'

'I also think we should make this picture public,' Tuvesson said.

'Speaking of which,' Klippan said. 'The media have been hounding me about a press conference.'

'I know. But that's going to have to wait until we can get our heads above water.'

'But people are worried,' Lilja said. 'They want to know what's going on.'

'The problem is that we do, too, and before I get in front of the cameras and expose my jugular, I want our affairs in better order. So let's move on to the stabbing in Hyllinge instead.' She turned to Klippan. 'How are you getting on? Have you found anything of interest?'

'No, so far we're no wiser than we'd be if we'd just read the papers. But hopefully the fog will clear once Ingvar has finished with the crime scene and I get access to the CCTV footage.'

'Good. Then let's wait for that. At this rate, I might even make it to my Högsell meeting on time. Finally, our most recent victim, Molly Wessman.'

'Right, well, we're not one hundred per cent sure that's murder, though several things point to it,' Fabian said.

'Let's put a pin in that particular problem and start instead with what you've found out about her.'

'Not much more than that she lived alone on Stuvaregatan 7 in the North Harbour, was thirty-two years old and had neither children nor siblings.'

'And no parents either?' Molander asked.

'She worked for Mavia Technologies in Landskrona and—'

'Hello, I asked you a question,' Molander broke in, waving as though to establish contact.

'I'm sorry, I didn't hear you,' Fabian said, trying to push down the thought that he was talking to a man he suspected of having killed not just his father-in-law, his lover and their colleague Elvin, but possibly many more besides.

'You know, like a mum and dad,' Molander reminded him.

'They died a year and a year and a half ago respectively down in Cádiz in southern Spain, where they'd lived since '92,' Fabian replied, trying to process how Molander could sit here and make jokes and pretend everything was normal.

'So where did she get the money?' Molander asked.

'What money?'

'A bit rusty after your sabbatical?'

'Fabian, the North Harbour isn't exactly the cheapest address in town,' Klippan explained. 'So given her relative youth, you have to wonder whether she might have inherited a fortune or something.'

'Not that I know. Her parents' house was mortgaged to the hilt. But I can tell you her salary went up considerably in the past two years.'

'Where did you say she worked?' Tuvesson asked.

'At Mavia Technologies in Landskrona. They're in the car industry. That's all I know.'

'Sounds like she had a meteoric rise.'

'But the company seems to be struggling. Their last three annual statements have shown a loss, and they've let almost half their staff go.'

'Maybe she stepped on someone's toes?' Lilja said.

Tuvesson nodded and made a note about *colleagues* under *possible suspects*.

'I don't know about the rest of you,' Klippan said. 'But I would like to know how she died.'

'This is what we know at the moment,' Tuvesson said. 'One of her neighbours, who happens to be a good friend of mine, was taking the bin out and noticed Wessman's door slightly ajar. At first, she didn't react, just walked past it to the rubbish chute. But on her way back, she saw a hand on the threshold, which prompted her to open the door fully and discover Wessman dead in her hallway.'

'And the cause of death, what do we know about it?'

'So far, nothing.'

'But as soon as we're done here, I'm calling Flätan,' Fabian put in. 'Even if he's not done, he should have something preliminary.'

'I'm going to have to ask you to hold off on that until tomorrow,' Tuvesson said.

'How come?'

Tuvesson sighed and exchanged a look with Klippan and Molander. 'It's his birthday, and no one takes their birthday more seriously than Flätan.'

'What about his colleague then? Arne Gruvesson or whatever his name is. Can't he step in?'

'You know how Flätan feels about Gruvesson. He would never consent to handing such an intricate case over to him.'

'By the way, did you hear what he said the last time Gruvesson came up in conversation?' Molander said. '*The only way that man should be allowed into the morgue is as a corpse!*'

Klippan and Molander guffawed.

'I agree with Fabian,' Lilja said. 'We're in the middle of three investigations. Of course we should be able to call him. It's not even a milestone birthday.'

'Since when is fifty-eight not a milestone?' Molander quipped.

'Were there visible injuries?' Klippan asked.

Tuvesson shook her head. 'Not that we know.'

'All right, this might sound stupid. But if there are no external injuries and we don't know the cause of death, how come you're so convinced it's murder? Why wouldn't our first guess be that she died of heart failure or suffered from a severe case of diabetes?'

'Believe me. I really wish it was an epileptic fit or a stroke. Unfortunately, that's just not it. We can't be one hundred per cent certain, of course, but there are things that point to someone taking her life.'

'Such as?'

'Such as the fact that she went to the police in Landskrona just before closing time last Wednesday to file a report,' Fabian said.

'Report about what?'

'It's not entirely clear, because it was never completed. As far as I can make out, she seemed to have felt someone was following her. Unfortunately, the officer in charge took neither his job nor her very seriously, so in the end, as far as I understand, she gave up and left the station in a fury.'

'Following as in stalking?' Lilja asked.

Fabian nodded. 'The problem is she couldn't give a description because she never saw the person in question. It was simply a "feeling" she had in the days before she died. The officer's put his personal comments in the margins of the report, describing her as *hysterical, incoherent* and *an attention whore*.'

Lilja shook her head.

'And why are we doubting his assessment?' Klippan said.

'Because of this.' Fabian took out and passed around a printout of the picture from Molly Wessman's mobile, in which she was sleeping soundly on her back in her own bed. 'According to the report, the alarm on her phone woke her up as usual, but when she picked it up to turn it off, she discovered her background image had been changed to this photograph.'

'I've examined the phone,' Molander put in. 'And the picture was definitely taken at 1.32 a.m. that same night.'

'And, if we choose to believe her,' Fabian continued, 'no one was in the flat apart from her.'

'So someone broke in to her home, snapped a picture of her sleeping with her own phone and then set it as her background,' Lilja said.

'Apparently.'

'Ingvar.' Tuvesson turned to Molander. 'How far along is the technical investigation?'

'We've only done what we had to so they could move the body. With things the way they are, I'm not going to make it out there until sometime tomorrow.'

'The locks. Did you have time to examine them?'

'Of course. And the answer to your next question is no. There was no sign of them being drilled open.'

'Could someone have picked them?'

'Yes and no.' Molander crossed his arms and leaned back in his chair. 'The tumbler lock's no problem. All you'd have to do to get it open is ask it nicely. But the deadlock's a different matter, and since she was clever enough to have a key instead of a thumb turn on the inside, a wire through the letter box wouldn't have worked.'

'So we're talking someone with keys.'

'Unless the perpetrator has that so-called super pick, which supposedly opens practically everything.'

'Do we even know if she'd locked both locks?' Klippan put in.

'She claims to in the report,' Fabian said.

'And then there's her phone,' Lilja said. 'How did he get into that without her PIN? Is that even possible?'

'Absolutely,' Molander said. 'And this was an iPhone, so it's not even much of a challenge. Especially not one running iOS 6, which was released just a week or two ago. Apparently, it's got more holes in it than a Swiss cheese. Would someone volunteer their iPhone? Fabian?' He leaned across the table with his hand extended, and Fabian pushed his phone over. 'The first thing you have to do is call Siri and ask what time it is.' He picked up the phone and pressed the home button until the phone beeped. 'Hi Siri. What time is it?' He held up the screen, which showed the time in Helsingborg. 'Then you click it and a plus sign will appear in the top-right corner. You click that to see what time it is somewhere else. But instead of choosing a location from the list, we write something else, anything really, like *fish guts*. Then we highlight the words, like so.' He showed everyone that the phrase *fish guts* was highlighted in the search bar. 'Then we click *share* and choose *message*. That will prompt it to ask for one of the names in the contact list. But instead, we'll type in a name that's not in the list. Let's keep it simple and write *Ravgni*.'

'How is that simple?' Klippan said.

'You don't see it? It's my name backwards. Anyway, we click it once and then again. Then we click *create contact* and *add picture*. And voilà. Now we just have to press the home button and we're in!' With poorly concealed pride, he demonstrated how he could click his way around the phone unhindered.

It took Fabian a moment too long to realize that wasn't such a good idea.

43

He was feeling confused again. And lost. And he didn't like it. No, he really didn't. He hated it, especially when, like now, he hadn't taken his medication. The streets seemed to swap places with one another, and the world was spinning around him. Like that boy. He had spun, too. Round and round, so quickly that after a while you couldn't even see him.

But he recognized his surroundings, he did. Because that was that sculpture with the red spinning wheel. It usually spun as well. At least it had when he was little. Now it wasn't moving. Stupid sculpture. If not for that old git staring at him, he would have walked up to it and pissed on it.

He wanted to go home but was afraid to. The police were probably there, rummaging around, and Igor would get angry and think it was him. Everything was so hard. And he didn't want to go back to the secure ward. They would just force him into that jacket and lock him up. And he needed to pee, so badly he almost couldn't hold it any longer.

He got up from the bench, left the small square and continued into an alley he recognized but couldn't place. There were trees there, and trees need to be watered. He hurried over to one of them, unzipped his trousers and dug it out before finally being able to relieve the pressure.

He'd been here before, lots of times. Right, to play arcade

games. That was it. They'd had that black-and-white space game Asteroids, and once he'd scored a thousand points and got an extra ship. His brother had played for hours on end with just one krona, with so many extra ships they didn't even fit on the screen.

Igor. Oh, he missed Igor so badly, even though he was mean sometimes. But he would never hand him over to the police. He was sure of that.

He had tried to call him lots of times, but his stupid phone refused to light up and he'd come close to smashing it on the ground. He knew it just needed charging, but he couldn't help thinking it was being mean. Why couldn't it just be on his side? He hadn't really used it that much.

Some idiot behind him was shouting that he was disgusting and should be ashamed of himself. As soon as he was done peeing, he was going to shut that loudmouth up with his stabby knife. But by then, the idiot was gone, go figure. Typical, but maybe just as well. What he needed was a charger. A charger, so he could call Igor.

Then he suddenly spotted himself.

Like a blurred echo from a time when he had more hair and had been on that medication that made him fat.

KNOWN PAEDOPHILE BEHIND THE LAUNDRY ROOM MURDER!

But that was him in the picture. It was. Was that why that old man had been staring at him?

Why couldn't they just leave him alone? Now he had to run again, and he didn't like running. It hurt his knees and made him all winded.

He must have been walking in circles. How typical. Now he was back in the square with that damn wheel that didn't even spin. But there, on the other side, there was a shop window full of mobile phones. They would be able to help him. And if not, he'd give them the knife.

He hurried over and walked past the salesperson, who smelled too strongly of perfume.

'Welcome to Telenor,' she said, sounding like an answering machine. 'Are you looking to buy a new phone?'

'No, just charging.' He pulled out one of the cords and plugged it into his own phone.

'I'm afraid we can't help you with that. But we sell chargers, both original and—'

'I told you, just charging!'

'All right, okay, sorry.' The salesperson backed away in fear as the phone came to life in his hand.

He didn't like her. She smelled too strongly and looked at him with eyes that weren't friendly. Not friendly at all, actually. 'You're stinky,' he said, pulling out his knife and starting towards her.

'I'm sorry, I didn't mean to upset you.' The salesperson held her hands up in front of her. 'Feel free to charge as much as you'd like.'

He stopped and hesitated for a few moments before deciding he was going to give her the knife anyway, but at that moment his phone rang.

'Hello? Who is it? Are you my brother? I want to talk to my brother.'

'*Assar, it's me,*' a voice said.

'Is that you, Igor? I tried to call you several times, but the phone was stupid and wouldn't let me. I hate this phone. Hate, hate, hate!'

'*Assar, calm down and tell me where you are instead.*'

'But why doesn't it say it's you? Why does it say unknown number?'

'*Because I'm not calling from my usual phone.*'

'Why not? Why aren't you calling from your usual phone? Why can't everything be normal?'

'*Assar, listen to me. Things aren't normal any more. You're wanted by the police; they're coming for you.*'

'I know. They're really mean.'

'*They are, and that's why I can't call you from my usual phone. Now tell me where you are so I can come and pick you up before the police do.*'

'You know the shop with lots of mobile phones by the square with that wheel that used to spin when we were little?'

44

Fabian couldn't for the life of him understand how he could have been so stupid. Not only had he voluntarily handed his phone over to Molander, he had let him click around for far too long before pulling his finger out and asking for it back. Molander had, of course, continued to swipe around while mockingly asking what kind of secrets he had on it.

One picture of the contents of Hugo Elvin's drawer. One single picture would be enough to let him know he'd taken over his secret investigation and was on to him. Which in turn could mean he was in as much danger as Elvin had been.

On the other hand, there was no way of knowing. Maybe Molander hadn't even looked at his pictures. Maybe he hadn't seen anything at all. It was impossible to gauge because he was acting normally and hadn't visibly or audibly reacted to anything on the screen.

In an attempt to silence his thoughts, he turned on the radio.

'*No, no, no, this isn't a political scandal. I'm not the one at fault here. What it is, is a miscarriage of justice!*' Sievert Landertz's agitated voice streamed out of the speakers as he turned off Österleden onto Södra Brunnsvägen. '*Early last Friday, when most of us were still in bed, there was a knock on my door. It was none other than the police, who without a word of explanation pushed me up against the wall and handcuffed me in front of my wife and my child. I've since spent two and a half days in detention!*'

'*And what do you yourself think is the reason behind your arrest?*' a male reporter was heard asking.

'*Think? I know exactly what this is about, it's about my political views.*'

Fabian turned right on to Gravörgatan and found a free parking space right outside Ramlösa Wok Express.

'*I would go so far as to claim that the actions of the police in this matter constitute a grave threat to this country's democracy. For that reason, I am going to seek compensation for false imprisonment. I'm also suing the detective who perpetrated this violation. Her name is Irene Lilja and I'm not going to rest until she's been punished and will never again—*'

He killed the engine and climbed out of the car. Without actually knowing how Lilja voted, he was convinced they weren't too far apart on the political spectrum. Like her, he didn't have much time for Sievert Landertz or his party. But this time, the man did seem to have a point, and if he decided to follow through on his threat, he hoped Lilja had better arguments than the ones she'd offered in the morning meeting.

He recognized the man sitting alone with a cup of coffee as soon as he entered the restaurant. It was the husband of Inga Dahlberg, the victim found on Ven. His name was Reidar Dahlberg, and even though he'd grown a beard in the intervening years, he looked like the pictures Fabian had found before making contact and setting up a meeting.

'You must be Fabian Risk,' a woman's voice said behind him.

He turned to the woman who was walking towards him. 'Yes, I am.'

'Beatrice Dahlberg, Reidar's wife of two years.'

'I see. How do you do.' They shook hands.

'As you can see, he's waiting for you. But before you start opening up a lot of old wounds, I want you to know Reidar has put that horrible story behind him and doesn't really want to talk about it.'

'Well, I'm afraid that's not up to him,' replied Fabian, who had already grasped that this woman was going to be trouble. 'In an ongoing murder investigation, you're obligated to answer police questions whether you want to or not.'

'I would appreciate it if you would at least go easy on him.'

Instead of responding, Fabian walked over to the table. 'Hello, Reidar,' he said, trying to catch the man's lowered eyes. 'I'm the one who called you. Fabian Risk.'

'I think that much is clear to him,' Beatrice said, taking a seat next to her husband.

Fabian sat down across from them and signalled to the waitress, who was on her way out, that he would like coffee, too. 'I understand it may feel strange to talk about this, so many years after the—'

'Yes, it really does. Doesn't it, Reidar?' Beatrice waited for a nod from Reidar before turning back to Fabian. 'As I said, two years ago Reidar decided to draw a line under all that awfulness and move on. And it's made him feel a lot better.' She put her hand on his.

'Good for you. But unfortunately, drawing a line under something doesn't make it go away,' Fabian said, pondering how to make her leave them alone. 'You see, some new information has come to light, which in turn has given rise to new questions. If all goes well, we might even be able to identify and apprehend the perpetrator.'

The woman let out a short laugh. 'That's what you said last time. If Reidar just answered all your questions. If he just let you search the house one more time. Then everything would be cleared up and the perpetrator would be arrested. But then, after that debacle of a trial, you gave up and left him with an open wound. And now you think you can just come here and open all of this up again.'

'I'm sorry, but how do you know all that? It was over five years ago. Did you know Reidar back then?'

'No, but he's told me. Reidar's told me everything. Like how you interrogated him and turned his life upside down. As though he were the one who raped her and nailed her to that… I'm sorry, Reidar, I'm just very upset.'

'Beatrice, I think it might be best if I spoke to Reidar alone.'

'My husband and I share everything, and right now he needs my support more than ever.'

Fabian sighed inwardly. 'Reidar, I would like to talk about you and Inga. About what things were like between you before she died.'

'Great. Things were great between them. Isn't that right, Reidar, things were great between you? Maybe not quite as great as between the two of us, though,' Beatrice chuckled. 'You see, Reidar's a wonderful man to live with, I can assure you of that.'

'That's lovely. But I would really appreciate it if you would let Reidar answer for himself.'

'There are many things in this world I would appreciate. For instance, I wouldn't mind a plausible explanation as to what you're really after.'

'As I said, new information has—'

'Come to light. Yes, you did say. The strange thing is, the papers haven't written about it. Not a word, as far as I know. Which they should have, given how sensational the murder was. Correct me if I'm wrong.'

'That's true. But for now, we've made the assessment that it's best if the perpetrator believes the case is closed. For that reason, we've elected to keep the investigation covert, and I would like to emphasize at this point how important it is that this conversation stays between us until the perpetrator has been arrested.'

Beatrice stared at him expressionlessly, as though she were on the other side of a poker table, pondering whether to call his bluff. Meanwhile, Reidar sat next to her, underlining the silence with his lowered eyes and closed mouth.

He looked strong and fit, with shoulders wide enough to make most men jealous. And yet there he was, hunched over, with a posture that made him look fifteen years older and would give any chiropractor or yoga instructor an instant headache.

The silence was broken by Beatrice's phone.

'Yes, this is Beatrice... Listen, can I call you back? I'm in the middle of a... Oh, right, I see...' She got up with a sigh and walked off.

'It's great you've met someone new.' This was his chance. 'She seems wonderful.' But he didn't have much time. She would be back soon, and the door would slam shut again. 'Reidar,' he continued, leaning across the table. 'The reason I'm asking about you and Inga is that there are some indications she was having an affair.'

Reidar finally looked up from his coffee and let the seconds tick by while he appeared to weigh up his options. Then he emptied his cup, stood up and walked out to the outdoor serving area. 'It's actually pretty nice out here in the sun.'

Fabian looked over his shoulder and saw Beatrice coming back towards the table so she could keep an eye on them.

'Don't worry. She's not a big fan of the outdoors. If it's not too hot, it's too cold. Not to mention all the bugs this time of year.' He let out a short laugh and signalled to her not to follow. 'But she's a good person and means well. I'm not sure how I would get by without Beatrice.'

'Reidar, I understand this is difficult for you. But I really do have to ask you to—'

'The last time the police asked me all these questions, I told them everything was fine.' Reidar closed his eyes against the sun. 'That things had never been better. Those were my exact words. It was a Saturday afternoon, and I was in the middle of a badminton game when my phone rang. A double, and after the break, it was going to be my serve. I heard everything they said, every word. About how they'd found her, washed up on Ven, nailed to that…' Reidar faltered and turned his back to the sun. 'But I wasn't able to take it in. I just wanted to cover my ears and close my eyes, so I hung up as though it were a wrong number and went back out on to the court and took my serve.' He shook his head. 'Three straight aces. Don't think I've ever served better. It was only when I got back home it started to sink in. That those words were so much more than words. The police were already there, waiting to bring me in for questioning. And I told them about how great things were between us. Said what I thought I should say. How passionately in love we still were after all our years together. That our sex life had never been better. Anything to keep them from suspecting me. From suspecting that I was the one behind that—' He broke off and looked like he had to focus all his energy on not crying. 'But it was all a lie.'

'Which parts weren't true?'

'None of it was. Not one word I said was true. She wasn't home that Friday when I got back from work. But did I get worried and call the police?' Reidar shook his head. 'I assumed she'd left me and would be back when she ran out of money. I wasn't even worried. Our relationship was so destructive that looking back now, I've no idea why she stayed. I made everything toxic and made sure I broke her to make her need me.' He turned around and looked Fabian in the eyes. 'She never came out and said it, but I could tell from the look in her eyes and read it between the lines. She hated me intensely. At times, I think she even wished I would die. And in hindsight, I have no problem seeing why. Living with me must have been torture. I'm a different person now, but back then I was a controlling, condescending prick. And to answer your question – of course I was convinced she was having an affair, so I watched her like a hawk.' He shook his head. 'Once, I even got it in my head that she was sleeping with our neighbour. Right, maybe you know him. Ingvar Molander. He works for the police, too, but he's a crime technician.'

Fabian ignored the question. He'd been given all the information he needed. He was about to thank the man for talking to him and wish him a good day, when a woman on a bicycle suddenly called out to them.

'Why, hello there!'

Fabian looked at the woman, who was wearing a bike helmet and sunglasses, but couldn't place her.

'It's Fabian, isn't it?'

He did recognize her voice, though.

'Hi, Gertrud,' Reidar shouted, waving. 'I figured you two might know each other.'

Of course Ingvar Molander's wife had to ride by at this precise moment. He almost couldn't believe it, but the very thing he'd been trying to avoid by not going to Reidar's house had just happened anyway.

'Hi there,' he finally managed to squeeze out, and he added a wave, frantically trying to think of some way of saving the situation. 'Long time no see. How are you these days?'

'Good, thank you.' Gertrud had now pedalled over to them. 'But I didn't know you two knew each other.'

'We don't,' Reidar Dahlberg replied. 'But they've reopened Inga's case. Apparently there's new information, which as far as I can make out is interesting enough that they're hoping it might lead to an arrest down the line.'

It was too late. The catastrophe was already a fact.

'Oh, really. Well, imagine that. I haven't heard anything about it.'

'Apparently they're keeping it quiet until the perpetrator has been caught. So it's not something we should be spreading around. Right? That's what you said, isn't it?'

Fabian could only nod and watch as the scorching meltdown ate through one containment wall after another.

45

MURDER AT ICA MAXI, HYLLINGE IN SHOCK!

LAUNDRY ROOM PAEDOPHILE STILL AT LARGE

POLICE THREAT TO DEMOCRACY! HEADS WILL ROLL!

FOR ONCE, THERE WAS so much going on, the tabloids were all running different headlines. All of them were, however, unanimous in their message about imminent societal breakdown, and two of them carried pictures of a neat and proper but incensed Sievert Landertz, just released from detention.

Lilja felt sure hers was one of the heads that was going to roll. He had already mentioned her by name on the radio; she would be shocked if he hadn't hung her out to dry in the papers as well. Landertz had a habit of attacking, and right now, she was in his sights.

She didn't care in the slightest. She didn't even have it in her to be upset. They were empty threats, attempts to clear himself and his son. For that reason, she resisted the urge to sneak into the Furutorp corner shop to buy up all their papers. Besides, she didn't have time.

The task of locating Assar Skanås's phone had gone as expected. Molander had been able to tell them straight away that it was unsearchable, which could mean anything from it simply being turned off or out of battery to it sleeping with the fishes at the bottom of Öresund.

What they had found was a logged position from when it was last connected, which turned out to have been that same morning, just after their meeting. At that time, it had been in the middle of the town centre, near Consul Olsson Square, where at 10.54 a.m. it had received a call from a hidden number before being turned off again twenty-one minutes later on Söder, where the police station was located.

It was now quarter past one, which meant he had a two-and-a-half-hour head start. That wasn't a lot of time, but certainly enough for him to cross the border and, at least in theory, be on his way to the other side of the world. But theory was one thing, practice another. A more likely scenario was that he was holed up somewhere, waiting for things to blow over.

She and Molander and Tuvesson had done a risk assessment and decided that she could go over there unaccompanied. Granted, with three simultaneous cases their workload had been a big factor in their decision-making, but she shouldn't be in any real danger.

She passed the funeral home on Furutorpsgatan.

Even so, her body was pumping out adrenaline, as though preparing for the worst, as she approached the given location at the lower end of Carl Krooks Gata.

The area had been pinpointed by five masts and looked like an oval with a sixty-five-foot semi-major and a fifteen-foot semi-minor axis. The centre of the oval was at the junction of Furutorpsgatan and Carl Krooks Gata, and even though she had no memory of ever having been there before, it didn't take her long to conclude that it was one of Helsingborg's most depressing intersections.

Four buildings, one on each corner, each uglier than the last. And that was despite three of them having large corner balconies. Even though the sun was out, there was nothing on them but satellite dishes, rubbish and the occasional pigeon. Clearly, this was a forgotten corner of the city and in many ways a perfect location for a furtive child murderer.

That said, he could, of course, simply have been walking that way when he realized he'd forgotten to turn his phone off. Maybe he'd been on his way to the South Harbour via the underpass. There were a handful of residential buildings there. But apart from those, that area of town was mostly offices, industrial buildings and, in the main, a lot of freight and container ships. A possible way out if you didn't want to leave signs of your departure.

If, on the other hand, he was holed up inside, there were, as far as she could make out, only two possible entrances within the confines of the oval. Furutorpsgatan 26 and Carl Krooks Gata 55. Of the two, the entrance on Furutorpsgatan was further from the centre of the oval, so she decided to start with the other one.

The building had five floors, and each floor had three flats. Among the fifteen names on the blue felt board with pinned-on plastic letters there were two *Perssons*, two *Nilssons* and no less than four *Svenssons*. On the third floor lived a *P. Milwokh*. She'd never heard the name before. At least not as far as she could remember. And yet it sounded vaguely familiar.

When she couldn't think of why, she continued towards the lift, which jerked to life and started ascending at an uncommonly slow and uneven pace. She'd never been scared of lifts, but this particular one added to her unease, which had been growing since she walked past the funeral home.

When the lift finally came to a stop, she couldn't get out fast enough. She proceeded to examine the three front doors, which looked like they were being cared for about as tenderly as the lift.

A. Andersson, B. Andersson and *C. Andersson.*

Was someone having her on?

The Andersson on the far left seemed the tidiest. Unlike the other two, he had neither bin bags nor shoes outside his door. If it even was a he? Judging from the postcard of roses on the door, it was more likely to be a woman. The Andersson on the right, on the other hand, was definitely a man, unless she was the owner of giant, *Guinness World Record* worthy, size-nineteen shoes. If not for the row of children's shoes, she might have rung the bell. Instead, she turned her attention to the bin bag outside B. Andersson's door.

She walked over, squatted down and opened it. A cloud of fruit flies swarmed up at her, causing her to back away instinctively, which made the bag tip over and spill its contents on to the floor.

In addition to various mouldy food remnants, she could see advertisement flyers from low-cost chain Alfo Gross, an old bottle of neon-blue nail polish and a push-up bra from H&M.

B. Andersson was most likely a relatively young woman who had nothing to do with the man they were after.

But, then, what had she expected? That he would jump out and turn himself in, just because she was poking through people's rubbish? No, she should just quickly scan each floor and then turn the door-knocking over to a couple of uniformed officers, so she could be put to better use in the office.

The first thing she saw when she reached the next floor down was the note on the middle door.

Nice one-bed sublet from 1 July. 5,300 kronor/month.

Without knowing if she was really going to call, she ripped off one of the tabs with the phone number before turning to the door on the right.

P. Milwokh.

She definitely recognized it. But just like when you ran into someone from primary school who looked different now or hadn't made a lasting impression, the name was little more than a combination of letters.

There was only one way to find out, she thought to herself, and she walked over and rang the bell. But she couldn't hear it ring, so she pressed the little beige button again, harder this time. Still no sound. She knocked instead, so hard her knuckles smarted.

When that went unnoticed too, she decided to do a search for the name instead, as soon as she got back to the office. But just as she turned to leave, the tiny pinprick of light in the peephole darkened.

So there was someone inside.

She knocked again. 'This is the police! Please open the door!' She held out her ID and waited a few more seconds, during which nothing happened, and then pulled out her phone. 'If you don't, I have no other choice than to call for back-up to break the door down.'

The peephole remained dark.

Was she mistaken? Had the peephole in fact been dark all along?

She had taken a step towards the door and grabbed the letter box when her phone suddenly lit up.

It was Hampus.

He, who never called, of course he would choose this moment to be in touch, when she had neither the time nor any desire to hear his voice.

She declined the call and turned back to the letter box, but then her phone rang again.

'Hampus, what are you doing?' she hissed into the phone. 'I'm busy and I can't—'

'*I know, but I think you'd better come home right now,*' he said, sounding unusually calm and collected.

'Why, what happened? Did something even happen? Or are you just having trouble finding the Coke? Because if that's the case, I can tell you we're out and you're just going to have to work up the energy to go to the shops and—'

'*As I said, I think you'd better come and see for yourself.*'

46

'EINAR GREIDE IN FORENSICS, *and yes, you have it right – I'm too busy to talk to you right now. And no, don't leave a message. If I don't have time to talk to you, why would I have time to listen to you?*'

There was a beep; Fabian ended the call. Flätan was known for his hatred of phones, mobiles in particular, and had made a habit of never taking his mandatory work phone home with him.

He called two more times just for the sake of it. At least that way he could say he'd called three times before he decided to go to his house.

He'd never been to Flätan's house before and wasn't exactly looking forward to it. The address had not been listed online, and no one at Helsingborg Hospital seemed to know it either, unless they'd in fact been given strict orders not to give it out under any circumstances.

His colleague Arne Gruvesson, on the other hand, had immediately given Fabian the number without objection. Indeed, he'd seemed almost giddy at the thought of Fabian going over there to bother Flätan at the weekend, and his birthday weekend to boot.

He parked on Traktörsgatan 38 and gazed up at the two-storey, side-facing brick house. It was quiet. Surprisingly quiet, considering how close to Söder it was. Once upon a time, the area had probably been teeming with children learning to ride bikes and playing hopscotch and tennis in the streets. Now they'd all flown the coop, leaving their parents to polish their cars while they waited for grandchildren to come and visit.

The only thing that didn't fit in was Flätan. He had neither a car nor children, and his garish clothes and long grey hair likely irked several of his neighbours no end. Knowing the coroner, though, he couldn't care less.

Fabian stepped through the small wooden gate and suddenly thought of Molander's wife, Gertrud, who had stumbled right into his meeting with Reidar Dahlberg. She had reacted, that much was undeniable. But whether it was to the fact that the investigation had been reopened or that she hadn't known about it was far from clear.

If the latter, there was a considerable risk she might already have called her husband to ask why he hadn't mentioned it to her. If the former, she would likely hold off on bringing it up until he came home from work.

If they even talked about things like that. It was conceivable that Molander, much like himself, avoided discussing his work at the dinner table. The question was if that would discourage Gudrun from bringing it up. It was impossible to know.

What was certain was that if she did tell him, he would have to let Tuvesson in on his secret investigation as quickly as possible so they could prepare an arrest order, praying they had enough evidence to secure a conviction.

He rang the doorbell, but couldn't tell if it was working. After a few attempts, he gave up and tried to walk around to the back instead, but a tall wall blocked his way, so he crossed over to the driveway on the other side of the house.

The garage was locked, as expected, and beyond that he was cut off by the neighbours' overgrown hedge. There really wasn't enough space, but with some effort he was able to push in between the hard, spiky branches and the garage wall.

A big back garden opened up on the other side. It was completely private and the trees were hung with hundreds of tiny disco balls that sent specks of light dancing across the lawn, which also housed, among other things, a tall wooden totem pole. A familiar electronic ambient groove was pulsing out of the surround speakers at a pleasant volume.

Trentemøller's *The Last Resort*. He had the album in his collection, and even though he hadn't listened to it in a long time, he rated it as one of the best albums ever to come out of neighbouring Denmark. That Flätan had even heard of it was impressive.

He walked on past some shrubs and spotted Flätan in a large hot tub full of steaming water, meditating with his eyes closed while a bronzed Adonis at least twenty years his junior massaged his shoulders, sitting right behind him in the tub.

The notion that he should probably sneak back out the way he'd come and heed Tuvesson's advice to wait until Monday occurred to him too late; the young man had already noticed him and stopped his massaging, which made Flätan open his eyes and give Fabian a tired look.

'Hello,' Fabian said, waving while he worked on his smile. 'I'm sorry, I didn't know you—' It felt like he'd just been caught red-handed and sent to the headmaster's office. 'If it works better for you, I can wait until you're done with—' he continued, and made a move to back away.

'That would unquestionably have been preferable. But unfortunately, you've already disturbed the energy fields.' Flätan signalled to the man behind him that the session was over. 'And for your sake, I hope this is important.' He pointed straight at Fabian. 'So important it can under no circumstances wait until tomorrow.'

The younger man climbed out of the hot tub, and even though Fabian looked away, he had time to note that his golden-brown body was as close to perfect as it was possible to get. His wasn't a body that spent its days lifting weights in a gym. No, it stayed fit some other way. Maybe climbing or yoga.

'*Coge el floreado*,' Flätan said in fluent Spanish. In response, the man fetched a floral bathrobe and held it up so Flätan could climb out of the tub. '*Mientras tanto puedes adobar la carne. Y luego pásame mi maletín, por favour. Ya sabes, el marrón*.'

The man nodded and walked away towards the house, seemingly unperturbed by the fact that he was stark naked.

'So? What's this about?' Flätan said, tying his robe and patting down his shoulder-length grey hair.

'Molly Wessman,' Fabian said. 'What was the cause of death?'

Flätan gave Fabian a look as though the question surprised him. 'Just so I've got this right. You come to my home. Uninvited. Possibly you ring the doorbell, but I don't know. Either way, you don't care that no one answers, you get in anyway. You don't give a toss that it's my birthday. That I was in the middle of my meditation. That I expressly told Tuvesson that it would have to wait until Monday. You didn't care about any of those things. The only thing you can think about is the cause of death. As though the entire case hinges on you finding out right now, instead of, say, eighteen hours from now.'

Fabian tried to find a reasonable objection, but could only nod, which made Flätan chuckle and move towards a pair of sofas littered with brightly coloured cushions.

'Annoying as it is, I have to admit that's what I like about you. Now, don't jump to conclusions. I still think you're pretty much as incompetent as most of the homicide detectives in this country. But at least you care. Which is more than can be said for some of your lethargic colleagues. Can I offer you some tea?'

'No, thank you.' Fabian sat down on one of the sofas, which was so deep it was downright impossible to sit upright.

'Severe dehydration.' Flätan picked up the thermos on the table and poured tea into one of the paper-thin cups until surface tension was the only thing keeping it from overflowing. 'The cause of death. Wasn't that what you were after?' He stepped up on to the other sofa and sank down into lotus position without spilling so much as a drop.

'Dehydration?'

Flätan nodded and sipped his tea. 'She'd probably been running a high fever beforehand, had the sweats, not to mention violent vomiting and diarrhoea.'

'So in other words, she was sick.'

'You can say that again.'

'So if I'm understanding you right, there were no signs of wrongdoing?'

'Oh, she was murdered, all right.' Flätan drank his tea. 'Remember Georgi Markov? You know, the Bulgarian defector who was murdered in 1978 on Waterloo Bridge in London?'

'Wasn't he poisoned with ricin?'

'Exactly, and Molly Wessman got more or less the same treatment. Except without the James Bond umbrella with a poison pellet in its tip. No, in this case, whoever did it kept it simple and just injected the poison with a syringe.'

The fit young man, who was now wearing an apron, returned with a briefcase, which he handed to Flätan before returning to the house.

'And when was this done to her?'

'Hard to say exactly. But probably twenty-four to thirty-six hours before she died.' Flätan opened his briefcase and pulled out a file. 'So, sometime Friday.'

The picture of Molly Wessman on her phone had been taken in the early hours of Wednesday, clearly a perfect opportunity to poison her. Instead, the perpetrator had, for unknown reasons, waited another two days.

'This is the pinprick.' Flätan handed him a close-up of Molly Wessman's right buttock, where a small red bump was visible.

'It must have hurt,' Fabian said. 'I mean, shouldn't she have reacted and gone to A&E as soon as she got sick?'

'That's assuming she was aware of what had happened to her. That someone had pricked her with a syringe. But if she was outside at the time, she might just as easily have figured it was a bee sting or some such. Then, when she fell ill, she didn't see the connection to the needle prick. Probably just thought she had the stomach flu or food poisoning, and nearer the end, she was too weak to get out of her flat.' Flätan drank the last of his tea and put the cup down. 'Are we done here?'

Fabian nodded and stood up. 'Thank you. I can show myself out.' He would probably have been welcome to exit through the house, but something told him there were things in there he shouldn't see, so he turned back towards the garage.

'So you're not going to ask if I found anything out of the ordinary?'

Fabian stopped and turned to Flätan, who was smiling and pouring himself another cup of tea. 'Such as?'

'I don't know. Anything.' Flätan shrugged. 'Isn't that your go-to question when you're flying blind with no idea of where to go next?'

'So what did you find?' Fabian walked back to the sofas.

'A small tattoo. And yes, I know exactly what you're thinking. Doesn't everyone have a tattoo these days? And you're right. In my profession, it's rare to come across a body completely free of ghastly butterflies, pathetic skulls and tribal patterns.' Flätan fell silent and leisurely sipped his tea. 'But this one stood out.' He put his cup down and handed over another close-up.

It was instantly clear to Fabian why Flätan had reacted. The tattoo looked like nothing he'd ever seen. No brightly coloured flowers, Asian characters or sage quotes here. In a way, it was bland and boring. And yet he struggled to tear his eyes away.

It was a classic shade of blueish-grey and consisted of two parts. The upper one was some kind of symbol, with a line penetrated by a downward-pointing arrow. The lower consisted of two numbers: 28. Nothing was straight or centred, and the whole thing gave an amateurish, unplanned impression.

'Where on her body was it?'

'Smack dab in the middle of her pubic mound, hidden underneath her, if I may say so, well-groomed pubic hair. I actually didn't notice it until I shaved her.'

47

When Lilja slowed down and turned off towards Perstorp, she had covered the distance from southern Helsingborg in just over twenty-two minutes. It wasn't just a personal best for her and the Ducati. It was also so far above the speed limit no police badge in the world would have saved her if she'd been caught.

But the call from Hampus had been ominous, to say the least. He'd worked hard to hide it, but there had been no doubt he was genuinely afraid. Normally, he'd prattle on like a machine gun, but this time he hadn't wanted to tell her what was wrong or why it was so important for her to hurry home.

On her way out of the city, she'd had her suspicions, but she'd tried to dismiss them as exaggerated and hysterical and to think about other things instead.

But she was getting increasingly worried about what she would find when she got home, and she wasn't able to relax until she turned down Jeans Väg and looked up at the house behind the juniper bushes.

Both the house and the garage looked the same as ever. The red brick and whitewash were as blandly boring as when she'd left.

Maybe it was that the second-hand dishwasher he'd insisted on buying had given up and started leaking. That wouldn't surprise her in the slightest. She'd thought it was a bad idea all along, especially since they'd just had their floors sanded. Or maybe it was just a— That was as far as she got before she rode up on to the driveway, put down her kickstand and saw the garden.

Someone had skidded around it on motorcycles in what could only be described as a rape of their lawn. In their wake, they'd left open wounds of torn-up tussocks of grass, puddles and tyre tracks that in places were so deep, they'd dug right through the soil to the layer of clay underneath. It hadn't rained much in the past couple of weeks, which meant they must have used the hose to do as much damage as possible. In other words, they knew what they were doing. Maybe she should be afraid. Maybe she should tell her colleagues, file a report and request police protection. Which was exactly what they wanted.

A frightened police officer.

She could already see the headlines. First pages with pictures of her devastated lawn. Reporters shouting over each other, trying to make out like they were on the side of good when all they wanted was a headline to sell more copies. Never mind if it stoked the hatred even more.

She was bloody well not going to play along, act the victim. Her best option was to counter it with silence and pretend like nothing had happened.

The problem was Hampus. He hadn't just been afraid. He'd been out of his wits terrified.

She opened the front door and stuck her head in. 'I'm here now!'

'Up here,' she heard a voice say somewhere behind her.

She went back out into the garden and looked around. 'Where are you?'

'Up here.'

She looked up and only now noticed him on the roof, sitting with his arms around his pulled-up knees, rocking back and forth as though trying to soothe himself. 'But what are you doing? Why are you up there?'

'Come up and see for yourself.'

She was about to argue, out of sheer habit, and ask him to come down instead. But something told her it would be better to oblige him. He looked like the slightest resistance might break him. In all their years together, she'd never seen him as pale and fragile as he was right now.

'All right, sit tight. I'm coming up.' She started climbing the ladder. 'And hey, I'm sure the lawn can be fixed.' When she reached the roof, she trod gingerly across the roof tiles towards Hampus. 'You've been talking about redoing it anyway, to get rid of the moss.'

Hampus didn't respond, just rocked back and forth with his arms around his legs and his eyes on the vandalized lawn.

'Hey… It's going to be okay.' She sat down next to him and was just about to put her arm around him when she realized what he was looking at. Suddenly, everything made sense. His violent reaction, which she'd found a bit over the top after getting back. The silence, which was so unlike him. His insistence that she see it for herself. Even why he was sitting on the roof became clear.

Down on the ground, she had interpreted the mayhem in their garden as exactly that, mayhem. The work of a couple of knuckleheads who had skidded around at random, trying to wreak as much havoc as they could as quickly as they could.

She couldn't have been more wrong.

Whoever it was who had roared around their garden, they'd known exactly what they were doing. Where to let their tyres dig extra deep into the mud; where they were supposed to destroy the lawn utterly and where they should leave a few patches. It was only now, looking down from above, that she could see what they had really done.

The entire expanse, from the stepping stones by the front door to the juniper bushes lining the street, was now filled with the biggest swastika she'd ever seen.

48

SOMEONE HAD TOLD HIM once that the buildings lined up in a row in the North Harbour were inspired by old ships. Fabian, for his part, thought they looked more like square grey lumps built out of Lego. At least from the outside.

After finding the entrance code among his notes, he discovered that the inside better reflected the poshness of the address. As Klippan and the others had intimated, it suggested Molly Wessman had, despite her relative youth, risen through the company ranks unusually quickly and may have stepped on a few toes on her way up.

But an embittered co-worker breaking in to her home in the middle of the night and hacking her phone to snap a background picture of her sleeping before lethally poisoning her two days later, it seemed too unlikely. The strange tattoo was a much more promising clue.

Granted, that downward arrow could have been nothing more than a vulgar sexual invitation. But that didn't explain the horizontal line or the two-digit number. Nor why the tattoo had been concealed underneath her pubic hair.

When he reached the third floor, he pulled out the keys Molander had given him, unlocked the door to her flat and entered.

Molander...

Over the past few hours, he'd done his best not to think about his colleague so he could give Molly Wessman his undivided attention. But the question of how he should handle the situation now that Gertrud knew the case had been reopened gnawed at him; when he stepped into the hallway and closed the door behind him, it was as though comprehension finally broke through his last barrier of denial.

What if Molander had already puzzled out that he'd taken over Elvin's investigation, Gertrud and the pictures in his phone notwithstanding? What if he was already planning his death? A death that, like Elvin's, would be made to look like suicide.

It wouldn't be hard to fabricate a motive, considering that his family was on the verge of imploding. Or was he planning an accident? If anyone could mess with brake cables without anyone ever finding out, it was Molander. Especially since he would be the one to conduct the technical investigation.

He decided to seize the bull by the horns and sound Molander out, so he pulled out his phone and dialled his colleague's number.

'*Hey Fabian. How are you getting on?*' The reply came before he'd heard a single ring. As though his colleague had been sitting poised to answer when he called.

'Hi, it's me, Fabian.'

'*Yes, I can see that and I was asking how you're getting on? Are you done in Wessman's flat?*'

'Almost,' he said, looking around to find something at least slightly relevant to bring up.

'*Almost? What have you been doing all morning?*'

Was the question genuine or was Molander toying with him? Judging from his tone, he sounded like he always did, whatever that meant. Molander was a master of irony. He never made much of a distinction between when he was joking and being serious, and it wasn't unusual for people to realize too late that they'd read him wrong.

'I saw to something else that couldn't wait first.' He squatted down to have a closer look at the shelf that lay in the middle of the floor among the shoes, with screws dangling from its brackets. The holes in the wall above gaped empty, indicating that Wessman had probably pulled it down on herself in her struggle to get to her feet.

'*Really, and what was that, if you don't mind me asking? Nothing serious, I hope?*'

The problem was that the shelf was already mentioned in the neighbour's statement. He needed something less obvious. Something that hadn't been discussed yet.

'Depends on how you see it.' He stood back up and deliberately paused to try to coax out a reaction. But the only response he got was a watchful silence. 'I stopped by Flätan's house, and it turned out he was practically done with—'

'*Seriously,*' Molander broke in. '*You went to Flätan's house today?*'

'Yes,' he said, and he heard Molander burst out laughing.

'*That's outstanding, Fabian. You really are the only one who could get away with something like that. Talk about wanting to be a fly on that wall. But since you're still alive, I assume he received you without overly strenuous remonstrations. Had he found anything of interest?*'

'He had, a tattoo hidden under her pubic hair,' he said and concluded that Molander was either a world-class actor giving the performance of a lifetime, or Gertrud hadn't said anything yet. 'It consisted of a horizontal line intersected by a down arrow and a two-digit number underneath.'

'*So we're talking a symbol with an associated number.*' He could virtually hear Molander lean back in his chair to think. '*The closest I have is a line intersected by two arrows pointing in opposite directions, which is the generally accepted symbol for crossing a border. The Physical Barrier Border Crossing icon, I think it's called. But that doesn't necessarily have anything to do with anything. What was the number?*'

'Twenty-eight.'

'*Twenty-eight... No, apart from that it follows twenty-seven and precedes twenty-nine, it means nothing to me.*'

'Don't worry about it. I just wanted to see if it made you think of anything.'

'*But that's not why you called, is it?*'

'Pardon?' He'd been about to end the call, pleased to have been able to convince himself Gertrud hadn't said anything yet. Now, instead, he was back to square one.

'*If that were the case, you would've called the moment you left Flätan's. Now, as far as I can make out, you're almost done with Wessman's flat, which implies you've been there a while, so logically, you should be calling about something related to that. Correct me if I'm wrong.*'

'I wouldn't necessarily say wrong,' he said, trying to buy time. Of course Molander was right. Of course he was calling to talk about something in Wessman's flat. The question was what. A white plastic card was sticking out of one of the shoes. It had probably fallen off the noticeboard when the shelf came off the wall. 'I did want to talk to you about the tattoo. But it didn't seem so urgent it couldn't wait until I saw you.' He picked up and studied the bone-white card, which simply read *Spades* in gold lettering. 'But you're right, that wasn't the only thing,' he continued and spotted a key deposit cylinder fastened to the top corner of the front door. 'When do you think you'll get here for the crime scene investigation?'

'*Tomorrow morning.*'

'All right, I just wanted to plant a seed in your mind for when you come.' It was more or less nothing. But right now, more or less nothing was better than nothing.

'*Okay,*' Molander said, waiting.

'Her front door has a key deposit cylinder. You know, a lockable tube where you can leave keys for your handyman or cleaning lady if you're not going to be in.'

'*Fabian, I know what a key deposit is.*'

'Okay, sorry. I just meant that someone could have been here to fix something and made a copy of her keys.'

'*Sure. But what do you want me to do about that when I'm there tomorrow?*'

Of course. What was Molander supposed to do about that? 'I just wanted to remind you to keep your eyes open when you're here,' he said, feeling himself sinking ever deeper into the quicksand.

'*Fabian, keeping my eyes open is my job.*'

'I know, I was thinking more about... about...' He swallowed and wiped the sweat off his brow with his sleeve. 'You know this thing about handymen and other people who shouldn't really have keys to her flat.'

'*Yes. And?*' Molander was starting to sound annoyed. '*Would you mind getting to the point? Everyone's on me right now, and I really don't have all afternoon.*'

'I just want you to react if there's something that's not right,' he said, clueless as to what that was supposed to mean. 'It could be anything in the flat. I mean in terms of fixing things. Do you get what I'm saying?'

'*No. But no need to fret. I'll keep my eyes open. Are we done here?*'

'Absolutely. I just wanted to tell you that.'

'*Great.*'

The phone call had been exhausting. The most important thing now was that Molander didn't seem suspicious and Gertrud had most likely not said anything. Which gave him time to think about whether to contact her or not.

He started studying the mysterious plastic card from every conceivable angle and in every conceivable light. But the only information he could see was the six gold letters.

Spades.

It could mean anything. From an illegal casino to an informal network for career women. Predictably, a Google search generated over three million hits. He went to Hitta.se instead so he could limit the search to the north-west part of Skåne. The number of hits was reduced to two.

The bowling club *Queen of Spades* in Allerum and *Club Spades* in Glumslöv.

He dialled the latter's number and was greeted by an answering machine.

'*Welcome to Spades, the club for all tastes.*'

49

'SHE'S GOING TO DIE.'

He was so sick of them and just wanted them to go away.

'*She doesn't deserve to live anyway.*'

Wanted them to leave him alone.

'*The only thing she deserves is you.*'

Stupid fucking prick voices.

'*You can do anything you want.*'

But, as usual, they refused.

'*Absolutely anything you want.*'

Though they did sound different this time; they did.

'*So long as it ends with her dying.*'

More intense and urgent.

'*We know you want to.*'

Nag, nag, nag.

'*That you've been looking forward to it.*'

It was as though they'd got stuck on repeat and weren't going to stop until he did what they told him to.

'*Looked forward to finally throwing all inhibition aside.*'

At least that usually shut them up.

'*You really do deserve it.*'

But he didn't always want to.

'*You of all people.*'

Sometimes, he'd done things just to make them shut up.

'*You know she's going to die.*'

The people in the ward had only themselves to blame.

'That it's the right thing.'

After all, they were the ones who insisted on letting him out every time. Not him.

'You know what to do.'

So, in a way, the voices were in fact on to something.

'And you do like children, don't you.'

His right.

'No one likes children as much as you.'

His goddamn right.

50

Tonight 4pm – 2am. Mixed. Odengatan 10, entrance on Heimdalsgatan. Welcome.

THE TEXT HAD BEEN sent from a withheld number just over half an hour after he'd left his name and number on the answering machine. At that point it had already been half four, which was why he'd gone straight from Wessman's flat, in the hopes of there not being too many guests yet. But as soon as he turned on to Heimdalsgatan in Glumslöv, he realized that had been wishful thinking.

A long row of cars and motorcycles were parked along the side of the road, in the tall grass. There was even a tractor and a couple of bikes with helmets dangling off their handlebars. Apparently, people were eager to get inside and get naked. He parked his car a few hundred feet further down the street and walked back. The last thing he wanted was to be boxed in and having to ask people to move their cars when they were in the middle of God knew what.

He squeezed through the gap between two cars and continued in through an opening in the ramshackle, overgrown fence. The reason they'd put the entrance in the back was probably the neighbours, who had no doubt done everything they could to get rid of the club, though things did seem surprisingly quiet. The idea of anything wilder than a dinner party and possibly a round of bridge going on inside felt like utter science fiction.

A well-trodden path led up to a grey door at the back of the house. A brass sign announced that he'd found Spades. He opened the door and stepped into the darkness beyond.

This was his first time at a swingers' club. Like most people, he'd toyed with the idea, and on one or two occasions he'd seriously considered whether it wasn't exactly what Sonja and he needed to kickstart their sex life after the baby years.

But he'd never gone so far as to mention the idea to Sonja. Mostly because he'd been convinced she would explode and accuse him of being distasteful and revolting and say that his pathetic midlife crisis wasn't her problem. What's more, he had no idea how he would react to seeing her with other people.

But in hindsight, maybe he should have suggested it. Maybe their relationship would have been different. Not to mention their sex life, which had descended into such a deep torpor over the past few years, not even electric shocks could resuscitate it. Or would it have made no difference, since, according to Matilda's philosophy, everything was preordained anyway?

Once his eyes got used to the gloom, he found he was in a hallway with black walls and that there was a dark red curtain in front of him. Soothing music and sensual moaning could be heard from the other side of it, mixed with the sound of skin slapping against skin at an increasing pace. And if he wasn't mistaken, at least one woman, possibly more, was close to climaxing.

Against his will, he felt his blood starting to stir. In an attempt to calm himself down, he refocused on why he was there and pulled the curtain aside.

'Welcome, Fabian Risk,' said the woman at the till. She looked about his age and was dressed in a tight latex corset, which matched her smiling red lips and elbow-length gloves. 'First time, I see.'

Fabian nodded on his way up to the till, pondering how she could tell. 'I'm afraid I'm only here to talk about a certain Molly Wessman. Do you know her?'

'Maybe,' replied the woman, whose smile was quickly replaced by a straight line. 'In this world, we don't discuss our guests with outsiders. So whatever secrets you might have, they stay between us. Might be good to know in case you ever work up the courage to come here to let your hair down.'

'Absolutely. But as it happens, Molly Wessman is dead, murdered.' He showed her his police ID. 'Priests, doctors and psychologists are some of the people whose right to professional secrecy is sanctioned by law. Swingers, or whatever you call yourselves, have no choice but to talk, unless you want me to press charges, that is.'

The woman briefly glanced down at his ID before looking back up at him. 'As I said, we don't talk to outsiders. So either you press your little charges, if that makes you feel good. Or you throw yourself into the unknown and become a member. Become one of us. Who knows where it might lead?'

Her smile was back, a visible confirmation that she could see right through him and his empty threats. As though he were even close to pressing charges.

'How much is a membership?'

'4,500 annually and 350 per visit. That includes a towel and bathrobe, oils and condoms. You'll have to bring your own Viagra.'

That wasn't only too expensive, the lead was also too flimsy to ask Tuvesson to compensate him. Even so, he found himself pulling out his card from his wallet, inserting it into the reader and punching in his PIN.

'There we go. That wasn't so hard, now was it?' She tore off the receipt and gave him his part along with his card. 'Your membership card will be waiting for you the next time you feel brave enough to stop by.'

'There won't be a next time. Now I would like you to answer my questions.'

'This is your bathrobe.' She placed a folded white robe and matching slippers on the counter. 'You'll find towels in the changing room.' She nodded to a door further down the hallway. 'Oil and condoms are available throughout the facility. And condoms are required, so just take as many as you need. But we'd appreciate it if you wouldn't mind discarding used ones in one of the bins provided. Other than that, there's only one rule: No means no. No one does anything against their will here. If you have any other questions, we can talk about them after you've showered.'

He was about to object when a couple in their thirties entered and flashed their membership cards.

'Hello, welcome,' the woman said and turned to get two more robes.

Fabian saw no other way than to follow her instructions. She definitely knew Wessman and unless he'd read her wrong, she had things to say about her. Or was he just fooling himself? Should he give up and go home?

The changing room was small but clean with lockers along the walls and a shower room with four showers. A wall-mounted TV was showing a film in which a muscular man was lying on his back, getting massaged by a woman. She sensually caressed his chest all the way down to his member, which though only half-erect was considerably larger than his own. Both the man and the woman were shaved smooth everywhere; their oil-drenched skin reflected the light when she took it in her mouth.

He wasn't big on porn, personally. Watching others have a good time instead of having a good time himself had never held much appeal. But he had trouble tearing his eyes away from this particular film. For a porn flick, it was remarkably tasteful and artistic, in terms of the lighting, the black-and-white filter and the choice of music.

He pulled off his jacket and unbuttoned his shirt. Then he took off his shoes and trousers and put everything in a locker. One of his socks had a hole on the heel; he pondered whether he should throw them out and go home barefoot. His washed-out underpants, which had once been blue with purple stripes, were hardly a source of pride either; taking them off was almost a relief.

What would Sonja say if she knew where he was right now? Would she even care? Probably not. She would probably just shrug and wish him luck.

He locked his locker and put the key in one of the pockets of the bathrobe on his way to the showers, where he stepped into the furthest stall and let the hot water wash over him. It felt good; he was finally able to relax.

Why was he fighting it, anyway? What was he ashamed of? He was practically divorced, looked okay for his age and from what little he'd seen in various changing rooms, he was well-hung enough to consider himself a bit above average.

He rinsed off the soap and heard the sound of love-making over the splashing of the water. At first, he assumed it was the TV. But when he moved his head out of the jet, he could clearly hear that it was coming from the adjacent sauna. It sounded like two women and a man and they all seemed to be enjoying themselves immensely.

A part of him wanted to pull his scruffy socks and ugly underwear back on and go home as quickly as possible. But only a small part. The rest of him instead turned off the shower and moved towards the wooden door, whose handle had gone dark from all the wet hands grabbing it. There were at least three people in there, maybe as many as five, and judging from the sounds, they were partying together.

He had never tried group sex. He'd never even come close to a threesome. If he was completely honest, it wasn't something he'd found particularly tempting, especially not if it involved another man. He couldn't say why. It had just never turned him on.

But that was then, all of thirty seconds ago. Now, his objections felt completely irrelevant. One or more men, women, it didn't matter. All he wanted was to go inside and join in. To experience all those things he had, for some reason, decided weren't for him.

He just needed a condom first, and like the woman at the till had said, they were right there, in a bowl within arm's reach. He picked up a wrapper, snapped it in half and started rolling the condom on to his throbbing cock. Of course he wouldn't do anything if he was unwelcome. But why would he be? There were clearly more than two people in there. And if not them, there were others. He hadn't even left the changing room yet.

He mustered his courage and grabbed the handle to open the door. It was stiff; he had to put his other hand on the door frame to yank it open.

A warm, humid wall hit him. A wall heavy with sweat and sex. The whole scene was one of the most revolting things he'd ever seen. And yet, he couldn't make himself stop staring, as though he were passing a traffic accident with severed body parts strewn along the side of the road.

It was a big heaving pile of flesh. Hairy backs, tattooed love handles and pimply behinds jumbled up in an orgy of bad taste. It took him several seconds to figure out that there were only four of them – two men and two women, all obese enough that ending up underneath them might be fatal.

Before any of them had a chance to notice him, he backed out into the shower room, pulled off the now much-too-big condom, wrapped his bathrobe around him and stepped into his slippers.

The event served as a reminder why he was there and steered him towards the red door that led out to a larger room with a black ceiling and red drapes along the walls.

The handful of lights in the room were so faint he had to stop and wait for his eyes to adjust again. People were spread out, conversing, holding cups of tea or coffee, as though this were a coffee break in a parish hall, with the slight difference that most people were naked.

There was a lot of paleness and obesity on which years of gravity had left indelible marks. Granted, some were tall and thin, but their posture seemed to be begging for back pain, and almost everyone, whether they were short and curvy or bald with guts so big they effectively concealed their private parts, had at least two or three tattoos.

From time to time, as if in response to a secret signal, a couple or an entire group departed for one of the adjacent rooms, and he was shot a number of inviting looks. But he pretended not to notice, and as soon as he saw the woman from the till enter and step in behind the bar, he walked over and sat down on one of the bar stools.

'Hi there, how are you getting on?' she said, serving the woman next to him a raspberry soft drink. 'Get laid yet?'

'That's not why I'm here.'

'Right, you're here for a murder investigation.' She chuckled. 'Everyone comes here with an excuse the first time, though I will admit I've never heard yours before.'

'Maybe because it's true,' he said. He waited until the woman next to him had left together with a couple in their forties. 'So if you wouldn't mind telling me what you know about Molly Wessman.'

'At the risk of disappointing, I don't know much more than you do.' She shrugged. 'She was one of our very first members, always showed up alone and was here maybe ten times, at a guess.'

'What was her orientation? I mean, was she into anything in particular? Something outside the realm of the normal?'

'And what exactly is outside the realm of the normal?'

'I don't know. Was she into BDSM? Did she like it rough? Or was she—'

'So BDSM isn't considered normal?'

'I don't know. This is your world. Not mine.'

'In my world, we don't ask stupid questions. "Did she like it rough?"' The woman shook her head as a short man with a beard and glasses came over with a homemade DVD.

'Would you mind running this in the video room?'

'Of course not, consider it done.' She took the disc out of the case, labelled CREAM #23, and inserted it into one of the players. 'So you and Sivan have been at it again, have you?'

The man lit up but didn't answer and then he disappeared.

'In your world, on the other hand,' she continued. 'There, a place like this is all about being deviants and getting off on, like, golden showers and strangulation.'

'If you wouldn't mind answering my questions instead of rating them,' Fabian said, spotting the two obese couples from the sauna entering through the red door. 'Then this would've taken no longer than a few minutes and you could have gone back to serving fizzy drinks and I could have gone home to my family, 4,850 kronor poorer.'

'Fine.' She met his eyes. 'If you ask me, she was completely normal. Just like you and everyone else here, she was interested in sex. Just like you, she did nothing her first time here, and when she came back, it was, as it so often is, very cautious and vanilla. But as time went by, she agreed to try all kinds of things. Just like you will.'

'Was she with different people, men and women, or always with the same ones?'

'She went with different people, men and women, just like it will be for—'

'Let's stick to Molly. Do you know if she ever thought things had gone too far, if she was afraid of anyone?'

'No, who would that be? One of the rules is that no one has to do anything they don't want to.'

'Never heard of people breaking rules?'

'Maybe out in your world. Not here.' She put out a sign that read *Serve yourself* on the counter. 'Are we done? Because I have guests waiting.'

Fabian turned around and saw a group of seven or eight people of different ages and in various states of undress waiting behind him. She was probably right. Not just about how safe this environment was compared to the world outside, but also about how it was probably his narrow-minded view of sex that had read too much into Wessman being a member of a swingers' club. Even so, he leaned over the counter and grabbed a pen.

'Just one last thing,' he said as he drew a line across a napkin and added a perpendicular arrow. 'You wouldn't happen to recognize this tattoo, would you?' He added the two-digit number under the line and handed her the napkin.

The woman glanced at the simple drawing, poised to hand it back without much thought and walk off with her guests. But instead, she froze mid-movement and looked from him to the sketch and back a few times before turning to the waiting group. 'I'm sorry, but you're going to have get started without me. I'll join you as soon as I can.'

The others nodded and left.

'Is that Wessman's?' She glanced over her shoulder as if to make sure no one had lingered.

'So you recognize it?'

'No.' She shook her head. 'I've actually never seen it before. But I've heard rumours. Are you sure it's Wessman's? Because I have no recollection of her having a tattoo.'

'Tell me about the rumours.'

'At least, that's what I assume they are. Like that he comes to this club. Sometimes, he's even been said to be in several places at once. But as I said, I always figured that was just a gimmick to draw people in.'

'But now you don't know any more.'

The woman shook her head, still staring at the drawing.

'And who is this legend?'

'I first heard about him about two years ago. He calls himself Columbus. No one knows who he really is, but a lot of people would give up everything for a night with him.'

'Why?'

Only now did she tear her eyes away from the napkin and meet his eyes. 'Rumour has it, it's like losing your virginity a second time. Like meeting a virtuoso who can push anyone beyond the limits. And who doesn't want that?'

'What limits?'

'Their own. Who else's?'

Molander had, in other words, not been too wide of the mark when he'd guessed the tattoo was a version of the Physical Barrier Border Crossing icon. 'And what about you?' he said and took the napkin from her. 'How much would you give up for one night?'

'The last thing I need is to venture beyond more limits. Besides, I'm an advocate for a varied diet.'

'Varied diet?'

'I'm sure it's just a rumour, like the other thing. But when he's done with you, you supposedly belong to him alone.'

51

THE E6 MOTORWAY WAS practically deserted when he drove home. Fifteen minutes later, Fabian turned on to Pålsjögatan and found an empty spot right outside the dark terraced house. But when he'd killed the engine and was about to unbuckle his seat belt, he felt a sudden reluctance to going home and turning in. After his visit to Spades, he had too many images flashing before his eyes, and he could picture Sonja lying with her back towards him while he stared at the ceiling, trying desperately to think about nothing at all.

He didn't know if that was the ultimate reason he turned the key in the ignition and drove on towards Johan Banérs Gata, where he turned left towards the sea. But he felt a lot better as soon as he got there and could roll down his window and fill his lungs with the briny sea air blowing in from the sound.

He turned on the radio, which was playing The The's 'Love is Stronger than Death'.

He'd never been a singer. Not even when his friends had dragged him to a karaoke place for his stag do had he agreed to get on stage. Now, though, he was singing with such feeling he had tears in his eyes all the way to Hittarp, where the music faded out to make room for the news.

'Tomorrow, Monday, will be the first day of the trial of the four Swedish teenagers of the so-called Smiley Gang

in Helsingør's County Court. The four stand accused of murdering three homeless people in Denmark. The prosecutor's most damning evidence is said to be the videos the accused disseminated online, which show them killing by means of what is best described as torture methods. Even so, the risk of a complete acquittal is said to be considerable. Rolf Sandén, Professor of Law, commented earlier today:

'"*The problem is that they were masked and will very likely blame one another. It's really not so different from some of the recent rape cases that have featured in the media, in which there were several perpetrators. There, too, we have seen a number of acquittals, as a lack of third-party witness statements has made it virtually impossible to determine who did what.*"'

He turned the radio off, slowed down and stopped by the side of the road near Svanebäck, where the land around him was so flat the grass appeared to meld into the mirror-like water, and even though he didn't think it would work, he found her number again and tried it. He had to talk to her and find out exactly what she knew about the case.

'*The number you have dialled is no longer in use. The number you have dialled doesn't exist. The number you have dialled is no longer in...*'

He tried information, only to be told that they couldn't find anyone named Dunja Hougaard in Denmark.

She had gone off grid and apparently had no interest in being found by him or anyone else. But why? Had something happened? Or was something about to happen? Either possibility was disconcerting. He decided to go over to Copenhagen as soon as he could to try to locate her.

Twenty minutes later, he turned on to Pålsjögatan again and parked his car in the same spot as before. He took his shoes off on the front steps so he wouldn't wake Sonja. Once he was inside, he hung up his coat and walked towards the downstairs bathroom without turning the lights on.

It had only been a few hours since his last shower; though he'd thought about it, he hadn't crossed the line and done anything Sonja or anyone else could find fault with. Even so, he felt dirty and was hoping a long, hot shower would rinse away the worst of it.

'Why are you so late?'

He turned around and realized someone was on the sofa. 'Sonja? Is that you?' She, who never slept downstairs, had stayed up, waiting for him to come home.

'It's okay if you don't want to say, and what difference does it make? As though I even have a right to ask.'

'I've just been working.' He went into the living room and couldn't help but feel a jolt of joy that she did seem to care a little. 'Did something happen?' He sat down on the edge of the sofa, which instantly made her pull her legs away and sit up.

'We need to talk.'

'Sonja, I'm aware I got too angry at Matilda when you came home yesterday. But there's something off about her, and to be honest, I'm really concerned.'

'Well, for once, I'm not talking about Matilda.' Sonja poured two cups of tea from a thermos. 'It's about Theodor.' She pushed one of the cups towards him. 'He's told me as well now and given me a slightly more nuanced version than the one you presented.'

'More nuanced?'

'Yes, I just think it's easier for him to talk to me about these things.' She sipped her tea. 'About how he fell in love with the girl in that Smiley Gang and was forced to be their lookout and ran into your Danish colleague, Dunja Hougaard.' She broke off and seemed to have to pause to summon the strength to go on.

'Did he also tell you he threatened her with that gun and tried to beat her up?'

'Fabian, listen to me. The things they've done seem horrible. Just heinous, I can't find the words to even begin to describe it. But that's not what this is about.' She met his eyes. 'Our Theodor was never part of it.'

'No? What do you call being the lookout and threatening people—'

'Please, just try to listen. He didn't even know. He was just in love, and as soon as he realized what they were doing, he tried to get away from them. The problem was they wouldn't let him leave but rather forced him to help them that last time. And now you want to make him turn himself over to the police.'

'Yes, of course. It's the right thing to do.'

'Is it? How can you be so sure?'

'The truth. No matter what we do, it's going to come out one way or another. Either he reports to the police and gives a statement, gets it out of his system and faces the consequences. Or he continues down the path he's on now and lets it eat him up from inside until he completely falls apart.'

'My God, you're so dramatic.'

'Am I? Or are you having trouble seeing things clearly because you behave exactly the same way as our son?'

'And what the fuck is that supposed to mean?'

'Sonja, as long as you choose not to tell me what happened between you and that art dealer, we're never going to be able to move on and you will just feel worse and worse.'

'We're not talking about me, we're talking about Theodor. Can we please stick to the subject at hand.'

'Fine.' Fabian spread his hands. 'I'll say it again: Justice must be allowed to be done, no matter how badly we want Theodor to—'

'So what's more important? Justice or your own son?'

'That's a false dilemma.'

'No it's not. So what's it going to be? Justice or Theodor? Go ahead, choose.'

'And what makes you think this is up to—'

'If you insist on this,' Sonja broke in, fighting back her tears, 'Theodor is going to fall apart. Just so you know. He's not going to be able to handle it.'

'Sonja.' Fabian moved closer to her on the sofa. 'It's not that I don't understand that this is hard.'

'Hard?' Sonja looked at him with revulsion. 'Is that what this is for you? "Hard"? Can't you see it's going to be completely devastating? Can you even picture Theodor in prison, serving, I don't know, a number of years for something he might not even be guilty of?'

'No, and do you know why? Because it's extremely unlikely that he would be given any kind of prison sentence. As you yourself said, his involvement will be considered minor compared to the others. And if he did end up in detention, against all odds, he wouldn't be in a prison, he would be sent to a young offenders' facility. And that's the worst-case scenario. The most likely outcome is that he gets a suspended sentence or acquitted completely. Both because he was coerced and because he did almost nothing. They will also take into consideration that he turned himself in and is willing to cooperate. But none of that is up to us, it's up to the courts. Just imagine what the world would look like if people disregarded justice whenever it didn't suit them?'

'Okay,' Sonja nodded, with tears streaming down her cheeks. 'At least I know where you stand.' She tried to wipe them away but gave up. 'I shouldn't even be surprised. It's always been like this. Work before all else. Before you, me and definitely before your children. Never mind if they go to pieces, so long as justice is done.'

'What's the alternative? To sweep this under the carpet and pretend nothing happened? Do you really think that's going to make him feel better? That the best option for him is to build his entire future on a lie? If he doesn't take the stand, the accused will blame one another and probably walk away scot-free.'

'Right, so now he's supposed to carry the weight of the entire justice system on his shoulders, too.'

'No, but he has a responsibility and is at a crossroads that he's going to have to live with for the rest of his life. And if this isn't the time to nudge him in the right direction, when is?'

Sonja shook her head and sipped her tea, which had long since gone cold.

'Sonja...' He tried to catch her eye in a last attempt at persuasion, but she refused. 'When you started seeing that art dealer, I knew immediately you shared more than an interest in art.'

'Great.' She met his eyes for a brief moment before looking away again. 'Back to that again.'

'But I didn't say anything. Instead, I let you stay out all night and come and go as you pleased with nothing but flimsy excuses.'

'I'm sorry, but what does this have to do with Theodor?'

'And do you know why? Huh? Do you?'

'What are you doing?' She stared him right in the eye. 'Why do you have to open up—'

'Because it felt easier! Not because I was indifferent and didn't care. Quite the opposite. I simply couldn't handle the conflict just then, even though you going behind my back felt so wrong and just fucking awful, to put it plainly.'

'All right, I think I get your point.'

'Even though I still loved you and wanted nothing more than for you to come back to me, I sat back and let it happen. I don't know what he did to you, and maybe you'll never want to tell me. But whatever it was, I was the one who let it happen and will never be able to forgive myself for not putting my foot down, for not forcing that conflict and sticking to my convictions. Never.'

Sonja still didn't say anything. But in her eyes, deep down, he thought he glimpsed an I'm sorry, and when she held her arms out to him, all his doubts vanished. Only now did he realize how much he'd missed having her close. How much he'd longed to just hold her. The smell of her hair. Her breath against his chest. Maybe he was imagining it, but he felt like she was back, and he could already sense a stirring of hope that maybe everything would be okay again someday.

52

While waiting for Tuvesson to finish her call and resume the meeting, Fabian's thoughts meandered back to Sonja. He couldn't remember the last time it had been like that. Him waking up, like he had that morning, in exactly the same position as when he fell asleep – on his back, with her head on his shoulder and his arm around her hip. Quite a change from his usual position, as far out on his side of the mattress as possible with his back to her.

Nothing more had been said. The words had all been used up by the time they'd got off the sofa and gone to bed. An intimate, almost magical closeness had enveloped them when she'd snuggled in next to him and let him put his arm around her.

The idea of sex had been there the whole time; in a way, it was the perfect set-up. Her body next to his, the building warmth and lust. They had both been ready and millimetres from breaking the ice. And yet it had never seemed more remote.

Minutes later, she'd begun to twitch as her breathing grew deeper. He'd lain awake for another hour or so, trying to understand what had happened. Whether this was the start of something new and they would finally be able to deal with all the things that had been left unsaid and build something together. Or whether it was simply a temporary ceasefire in their cold war.

One thing was clear, however. If Theodor didn't see the light and agree to turn himself in, there was nothing he could do about it. It didn't matter that he was right, or that he, too, risked being charged with crimes if it ever came out that he'd known about his son's involvement. Until he and Sonja agreed, all he could do was wait.

That troubled him; he could only hope she would eventually come to her senses.

His worry about that had, however, been replaced with a different one the moment Molander entered the conference room and sat down diagonally across from him. When they'd spoken on the phone the day before, he'd been almost certain his colleague didn't know anything. Since then, Gertrud had had plenty of time to fill him in.

During the meeting, he had tried to analyse every detail of his colleague's behaviour, but had, in the end, concluded that his only option was to visit Gertrud as soon as possible to try to suss out if she'd brought it up.

That aside, the morning meeting had been unusually efficient. None of them had had the time or peace of mind to enjoy the first get-together of the week or make small talk. Lilja had for some reason spent most of the time staring at her phone, and both Molander and Klippan had, with the help of Tuvesson's expert direction, been surprisingly succinct and focused, which was why they'd reached the last point on the agenda after just twenty-five minutes and were now waiting for Klippan to connect his laptop and show them clips from the ICA Maxi CCTV tapes.

Lilja had already told them about how her search for Assar Skanås's turned-off phone had led her to a building on Carl Krooks Gata, and that the only thing of interest she'd found there was a one-bed flat for rent. After a short discussion, they'd agreed not to divert resources to door-knocking in the area. But they would make sure to maintain around-the-clock readiness to act if the phone became active.

Molander had also, with the aid of the network provider, secured the call lists for the past week to and from the number in question. They'd shown that Skanås had called Björn Richter, the man with the dolls who lived in the same building as Moonif Ganem, several times. He had even tried to call him at 7.18 a.m. on the morning of the murder.

One theory was that Skanås had travelled to Bjuv to visit the man with the dolls, and when he was not in, he'd lingered in the stairwell until Moonif came down with his recycling. Either way, it was clear the two knew each other, which was why Tuvesson had immediately dispatched two uniformed officers to search Richter's flat.

Then Klippan had recounted the conversations he'd had with some of Molly Wessman's co-workers, who had all spoken of her competence and ability to execute both cutbacks and restructures. Some had, however, mentioned that she had not seemed like herself in the days before the murder. She had allegedly acted nervously and after calling off her presentation to the board halfway through had left the office in a hurry.

He had told the others about his meeting with Flätan, who had concluded that Wessman had been poisoned with ricin, probably at some point on Friday afternoon. He had shown pictures of her concealed tattoo and informed them that it suggested she had been in sexual contact with a certain Columbus, who, as rumour had it, could make anybody push beyond their own sexual limits.

It was undoubtedly their most promising lead, though Tuvesson had remained sceptical and asked him to keep looking into how much truth there really was to the rumours and whether this Columbus was even real.

'All right. Great, then we know. Thank you.' Tuvesson put her phone down and turned back to the others. 'I'm sad to say, people, Assar Skanås is not hiding at Björn Richter's house, playing with dolls.'

'Did they check his basement storage area?' Lilja said.

Tuvesson nodded and glanced at her watch. 'Klippan, how are you getting on with that?'

'I think I've got it working now.' Klippan picked up the remote and started the overhead projector, which made his desktop picture – his dog, Einstein, chasing a tennis ball – appear on the wall.

'Is this going to take long?' Molander downed the rest of his coffee and looked at his watch. 'Because my guys are actually sitting around right now, waiting to get started on Molly Wessman's flat.'

'It will take as long as it takes. So I would suggest not wasting any additional time.' Klippan started the 14.32 seconds long video, which had no sound, low resolution and a colour resolution that left a lot to be desired.

Even so, Fabian couldn't deny there was something fascinating about the images from the ICA Maxi CCTV cameras. There was something almost feng shui about the man's movements as, completely without warning, he pushed his way through the queueing crowd, placed one hand on the glass counter, swung himself over it as though it were the easiest thing in the world, snatched up the long, thin blade from the cutting board and stabbed the victim in the throat. All in one fluid motion that must have taken hours of practice to perfect.

The most remarkable aspect was the total lack of hesitation during the actual execution, even though there were at least ten witnesses within close range. That took not only nerves of steel but above all careful planning. At the same time, there was something spontaneous about the whole act. As though it were just a spur of the moment thing.

'Do you have any footage of him entering the shop?' he said, while furtively studying Molander, who seemed completely absorbed by the clip, even though it was the third viewing.

'Absolutely. But just so you know, it's over five minutes long, and not particularly eventful. But let's have a look at that, too.'

The way the perpetrator passed through the entrance, grabbed a basket and continued into the shop in his baggy hip-hop clothes, black gloves and hoodie with its hood pulled up over his head was confident and bold. As though he had a concrete goal in mind.

At the same time, there was nothing about his movements among the shelves that suggested he was there for anything other than food shopping. First a litre of Oatly oat milk and freshly squeezed juice from Brämhult in the dairy section. Then he walked over to the bread aisle and grabbed a bag of Fazer rye rolls before continuing towards the meat counter.

But instead of taking a number, he just glanced at the meat counter on his way to the vegetable section, where he put his basket down and squeezed some avocados before walking over to the mountain of vine tomatoes and selecting some with great care.

After tying his bag of tomatoes closed, he walked towards the potatoes. But halfway there, he changed his mind mid-step and turned back towards the meat counter, where he pushed the button for a ticket and waited his turn.

It was virtually impossible to get a good look at his face at any point during the clip. Whether that was because he knew where the cameras were and made sure to keep his back to them or through sheer happenstance was impossible to say.

Forty-three seconds later, he pushed through the crowd without warning, jumped over the counter and stabbed Lennart Andersson.

The blood fountained out of Andersson's throat for several seconds before he managed to pull the knife out himself, throw it away and clap one hand to the wound, his eyes baffled and terrified in equal measure. There was nothing to suggest they'd met before. Then the perpetrator picked up another knife from the cutting board and struck again and again while the victim, despite grievous injuries, managed to stay upright and fight back.

But when the perpetrator managed to get the knife in between his ribs on his fifth try, he collapsed out of shot. After that, the only thing they could see was the perpetrator snatching up a cleaver and raising it above his head.

'Maybe that's enough.' Klippan paused the video and turned to the rest of the team. 'I don't know about you, but I have two things I think merit discussion.'

'Good. Let's start with them,' Tuvesson said.

Klippan nodded and backed the video up slightly. 'This is the first.' He paused at the exact moment the perpetrator plunged the knife into Andersson's throat. 'Can anyone see what that is?'

'What, should we?' Tuvesson leaned forward to have a closer look at the frozen image, which looked more like one of those banned horror films from the infancy of VCR technology.

'Sure, I would go so far as to argue it's obvious enough you don't have to tear your hair out to see it,' Molander said as he put his reading glasses on and started flipping through his papers.

'Good,' Klippan said. 'Has anyone other than Ingvar been paying attention?'

'Klippan, come on,' Lilja said on a tired exhalation. 'Can we save the quizzes for the Christmas party and do our jobs instead?'

'Ingvar even gave you a clue. But all right.' Klippan took out and passed around one of the crime scene photographs, in which Lennart Andersson could be seen lying on his back in a pool of blood with a meat fork implanted next to his nasal bone. 'Now do you see?'

Fabian and the others nodded, instantly identifying the clue Klippan had referred to.

In the picture on the paused screen, the victim appeared to have thick hair covering his entire head. But in the post mortem picture, most of the hair, other than some on the sides, was missing.

'He wore a toupee?' Tuvesson said.

'Looks like,' Klippan replied.

'So you're saying the perpetrator took it with him.'

'It's a possibility.'

'You're thinking about Molly Wessman's cut-off fringe,' Fabian put in.

'Exactly. Maybe there's a connection.'

'What kind of connection would that be?' Tuvesson wanted to know. 'Apart from the hair, there are no similarities whatsoever.'

'I don't know.' Klippan shrugged. 'Maybe the victims knew each other? Maybe they were connected to the perpetrator in different ways. Or maybe they simply—'

'You'd do better to stop there,' Molander said, taking his glasses off just as the phone vibrated again in Lilja's hand. 'Because there's no connection. Not even with the hair.'

'What, you found the toupee?'

Molander nodded. 'Apparently, it had slid under the counter. Sorry, Klippan. Didn't mean to rain on your parade.'

'Don't worry about it. It was just a theory.'

You disgusting little Jew cunt. Let's see how cocky you are when we've fucked every hole you have bloody. When we've pissed on you and fisted you so hard with our knives there's not a drop of Jew blood left in you. Then we'll see how much your police badge can help you.

P.S. I hope you like your new lawn.

'Irene, what's the matter?' Tuvesson said. 'Are you okay?'

Lilja looked up from her phone. 'I'm just a bit tired.'

'Are you sure?'

'Absolutely. Let's keep going so we can wrap this up sometime today.'

'All right,' Klippan said and pressed play, which made the perpetrator resume stabbing his victim. 'As you may be aware, the witness statements are contradictory to say the least when it comes to the perpetrator's appearance. Some describe his nose as large and others as small. One mentions an underbite, another an overbite. The only description they all seem to agree on is "odd". Apparently, they all feel he looked odd. And I didn't understand what they meant until I saw this.' He paused the video and proceeded frame by frame.

For the first and only time, the perpetrator turned his face to the CCTV camera for a fraction of a second, and it was suddenly obvious what Klippan meant.

The man's appearance really was odd in a way that was hard to describe. He was dark, but that wasn't it. It was all the other things. Like his nose, which was a bit crooked and looked like he'd just lost a boxing match. Or his right cheek, which drooped lower than his left. Not to mention his eyes. His face was definitely *odd*. As though it didn't belong to the perpetrator.

'See this?' Klippan aimed his laser pointer at the perpetrator's arms, which were raised above his head, holding the cleaver, and stopped at a lighter section in the gap between the sleeve of his hoodie and his glove.

'Yes, it's his wrist,' Tuvesson said.

'Right. But can't you see the difference in skin tone? Can't you see how much lighter this is than his face?'

Tuvesson nodded. 'Are you saying that his face isn't his?'

'Exactly. It's just a mask. Or, I don't know about just. I don't think that's something he picked up in a gag shop. If you ask me, it was made by a professional mask maker.'

'Which means the whole thing was planned and not a sudden impulse.'

'Precisely.'

'Which suggests there might be some kind of connection between the victim and the perpetrator,' Molander put in.

'Such as?'

Molander shrugged. 'It could be anything. An unpaid gambling debt. Or why not an affair with the neighbour's wife that was discovered?'

An affair with the neighbour's wife. Fabian almost couldn't believe that's what Molander had said. Was it a Freudian slip or was he toying with him? Was this his way of showing he knew and was so many steps ahead he wasn't even concerned?

'But listen,' Lilja suddenly interjected, looking up from her phone. 'Don't you think this whole thing feels a bit... How do I put it, schizophrenic, somehow?'

'Schizophrenic?' Tuvesson reached for the coffee thermos and loosened the lid. 'What do you mean?' Only to discover it was empty.

'I'm not sure, but there's something here that's not right. Or at least it doesn't make sense to me. I mean, if you're planning to kill someone, surely you wouldn't choose to do it in front of CCTV cameras and a bunch of witnesses at ICA Maxi.

'Maybe it was just to confuse us and make it look spontaneous?' Molander suggested.

'But aren't there a hundred easier ways of doing that? Like a hit and run with a car. Or, if you prefer knives, it wouldn't take much of an effort to make it look like a botched robbery. If you want to make it really easy, you could always pretend to be some drugged-up junkie attacking whoever's in your way.'

'That's true,' Tuvesson said. 'But strange as it may seem, he did choose to commit the murder at ICA. It's our job to figure out why, whatever the underlying reason may be.'

'Have you considered that it might be the other way around?' Fabian said, and suddenly he had everyone's undivided attention. 'What if he wanted to be seen? What if the whole point was to have as many witnesses as possible?'

'Then why go to the trouble of wearing a mask?' Molander countered. 'Not to mention the cameras. He should have turned to them if that were the case.'

'CCTV cameras the police can use to zoom in and analyse is one thing. Witnesses at the scene is something else entirely. But I would say we're asking the wrong question. Instead of asking why he wore a mask, we should be asking ourselves why he wore a dark-skinned mask.'

As though everyone needed a moment to take in what Fabian had just said, silence fell and lasted until Lilja broke it.

'If I'm understanding you right, you're saying the underlying motive might be racism.'

'I know you've been on that track all along, and even though I don't think we should make too much of this, we should at least give it serious consideration.'

'The only problem is that Assar Skanås is a paedophile, not a racist,' Klippan said. 'Besides, he would never be able to pull off something this sophisticated.'

'Who said it had to be him? He might not even be the person who killed Moonif Ganem. All we know for sure is that he was in the laundry room that same morning.'

'Fabian, what are you trying to say?' Tuvesson said. 'Are you suggesting there's a connection between the murder of Moonif Ganem and the murder of Lennart Andersson?'

'Not necessarily. But if you look at them side by side, it's hard not to see links. First he kills a young boy in the most brutal and sensationalist way imaginable. It wasn't important who the boy was. The only thing that mattered was the colour of his skin. Then we had the fire, which killed three asylum seekers. And now he responds by donning a dark-skinned mask and killing Lennart Andersson, a white middle-aged heterosexual man, in front of a bunch of witnesses.'

53

How would a person react if they found out their life partner had murdered at least three innocent people, one of whom was their own father? Would they even be capable of taking it in, or would they dismiss it out of hand as a misunderstanding?

On his way to see Gertrud Molander, Fabian had pondered how to broach his subject without spooking her, and whether there was a way of finding out what she had told her husband without also spilling everything he knew.

But he had been forced to conclude that whatever he did, there was an imminent risk he would make the situation worse. Still, he had no choice but to try. If he did nothing, it would be only a matter of time before Molander finalized his plan for his demise. Seen from that perspective, he'd dawdled too long already.

He opened the gate and continued up a garden path made of slabs of slate, which despite their irregular shapes seemed to fit together so precisely that not one blade of grass had managed to push its way up into the sunlight. When he reached the door, he overcame his last shred of hesitance, rang the bell longer than necessary to make sure she heard and backed up a step so he wouldn't be in the way of the door, which in true Molander spirit was newly treated and smelled of oil.

The silence that followed was palpable, and he was struck by how no silence was like the silence in the gap between ringing a doorbell and the door opening. How long was he going to wait before ringing again? A minute? Two? Thirty seconds?

And how should he stand? It didn't matter which foot he put his weight on, he felt stiff and uncomfortable regardless. And his hands. What was he supposed to do with them? He tried letting them hang straight down, but that felt exposed and vulnerable. Shoving them in his pockets didn't work either. Not his front or back trouser pockets or his jacket pockets.

At length, he stepped forward and rang the bell again. This time, he kept his finger on the button for so long it left a round indentation in his fingertip when he stopped.

Had she seen it was him? Was that why she wasn't opening the door? Had she figured out why he was there and called her husband, who had promptly left Wessman's flat and was now on his way home?

Her car was definitely parked in the driveway and he could see lights on in some of the windows. There was, however, no sign of the bike she had used the day before. Maybe she was running an errand. It hadn't started raining yet. But it was in the air, like an omen, just waiting to start pouring down; she would have to hurry home if she didn't want to get soaked.

That was probably why he was feeling cold. Considering they were only days away from Midsummer's Eve, the weather was unusually chilly. Or maybe it was the same as every other year – overcast and four or five degrees warmer than Christmas. Even so, he could feel a droplet of sweat trickle from one of his vertebrae down his spine.

He, who was never usually nervous, was now trembling so violently he had no choice but to stick his hands in his pockets as the door slid open and Gertrud appeared, wearing an apron and curlers, staring as though she didn't recognize him at first.

'My goodness, Fabian, is that you? I had no idea who might be calling at this hour.'

'Hi, Gertrud.' He held out his hand, even though it was far from steady. 'Do you have a moment?'

'Yes, I suppose. What's this about? Nothing serious, I hope.'

'I'd prefer to discuss it inside. I think it might be starting to rain any second.'

'Of course, I'm sorry, do come on in.' She let him into the hallway and closed the door. 'Let's go into the living room. Oh, would you like some coffee?'

'No, thank you, I'm good.' He took his shoes off, only to discover he was still wearing the sock with the hole on the heel. 'This won't take long.' He continued into the living room, which was beige, past the breakfront that housed Gertrud's collection of crystal owls, which, if she was to be believed, had grown out of control because their friends insisted on sneaking a new one in every time they came to visit.

'Isn't he a sweetheart?' Gertrud put down a tray with a jug of water and two glasses.

'I'm sorry, who?'

'Reidar, who else? The man you were talking to yesterday.' She sat down on the edge of the sofa. 'Water?'

'No, thank you, I'm good,' he replied, for the simple reason that his hand was still shaking too hard to hold a glass without spilling. Instead, he took a seat in one of the armchairs, pondering whether she had brought up Reidar because she'd already figured out why he was there and wanted to help him along.

'I have to say I find it impressive that he's managed to move on and even find a new woman and everything. Not everyone does, even after an ordinary divorce. I honestly don't know how he gets out of bed in the morning.' She put her hand to her chest and shook her head. 'It's so awful to think about.'

Or was she in fact prepared for his visit and trying to gauge his suspicions?

'I don't know how I would get by if something happened to Ingvar. But at least you've reopened the investigation. That's a step forward.'

'It is, and that's actually what I wanted to talk to you about.'

'Oh? Did something happen? I mean, do you know who did it, or did you even arrest him already?'

'Gertrud, I'm afraid I can't—'

'And what does any of it have to do with me? Ingvar never mentioned anything. I just happen to live next door and—'

'Gertrud.' Fabian held up his hand to her; it was finally feeling reasonably steady. 'As I'm sure you understand, I can't discuss the exact state of the investigation.' Her anxiety had a calming effect on him. She was not play-acting, nor did she have an ulterior motive. 'What I can tell you is that due to various technical details, we've chosen to keep a very low profile and won't be making any statements to the public at all. For that reason, I wanted to ask you not to talk to anyone about the case or tell them it's been reopened.'

'Of course, I wouldn't dream of it. What kind of ninny do you take me for? I've been married to a police officer for nearly thirty years. How would it look if I went around blabbing to all and sundry about everything Ingvar tells me?'

'So, you and Ingvar, you do discuss things that are meant to be confidential?'

Gertrud sighed. 'Fabian. Don't tell me you never tell Sonja anything she shouldn't really know.'

'I'm sure that's happened. But for her sake, I try to keep it to a minimum. And since we're on the subject, have you mentioned this to Ingvar?'

'I'm not sure I follow. Have I mentioned what to him?'

'The investigation. That it's active again.'

Gertrud looked at him as though she felt a need to recalibrate her understanding of his visit, only now realizing she had to weigh her words carefully. At that moment, raindrops began to patter against the window. Then she suddenly lit up and let out a laugh. 'No. You know, I've barely seen him for days. Honestly, I have no idea when he came home last night. But it must have been in the wee hours, because I was out cold.'

'So you didn't see him at all yesterday?'

'No, I did, he came home for dinner as usual. But then there was an alert or something on his phone and he had to go.'

'What kind of alert?'

'No idea. You should ask him.'

'So you just didn't have time to tell him.'

'I suppose you could put it that way.'

She hadn't told him after all. 'That's good,' he said, nodding. 'And I would be very grateful if you would continue to keep it to yourself.'

'Why? You work on the same team, for Pete's sake. And now here you are, telling me I absolutely can't tell him.' She shook her head. 'I honestly don't understand what's going on.'

'Gertrud, I know this may seem strange.' He had to stay calm now and not speak too fast or too slow. The slightest hesitation and she would see right through him. 'The reason is that it's still such early days, it's not clear you can even call it an investigation yet. And before I have more to show, I would prefer to keep as much as possible to myself.'

'You're telling me Tuvesson and the team don't know?'

Fabian nodded. 'Given how full our hands are already, Tuvesson wouldn't be best pleased to find out I spent a whole hour with Reidar yesterday.' She still wasn't convinced. He could see it in her eyes and decided to gamble on his hand being steady enough to pick up the jug and pour himself a glass of water. 'And I don't know what Ingvar's like at home. But at work, he likes to talk, and I wouldn't be surprised if he accidentally let something slip during a coffee break.'

'Don't worry,' Gertrud said with a chuckle. 'I promise I won't spill the beans.'

'It's not about spilling beans, it's about—'

'Fabian. I understand exactly what this is about.' She looked at him with a gravity he didn't know how to interpret. 'If my silence can help you find out who did it, you have it.' She swallowed and closed her eyes. 'I'm never going to forget the day Ingvar came home and told me what had happened.' But she couldn't stop her mascara from running and eventually managed to pull out a tissue. 'That the long-haired coroner had managed to identify the body that had drifted ashore on Ven. You see, they weren't just our neighbours. We had dinner together and Inga and I went to yoga every week. I still don't understand how anyone can put another human being through what she had to go through.'

'When did he tell you?'

'It was a Monday afternoon almost five years ago. Five years. It still feels like yesterday. I was unpacking and doing laundry after a long weekend in Berlin, which Ingvar had arranged as a surprise, when he suddenly appeared in the door to the laundry room and asked me to come into the kitchen and have a seat. He had even poured a glass of—'

'Hold on a second,' Fabian broke in, putting down the glass of water he still hadn't drunk from. 'When were you in Berlin?'

'Thursday night to Sunday afternoon. Ingvar had arranged everything, for our anniversary. Hotel, plane tickets and even several dinner reservations. So unlike him, now I think about it.'

'So you're telling me you and Ingvar were in Berlin when the murder took place?'

'Yes, what about it?'

'Nothing. I just didn't know that.' He tried to squeeze out a smile, even though he could see his whole investigation falling apart before his eyes. 'I was still in Stockholm at the time.' If Molander had an alibi for the murder of Inga Dahlberg, everything else fell like dominoes. No matter how hard he and Elvin had fought to line them all up, one after the other. If Molander wasn't the killer, there was no motive. It just couldn't be true that he'd been in Berlin. 'I'm sorry if I'm being slow, but are you one hundred per cent sure that was the weekend you went to Berlin?'

'Like I just said, I remember it like it was yesterday.'

'And you were together the whole time, you and Ingvar. You never split up and—'

'Fabian, what are you getting at?'

'Nothing. I'm just—'

'Just what? What is this? I don't know where you would have got such an idea, but it actually sounds like you're suspecting my Ingvar.'

'No, no, no, absolutely not. God, no,' he tried to reassure her. 'I'm just puzzled because it doesn't match the information I have.'

'What information?' She stood up and pointed straight at him. 'Ingvar and I were in Berlin, whether you want to believe it or not.'

'Great, understood. I just wanted to make sure.'

'I can even show you a picture.' She walked past him to the bookshelf and picked up one of the framed photographs on it.

'Gertrud, there's really no need. I believe you.'

She put the photograph in his lap. 'You can see for yourself.'

'Gertrud, I'm sorry. I didn't mean to make it sound like I didn't believe you.' He looked at the picture, which showed Gertrud and Molander drinking coffee with a half-eaten apfelstrudel sitting between them. 'I was just surprised you were in Berlin that particular weekend. That's all.'

'I don't know if you've been there, but that picture was taken at Café Einstein Stammhaus, one of the few classic cafés in Berlin that survived the war.'

'I have been there, actually,' he said, studying the picture that gave Molander exactly the alibi he needed.

'I clearly remember Ingvar telling me about Goebbels giving his mistress the building as a gift before it was turned into a casino. It felt very historic. And, here, look.' She turned the frame over, undid the back, took the picture out and put her index finger on the date stamp *24 AUG 2007* from the camera at the bottom of the picture. 'I'm sure you know this better than I do. But I do think that was the very day Inga Dahlberg was murdered.'

Fabian nodded. She was right. It was that very day. He should feel happy and relieved. Maybe it wasn't his colleague after all. But the only thing he felt was disappointment. Until now, he'd been convinced both he and Hugo Elvin had been on the right track. One puzzle piece after the other had fallen into place, and a motive as terrifying as it was plausible had slowly crystallized. But now the rug had been pulled out from under the whole case and he was left with nothing.

'And unless I'm misremembering, there are more pictures,' Gertrud continued. 'I actually think we have a whole album. Just don't ask me where.'

'Don't trouble yourself.'

His phone started vibrating in his pocket, but this definitely wasn't the time to pick up.

'Is that your phone ringing?'

Fabian nodded and had pulled it out to decline the call when he saw that it was Molander. 'Hi, I thought you were busy with Wessman and not to be disturbed under any circumstances,' he said, while scanning the photograph for anything irregular.

'*That's absolutely right,*' Molander replied. '*But for me to call and bother you is a different kettle of fish altogether.*'

It might be anything. An outline that looked photoshopped, missing shadows or lighting that didn't match the rest of the scene.

'Have you found anything?'

'*And then some. I would suggest you drop whatever it is you're doing and get yourself over here on the double.*'

Anything that could burst this damn alibi so the stinking truth could seep out once and for all.

54

Fabian parked behind Molander's white van and killed the engine. The radio, on which Tuvesson was being chewed out because the hunt for murder suspect and paedophile Assar Skanås was now on its fifth day, fell silent as the wipers stopped halfway across the windscreen, making the rain, which had turned torrential, form little pools that merged and grew bigger until surface tension was overwhelmed by gravity.

Molander had sounded excited and happy on the phone. Not a hint of suspicion had shone through. Perhaps he was just being his usual self, proud and impatient like no one else to show off the findings he had supposedly made.

Even so, he was far from ready to trust that impression. For Molander to have called when he was actually at his house, discussing him with Gertrud, could, of course, have been a coincidence. But it could equally well have been because his colleague had been listening to their conversation via some hidden microphone and decided to cut their meeting short before it could go too far.

If so, the question was what Molander's plan was. It seemed unlikely that he would choose to liquidate him in Molly Wessman's flat, though he couldn't disregard the possibility. One person had already died there recently, and besides, Molander himself was in charge of the investigation. What made it unlikely was his two assistants; so long as they were present, he should be safe.

Even so, he took out his gun, pushed in a loaded magazine and placed it in his shoulder holster, under his jacket. Then, as an extra precaution, he sent Tuvesson a text saying Molander claimed to have found something interesting at Wessman's and that he was on his way over to check it out.

He left his car with the key in the ignition and hurried towards the front door. A distance that, despite being barely more than fifteen feet, was long enough for him to get soaked. A doorstop was propping the front door open and outside the lift, next to a tool bag, stood a number of buckets adorned with red warning triangles, so he took the stairs.

Outside Wessman's flat, he waited to give the water a chance to drip off before running his hands through his hair, turning on the recording function on his phone and entering.

He had considered not going, naturally, but had concluded that would only serve to raise a lot of questions, if Molander really had found something.

Bringing Klippan and someone else from the team had also crossed his mind. That would likely stop Molander from executing his plan, if in fact he had one. But only temporarily. If the man had decided to take his life, making sure they were never alone was not a sustainable solution, and nor was running away.

No, that left him with just one option – direct confrontation. And that might as well happen now as some other time. Paradoxically, it might be to his advantage, since he hadn't been able to come up with any binding proof yet. A failed murder attempt would be more than enough to arrest him and launch an official investigation.

So his best option was to get ready and not hesitate to take charge the moment something out of the ordinary happened. Whatever *out of the ordinary* might mean when it came to Molander.

'Hi there, come in, come in!' Molander pulled off the hood of his protective suit as he walked towards him through the hallway. 'Emil and Janos just popped out for lunch, so we have the whole place to ourselves.'

Fabian nodded and stepped on to the protective transparent plastic covering the hallway floor. Of course it was just the two of them. 'You wouldn't happen to have a hazmat suit for me, too, would you?'

'Nah, as long as you stay clear of the bedroom, you'll be fine. That's where we're still working. But we're all done in here, so feel free to walk around.'

Silence fell. Fabian took the opportunity to take a step back. Arm's length felt like a minimum requirement. 'What have you found?'

Molander lit up. 'Come over here. I'll show you.' He backed into the hallway and beckoned him over with a wave.

Why couldn't he just tell him? If it wasn't so typically Molander to drag these situations out, he would have refused to go any further. As it was, he had no choice but to obey.

'You asked me to keep my eyes extra peeled, remember?'

Fabian nodded, though he had no earthly idea what Molander was talking about.

'Don't look so surprised. Don't you remember? When you called me up and went on and on about that key deposit.' Molander pointed towards the front door. 'To be honest, I didn't understand why you insisted on yammering about it and about potential handymen who might have had access to her home keys. But it just goes to show.' Molander took a step towards him. 'We're not always supposed to understand things right away. Or like someone once said: *When you choose to be puzzled, life works out in mysterious ways.*'

'Ingvar,' Fabian said and backed up another step. 'Why am I here?'

'Well, well, aren't we cranky today.' Molander shot him a smile over the top of his glasses, which looked like they might slip off the tip of his nose at any moment. 'You see, it's unusual for me to be in this position. Only the second time ever, to be precise.' He held up two fingers. 'Which makes the whole thing especially sensitive.'

Fabian thought he understood his meaning all too well. A couple of months ago, Hugo Elvin discovered Molander's secrets. And now it was his turn to confront Molander. The problem was that he found himself unable to pull out his gun and take charge. After all, Molander hadn't said or done anything so far that warranted an arrest.

'But, luckily, it's just the two of us here, which actually makes this easier for a proud man like myself,' Molander continued. 'Because the truth is that if you hadn't insisted on me paying extra close attention to that particular object, I would very likely have missed it.'

Fabian was thrown back into confusion, fumbling around for something to hold on to. Maybe that was exactly what he was trying to do. Confuse him and make him lose focus.

'See that wire up by the ceiling?' Molander gestured towards a point behind him on the right.

It was the last thing he wanted to do, but he had no choice but to turn his back on Molander. And there was, indeed, a wire, a completely ordinary white electrical cord running along the right side of the hallway where the wall met the ceiling, before disappearing through a hole.

'That happens to be a high-speed cable for her broadband. A so-called fibre-optic cable.'

'Okay. Sure,' he said, in an attempt to sound interested, as he turned back to Molander.

'Nothing strange about that. In a few years, everyone will be on a fibre-optic network. But when I noticed where that cable was running, I felt I had to have a closer look. It's been installed the usual way, by running cable up from the basement, where the hub is, through the lift shaft and from there out to each floor. And to keep installation costs low, the modem and router are usually placed somewhere in the hallway, in a cupboard or some such. But as you see, in this case, they've instead run it in through the flat, all the way to the bedroom. They did a good job, too, so we know it wasn't cheap.'

'Maybe she wanted the router in the bedroom and was happy to pay extra for it.' Fabian shrugged. Where was he going with this? What on earth was all this about?

'Maybe. I've certainly always had terrible reception in my bedroom. At least according to Gertrud, who insists on playing Wordfeud in bed half the night.' He shook his head. 'But that doesn't explain why the cable runs through the wall.' He pointed up at the ceiling to where the cable disappeared through a hole.

'What's on the other side?'

'Precisely, what is on the other side? Finally, we're getting somewhere.' Molander tapped his temple. 'Come with me and see for yourself.' He backed further into the hallway, past a door that he pushed open with one hand. 'What are you waiting for? Here, I thought you were really curious.' Molander beckoned him into the room like he was luring a child with sweets.

Fabian unobtrusively put his hand to his chest to make sure his gun was where it should be before walking up to Molander and looking into the bathroom, which had spotlights in the ceiling, hand-painted tiles at chest level and a toilet, bidet and washbasin lined up along the wall on the right. On the other side was a washer and dryer with a few white plastic buckets on top, and straight ahead, a spacious whirlpool bath. In other words, a lovely upmarket bathroom where nothing seemed out of the ordinary.

Here, too, the floor was covered in plastic, a habit of Molander's when they were done with a room but not the rest of the property. The point of the plastic was that you could go in without contaminating anything. Fabian wanted nothing more than to get out of there. But to see the cable Molander was talking about, he had to step inside completely and turn around.

The light from the spotlights in the ceiling blinded him and forced him to shield his eyes with one hand. It was warm, too, several degrees warmer than the rest of the flat. Especially down by the floor. Was the underfloor heating turned up to the max? If so, why? He was utterly confused and felt his tongue stick to the roof of his mouth while sweat soaked his already damp clothes.

What he really needed was to sit down and drink a big glass of cold water. But he couldn't afford to let his guard down. Never mind that the heat was making him nauseous. What he had to do was stay focused, keep trying to understand what Molander had planned for him and wait for the right moment.

And he did understand, as soon as he saw the cable. The way it came out of the wall as expected and continued along the ceiling through a small box before disappearing out through another hole further in. Suddenly, everything made sense. All the talk about his call on Sunday and his own incoherent thoughts about a handyman with an extra set of keys, the cable and the protective plastic on the floor, the turned-up heat and those buckets he now noticed had the same warning triangles as the ones in the stairwell.

'Now do you see?' Molander said behind him.

And he did see. He saw that his colleague had used that bloody cable to lure him into the bathroom so he could push him into the bath.

Hydrofluoric acid. Wasn't that so highly corrosive you couldn't store it in glass jars, only in plastic buckets? So corrosive it could dissolve a human body into a bloody, viscous slime so you only had to remember to pick out the bones before flushing the rest down the toilet?

He stuck his hand inside his jacket and closed his fingers around the butt of his gun. He didn't know if he had enough evidence. But it didn't matter. He couldn't wait any longer. If he didn't act now, Molander would be coming at him with some kind of syringe or chemically soaked piece of cloth.

'Isn't it odd?' Molander stepped into the bathroom with him.

'I think that's putting it mildly,' Fabian said as he started to pull his gun from its holster.

'Right?' Molander turned around and pointed at the ceiling. 'I mean, why run a cable like that? My first thought was that it was completely pointless. Just drilling through that wall, which is load-bearing, by the way, requires a rotary hammer, and then out again through the same wall over there.' Molander shook his head. 'Completely incomprehensible. If not for that little box in the middle. Because that's where the explanation is found.' He suddenly turned to Fabian. 'Are you feeling all right?'

'Pardon?'

'Well, your face has gone completely white and you look like you're about to pass out.'

'No, I'm okay, just a bit overheated.' He let go of the gun.

'I know, it's a sauna in here. It's Janos who keeps turning the underfloor heating up to see how warm it can get. Apparently, he's planning to renovate his bathroom at home. But never mind that. Either way, I took the liberty of having a closer look at that box, and as soon as I opened it up, I knew what it was.'

Fabian nodded and wiped the sweat off his forehead with his jacket sleeve.

'So, if you haven't figured it out yet, this is the time to ask.'

'I'm sorry, but I don't know if I understand what—'

'God, you're really not yourself today.' Molander shook his head. 'It was the same thing in the morning meeting. I don't know where you'd gone. But you certainly weren't present.'

'You'll have to excuse me, but I have a lot of things on my mind right now and I would appreciate it if we could get back to what we're here for. Which is to say—'

'You mean the eye,' Molander broke in.

'Um, what?'

'You heard me. In that box, there's a tiny web camera, the smallest one on the market, and it's looking straight down at whoever might be having a nice, cosy soak in the bath. Delightful, no?'

'Okay, hold on. What, a webcam? Are you seriously telling me there's a—'

'Yep. And if that's not bad enough, there's another one exactly like it in the bedroom.'

55

KIM SLEIZNER PARKED HIS car in a disabled parking bay outside Restaurant Thai Pan on Thorupsgade, placed the permit he had wheedled out of his doctor when he had his hip operation on the dashboard and continued on foot along Korsgade. After about fifty yards, he took a right on to Blågårdsgade and immediately felt his gorge rising, bubbling like boiling bile.

There were few places he disliked as much as Blågårdsgade. Granted, there was something picturesque about all the outdoor serving areas full of young people who didn't know better than to waste their lives drinking yet another overpriced macchiato made with organic beans some fucking Indian cat had shat out. Sure, he'd been young once and could, if he really put his mind to it, dig up one or two positive memories from all the wet nights out he'd spent in this neighbourhood.

But he had a very strong desire to tear the whole place down. Level it like a ground zero and build something new. A parking garage or whatever; it didn't matter so long as no trace remained of the old. His hatred, because it really was hatred, did not spring from all the shootings that took place around here or the fact that one of the city's criminal gangs had made the neighbourhood its base.

No, it was all Dunja The Cunt Hougaard's fault. She'd ruined his sleep and drawn dark circles under his eyes that no concealer in the world could hide, and the closer he got to her flat on Blågårdsgade 4, the darker his mood became.

After the events in Helsingør the month before, when he managed to prevent her from getting the credit for solving a case about homeless killings, he had decided he wasn't going to have anything more to do with her. He had successfully stymied her career progression, and now he would keep as far away as he could, observe her from a safe distance and watch as she shrivelled up and eventually died in a pool of her own failure.

But her deafening silence had given him no peace. No matter how dearly he wanted to, he could no longer sit on his hands, content not to rock the boat, while attempting to convince himself that all was well.

Vanishing without an electronic trace was considerably harder than people might think. Getting an anonymous pay-as-you-go SIM card for your phone and closing your accounts on social media was one thing. Cutting up your credit cards and not touching the money in any of your accounts was something else.

At best, he had nothing to worry about. A month was, after all, not a very long time. Perhaps she was just curled up in the foetal position at home, trying to comprehend how he'd managed to best her yet again.

It did still say *Carsten Røhmer & Dunja Hougaard* on the entry phone. But there was no need to call up and give her advance warning. He had been sure to make a copy of her house keys as soon as she started in his department in 2009.

He had done that with all of his employees, but, with very few exceptions, Hougaard's had been the only keys he'd ended up using.

This time, the door to the building wasn't properly closed, so he could walk right in and climb the stairs to her front door, where his key slid into the lock as if into a willing virgin. Two silent seconds later, he was standing in her hallway, breathing in the air.

It smelled of clothes that hadn't dried completely and of frying grease. This was exactly what he'd pictured and how he'd hoped she lived. In misery.

But it didn't look like he remembered. Or did it? Hadn't she had a number of framed Louisiana posters in the hallway? Now it was hung with pictures of the Great Wall of China, elephants and various temples at sunset. It was unbearably tacky; a red Chinese lamp with tassels and things hung over the kitchen table, which was covered in a red elephant-print oilcloth.

'What the fuck are you doing in here?'

The words came from a short, slightly pudgy Chinese man with a squeaky voice and wild hair.

'Good day, my name is Kim Sleizner.' He walked up to greet him, even though he could still hear the toilet flushing in the bathroom and was well aware that hygiene was not a priority for Chinese people.

'I don't care what your name is, Kim Sleizner or Kim fucking Sleizner.' The Chinese man waved his index finger in the air. 'I want to know what the hell you're doing in my flat.'

'I'm sorry, I'm an old friend of Dunja's.' Sleizner tried hard not to laugh. 'I was just in the neighbourhood.'

'Hm, interesting.' The Chinese man stroked his little goatee and nodded in an over-the-top display of thoughtfulness. 'Then maybe Kim fucking Sleizner can tell me how it is that you "happen" to wander straight into my flat?' He crossed his arms and fixed Sleizner, who gave him one of his patented smiles in return.

'I apologize, it wasn't my intention to intrude. The thing is that my very good friend Dunja Hougaard used to live here, at least until about a month ago. And since she's trusted me with her keys—' He waved the keys around. '—and no one opened when I rang the door, I just wanted to make sure everything was—'

'Rang the door. How odd. I certainly didn't hear it ring.'

'Maybe I accidentally hit the light button.' Sleizner shrugged and could feel his patience hanging by a fragile thread. 'But let's get to my reason for stopping by. You wouldn't happen to know where Dunja is, would you?'

'And why would I know that, when I don't even know who she is? That's like asking an elephant if it can fly to the moon.'

'But you do have her name on your door, so you must know something.'

'I do not have her name on my door. Why would I? The fact is that there's no name at all on my door right now, and that's none other than Kim Sleizner's fault.' The man, who was at least two heads shorter than Sleizner, was now standing very close to him, jabbing his index finger into his chest. 'Because if you hadn't come bumbling in here, babbling nonsense, it would have been up by now.' He walked over to the hallway table, pulled a brass sign from a small plastic bag and held it up in front of Sleizner.

Qiang Who, it read, and Sleizner could only nod. 'All right, but on the entry phone downstairs, it does say Dunja Hougaard, that much I know.'

'And how is that my fault? I've been on to the landlord about it more times than there's letters in the word elephant.'

'Okay, okay, okay,' said Sleizner, who'd had enough of the bickering. 'So you don't know anything about Dunja Hougaard?'

'Only that she seems to have a habit of handing my keys out to any passing stranger.' The man ripped the keys out of Sleizner's hand.

'Well, that's that, then.' Sleizner was about to take a step back. But he couldn't bring himself to back down from a short fucking elephant Chinese guy. He just couldn't. 'Then the keys have found their way home at least. That's good to know.'

'That's one way of putting it,' said the Chinese man, who insisted on standing so close to Sleizner he could smell his foetid breath, despite the height difference. 'I prefer "Bye, not at all nice to meet you. See you never."'

This idiot was worse than a goddamn mutt whose brain was too small to work out that instead of barking, it should run away as fast as it could.

There was very likely no one else in the flat, and he would have no problem surprising and incapacitating the pudgy little Chink with a forceful kick to the shins. But he wasn't quite there yet, though he was already looking forward to accidentally using slightly too much force when he locked the Chinaman's arms behind his back and hearing the crunch of a shoulder dislocating.

'Absolutely, no need to worry. Of course I'm leaving,' he said, surprised at his own patience. 'But before I do, I just want to ask you something. We can think of it as you returning the favour since I brought you your keys. Would it be all right if I looked around? Just for a bit, five, six minutes, no more.'

The man looked up at Sleizner, picked his nose, rolled his findings into a small ball between his thumb and forefinger and flicked it away. 'You're slower than a retarded elephant. What part of "goodbye" don't you understand?'

'I understand perfectly,' Sleizner said, and caught himself already planning how to clean up the blood spatter on the walls and get the body out of the flat. 'But the thing is, she borrowed a CD and some other things off me and she might have left them here.'

'A compact disc of what?'

'Pardon?'

'You said she'd borrowed a CD. What CD?'

'Well, um...' Why had he said that? He didn't even like music. 'Huey Lewis and the News. Some best-of collection. But it was signed, from the last time I saw them live, so it had a lot of sentimental value.'

Surprisingly, the man seemed to ponder that. Instead of just spitting out a no, he stood there scratching his pathetic goatee.

'Wow,' he said at length and nodded. 'Huey Lewis and the News, that's one of my absolute favourite bands.' He held out his hand and smiled. 'And you've seen them live. That's more than I can say.'

Sleizner reluctantly took the bogey hand in his and hoped the handshake wouldn't be followed by a hundred idiotic questions he couldn't answer. 'Sadly, I haven't seen any of their albums around. Except my own, of course. But I did find a shoebox on the top shelf of the wardrobe. Something in that might be yours. Wait here, I'll go get it.'

The man disappeared into the flat. Sleizner seized the opportunity to poke his head into the living room and concluded that the bloke was obsessed with elephants. Everything, from the curtains and the rug to the cushions on the sofa, was covered with elephants of various colours. The same thing with the souvenirs in the bookcase and the figurines next to the TV. Elephants, elephants and more elephants. Even the legs of the coffee table were in the shape of elephant feet.

'Here.' The man handed him a shoebox.

So the little slut had left something behind after all. He didn't know what to expect. But with luck, it might be something of interest. An address, a phone number, a receipt from Netto or discount stamps from Joe & the Juice. It didn't matter what, so long as it was an embryo of something that could point him in the right direction.

At the top were a number of unused postcards that were really advertisements in disguise. A wristwatch had stopped at seven minutes to eleven on the twenty-first. There were also some pens, a chewed-up eraser and a box of Ga-Jol that rattled when he shook it. At the bottom, he found a notepad with about half its pages torn out; when he held it up to the light, he finally reaped the rewards of his labour.

Just as he'd hoped, she had scribbled something down and then ripped the page out, thinking she was leaving no trace behind. That stupid fuckwit had pushed down so hard on her pen he could read the grooves in the paper without difficulty. It was a ten-digit number. Probably a personal identity number or a mobile phone number. It didn't matter which. Regardless, it would move him forward.

'Thank you very much. You've been extremely helpful.' Sleizner tore out the page and was just about to hand the shoebox back when he discovered even more notes on the next page. And these were fully visible in ink.

You can try if you want
But this is neither a personal identity number nor a mobile phone number
Just a random string of numbers
So for your own sake, stop looking
Because you're never going to find me
But I'm going to find you
When you least expect it
Where it hurts the most

56

FABIAN CLIMBED OUT OF his car, noted that the rain had stopped and locked the doors with a feeling of being precariously balanced on the edge of a cliff with his eyes blindfolded. He was alive but he didn't know whether to feel relieved or disappointed that Molander hadn't shown his true colours. Everything was in flux again.

Even the murder of Inga Dahlberg had turned into a giant question mark in the form of an alibi from Berlin, and until he could break that, he had no choice but to try to go about his business as usual, just like Molander.

The hidden webcams were without doubt a very significant lead in the investigation. His first thought had been that Wessman must have chosen to instal them in her bathroom and bedroom herself. An exhibitionist streak would hardly be surprising, given her tattoo and membership of Spades. According to Molander, considerable time and money had been spent on concealing the cameras, but that could have been to avoid disturbing potential visitors.

But since Molander had been unable to locate the server the cameras sent their information to, and hadn't managed to turn them off, short of cutting the wires, they had agreed that Wessman was most likely unaware she was being watched.

It was also clear that the cameras had been installed together with the building's high-speed internet cables. A job that, according to the chairman of the housing cooperative, had been completed over the course of a week in the autumn of 2009 by Fiberbolaget AB.

He had called the company, trying to reach the owner, Eric Jacobsén, but according to the woman at the switchboard, he was out conducting an inspection and wasn't expected back until sometime that afternoon. She had declined to give them a mobile phone number. She had, however, offered to pass on a message and ask him to call them back.

Eric Jacobsén was a common name, but only one of them had an income that allowed him to live on Slottsvägen in Laröd, just north of Helsingborg. It was on the right side of Larödvägen, in the old part of town, by the water. Judging from the cars parked in the driveways in front of the houses, Jacobsén wasn't the only one in the neighbourhood doing well for himself, though it did appear he was slightly ahead of the pack.

There were no fewer than four cars parked in the driveway of number ten. Next to the black van with the Fiberbolaget logo was a large, dark blue Lexus, a shiny red Lamborghini and a well-maintained, pale yellow Volkswagen Beetle.

On the front door was a classic old knocker in the shape of a brass fist, but before Fabian could grab it, the door was thrown open by a broad-shouldered man in a suit and white shirt exiting with a briefcase in his hand.

'Excuse me, you wouldn't happen to be Eric Jacobsén, by any chance?'

'I am.' The man stopped and gave Fabian a puzzled look. 'What's this about?'

'My name is Fabian Risk, from the Helsingborg Police.' He held up his ID. 'Do you have a minute?'

'Not really.' The man ran a hand through his blond hair. 'I'm actually running late for a meeting with a client. Apparently, I'm an incurable time optimist. Can it wait until tomorrow or, even better, the end of the week?'

'I'm afraid not. But hopefully it won't take long. Am I right in thinking you were the ones who installed the high-speed broadband on Stuvaregatan down in the North Harbour last autumn?'

'Probably. We're hooking up most of north-western Skåne at the moment. But hey, let me make a suggestion. How about you come with me in the car, and we can talk on the way? And in case I don't have time to drive you back here, which I likely won't, the taxi's on me. Win, win, I reckon. What do you say?'

'All right.' Fabian climbed into the passenger seat of the van and didn't even have time to buckle his seat belt before Jacobsén started reversing out of the driveway.

'First stop, Husensjö, which should give us about fifteen minutes.' He shifted into first and roared off down the street. 'Where were we?'

'Stuvaregatan.'

'Right.' Without easing off the accelerator, he connected his phone to a hands-free and dialled a number. After just one ring, a woman answered.

'*Hi Eric. What can I—*'

'Stuvaregatan down in the North Harbour,' Jacobsén broke in. 'Would you mind checking if that's something we'd have on our conscience?'

'Of course. As soon as I finish the PowerPoint for the board—'

'No, Lina, right now, please.'

Someone outside called out, 'Hey! Eric! Wait!', which made Jacobsén slam on the brakes so hard the tyres screeched. He rolled down his window.

'Hello there,' he said to the man hurrying up to the van, dressed in gym clothes and a baseball cap. 'Everything okay?'

'Absolutely. No complaints. I just wanted to check with you if Wilhelm could go home with Rutger after football practice on Wednesday. I have to pop over to Brussels and won't be back until Thursday afternoon, and Emilie has Pilates, or whatever it was she said.'

'No problem. I'll take him, too. Emilie can come and pick him up after dinner, or maybe she wants to come over and eat with us. Either way is fine by me, so long as you're back for the pool party on Saturday.'

'Of course. I wouldn't miss the event of the year.' The man turned to Fabian and stuck his hand in to introduce himself. 'Hi. Axel Stjärnström, Eric's neighbour.'

'Just mind what you say to him.' Jacobsén raised a warning finger. 'He's a police officer. Hey, by the way, this isn't an interrogation, is it?'

'That depends.' Fabian smiled as he shook Axel Stjärnström's hand. 'Hi, Fabian Risk.'

'Blimey, I'd better watch myself,' Jacobsén said.

'It's fine, I'll vouch for him and be his character witness if necessary,' his neighbour chuckled. 'To be honest, I can't imagine a better neighbour than Eric, that's for sure. Without him, this street wouldn't have been what it is today. And hey, speaking of which—'

'*Hello, I'm back*,' the assistant said over the speakers.

'And did you find anything?' Jacobsén let the clutch out and the car started moving at a crawl. 'Axel, we'll talk more when you're back from Brussels.'

His neighbour gave him a thumbs up as Jacobsén rolled up his window and sped away.

'*Yes, we were there.*'

'When?'

'*Two and a half years ago, in October of 2009.*'

'Well, what do you know. That's more than I remember.' Jacobsén turned to Fabian. 'Happy with that answer?'

Fabian nodded, even though it took him a while to remember what he'd actually asked, what with all the neighbours and assistants.

'Thank you, Lina. As always, a rock. And, right, if you could make me an avocado sandwich and a soft-boiled egg before my meeting this afternoon, I would be eternally grateful.'

'*Just don't promise too much.*'

'Kisses.' Jacobsén ended the call while turning south on road 111 and flooring it. 'Just so you know, I'm counting on not getting fined while you're in the car.' He chuckled and pulled out into the overtaking lane.

Fabian left his comment unanswered. He knew Jacobsén's type all too well. Successful and brash. No obstacle was so great it couldn't be overcome by a smile, a firm handshake and a gung-ho spirit. If it works, it works.

'I don't want to leave clients waiting too long and risk them taking their business elsewhere. You know, right now, the fibre-optic market is so overheated, there's a line of companies waiting to take our place.' He was tapping his fingers on the steering wheel. 'That's why we have to make sure we're always the best, the cheapest and the fastest.'

A lorry was pulling into the passing lane ahead of them, but gave up when Jacobsén accelerated and flashed his high beams.

'You know, I started the company in 2001. Everyone thought I'd lost my mind. How could I quit my job at Sydsec Security? But I was so damn fed up with having an incompetent manager making all the important decisions. I swear, a dart-throwing monkey could've done a better job. It was seven years before it took off, but then it really did take off. Suddenly, one computer in each home wasn't enough, everyone needed their own, and since then we've gone from strength to strength. Completely insane.'

'Who does the actual installations?' Fabian asked, noting that their speed was already way above the permitted limit.

'At first, it was just me, like I said. Now we have fifteen guys out running cable seven to four, five days a week, sometimes seven, and by the end of the year I reckon there'll be twenty of them. It's amazing, obviously, though these days my job consists mainly of standing around being the face of the company, wearing a suit and a beaming smile. But enough about me. What is this all about? Really. I mean, what do you want from me?'

'We're in the middle of a murder investigation, and I'm hoping you might be able to help solve some of the mysteries.'

'Is it that murder at ICA Maxi in Hyllinge? Lennart, or whatever his name was. I was actually there with my son, the day before it happened.'

'No, this is a different case. The victim's name was Molly Wessman and she lived on Stuvaregatan. Does that ring any bells?'

'No, can't say that it does.' Jacobsén pulled back into the inside lane to let another car pass. 'So I'm not sure how I can be of service.'

'I need to find out who installed the broadband in her flat.'

'Then you don't want to talk to me, you want Lina, who was just on the blower.' He took out his phone again and dialled the number while he pulled back into the overtaking lane to make room for a car merging from the slip road.

'*Hi Eric, what can I—*'

'Sorry, I know you have a thousand things on your plate. But you know that job on Stuvaregatan?'

'*Yes?*'

'Would you be able to find out which of the guys did that?'

'*Absolutely. Lucky I still have the file out.*'

'Right.' He shot Fabian a wink.

'*Stuvaregatan, was it? What number?*'

'Seven.'

'*All right, looks like there were two of them. Jocke Olsson, and then that—*'

'It's a specific flat, and what I'm wondering is whether our records from two and a half years ago are that detailed.'

'*I can assure you they have been for as long as I've been around.*'

'Didn't I tell you she's a rock?' Jacobsén turned to Fabian. 'With Lina on your team, you'd solve every case, I promise you.'

Fabian nodded, busy trying to figure out if he'd actually mentioned anything about it being number seven.

'*Which flat is it?*' Lina asked.

'A certain Molly Wessman.'

'*That's what I thought. It was that bloke whose name I can never remember. Christofer Comorowski.*'

'Great, then we know. Thanks for that. And, right, don't forget about the avocado sandwich.' He ended the call and indicated right to turn off the motorway.

'This Christofer. Is he one of your employees?'

'No, he's just a guy we call in when we get too busy.' Jacobsén turned down Filbornavägen and continued to Sockengatan, where he made a left. 'Can I ask what he's suspected of? Not murder, I hope.'

'No one said he's under any kind of suspicion. I just need to get in touch with him. Do you have his information – phone number, personal identity number and address – or should I be talking to Lina?'

'Normally, she'd be the one to talk to, but unfortunately not in this case. When it comes to Christofer, we only know that he's from Poland or Ukraine. To be honest, I'm not entirely sure Christofer's his real name.'

'No? How come?'

Jacobsén turned on his hazard lights, slowed down and stopped at a bus stop, staring blindly into space. 'You know, the moment you mentioned Stuvaregatan, I had a hunch we'd end up here. The truth is, I paid him under the table. I know, it's wrong, but I had no choice.'

'Don't worry,' Fabian said as disappointment washed over him. 'I'm not after tax dodgers. The only thing I'm interested in is getting hold of—'

'I just want to be clear that it wasn't about dodging taxes. I contribute plenty, that's for sure. I've also offered him permanent employment several times, but apparently job security isn't something this man craves.'

'Eric, just tell me how to get in touch with him. You can discuss the other aspects with your accountant.'

Jacobsén heaved a sigh and turned to Fabian.

'The problem is, he's the one who gets in touch with me.'

Fabian thought about whether he had any other questions to ask, but decided all that was left to do was to unbuckle his seat belt, climb out of the car and hope it wouldn't take too long to get a taxi.

57

Fabian put the frozen block of mince in the pan; it began to sizzle and sputter in the hot olive oil. He'd assumed Sonja would already have started dinner when he got home. Instead, he'd found a kitchen in which bread crusts, open jars of marmalade and sweaty cheeses jostled for space with dirty plates, half-melted butter and glasses filled with juice residue, eggshells and old teabags.

He'd found Sonja asleep in their bedroom, as though she hadn't been up since he'd left her that morning. He'd woken her up gently and asked how she was feeling. But she had just shaken her head and asked to be left alone, so after twenty minutes of cleaning up, he was now scraping layer after layer off the frozen lump of mince in an attempt to make something edible.

Even though he was in the middle of a murder investigation, he had decided to try to come home for dinner so the family could come together at least once a day. And this particular evening, it hadn't been much of a challenge since every lead they found invariably led them straight to one dead end after another.

He pushed the chopped onion off the cutting board, crushed the garlic cloves, which were really too dried up, and seasoned with paprika, chilli and a stock cube.

Someone had kept Molly Wessman's home under

surveillance. And this person now had a name. A name that was unusual enough that it shouldn't be too difficult to locate him. But a search for Christofer Comorowski hadn't generated so much as one hit in any of their databases. The same thing was true of Wessman's concealed tattoo, which had supposedly been put there by some mythical sex athlete who called himself Columbus.

He gave up his search for tinned tomatoes and instead filled the pan with water, tomato puree, what was left in a jar of sundried tomatoes, five tired carrots he peeled and grated, and an expired can of kidney beans.

Then it hit him. As he was tasting his improvised sauce, which needed another stock cube and a few dashes of cayenne, he suddenly saw a possible connection between the two leads.

Christofer Comorowski and *Columbus*.

Was that the link they needed to move forward?

Christofer Columbus.

Was that how the two things fitted together? Were the two of them in fact the same person?

It was only when the toaster snapped up behind him that he noticed Theodor was in the kitchen, about to spread Nutella on his freshly toasted bread.

'Hi, Theo. It's nice to see you. I didn't hear you come in.'

'Okay,' Theodor said, meticulously spreading a thick layer of Nutella on one of the slices of toast.

'Just so you know, dinner will be ready in fifteen, twenty minutes.'

'But I'm hungry now, so it's cool.'

Cool? He wanted to reply that it was anything but cool. That they were in a nosedive and risked crashing any second if they didn't make some changes soon. That he was going to sit down for dinner with his family whether he wanted to or not. That all that sugar was going to give him diabetes if he didn't watch himself. But he didn't say any of that. Instead, he just stood there, paralysed.

'I don't know if you've heard on the news,' he finally managed, even though he'd promised himself not to bring it up while Sonja wasn't on his side. 'The trial in Helsingør is underway now.'

'Right. What do you know.' Theodor started building a small mountain of orange marmalade on the other slice of toast.

'Like I feared, they're blaming each other in their first statements. The only thing they're all certain of is that they themselves did practically nothing.'

'Right, that's what you said. Good for you.' Without so much as a glance in his direction, Theodor put his toast on an empty plate and poured himself a big glass of milk.

Fabian felt something break inside him. 'Is that all you've got? An ironic comment whose only purpose is to put me down?' A small crack that grew until the whole dam burst. 'Do you really think this is funny? That it's ha, ha, ha.' But he mustn't let his feelings take over. Not now. 'Do you realize what this means? Do you have even the slightest inkling of what this will lead to?'

Theodor dumped spoonful after spoonful of chocolate powder into his milk.

'They're going to be acquitted. Do you understand that? Unless you, who knows who's who and who did what, choose to come forward, justice won't stand a chance. Even after they took turns jumping on that homeless man's chest until every rib was broken, they're going to be acquitted and walking these streets again in just a few months. Despite forcing another homeless man into a shopping trolley, chaining him to it and pushing it out on to the E4 motorway during rush hour. Despite all that, all you can do is shrug and make sarcastic quips.'

Without knowing how it had happened, he was suddenly standing behind Theodor, watching himself grab his shoulders and turn him around.

'Look at me when I'm talking to you,' he said, much too loudly. 'I said, look at me!'

But Theodor's empty eyes were as evasive as a magnet of the same polarity as his own.

'This is real, don't you understand that?' he continued, shaking Theodor in an attempt to provoke a reaction. Anything, any response at all. 'Or do you think this is some bloody video game where you can just start over if you run out of lives? Huh? Answer me!'

Theodor finally met his eyes. Finally, a reaction and some kind of contact.

'Are you done?'

The question hit him like a slap so hard his cheek was still stinging as he watched Theodor walk towards the stairs with his plate in one hand and his glass of chocolate milk in the other. As long as Sonja was on his side, there was apparently no limit to how badly he could behave.

The soft xylophone jingle sounded familiar, but he was unable to place it until he realized it was his own doorbell. True, they'd been in Helsingborg for almost three years, but people rarely rang the door.

The girl with the blonde plaits out on the porch looked to be over twenty; he had to remind himself she was classmates with Matilda and only thirteen years old. Part of it could be blamed on her colourful 1960s' dress and the worn leather waistcoat. But the main reason was her calm gaze.

He hadn't seen her since that fateful night when Matilda was shot. They'd been in the basement, playing with her Ouija board, when the perpetrator had burst in on them and forced them up to the living room with Sonja.

'Hi, Esmaralda,' he said, holding out his hand. 'How are you?'

'Much better now I know Matilda's all right and going to recover.'

'I thought you knew that all along. Can't you just ask your ghosts? Greta, or whatever her name is.' Fabian chuckled in an attempt to rescue his inappropriate attempt at a joke. But it fell painfully flat. 'I suppose you're here to see Matilda,' he continued, trying to ignore the fact that Esmaralda somehow managed to look down on him, even though she was significantly shorter.

'Hi Esma! Come in.'

Fabian turned to Matilda, who was standing behind him.

'Fabian, would you mind moving out of the way so she can get in?'

'Of course. I'm sorry.' Fabian backed into the hallway. 'But just so you know, dinner will be ready in twenty minutes, so she'll have to go home.' He wanted to bite his tongue. But it was too late. His frustration at Theodor and the whole situation had seeped out.

'If we're done,' Matilda said as Esmaralda stepped inside. 'And if we're not, I'm sure there's enough for her, too.'

He wanted to shout out *no there goddamn isn't*. She was barely a teenager and he was getting awfully close to fifty. No one was going to tell him about *his* dinner that *he* had cooked. And it wasn't fucking okay to just hole up in your room and gobble down sugar either. It wasn't about whether or not there was enough food. Esmaralda was going home, and she could take her bloody Ouija board with her.

But this time, he managed to rein in his feelings. 'Of course there's enough,' he said in as calm and sympathetic a tone as he could muster. 'But I think Esmaralda understands that we need it to be just family, considering everything that's happened.'

The ding from the phone in his hand was so quiet he almost didn't hear it. Even so, Matilda seized the opportunity to pull Esmaralda upstairs and was gone before Fabian had time to react. If the text he'd just received hadn't been from Gertrud Molander, he would have run after Matilda and made it clear to her that he was serious.

As it was, he hurried down into the basement instead.

58

Irene Lilja turned into the driveway, put down her kickstand and got off the Ducati. She was late back, considering she'd left the station over two hours ago. And the reason wasn't that she'd been stuck in traffic or that she'd run out of petrol.

No, she had simply felt a need to be alone, which was why she'd given in to a sudden whim in Åstorp and instead of taking the 21 eastward had turned left on the 112 going north.

It was the texts that refused to stop coming. She'd received six so far. Each more threatening than the last. She wasn't just going to be raped when she least expected it. She was going to be whipped, stoned and fucked until her stinking fucking Jew cunt was nothing but mincemeat. She was going to be pissed and spat on and kicked, and it had carried on like that all day.

She hadn't told anyone so far. Neither Tuvesson nor anyone else on the team knew about the threats, except for the ones Sievert Landertz had delivered openly in the newspapers. It wasn't that she didn't take them seriously or find them disconcerting. On the contrary, she was deeply shaken and probably in some kind of shock.

That thought had occurred to her when she suddenly burst into tears after driving all the way up to the Kullen lighthouse and taking a seat on one of the viewing benches to let the sea winds blow through her while she gazed out across a sea where the white-crested waves were wild and eternity could be touched.

But under no circumstances was she going to give in to the fear and let it win. If she told Tuvesson, she would be forced to implement countermeasures, which in turn would lead to more headlines. Exactly what they wanted. They fed off the attention. Putting up a fight and having uniformed officers guard her door was tantamount to baring her throat, which would only make them stronger.

What was the point of scaring people if no one was scared? What was the point of a demonstration with your right arms in the air if no one was watching? No journalists, no flashing cameras and no raucous counter-protests.

She pulled off her helmet, locked her bike and continued into the garden, where Hampus was working to restore the lawns. Flies were buzzing around him, drawn by the sweat steaming from his vest top. He must have been at it for hours. The garden no longer looked like a construction site and the lawn was back in place.

But the swastika was still visible, from some angles even more clearly than before. Whether because of the grooves in the ground or just because it was more trampled and muddied where Hampus had put in the most effort was impossible to say.

It was as though the whole lawn had been branded forever. As though it didn't matter how much they dug, raked and tried to level the ground. The swastika was there to stay, and the grass would always be slightly shorter or greener or have fewer dandelions there.

'Oh, great, now you show up.' Hampus stuck the shovel in the ground, turned to her and pushed his hair out of his face. 'Where the fuck have you been?'

'I've been at work,' she said and spread her feet slightly wider to signal that she wasn't in the mood for his bullshit. 'We have a few things to get on with, in case you haven't noticed.'

'How busy can you be if you felt free to leave more than two hours ago.' He gave her a smile and pushed some *snus* up under his lip. 'That's right. You see, I took the liberty of calling up and asking that little synth dweeb you have in reception. According to him, you left a long time ago.'

'Fine, I took a little detour up past Kullen. I needed some alone time.'

'You did, did you? Interesting. And it never occurred to you that maybe you should come home and help with this instead?' Hampus gestured towards the lawn.

'No, actually.' She shook her head. 'And why should it have? You're the one who absolutely needed a house and garden, not me. Have you forgotten that this is your little project?'

'Mine?' Hampus jabbed his chest so hard with his index finger it must have hurt and took a step towards her. 'What the fuck do you mean, mine? This is your fucking fault! If not for you and your bloody job, none of this would've happened!'

Rage was pumping so hard through the veins on his neck she wouldn't have been surprised if one of them had suddenly burst.

'That's one way of looking at it,' she said, even though she'd decided not to bring it up. 'Personally, I fail to see how it's my fault just because I'm doing my job in a murder investigation that happens to be leading me into brown waters.' She had decided to not even mention it, but rather let all his other flaws and their destructive dynamic be the reason she left him. But she couldn't hold back any longer.

'Your job?' Hampus shook his head and looked almost happy, as though he was about to burst out laughing any moment. 'Far be it from me to tell you how to do your job.' But the smile was nothing but a last feint before the decisive shot. 'But hand on heart. Was holding Sievert Landertz for so long really warranted?'

She couldn't stop herself. Even though she knew it was wrong, it was too late.

'I for my part can't blame him for feeling hard done by,' Hampus continued.

'Of course you can't. Why would you? You fucking voted for him!'

'What?'

Finally, that disingenuous smile was wiped off his face. Finally, the wall had cracked and he was standing there naked, fumbling for something to hold on to. 'Why do you look so surprised?' She didn't give a toss about the consequences. 'Yeah, I know you're a member of the Sweden Democrats. You see, I took the liberty of having a look through their membership list and who did I find there if not Hampus the closet racist.'

'Fuck you,' he said and now she could see it. The blackness in his eyes.

'Fuck me? I'm the one who should say that to you. You're the one who's been going behind my back, not the other way around. Don't you get it? Don't you get that this is what you voted for?' She pointed to the swastika in the lawn. 'So to be completely honest, I don't understand why you're working so hard to get rid of it. Frankly, you should be proud and stand out here Sieg-Heiling every morning when—'

She couldn't claim she wasn't prepared.

Even so, when his fist struck her face, she was surprised.

59

The album wasn't easy to find, but it's all about perseverance. I've taken pictures of all our Berlin photos, so you can see for yourself that my husband and I really were there. In case you were still in doubt. Best wishes, Gertrud.

ATTACHED TO THE TEXT was a number of images of photo album pages, which looked to be filled with pictures of Ingvar and Gertrud Molander in Berlin. In one picture, they were holding hands in front of Checkpoint Charlie; in another, they were having pints at one of Berlin's many beer halls. All the pictures bore the same kind of date stamp along their lower edge as the framed picture from the classic Berlin café.

Fabian had similar pictures with date stamps in some of his albums, but they were all from the 70s and 80s, not from 2007. Most people, apart from perhaps the members of Celluloid, had long since stopped sending their photographs away to be developed and putting them in albums. And yet, that was what dyed-in-the-wool technology geek Molander had done.

Doing so had given him an alibi that was virtually waterproof. At least at first sight. It wouldn't surprise him if the Berlin getaway was nothing but misdirection orchestrated by Molander. An illusion that at first glance looked plausible, but that at the end of the day rested on nothing but smoke screens, mirages and thumping music.

Like all magic tricks, the key was to pay attention to what the illusionist wasn't pointing to. To the details outside the spotlight. For that reason, he'd transferred the pictures from his phone to his desktop computer, where he could use the bigger screen to scrutinize them down to the last pixel.

Like the picture from the café, the rest of the Berlin pictures showed no obvious signs of tampering. No matter how much he zoomed in, he had to conclude they were the genuine article.

The same was true of the date stamps at the bottom of the white frame. A comparison with his own old pictures confirmed that they were identical. The dates ranged from 23 to 26 August 2007, and all days, including 24 August, when the murder took place, were represented.

It wouldn't be difficult to change the camera's internal date and go to Berlin the weekend before or after instead. But that was unlikely since it would leave Molander in a position where he had to get Gertrud on board and trust her ability to lie about when they'd been there.

That said, there was another angle as far as the time was concerned. An angle that only occurred to him now as he zoomed in on the picture from the Berlin café with its mirror walls, marbled columns and stately crystal chandeliers.

It wasn't Gertrud and Molander, with their cups of coffee and half-eaten apfelstrudel, that interested him; it was the man at the little table behind them. Or, rather, the man's wristwatch. Its hands showed quarter to nine, and judging from the light and the prevalence of coffee cups rather than wineglasses on the tables, it was before noon.

In another picture from the same day, Gertrud was standing with her glasses pushed up into her hair, studying a tourist map in something that looked like a hotel lobby with clocks showing the time in New York, Tokyo and Berlin. The hands showed eleven minutes past seven, which was probably just before they left for the café.

There were three more pictures from 24 August. In one, they were posing in front of the bombed church spire rising from the asphalt, roofless and hollow, a reminder of how present the Second World War still was in the German capital.

The only thing that looked renovated was the clock face, which shone like newly polished gold, in sharp contrast to the sooty stone façade. Its hands showed twenty past nine, and here, there could be no doubt it was in the evening. Both Gertrud and Ingvar were now dressed up for a fancy outing, having shed the windcheaters and ergonomic shoes they'd been wearing that morning. She wore a purple evening gown, high heels and a leather jacket, he a blue suit with a bow tie and patent leather shoes.

In the second picture, they were sitting at a bar raising their cocktails to the camera, and in the third, they were eating *plateaux de fruits de mer* in a restaurant. The rest of the pictures were from the other days and showed them doing touristy things in Berlin.

The pictures more or less documented their days from morning to night and were taken reasonably regularly, no more than a few hours apart. At least as far as Thursday night, when they arrived, Saturday and Sunday were concerned. The Friday, on the other hand, was a different matter. It had a gap of no less than twelve and a half hours. Between the café visit at quarter to nine in the morning and twenty past nine in the evening, there wasn't a single picture.

What had they been up to during all those hours?

Granted, it was their anniversary, but he found it hard to believe they'd spent the whole day between the sheets in their hotel room.

He clicked over to Momondo and did a search travelling from Berlin to Copenhagen and back on a random Friday in August. The list of departures showed that the route was primarily served by SAS, Norwegian, easyJet and KLM. Norwegian had no flights under four hours since their routes required a stopover in either Stockholm or Oslo, and KLM didn't have a single flight in the twelve-hour window.

With SAS, on the other hand, leaving Berlin at 1.30 p.m. would put you in Copenhagen exactly one hour later. If you travelled without check-in luggage, you should be able to leave the airport by car twenty minutes later. The drive across the bridge up to Ramlösa Brunn Park, where Inga Dahlberg was allegedly attacked, took exactly an hour, according to Google Maps.

There was an easyJet flight from Copenhagen to Berlin at 7.05 p.m. If Molander had checked in online and printed his boarding card, he wouldn't have needed much more than half an hour to get through security and reach his gate.

That left him two hours to attack, drug and transport Inga Dahlberg from the park to the secluded spot by the Rå River, rape her and screw her arms and legs to the freight pallet, push her into the river and clean up after himself before getting back into his car and racing to Copenhagen Airport.

It was tight, unbelievably tight. Theoretically speaking, it could work. In practice, a thousand and one things could go wrong. An accident on the E6 motorway and he would have been stuck in traffic and missed his flight. A passer-by straying too close, or just an unexpected reaction from Dahlberg. But as was so often the case with Molander, the difference between theory and practice was virtually non-existent.

60

Gertrud brushed some more blush on her cheeks and studied the result in the mirror. She wanted to look beautiful and appealing but under no circumstances too dressed or made-up. It was a hard balance to strike since she was not in the habit of using anything beyond mascara and a bit of eyeliner on an ordinary Monday like this one.

To make sure Ingvar didn't start asking questions, she dressed down in a pair of blue jeans and a white shirt, which she left untucked. Same thing with her hair. No washing, blow-drying or styling. Instead, she put it up with two chopsticks, as though she was in the middle of cleaning and her appearance was the last thing on her mind.

It was the same with dinner. She couldn't remember when she'd last fussed this much over tiny details. Not just with the cooking, but the ingredients and above all, the planning. It mustn't come off as too lavish or festive. At the same time, it had to be both delicious and take a long time to eat so she wouldn't feel rushed.

Because that was the aim of the game. To draw things out for as long as possible so she could find out what Ingvar's colleague Risk was up to.

Somehow, he'd managed to hit a few nerves she had only realized were raw in hindsight.

Like that weekend in Berlin five years ago.

Ingvar had really bowled her over that time, when in the middle of making dinner he'd asked her to come with him to the car, where a packed bag and plane tickets had been waiting for them. It certainly wasn't the norm for him to surprise her with a getaway. Or anything, for that matter. The few times he'd remembered to buy her flowers on their anniversary could be counted on one hand. Consequently, it was with a sense of wonder and anticipation that she'd sat down in the seafood bar at Copenhagen Airport and ordered a glass of champagne.

The weekend had been lovely. Not only had they eaten well and seen too many attractions to count. They'd also had time to take lots of pictures, something they normally never did. And for once, Ingvar had even developed them and put them in an album.

And yet there was something that chafed at her when she thought about that Berlin trip. An unsettling dissonance she'd never been able to put her finger on, which had made her almost repress the memory of that weekend. In the past few years, she actually hadn't given it a thought, until this afternoon, when Fabian Risk stopped by with his ambiguous questions.

Looking back, it was so hazy. She had suddenly felt ill, that much she remembered. She had suspected that apfelstrudel at Café Einstein, and after that they'd been forced to go back to their hotel where she had gone to bed, trembling and clammy.

She'd felt so stupid; anxiety at being ill when they were travelling and were supposed to be having a nice time had completely overwhelmed her. But Ingvar had been so understanding and lovely, reassuring her that she probably only needed a lie-down and that she would be back on her feet in no time.

Afterwards, she'd pondered the strangeness of his behaviour. It had been so unlike him. He, who was usually anything but gracious about her being ill. He, who always behaved like it was his world falling apart, not hers. As though she had deliberately come down with something or was just too lazy to get up.

In Berlin, he'd been completely different. He'd been tender and kind and not annoyed in the slightest. He'd helped her get undressed, tucked her in and brought her water. As though he wasn't really surprised.

She hadn't realized she'd dozed off until she woke up. In fact, she'd been so out of it, she was confused about where she was at first. Her memories hadn't started drifting back until Ingvar had come and sat down on the edge of the bed and told her she was in a hotel room in Berlin. It had taken her several minutes to accept that she'd been 'out' for over ten hours.

Ingvar, on the other hand, had just sat there on the bed like everything was fine and asked her how she was feeling, and if she felt like hitting the town and celebrating their anniversary. And to her own great surprise, she'd felt surprisingly fine after drinking a few glasses of water and taking a shower. After that, they'd had an amazing evening together; she'd even been hungry and dared to tackle a *plateau de fruits de mer*.

It was only a year or so later when she'd had her appendix removed that she was struck by how similar her sleep in the hospital had been to the one she'd experienced in Berlin. Synthetic and jet-black, as though someone had simply switched her off without her being aware of it. The only difference was that for the surgery, she'd been out for a fraction of the time.

'Well, well, what's all this?' Ingvar exclaimed the moment he stepped into the hallway and noticed the set dinner table, the bowls of raw chicken, pork and beef, aioli, garlic butter and chilli mayonnaise, and in the middle, the pot being kept warm by the blue flames underneath. 'Fondue. Can't remember the last time we had that. What are we celebrating?'

'Nothing at all,' she said and tried to accompany her reply with a carefree laugh. 'No need to panic.' The napkins. It must have been the napkins. Why hadn't she just brought out the kitchen roll instead?

'That's a relief. I was worried there for a second.' Ingvar hung up his coat and came in. 'I thought I'd forgotten our anniversary or something.'

'No, I was just cleaning the kitchen cupboards and I found our old fondue pot and thought, why not?' She shrugged. 'Sit down and I'll get the rest.'

Ingvar sat down and started fiddling with the tiny forks with coloured handles. 'I'll take the blue and you can have the red. Sound okay to you?'

'Absolutely,' she said on her way back with the jacket potatoes.

'Wow, this is some stroll down memory lane. Remember when we were in France on that skiing holiday? Wasn't that the very first time we had fondue?'

'It was, but I've updated the recipe a little – more red wine and less oil – so if it weren't for the potatoes, it would be proper GI food.'

'I know it's only Monday, but this kind of dinner practically requires a glass of wine, don't you think?'

'So long as we don't make it a habit,' she said with a smile and sat down across from him. 'It's a slippery slope.'

Ingvar chuckled and got up. 'That almost sounds like we should go for a whole bottle instead.' He winked at her and left the room.

Gertrud pinched her arm to keep herself from being too swept up by the jovial mood.

'How about a Marchesi Antinori from Tuscany?' Molander held out the bottle like a waiter. 'It's what you would call a medium-bodied wine with hints of cherry, plum and herbs. It's aromatic and flavoursome and has a long aftertaste with notes of wood.'

'I'm sure that'll do just fine.' She tasted the little splash he poured into her glass. 'Mm, delicious.'

Molander filled their glasses and they proceeded to spear meat on their forks.

'How was work today?' Gertrud lowered her fork into the hot broth and started a new one with mushrooms, plum tomatoes and tiny onions.

'It was all right. A bit too busy at the moment.'

'So it seems. How many cases do you actually have now?'

'A thousand, it feels like. And they're not straightforward ones either. But then on the other hand, who ever said straightforward things are better?'

'Indeed, you usually like a challenge.'

'Believe me, any one of those cases would have been plenty.' Ingvar lifted out one of his forks to check if the meat was done.

'And Fabian? Is he still on leave, or—'

'No, no, he's back and leading one of the investigations, though I have to say his efforts seem a bit half-hearted.'

'Oh, how so?'

'Well, you know, he's unfocused and his mind seems to be elsewhere.' Ingvar cut an x in a jacket potato and pushed the sides in to make it open. 'But I suppose it's no wonder, considering what his family's been through.'

'Right, God, what a nightmare.' She lifted out both her forks and slid the meat and vegetables on to her plate. 'It must've been awful. And his daughter, what's her name again?'

'Matilda.'

'Right. How is she doing? Is she okay?'

Ingvar nodded as he followed Gertrud's example and harvested his forks. 'As far as I understand, she's going to make a complete recovery.'

'Thank goodness.' She dipped one of the pieces of beef in the chilli mayonnaise and started chewing. But just like all the questions she could no longer ignore, not to mention the anxiety at what the answers might be, the sinewy piece of meat was impossible to swallow down, as though it were made of rubber. The silence grew too long; eventually she had to force the beef down whole with the aid of a large gulp of wine. 'So which case is Fabian in charge of, then?'

Ingvar put his glass down and studied her with eyes that penetrated her skin and not only read her mind but gauged her blood pressure, breathing and stress level. No one could see right through people like Ingvar or was better at knowing exactly which buttons to push to get them where he wanted.

It was her question, of course. When she thought about it, it was completely uncalled for; if Ingvar hadn't been suspicious up until that point, he certainly was now.

'Gertrud, do you even know what cases we're working on?'

'I know a bit.' She took another sip of wine. 'It's all over the papers, you know.' Right now, she would take anything that could help calm her nerves. 'There's that terrible business with the immigrant boy in the washing machine, and then the man who was stabbed to death right in front of people at ICA Maxi, just like that. I mean, Lord, what's the world coming to?' She was babbling again.

'You're not the only one asking that question.' Ingvar fell silent and studied her so intently with his damn X-ray vision she didn't know what to do with herself. Every movement felt unnatural, and the pain in her lower back was screaming ever more loudly to be stretched out. But she couldn't start doing back exercises in the middle of dinner.

'Are you not going to eat?'

Right, eat. How could she have forgotten about that? 'I just wanted to let my potato cool down a bit.' Like Ingvar, she opened her potato like a flower and placed a lump of garlic butter in the opening.

'Cool down? Isn't the point for the butter to melt?' Molander popped a piece of chicken into his mouth. 'Fine, since you're so eager to know, Fabian's working on an investigation we haven't let the media in on yet.'

'Oh really, what is it?'

'Damned if I know. At the moment, all we're really sure of is that the victim, a woman, died from something as unusual as ricin poisoning. And both her bedroom and bathroom were under surveillance.'

'Surveillance? By whom? Who would do something like that?'

'That's exactly what we're trying to find out.'

'And how is that other investigation going?'

'What investigation?'

'You know, the one into the murder of Inga Dahlberg.'

'What are you talking about?' Ingvar put down the glass he'd just been about to drink from. 'As you're very well aware, that case has been closed for years.'

'Oh right, of course.' She shrugged and focused on swallowing another piece of meat. 'I was just thinking it might have been reopened. Those things do happen, after all. I mean, you find new clues and leads, which in turn—'

'Gertrud, I see what you mean.'

'But I guess not, then.' She was babbling again.

'Not to my knowledge.'

'Okay then, great, now I know.'

'Yes, now you know.'

They resumed eating, and the silence grew so intense the sound of every little bite, every sip she and Ingvar took was amplified as though there were microphones inside their mouths. He was cross and didn't want to talk about it. But she couldn't stop. Not when she'd made it this far.

'Imagine, though, how good it would feel if we could have some closure,' she said and lowered a new fork with only chicken on it into the pot. 'What that would mean for Reidar. Such an awful business. Yes, I know he has a new woman and all, but still. Just to know who it was and let justice run its course. Not to mention you and your colleagues. You worked so incredibly hard back then. Didn't you?'

'Yes, but you're forgetting something very important.' Ingvar put a mushroom in his mouth.

'And what would that be?'

'That we solved it.'

'I'm sorry, I'm not following. What do you mean, solved it?'

'The case. Maybe you've forgotten, but we actually did identify the killer and we arrested him. His name was Benny Willumsen, he was from Denmark but lived in Malmö – on Konsultgatan 29, if memory serves. He's passed away since, sadly.'

'But? So you mean the man you had to—'

'Release. Exactly.' Ingvar downed the last of his wine and topped himself up. 'The problem was that he had an alibi the court considered strong enough.' He shook his head and had another sip of wine. 'So unfortunately, Reidar's never going to get justice.'

'But it couldn't have been him, then. If he had an alibi, I mean.'

Molander laughed. 'Well, I suppose that's one way of looking at it. On the other hand, being able to present an alibi is hardly the same thing as being innocent.'

'Hold on a minute. If you have an—'

'Sweetheart, listen to me.' Ingvar leaned forward over the table. 'If you're well prepared and know how to go about it, fabricating an alibi's not that difficult. I would almost claim it's in fact rather easy.'

'But Ingvar, you don't mean to say that—'

'Yes, that's exactly what I mean to say,' he broke in and topped up her glass as well. 'You'd be surprised to learn how little it takes for a court of law to swallow a fake alibi. Believe me. I know what I'm talking about.'

He raised his glass, and she followed his lead, toasted and drank, terrified he would be able to tell from looking at her that she was finally, after all these years, starting to come to grips with what had really happened that weekend in Berlin.

61

After covering his hair with a stocking, he pulled on the grey curly wig and adjusted it in front of the mirror until it was perfect. He immediately looked completely different. It was strange to think, really, how much of a person's personality was in their hair. Just a few strands, which when they fell out could rob most men of their confidence.

He was already wearing tights, fake breasts and his belted pale blue dress. He'd even put on base make-up: a light face cream and even lighter powder.

Yet despite all that, he'd still looked like a confused transvestite or possibly someone on their way to a costume party. It was only when he put on the wig that everything started to fall into place, and once the pale sun hat was on properly, too, along with the earrings and pearl necklace, his transformation was complete.

The dice had said *old lady*, but now, studying his reflection in the mirror, he had to change that to *sweet little old lady*.

Just two days ago, the dice's decision had made him blow a gasket. No matter how he'd turned it over in his mind, he'd been unable to think of it as anything but deeply unfair.

Sure, he'd rolled an X, and the side mission had been crystal clear. But still. After all his hard work and achievements, it felt like a big slap in the face, whose only purpose was to show him he shouldn't get too big for his boots.

But on reflection, he had, despite everything, concluded it was exactly what he'd needed. A slap in the face and a reminder that he had to stay humble. That he was nothing but a passenger who would never get anywhere near steering the ship.

Besides, the dice had been proved right yet again. Having designated a side mission that had seemed virtually impossible to complete, especially given that he had only two days to prepare, he could now, with only a few hours left, honestly say the whole thing had come off a lot better than he would have dared to hope.

The fact was, he'd been so fabulously lucky that a lot of people would have insisted he must have been blessed somehow, and if he'd been a believer, he would probably have agreed. Practically everything had simply fallen into place, and the only things left to do were to pack his backpack, touch up his powder and put on his beige coat and pale blue pumps.

After that, it was out of his hands.

62

Fabian didn't know how many times he'd studied the black-and-white pictures of Inga Dahlberg climbing out of Molander's car that summer night. He hadn't just scrutinized them through a loupe; he'd scanned them, too, using such high resolution he'd almost maxed out the space on his hard drive.

When he went through the files again, zooming in on various details, it was like looking at his own reflection. There was nothing new. No surprises. He knew who the woman was, why she was there, who she'd met and who'd taken the pictures. Even so, he was convinced there was something there he'd missed. Some small detail he'd overlooked.

It was growing light outside the basement window, even though it was only just gone half four in the morning. Two more days, then it would turn and start getting darker. It was the middle of summer and the days were at their longest, and yet he felt melancholic about it being downhill from here.

But that wasn't the only reason he'd lain sleepless for hours and finally got up and trudged back down to the basement. His thoughts had revolved around Molander. Now that he'd found an opening in his Berlin alibi, there wasn't much doubt left.

The problem was that despite all the hours he'd put in,

he still didn't have a shred of concrete evidence. None of the many things he'd uncovered and concluded came even close to being able to hold up in court.

He'd managed to fill in some of the gaps, true, and he'd collected enough material to make a strong circumstantial case. But no matter how strong it was, what he had was in no way tantamount to concrete proof.

It was like the Berlin alibi. He could show that there was a reasonable possibility Molander had in fact not been in the German capital when Inga Dahlberg was murdered. But as long as Gertrud insisted she'd been with him the whole weekend, he had nothing.

Hugo Elvin must have, though.

There could be only one reason Molander would have risked going so far as to off his colleague: that Elvin had found something incriminating enough to constitute a real threat. The question was where he'd hidden his evidence. Certainly not in his desk drawer, anyway.

Every time he'd gone through its contents, he'd been forced to conclude that all the clues, pictures and notes belonged to the category *strong suspicion*. Even so, he'd decided to go over it all again.

He put the pictures of Inga Dahlberg aside and took out Elvin's diaries, flipping through them one page at a time, reading his brief and sometimes cryptic notes again. But they held nothing he hadn't already looked into.

Finally, he took out the key ring with the seven keys marked with different-coloured cloth tape that divided them into groups. One of the three green ones, which all had handwritten question marks on the tape, had opened the locker at the Celluloid photography club that had belonged to Gertrud's father, Einar Stenson. The other two were, indeed, still question marks. The same was true of the two white ones, one of which had a fish on its tape marker while the other had a code: 759583.

Maybe it wasn't a code at all, but a phone number. He tried calling it with the local area code, but was greeted by an error message informing him the number didn't exist. He got the same result when he tried the Malmö, Landskrona, Göteborg and Stockholm area codes, after which he put the white keys aside and focused his attention on the two blue ones, the ones he'd given the least thought.

The larger of the two was also marked with numbers. This time four of them: 0388. The key was a normal pin tumbler key and the four numbers were likely an entry code to a building or some such. The question was, which building?

The smaller one was more noteworthy. The head was asymmetrical, oval in part. It almost looked like a cranium in profile. He took out his magnifying glass to get a closer look at the details. There was no doubt it was old. Scratches, dirt and oil covered the surface. Nothing strange about that. What was strange were the small white dots, which under his magnifying glass looked like tiny crystals.

When he gingerly touched one of them with the tip of his index finger, it skittered down on to the table like gravel. Maybe he should have let Hillevi Stubbs run an analysis of whatever substance it was, but instead he ran his own by gathering them up with his index finger and placing them on the tip of his tongue.

As expected, they tasted salty.

He couldn't say if it was the peculiar shape of the key's head or the salt that gave him the idea. Probably a combination of the two. Either way, he took the key off the ring and started removing the tape, which after so many years left sticky glue marks in its wake.

But once the head was reasonably clean and he could see the Neiman logo in which the first N continued to form a kind of roof over the rest of the letters, he was sure.

The key was an ignition key, probably for an old Volvo Penta, one of Sweden's by far most common inboard motors.

Two years had passed since he'd left Stockholm for Helsingborg and started working with Hugo Elvin. Two years of lunches, coffee breaks and long sit-downs. Not once had Elvin mentioned anything about owning a boat. Nor had Molander, for that matter, if it turned out to be his. On the other hand, both men had turned out to harbour so many secrets, he'd long since stopped feeling surprised.

63

She couldn't place him, yet she felt she recognized the man in sunglasses who was sitting on the bench next to a backpack, smiling, wearing a beige jacket and trousers that were hiked up a smidge too high. What if it was that paedophile the police were after? No, he wouldn't dare to be out in broad daylight like this, with people all around him. Like the lady who was sitting down next to him, forcing him to put his backpack on his lap. No, it was probably just something about him that told her she should keep an eye on him and stay vigilant.

Victor and Samuel were the ones closest to him and, as usual, they were fighting about who was going to pedal the tricycle and whose turn it was to push. Sonja and Niki were there, too, shrieking as Ruben chased them. Right now, it was the most fun either one of them had ever had, but she would bet her great-grandmother's wedding ring on one of them bursting into tears in less than a minute.

They were one man short, and there was almost nothing worse. What's more, if she knew Josefin right, she wouldn't bother to show up at work again until the end of the week. *Fever and achy all over, probably the flu*, she'd groaned on the answering machine that morning. How stupid did she think they were? As if they didn't know she'd got lucky with some pathetic Tinder hook-up and was now far too hungover to work.

To be honest, it was beyond her how Josefin of all people could have such an easy time finding men who were willing to give her a ride. She, on the other hand, had tried everything after her divorce, from spending hours making a dating profile to placing a classic personal ad in the local paper. She'd even gone down to Dickens and got trashed enough to brave the dance floor.

Josefin, on the other hand, all she had to do was snap her fingers and spread her legs a little for all and sundry to come running. She wasn't even good-looking. Apart from being thin, too thin to be honest, she had nothing. She barely even had a hairdo. And yet, there she was with yet another memory between her legs, pretending to be ill.

It was so like her not to give a toss that Tuesdays were park days and the whole group was off to the park, even though just two hours ago it had been raining so hard she'd been convinced it would be on the news. The only reason they hadn't cancelled and played indoor games instead was the deluge of displeasure they'd get from the parents who would inevitably jump down her throat at the next parent – teacher meeting.

And of course all the children were present. Even Rigmor, who had such a bad cold her dried-up snot would fit in brilliantly as a prop in *The Exorcist*. They should have wiped it a long time ago. Or rather, *someone* should have wiped it, but that *someone* apparently felt she should be the one to do it.

As though she hadn't already put on more than her fair share of the rain clothes, made a packed lunch for Asta whose parents had, as usual, chosen to forget, and made sure they packed the first-aid kit, which had already come in useful when Edvin tripped and caught himself with his hands. My God, he'd howled. No one could scream as much over as little as that helicoptered brat.

No, she was at the end of her tether. The pain in her knees rivalled her heel spur, and every part of her body was exhausted. Exhausted from taking care of everyone's children but her own. Exhausted from all the screaming and from never having an uninterrupted adult conversation.

She couldn't even think about tutelage. Sure, it was nice on paper, ever so fancy and sounded great in the sales pitch when parents came in for tours. In reality, it was often about sheer survival. Getting through the day without too many disasters.

It was easier said than done when the children refused to stay in one place for longer than two seconds. They dashed around like crazed squirrels, screaming, completely impossible to keep an eye on. Especially here at the Slottshagen playground, where they could easily wander off into the rest of the park.

At least the man with the backpack was leaving. One reason for cheer. He'd probably noticed she was watching him and felt innocently accused. But she couldn't care less. Innocent or not, there was no reason for him to hang around the playground when the whole park was full of benches.

She turned to the sun, which had just found an opening between the clouds, and felt its warmth on her face. It might be a really nice day after all.

'Angela! Siri needs to go to the bathroom.'

She turned around and saw Harald with Siri in his arms.

'Do you want to take her or should I?' he continued, pushing his fringe out of his eyes.

Harald, who she didn't know what to make of, even though they'd worked together for almost a year and a half. He was unquestionably amazing in every way. Enthusiastic and so full of energy he had to round off every shift with a trip to the gym. The children adored him and even though he didn't have any formal training, there was no denying he was an enormous asset. Even so, she felt unsure about him.

'It's all right,' she said and started walking towards them. 'I'll do it.'

She couldn't help it. It didn't matter how politically correct you were. How happily you embraced the ideas of gender equality and eventual world peace. You just couldn't deny that Harald was a man and that with very few exceptions, child molesters were men.

'No, not Angela,' howled Siri, who had disliked her since her first day. 'Harald help me.' On the other hand, she'd never liked Siri either.

'I mean, really, I'm fine doing it.' Harald hoisted the girl up on his shoulders as though the overfed little lump weighed nothing at all.

'No, I'll take her. I have to go myself anyway,' she lied, and she pulled the protesting Siri down from Harald's shoulders.

No one could tell her she didn't know what she was talking about. Not after what happened with Krister. And she'd worked with that man for more than five years. Five years, during which he'd been the children's favourite, always happy to pull out his guitar and sing a song or read a book aloud with intense feeling, unless, of course, he made up his own story. He of all people had done things to the children that were so horrible she still wasn't over it.

Some of her co-workers had even told her in confidence they couldn't help suspecting him of the unthinkable. And every time she'd defended him, on occasion taking it so far she'd ended up in a conflict situation with the co-worker in question.

Never again, she'd promised herself after that rude awakening. Never again would she stick her head in the sand without a clue about what the children were suffering. That was why she never left Harald alone with the children if she could help it. Without making a big deal of it, she always made sure she or someone else on the team was present, too.

Harald obviously wanted to know what her problem was and had gone so far as to ask her bluntly in one of their staff meetings. But she had stubbornly denied it had anything to do with him being a man. Instead, she'd referred to her interpretation of the curriculum, which said the children should always be supervised by at least one fully trained teacher, and until he was fully trained, there wasn't much she could do about it.

As expected, Siri refused to pee. To avoid an accident on the playground, she forced her to stay on the loo until she couldn't hold it any longer and eventually emptied her bladder. She couldn't say why, but a nagging feeling of having made the wrong decision was growing stronger with every step she took on their way back towards the playground.

To make matters worse, she couldn't hurry back. Of all the children she'd looked after over the years, Siri was the only one she'd never been able to pick up without scratching and loud protests. So they walked on at a snail's pace.

An eternity later, with her heart pounding in her ears,

they passed through the leafy archway. Siri immediately let go of her hand and scampered off to play with Quentin and Nova, who'd collected a pile of stones and were now busy arranging them in a straight line.

She saw Harald playing with Samuel, Ruben, Lisen and Sonja at the other end of the playground, and Ebba, Alva, Niki and Victor were on the big swing, waiting for a push. She spotted Vincent's bright ginger mop of hair on its way across the bridge to the miniature copy of Helsingborg's medieval tower, Kärnan, to go on the slide. And Melvin was in the sandpit.

At first glance, everything seemed calm, almost calmer than usual. And yet, every alarm bell in her head was ringing so loudly it was difficult to think.

The bench where the man with the backpack had sat was now occupied by two mothers with buggies that must've cost the equivalent of providing for an entire African village. But who wasn't there? Who was missing? It was someone, she was sure of it. Every cell in her body was screaming at her that something was about to go terribly wrong.

Ester. Was Ester the one she hadn't seen? She almost always played with Lisen, but right now Lisen was with Sonja, waiting for Harald to tag Ruben and Samuel. Fuck, fuck, fuck. Not again, she thought, spinning around one more time.

'Harald,' she called out, in a voice that had already given up hope. 'Have you seen Ester?'

'Ester?' Harald replied, scanning the playground with a bewildered look on his face.

'Yes, Ester Landgren with the yellow jacket and the blue tights,' she said, even though she was sure he knew.

'She was playing tag and was going to run and hide.'

'*Where*, Harald?' she said, grabbing hold of his jacket. '*Where* did she run and hide?'

'I don't know.'

'You don't know?'

'No, I had my eyes closed and was counting to twenty. But I'm sure she's here somewhere.'

'She *was* here somewhere! Where she is *now*, we apparently have no idea!'

'The tower. Did you check the tower? Sometimes they hide in there.'

No, she hadn't checked the tower, and on her way there, she wasn't even able to try to hope they'd find the little girl. She'd already given up and could only watch as one scenario more horrible than the last played out in her mind. Even so, she burst into tears when, seconds later, she looked through one of the openings in the tower and confirmed what she already knew.

Her legs wouldn't carry her; she collapsed in the sand. She couldn't even answer Harald when he called out he was going to look outside the playground to make sure she wasn't hiding behind a tree.

There were, of course, any number of places to rule out before they could be absolutely sure. Then the police would be called and an alert would be sent out. But it was mostly for appearances' sake. So they could clear their own names and claim they'd done everything. Whatever that was supposed to accomplish when what must never happen had just happened.

Again.

64

THEY WERE LOOKING. SHE could tell they were all looking, almost staring, even though they were doing everything they could to hide it. She had to admit it wasn't exactly surprising, given that she normally never wore make-up, other than maybe a hint of lipstick if she was going to a wedding or some such. Today, she'd attempted a proper pancake.

But no one said anything. They all just sat there, waiting for the meeting to start, slurping their coffee like they were on a hike and the lukewarm liquid scalding hot. And she could see why. What were they supposed to say? Even if they did suspect what was hidden underneath the layers of concealer and powder, they could hardly do anything other than keep their mouths shut.

It was the first time Hampus had ever hit her. But it wasn't the first time he'd raised his hand in anger, though until now he'd always chosen to take out his frustration on the nearest piece of furniture instead, or whatever else happened to be within arm's reach.

But this time, his fist had completed its trajectory through the air without interruption, and in some twisted way, she felt relief, some kind of gratitude, that he'd finally crossed the line and nothing in the world could make it undone.

She'd left him more times than she could count. But he'd never accepted it was more than empty threats, which in some ways it had been. Because despite all the problems and ugliness, there had still been a part of her that loved him. But that was then. Everything was different now.

As expected, he'd launched into extravagant apologies and promises it would never happen again. Not to mention his pathetic justifications about his blood sugar being low after working on the lawn all day, or how terrible he'd been feeling recently because she made him feel so rejected. Which somehow made her complicit. After all, it took two to tango and yada, yada, yada.

He could say whatever he wanted. It made no difference. It was over. So incredibly fucking over.

'Irene?'

Lilja looked up at Tuvesson, who had turned to her.

'Are you okay?'

'Yes, you keep asking me. Why wouldn't I be?' It was only at that moment she realized the rest of the team were looking at her too, without even trying to hide it.

'You just seem so… absent. Did something happen?'

'No, like what?'

'I don't know. But I would personally find Sievert Landertz's attacks in the papers pretty difficult to handle.'

'Whatever. I couldn't care less about what he says.'

'Okay, great. It's obviously empty threats, but if anything happens, don't hesitate to ask for help, okay?' Tuvesson turned to the others. 'Where were we?'

'The crime scene investigation at ICA Maxi,' Molander said and turned to Lilja. 'Which has determined that the perpetrator exited through the staff entrance and fled on his bike.'

'I know,' Lilja lied and emptied her coffee cup.

'And what do we have on the victim, Lennart Andersson?' Tuvesson asked.

'Not much, other than that he was divorced, did a lot of sports and seemed to have a burning passion for genealogy,' Klippan replied. 'I've talked to his ex-wife, who fell apart when she received the news. According to her, he was one of the best people she knew.'

Tuvesson nodded. 'Any new theories about possible motives? Apart from trying to start a race war, as Fabian has already suggested.'

'No, not so far. But the ex-wife gave me a list of all his friends and acquaintances. I'm crossing them off one by one. I've also requested all the CCTV footage from the week before the murder. Hopefully that can give us something to go on.'

'All right. Let's move on to Wessman and the hidden webcams, more of which, if I've understood correctly, have been found in other flats.' Tuvesson walked up to the whiteboard, where she made space for more victims next to Molly Wessman's photographs and notes.

'Yes, so far I've identified four other women who were under surveillance,' Fabian said, studiously avoiding the looks Molander gave him as soon as he opened his mouth. 'If Lina Parnerud at Fiberbolaget is to be believed, Christofer Comorowski has installed fibre-optic cables in twelve buildings during her time with the company. How many flats he did before that is anyone's guess.'

'And these latest ones, are they bedrooms and bathrooms, too?'

'Yes,' Molander said, finally taking his eyes off him.

'And how are you getting on with the webcams?'

'I don't know about getting on. I haven't even looked at them yet.'

'Why not?' said Lilja, topping up her coffee.

'Firstly, because I believe we can assume it's the same set-up and models as in Wessman's flat.'

'And secondly?'

'I'm going to leave that one to Mr Risk, since he was the one who expressly asked me to leave them be until further notice.' Molander turned back to Fabian. 'Don't worry. I'm in complete agreement. Sometimes, it's best to let a sleeping bear lie.' He fired off a smile and an almost imperceptible wink.

'I'm not worried whether you agree with me or not.' Fabian returned Molander's look but let the smile pass by unacknowledged, then turned to the others. 'I'm concerned he'll realize we're on to him if we start taking down and examining too many of the cameras.'

'That's true,' Tuvesson said. 'But how do the women in question feel about it?'

'I know how I would feel,' Lilja said.

'One checked in to a hotel, another decided to go visit her parents in Båstad until this is over. The other two have agreed to carry on as normal.'

'If you can even do that with a camera in your bedroom.'

'Sure, that's debatable. But they've promised to try, and I have promised them police protection in return.'

'Okay.' Tuvesson sighed and turned to Molander. 'Then the question should be how you're getting on with Wessman's webcams, because I assume you've at least examined those.'

'I have indeed, and I have to say I'm pretty impressed by this Comorowski, if he is in fact the one who constructed and installed them, that is.'

'And the server, or whatever it is these cameras are sending their pictures to, have you been able to locate that yet?'

'No.' Molander smiled widely. 'And that's the reason I'm so impressed. As you may know, most webcams are USB based, which means you need a processor and quite a bit of electronics to turn the data into something that can be transferred over an ordinary ethernet cable. Just connecting electricity to the camera itself can be a challenge, given that the IEE 802.3at PoE+- standard can't deliver more than 25 watts.'

'Ingvar, please get to the point.'

'Sorry, that last part was parenthetical. But the rest is pretty much the point, because the same processor is also programmed to create a VPN tunnel and TOR router. Smart, no?'

Tuvesson exchanged looks with the others. 'Does anyone know what he's talking about?'

'It's really not that complicated. A VPN tunnel is an information channel that encrypts all data transported through it, which makes it impossible for a third party to check the content. The problem is that the sender address and the recipient address at the beginning and end of the tunnel aren't anonymous, so they can be traced with the right software. To get around that, Comorowski's added a so-called TOR router to the signal chain – *The Onion Router*, as it's really called. It anonymizes both the sender and the receiver by bouncing the information back and forth between proxy servers. That way, he's not only made sure the contents are undecipherable to any prying eyes, he's also made it impossible for us to trace him.'

'So the only thing you've found out is that we can't find out anything else.'

'That's another way of putting it.'

Tuvesson did nothing to hide her irritation. 'What about that tattoo, then? Did any of the other women have one like it?'

'Unfortunately not,' Fabian said.

'That means we have to drop the hypothesis that Christofer Comorowski and Columbus are the same person.'

'Isn't that a bit hasty?'

Tuvesson shrugged. 'As far as I can see, there's nothing to suggest a link between them.'

'No?' Fabian said. 'We have one bloke installing hidden webcams in the homes of single women and another who moves in the swinger circuit, branding women like cattle after having sex with them. I would say there are plenty of points of contact.'

'One sounds more like a voyeur and the other more like a practitioner, if you ask me.'

'Perhaps. At the same time, though, there are countless examples of observers tiring of sitting on the sidelines and deciding to get involved. And we have the names. I know it sounds far-fetched, but *Christofer Columbus*. It just can't be a coincidence.'

'Why not?' Lilja asked.

'Because I think we can assume Columbus is a name someone's given themselves, and self-given monikers always have significance, whether conscious or subconscious.'

'All right, let's keep that door open for a while longer. After all, you have a few more names on your list,' Tuvesson said. 'Make sure you contact them as soon as possible. It might be that some of them are branded.'

'But there's one thing I don't understand about all of

this.' It was the first time Klippan had spoken in a while; the others turned to him as if they'd forgotten he was in the room. 'What's the motive?' he continued. 'Let's assume it's the same person. What's his motive?' He looked them all in the eyes. 'He spies on a bunch of women in their homes. I'm with you so far. Most of them are, as far as I understand, between twenty and forty years old, and they're all reasonably good-looking. No obese couch potatoes, but real Bettys, as my father would have put it. Nothing weird about that, either. At the same time, going by Fabian's theory, he's moving around in swingers' circles where, if rumour is to be believed, women line up to have sex with him and have their privates branded. I've never heard of anything like it, but there's a lot to hear in this world before your ears fall off, so let's roll with it. But, and this is where you lose me, why would he kill Molly Wessman?'

'Wasn't it something about them belonging to him?' Lilja said. 'That's why he brands them, right?'

Fabian nodded, even though he felt Klippan had in fact pinpointed the weakest link in the motive chain.

'And I suppose that's why he keeps an eye on them,' Molander said. 'To make sure they don't stray.'

'But in that case, they should all be branded, not just Wessman,' Klippan said.

Fabian nodded. Klippan was right. No matter how you looked at it, it didn't add up. On the other hand, logic wasn't always the foundation of a perpetrator's motives. In fact, the opposite was usually closer to the truth.

'Besides,' Klippan continued, 'I have a hard time imagining Wessman would be the first and so far only woman who has ever stepped out on him. Especially considering how many there must be, if we assume the numbers are ordinals.'

'Or—' Tuvesson said, but broke off when Molander's phone beeped and he picked it up.

'Or what?' Klippan said.

'Maybe she's just the first one we've come across.'

65

'HELLO? EXCUSE ME?'

Fabian heard the distant voice but chose to keep walking across the car park outside the station. Flätan had just agreed to meet to go over a list of recently deceased women whose deaths had not been considered suspicious. Naturally, he would never admit that he himself had been incorrect or missed something. His colleague Arne Gruvesson, on the other hand, had, if Flätan was to be believed, a habit of overlooking the most obvious of cases.

'Hello, have you a moment, please?'

Fabian, who had just opened the car door, turned around and saw a man hurrying after him across the car park.

'I understand you're busy. But this will just take a few minutes.'

'I'm sorry, I don't have jump leads, if that's what you're looking for,' Fabian said before realizing he recognized the man.

'Hi, we met yesterday. Axel Stjärnström, Eric Jacobsén's neighbour.'

'Yes, I remember.' Fabian shook hands with the man who the day before had come trotting up to Jacobsén's car in gym clothes and a baseball cap; now, he was wearing a suit. 'What's this about? I'm afraid I'm on my way to a meeting.'

'I'll try to keep it brief,' Stjärnström said, catching his breath. 'I obviously said some things yesterday. About Eric, I mean.' He straightened his tie even though there was no need. 'I'm not sure how to put this, but last night I realized I might need to modify part of what I told you.'

Fabian nodded, though he had no recollection of what the man had said.

'As I'm sure you remember, I had nothing bad to say about him, and he really is an amazing person in many ways, full of energy.'

'I'm sorry, what are you getting at?'

'*There's no such thing as a free lunch*, someone told me once.' Stjärnström fixed Fabian intently. 'I didn't understand what they meant at the time. But now, a few years since Eric moved to our street, it couldn't be any clearer. Nothing's free. Right? Everything comes at a price.'

'I'm sure that's true, but as I said—'

'And when it comes to Eric, I would say the price is very, very high.'

'In what way?'

'How can I explain it? It sneaks up on you. At first, you don't give it a second thought. Everything's the same as ever, just a bit better and more fun. You know, a little bit ritzier and more exciting. The only thing you find yourself pondering is why you waited so long to start enjoying life. But at that point, it's already too late. You just haven't realized it yet.'

Fabian had no idea where the man was going with his rambling line of thought. He wanted to interrupt, thank him for talking to him and wish him luck in life.

'Do you know how cuckoos operate?' Stjärnström continued, without waiting for a reply. 'The female lays her eggs in other nests when the parents are out finding food, and she pecks holes in and eats one of the other birds' eggs so they won't know the difference.'

'Yes, I'm familiar with it. But I'm not sure what all of this—'

'That's what Eric's like. Just like a cuckoo chick, he makes sure he hatches a few days before the others so he's a little bit bigger. But no one notices. Not until he's pushed all the other baby birds out of the nest, and what's the point then?'

Fabian nodded. 'Okay, so that's what you wanted to tell me?'

Stjärnström nodded.

'All right, then. Thanks for that.' Fabian shook the man's hand and climbed into the driver's seat. He was already five minutes late, and it would take him at least fifteen minutes to get to the hospital to receive his scolding from Flätan.

He put the key in the ignition, turned it and reached for the door to close it. But Stjärnström blocked him. 'I'm sorry, if you could just move a little, so I can—'

'For me, he crossed the line when he started flirting with my wife.'

'Yeah, that doesn't sound great. But you'll have to excuse me, I'm running late.'

'And you should know that Eric doesn't leave it at a few stolen looks.' Stjärnström pressed on without paying any attention to Fabian's obvious need to leave. 'Instead, it became increasingly open, as if I wasn't in the same room, or his own wife for that matter. At the same time, he started hinting to me that I'd gained weight and that I never bought my beautiful wife flowers and was taking her for granted.' He shook his head. 'The only thing I could do was laugh it off and raise my glass to him. I mean, you don't want to spoil the mood when you've been invited over for dinner and everything.'

'No, I suppose you don't.' Fabian realized Stjärnström wasn't going to move until he was good and ready, so he killed the engine.

'The problem was, Emilie took it to heart. She ate up all that smarm of his, and in just a few months, he'd managed to make her look at him the way I've wished she would look at me for so many years.'

'Have you tried to talk to him and tell him what it's like for you? Try to make him see that his behaviour is out of line?'

Stjärnström let out a short laugh and shook his head. 'You can't talk to Eric that way. He slips away, feints and sidesteps and before you know it, you're naked in his sauna with an IPA in your hand, planning a trip together.' He fell silent as though he were summoning the strength to go on. 'But in the end, I brought it up with Emilie, and she swore she wasn't interested in him in the slightest. Just like me, she found him too vulgar and gauche. And I was foolish enough to believe her, talk about naïve, and then only a few months later, I discovered... It was during a dinner party at our house. It was just me, Emilie, Eric and his wife. We were discussing the killing of Osama bin Laden, when I realized his foot was between my wife's... legs.' He swallowed again but was overcome with emotion. 'And she was sitting there pretending nothing was happening. Bloody hell.'

'Maybe you should go talk to someone about this.'

'Maybe. Yes, I suppose I should. But I honestly don't

know what good it would do. It's not like I've done anything wrong.'

'You haven't considered moving?'

'Every day. But Emilie won't hear of it.'

'I meant move as in move out, leave her.'

Stjärnström met Fabian's eyes. 'We might be going through a rough patch right now, but we have two children, a mortgage and a life together and I guess I'm still hoping it's going to work itself out somehow. Anyway, I went through her phone a few nights after that incident. To my surprise, they'd only texted about the children and dinner parties I was invited to as well. I couldn't find any emails at all.'

'So what did you find?'

'A picture. One that was different from all the others. At first, I didn't understand what it was. It didn't look like anything at all, until I realized it was a close-up of a pubic mound... Or, to be precise, Emilie's pubic mound, which was shaved and had a tattoo.'

66

Assar Skanås opened his backpack, took out the two plastic bottles filled with water and put them next to the girl. It was her. He was sure it was her. The one the voices had told him deserved it. The one he could do whatever he wanted to.

But he was a nice man, he was, and he was going to be nice to her. At least during the act. Of course she should enjoy it too. Afterwards… Afterwards was afterwards.

Blood. He didn't like blood. It had trickled from the wound down across her ear and dried. But not enough to make anyone react. Everyone had looked away or fiddled with their phones, assuming he was an ordinary dad carrying his tired daughter.

He hadn't wanted to hit her. He hated fighting. But she'd clawed and screamed, she had, so loudly his ears hurt. He hadn't meant to hit her so hard. He never did and yet that's almost always how it turned out.

The wristwatch Igor had given him had struck her temple so hard she was still unconscious. It was the watch's fault. Not his. He liked children and preferred to play with them when they were awake.

He took out the plastic bowl and emptied one of the water bottles into it. Then he opened the front pocket of his backpack and coaxed out the pump of the liquid soap dispenser.

Lavender, the best smell in the world. Nothing smelled better; the fragrant lather in the bowl immediately made him feel calmer as he carefully and methodically washed his hands, one finger at a time, one nail at a time. He wanted to be clean, as clean as possible. She was, after all, a virgin, and there was nothing purer than that.

He'd always thought so. But he'd never told anyone. It was his little secret. Ever since that time at the pool, he'd resisted, he'd been good. Really good, as several people had told him; he had pretended to agree with all of them about how wrong and forbidden his particular desire was. As though desire could be wrong. As though it was so much worse than the desire to eat meat or travel to the other side of the world on your holiday.

But nothing mattered any more. The voices had finally told him to stop pretending. They had told him what he'd always felt deep down inside. But they had sounded different this time; they had talked slower than usual and almost never over each other. But they'd been on his side, they had, unlike all the babbling psychologists.

She was his, they'd told him. His, his, his. The only reason she'd been born was so she could please him, and once it was done, she was spent like when the most precious flower is picked from the meadow and wilts in its vase.

He'd hurried as far from the playground as he could. Away from all the stupid people who wanted to take what was his. But the trees in the park, or maybe it was all the gravel walks, had made him confused again, and soon everything had been spinning and swapping places.

It was only when he mustered the courage to stop and raise his eyes that he'd spotted Kärnan, looming above everything else. Then he'd finally realized where he was. Oh, how he loved that old tower that made everything stop spinning.

He undid his belt, pulled down his zip, then his trousers and his underwear.

His lust hadn't morphed into arousal yet. He couldn't even see it for all the hair. He fumbled around with one hand, tugged on it a little to wake it up and pulled the skin back. The rank smell of uncleanliness blended with the lavender, making him feel dirty and unworthy. But he was sure it would get better as soon as he started washing and soaping it up.

He hadn't known where to go, but just like a few days ago, everything had sorted itself out. Suddenly, he'd been walking down those stairs towards the city centre, and he'd been so tired from carrying the girl he'd almost taken a tumble. But he'd made it all the way down to the first turn.

After that, he'd carried on towards the second turn, but he'd been forced to turn back because a group of men in suits and construction helmets had blocked his way and stared. If it hadn't been for the girl, he would have stabbed them up.

He'd almost dropped her several times on the way back up, he'd been so tired; he'd had to stop and catch his breath before the last flight of stairs. That's when he'd noticed that one of those doors that were always closed was ajar.

Maybe it was the men in the construction helmets; he didn't know. Either way, no one had seen him squeeze in with the girl and hide behind a pile of furniture and boxes. Shortly afterwards, he'd heard someone enter, pick something up and leave again.

He, for his part, had continued further into the building and climbed a spiral staircase to a dirty, cluttered room. But the high ceiling, the red brick walls and the window with a view of the whole city still made him feel like a king.

He picked up the bowl of water, held it between his legs and rinsed off the soap. It was exactly as delightful and exciting as he'd hoped, and once he'd air-dried, he wasn't just clean but also hard enough to do what he'd been waiting for, for so long.

Now, he just had to prepare the girl.

67

That Eric Jacobsén might in fact be the notorious Columbus almost seemed like a bad joke. An impossibility. He had absolutely not come across as some sort of sex god who could make the women who made pilgrimage to him push beyond their sexual limits and let themselves be tattooed. But there was no doubt the tattoo his neighbour Axel Stjärnström had found on his wife was the same as Molly Wessman's, apart from the number, 103.

He parked the car outside Jacobsén's house in Laröd and noted that both the Lexus and the red Lamborghini were missing from the driveway. According to Molander, however, Jacobsén's phone was in his home and in the past half hour he'd made two phone calls to Axel Stjärnström's wife, Emilie.

During his previous visit, Fabian hadn't had a chance to use the door knocker. It was surprisingly loud and made him back up a step and instinctively reach for the handcuffs in his jacket pocket.

But instead of Jacobsén, a blond boy of about ten opened the door. Franz Ferdinand's 'Take Me Out' was roaring out from somewhere inside the house with an accompanying guitar riff that was one of the least on-key things he'd ever heard.

'Hi, my name is Fabian Risk. What's your name?'

'Rutger.'

'Your dad, he wouldn't happen to be home, would he?'

'No.'

'Rutger, it's your turn!' someone shouted after the music finally died down.

'Oh no? Then where is he? Your dad, I mean.'

The boy shrugged. 'At work or out somewhere.'

'And your mum? Maybe I could talk to her?'

'She's not home either.'

'Ruuutger! Otherwise I'm going again!'

'No, it's my turn!'

'You wouldn't happen to know when one of them might be back, would you?'

'No, but I have to get back to my friend now.'

'I understand. Would it be okay if I came in and waited?'

Rutger was considering that, apparently unsure how to respond, when Joan Jett & The Blackhearts' 'I Love Rock 'n' Roll' started up with a guitar accompaniment that completely butchered the song. 'It was my turn!' Rutger disappeared into the house, leaving the door open behind him.

Maybe Jacobsén was home after all. Maybe his son was just so absorbed in the video game he was playing with his friend he hadn't noticed his father coming back. After all, his phone was here and he'd called the neighbour's wife less than half an hour ago.

He closed the door behind him and looked around the hallway. Clothes and shoes were strewn across the floor. He took off his shoes, too, placed them neatly by the wall and continued into a living room so big it was furnished in sections.

Near the fireplace, a number of big cowhide cushions were scattered on the floor. Beyond them, by the open-plan kitchen, was a long dining table with seven lamps hanging over it in a row from the slanted ceiling.

At the other end of the room, two corner sofas formed a big U in front of the rolled-down projector screen on which an overhead projector was showing Guitar Hero while the surround sound system blasted out the Joan Jett song, which came to an abrupt end when Rutger's friend apparently hit the wrong buttons once too often.

He'd heard about the game but hadn't seen the fun in pressing a few plastic buttons to the beat of dated rock songs. Still, he couldn't help walking over to get a closer look.

Rutger was considerably better than his friend; when he took over the guitar and started playing 'Message in a Bottle', hammering the buttons like his life depended on it, Fabian almost wanted to have a go himself. But instead, his eyes were drawn to a phone that lay discarded on the sofa among all the cords and controllers, which lit up as it received a text message.

There was nothing strange about Rutger having a phone. Nor was it any wonder it was the latest iPhone 4, which was far from cheap. No, what made Fabian react was the background picture of Jacobsén's wife.

'Rutger, is that your phone?'

'No, it's Dad's,' Rutger said without missing a beat on the controller.

'I thought you said he wasn't home.' Fabian picked up the phone and read the text.

'He's not.'

Could you tell Wilhelm to be home by dinnertime at the latest? Emilie.

'All right, so it was you calling Wilhelm's mum a while ago?'

Rutger stopped playing and turned around. 'How did you know that? Wille, did you rat me out?' He turned to the other boy on the sofa.

'Don't look at me. I didn't say anything.'

Rutger turned back to Fabian as the Police song went down in flames behind him. 'Did Dad send you? Okay, listen. My phone's broken and I just had to borrow it to call Wille over.'

'Don't worry.' Fabian held his hands up. 'Your dad didn't send me here to spy on you. As I said, I came to see him.'

'Because I didn't poke around in it, and I promise I'll charge it and put it back in his office.'

'That's fine by me.'

Rutger breathed a sigh of relief and handed the controller to Wilhelm. 'Your turn.'

'But there's one thing I don't get,' Wilhelm said as he adjusted the strap so the controller would be the right height. 'If you want to see his dad, why are you here when you know he's not home?'

'Yeah, actually, why are you here?' Rutger chimed in.

'See what this is?' Fabian handed him his police ID.

'You're a police officer?'

Fabian nodded.

'Wow… Check it out.' Rutger passed the ID to his friend. 'So what, you're, like, investigating a crime?'

'Yes, I suppose you could say that.'

'What kind of crime?' Wilhelm said. 'Did someone get murdered?'

'I'm afraid that's confidential.'

'And what do you want with my dad?'

'I was hoping he could help me straighten a few things out. But maybe you two could help me instead?'

Rutger lit up. 'What do you want us to do?'

Fabian held up the mobile. 'First, we should, as you said yourself, put this back where it belongs. We don't want your father to come home and find it has no charge. So if you could start by showing me to his office.'

'Okay.' Rutger jumped over the back of the sofa like he was doing parkour and jogged across the living room towards a spiral staircase.

Fabian followed him down to the basement, past a spa section with reclining chairs, a sauna and sliding glass doors opening on to the pool area outside. A few doors and a short hallway later, Rutger stopped and turned to him.

'But you have to promise not to tell him I have a key.'

'I promise.'

Rutger pulled a small bunch of keys from his pocket, found the right one, turned to one of the doors and put the key in the lock. Fabian noted that it was a proper lock, the kind you would normally see on a front door.

'But hold on, Rutger,' Wilhelm said as Rutger was about to turn the key. 'What if your dad's the suspect?'

Rutger turned to Fabian. 'Is he? Is my dad the suspect?'

'No, he's not.'

Fabian didn't like to lie. Especially to children. That said, Jacobsén had passed the stage where he was merely a suspect, so that should excuse part of the lie. 'And as I'm sure you understand, I can't tell you exactly what this is about.'

The boys looked at each other and when Wilhelm finally nodded, Rutger unlocked the door.

'Thanks.' Fabian entered the room. 'Why don't you go back upstairs and play your game and I'll let you know if I need more help.'

'Or we can wait here until he's done.' Wilhelm crossed his arms.

'Nah, come on, let's play,' Rutger said and disappeared with Wilhelm hard on his heels.

'But do come down and tell me the moment one of your parents shows up!'

'Okay!' Rutger shouted back from the spiral staircase.

Fabian turned on one of the two desk lamps and immediately noticed how neat and tidy the office was. Unlike the hallway and the living room, there was a kind of compulsive order in this room, with everything meticulously in its place.

Apart from that, it looked more or less like a normal study. Desks with computers, filing cabinets and a printer, bookshelves filled with binders sorted according to colour and the inevitable piles of bills and unopened envelopes. The only thing that stood out was a small workbench strewn with electronics, soldering irons and circuit boards.

He turned on the computer, which, as expected, asked for a password. He skipped the most common ones like *123456*, *password* and *football* and instead tried *Columbus*.

Incorrect password

Too obvious. Jacobsén was smarter than that. It could be anything, of course, a random string of numbers and upper- and lower-case letters. In a way, randomness was an impenetrable wall. But Jacobsén seemed too structured and controlled to let randomness rule him. On the contrary, he'd talked quite a bit during their drive about the importance of seizing control and being in charge of your own life.

Christofer1492.

He considered it. That could absolutely be the password, but it could also be something else entirely. He did feel fairly certain about three things. If any of the letters was upper case, it would be the first one; if there were numbers, they would be at the end. That was almost always the way of it when people made their own passwords. He also felt convinced it would be connected to Columbus one way or another.

Incorrect password

Jacobsén had proudly told him about when he first started the company and no one had believed in him. Maybe he viewed that as the kind of conquest Columbus made in 1492. As the point when he seized the tiller of his life and started charting his own course.

Christofer2001.

Incorrect password

But when he thought about it, the company might not be the most life-changing part of Jacobsén's life. Money, success and above all the opportunity to ogle women he didn't know, absolutely. But the most pivotal event should have been when he became *Columbus*. According to the woman at the swingers' club, the rumours about him had started circulating about two years earlier.

Christofer2010.

The screen went dark for a few seconds and then lit up again, showing a desktop picture of an oil painting of three ships on the open sea. He immediately realized they must be Columbus's ships, the *Niña*, the *Pinta* and the *Santa María*.

He was in.

68

ASSAR SKANÅS PULLED THE cloth bundle out of his backpack, unrolled it on the table next to the little girl and made sure the tools were all neatly ordered and within easy reach. There were pruning shears, two kitchen knives of different sizes, an awl, a hatchet, a hammer and a hacksaw. Lined up like that, they looked scary, they did, and he didn't really like them. But once he got to them, she wouldn't be feeling anything anyway.

He looked out of the window, down at the people scurrying about like crazed ants far below him. No one even seemed to have time to stop and look at the police cars with the flashing blue lights that were pulling up in the middle of the square.

What if they were looking for him? Could that really be the case? No, it must be someone else. Either way, they wouldn't find him. Ever. He didn't need to worry. Not even one bit, actually.

The little girl's navy-blue tights with white horses slipped off with a crackling of static electricity. Her legs were white like mother-of-pearl, which made the three bruises below her right knee stand out more. Why hadn't he brought something to cover them up with?

Her dress, also with a horse motif, he cut off. Same thing with her panties. One snip on one side, one on the other and they were gone with a little tug.

Apart from the bruises, the sight before him was the most beautiful he'd ever seen, and it made his desire grow so strong he felt certain it had never been stronger. He wanted to be inside her, and he wanted it now. Immediately.

But that was bad. He knew it would be bad and too quick if he didn't check himself. Instead, he took it in his hand and started pulling back and forth. First with calm, careful movements. But the sight of her soft ivory skin made him go faster and harder and in the end, he couldn't hold it back.

Catching his breath, he could feel it soften as the blood left it, swollen and half-erect after the rough treatment. He looked out of the grimy window and noted the arrival of another flashing car as the police officers fanned out in different directions.

He cut out a piece of fabric with the pruning shears and used it as a rag to wipe her clean. Then he opened her mouth and counted five moist breaths before he balled up the rag, pushed it in and covered the whole thing with two large strips of tape.

The girl switched to breathing just as calmly through her nose, without any reaction. Had he really hit her so hard she was in some kind of coma? It had its advantages, but it reminded him too much of death, and he didn't like death. Not at all, as a matter of fact.

He picked up her right arm and pulled it to turn her lifeless body 180 degrees, which made her head brush against him. Then he rolled her on to her stomach and pulled on both arms until her head dangled free over the edge of the table.

Then he picked up the bowl with the lavender scented water and eased it down and in underneath her head. He held it with both hands to avoid spilling, knelt down and raised it until her whole face was under water.

Please, don't let her be in a coma. If she was, he'd have to hurry before she turned cold and stiff. Because he'd heard about that. Dead people went all cold and stiff; he didn't like that at all.

Then she finally coughed and came to with a violent jerk. He could see the muscles between her shoulder blades tense up like springs as she pulled her head out of the water and looked at him.

He smiled at her, his warmest smile, so she would understand that this was something beautiful. Something for her to be happy about. But she didn't look happy. Even though he was stroking her hair ever so gently, she managed to spit out the rag and scream at the top of her lungs. And he didn't like screaming.

Not one bit, as a matter of fact.

69

After twenty minutes in front of the two computer screens, clicking through folders and files, Fabian had found nothing more sinister than accounting, client lists and myriad pictures of Jacobsén himself, his friends and family by the pool and on various holidays.

Nothing from his alter ego Columbus. Nor any external servers, either physically present in the office or in the cloud, and the search history showed only innocuous visits to Facebook, Google and news sites.

He started closing down all the open windows to turn his attention to the contents of the bookshelves and cabinets instead, when one of the windows marked *Docs archive* caught his attention.

It contained all the files on the hard drive, the ones he'd just been going through. But it wasn't an item in the list that had made him react, it was one of the settings in the top right corner that controlled what was being shown. He'd never reflected on there being such a setting, but there it was.

Hidden items, it said, under *Details* and *Current view*.

He ticked the little box next to it and started scrolling through the list again; at first glance, it seemed unchanged. But a minute later, he noticed a folder he was sure hadn't been there before. It was called *Santa María* and was one of the largest folders on the hard drive with its three hundred gigabytes. He opened it, which made a number of subfolders appear in a new window. He chose the top one, marked *TAT*, whose contents had last been changed three days earlier.

A long list of subfolders opened up, all labelled with a number. He chose one at random, which turned out to contain pictures of a woman sprawled on a leather sofa. There were clamps on her nipples, and in another picture, she looked straight up into the camera while taking the man who was holding it into her mouth.

Every last folder turned out to contain pictures of women in various positions. It was everything from Asian to dark-skinned women, blondes to redheads. Some wore knee-high boots, others vinyl and leather, but most were completely naked. Of Jacobsén, if it was him, nothing more than a hand, a sculpted torso and from time to time an erect penis adorned with a tattooed arrow could be seen.

All the women seemed to be alive. Some had their eyes closed, true, and some looked worried or even scared. But nowhere did he see anyone who seemed drugged or generally out of it. On the contrary, most of the eyes he zoomed in on were glazed with desire, lust and unadulterated horniness.

One picture united them all. A close-up of the women's exposed pubic mounds, which had just been shaved and tattooed with a line penetrated by an arrow and a number.

He scrolled down the list to folder number 28. As expected, it was Molly Wessman. She was lying on a rough wooden table with both arms and legs tied, being whipped. But in none of the pictures did he see anything fundamentally different from the others that might explain why she had to be poisoned and killed.

He closed the window and opened the folder marked *DATE*. It contained only a programme called Opera, which turned out to be a browser. Fabian used Internet Explorer, even though he'd heard there were several others that were much better.

He couldn't find any bookmarks, but the search history showed a number of different dating sites.

He chose *Badoo*, where a number of women's profile pictures had been selected as favourites. They were all better-looking than average, though some of them had enlarged their breasts and lips a bit too much.

Ingela Kjellson had, among other things, listed *sex* as one of her main interests. Another was *role play* and a third *threesomes*. The same was true of *Tina Frej, Hanna Idun* and *Sofia Öhman*. Apart from *films, romantic dinners* and *music*, all the women Jacobsén had selected listed different forms of sex among their interests.

It didn't look like he'd been in contact with them at all. He did, however, keep extensive notes about each of them. Among other things, he'd found out their home addresses, whether they rented or owned, who their landlords were or who was on the board of their housing cooperatives, and finally, what kind of internet service they had.

So this is where Jacobsén trawled for victims.

He went back to the original folder *Santa María* and opened one of the other subfolders, which was labelled *TOR*. *The Onion Router*, it said at the top of the browser-like window. He'd never visited before, but he instantly knew it was the dark net.

Of course this was where Jacobsén hung out. Anonymous and impossible to trace among the illegal weapons dealers, people traffickers, paedophiles and so-called Red Rooms, which featured live executions.

One of the bookmarks was marked *Live*; when he clicked it, both screens went dark. But then, as the transfer speed caught up, the pixels came back to life and a grid of five-by-five squares appeared on either screen. What he was looking at was live feeds from around fifty different bed- and bathrooms.

Each square was marked with a first name like *Stina, Greta, Ingela, Fia, Ylva* and so on. The square marked *Molly* was black and marked with a red X.

Most of the squares showed empty rooms, but then it was the middle of the afternoon. *Lisa* was home, though, and in the process of getting out of the bath, scraping water off her breasts before wrapping herself in a towel. *Carina* seemed to be asleep, and *Amanda* was reading in the bath. *Kelly*, on the other hand, was hosting two men in their thirties who were taking her in both holes.

Despite the grainy image, he almost felt like he was hiding behind the curtain in her bedroom. Before the cloying feeling of aversion and shame had a chance to grow too overwhelming, he closed the TOR browser and instead opened the folder labelled *MOV*.

It contained a list of around fifty subfolders, also labelled with first names. He scrolled down to Molly and opened it. It contained videos that looked like they had been culled from the hidden webcams in her bedroom and bathroom, in which she was either pleasuring herself or having sex with one or several men and sometimes women as well.

The most recent clip was almost exactly two years old and showed a man wearing nothing but a leather waistcoat, a cowboy hat and a hip holster with a revolver in it, taking her from behind in what looked like an act of very rough anal sex.

In order to get as deep as possible, the cowboy was holding her hips with both hands and thrusting so hard his revolver slapped against her every time he hit bottom. But Molly didn't seem to mind. On the contrary, her pleasure seemed predicated on his roughness.

After a while, he pulled out, grabbed her hair with one hand and pulled her towards him. With the other hand, he pulled out the gun and put it to her temple while she took him in her mouth.

From time to time, he pushed her head so far down that Fabian could clearly see her gagging, and he only pulled her up by the hair when he came and—

'What the hell is going on here?'

Fabian turned around to see a woman standing in the doorway, staring from him to the violent sex on the screen and back again.

70

LILJA WAS STANDING IN the middle of the square, letting her eyes rove across the façades. Assar Skanås's phone turning on had seemed almost too good to be true. Molander had received the news in the middle of their meeting, after which they'd hastily wrapped things up and hurried off. Finally, they were going to catch him.

But her joy had been short-lived. Not long after, word about Ester Landgren disappearing without a trace from the playground up in Slottshagen near Kärnan reached them.

Molander had narrowed it down to a circular area centred on the eastern part of Stortorget Square, between the Trygg-Hansa building and the Elite Hotel. With a radius of a hundred and fifty feet, the circle stretched from the statue of Magnus Stenbock all the way up to Kärnan, which in turn meant the two events were too geographically close not to be connected.

Compared to the search area on Söderåsen, this was nothing. That said, the city centre was far from easy to search. The square and the stairs leading up to Kärnan were no problem. Apart from some vegetation and various nooks and crannies, they were relatively open areas; two uniformed officers had been able to clear them in minutes.

No, it was the other part of the circle, between the Maria Church and Strömgränden, that presented the greatest challenge. It contained everything from hotels, offices and private residences to shops, basements and courtyards.

No matter what approach they took, it would take hours to search everything. Besides, they couldn't use all the resources available to them, because more than half of the uniformed officers had been tasked with securing the perimeter so Skanås couldn't escape. Because they were going to arrest him. She wasn't worried about that. Her concern was rather what he would have time to do to the girl before they found him.

According to Molander, the phone hadn't moved for the past hour. That made it easier to organize the search. But it also meant he'd likely found a place where he could live out his sick perversions. Or, alternatively, he'd just tossed it in a bin somewhere to throw them off his scent and was actually somewhere else entirely.

'As many as you can spare,' she heard Klippan half-shout into his phone as he came walking towards her across the cobblestones. 'No, I need them right now.' He ended the call and turned to Lilja. 'I have one team searching both hotels and one tackling the H&M and the offices in the Trygg-Hansa building. But it's going to take time.'

'I figured. How many more are on their way?'

'About ten. I was thinking they could form a third team and take on the smaller properties. But it's going to be at least thirty minutes before they're here, and just getting access to all the facilities is going to be a nightmare.'

'Yes, Klippan, I know it looks bleak, but what are we supposed to do?'

'What would you say to just calling him?'

'What would I say to that? I would say I think he's going to realize we're on to him and that we have his number, which will make him turn it back off, and right now, I'd say that's the last thing we want. You?'

'I'm convinced he's known we're on to him for a while. All he has to do is open a newspaper. And it will hardly come as a shock that we have his number, since it's in the phone book. What's weird is that he's turned it on again, which suggests he's not in control of his own actions. Sure, we run the risk of him turning the phone back off or getting rid of it the moment he realizes it's us. But that should still give us a few valuable seconds of information about where he might be. Besides, we'll have a chance of persuading him to give up.'

Lilja nodded, even though she found it hard to tune out all the potential consequences. 'All right, let's give it a try.' There was no time to debate the merits. If they wanted even a slim chance of getting to him before it was too late, they had to take a shot in the dark and cross their fingers. 'Let's do it in Ingvar's lab, so he can record and analyse.'

Klippan nodded. 'He's ready and standing by.'

So they'd already discussed it behind her back and made the decision. What if she'd said no? Would they just have done it anyway?

'It's like this,' explained Molander, who was sitting by the control panel in the van with headphones around his neck and his eyes on one of the screens, which showed a map of the search area. 'I've prepared a number of unregistered numbers in case we have to call—'

'What do you mean, unregistered?' Lilja broke in. She took a seat on one of the little stools as Klippan pulled the sliding door shut behind her.

'They're anonymous and can't be searched. At the same time, though, they turn up like any normal number on the screen, rather than it saying "unknown number".' He handed the headset to Lilja. 'If you're ready, let's do this.'

As soon as she heard the first beep, she cleared her throat to make sure everything was working. When the third ring rang out, she could almost picture Assar Skanås interrupting whatever he was doing and considering whether to pick up his ringing phone or not.

'*The number you are calling is not available at the moment. Please try again later.*'

Molander ended the call and turned to the others.

'Shouldn't we give it another go?' Klippan said.

'No, we shouldn't,' Lilja replied.

'Why not? What if it was on silent and he didn't get to it in time?'

'I'm actually inclined to agree with Klippan,' Molander said, nodding to underline how right he was.

'Oh, you are, are you?' Lilja said, looking for the right argument to prove to them why it was such a bad idea. But before she could find any at all, the phone started ringing. 'Is that him?'

Molander nodded and pressed *accept*.

'*Hello?*' The voice on the other end sounded winded and stressed.

'Assar, is that you?'

'*Who is this?*'

'My name's Irene Lilja and I'm calling from—'

'*Why? What do you want?*'

'I just wanted to know how you're doing and where you are?'

'*Not now. No time. We'll have to talk some other time. Goodbye.*'

'No, Assar. Hold on. Can't you—'

'*Everything's fine. Great. Never better. I think I have to hang up now.*'

'The girl, Assar. Do you have her?'

'*What girl?*'

'Ester Landgren, the one you picked up at the playground.'

'*I don't know what you're talking about. I don't have a girl.*'

'The one with the red hair and the blue tights with horses on them.'

'*I told you, I don't have a girl! I know it's not allowed.*'

'But lying's not allowed either, is it?'

'*I don't know what you're talking about. You're mean and probably have the wrong number.*'

'No, I don't, and you know exactly what I'm talking about.'

The line went silent; the only sound was Assar Skanås's heavy breathing.

'Assar, listen to me when I tell you how it's going to be.' She made sure to inject a dramatic pause. 'If it turns out you're lying to me about the girl, I'm going to make sure you can't watch any of your children's films for the rest of the month. And you can forget about sweets.'

'*What, why? She's mine. The girl belongs to me, just me!*'

'Assar, I hear you. But you do understand that you have to let her go, don't you?'

'No, *I'm not letting her go. Do you hear me? Never ever! I've waited longer than anyone and now it's my turn to do what I want. What I want! The voices said so, so there.*'

'But Assar, we—'

'They're in charge, not you!'

The call ended.

71

'I HONESTLY DON'T KNOW where to start. This isn't something I like to talk about, as I'm sure you can understand.' Karolina Jacobsén, dressed in a knee-length skirt and bone-white blouse, straightened her dark, shoulder-length hair, even though it was already perfect. 'But Eric's behaviour around intimacy and sex has never been particularly normal.'

Fabian had tried to shut down the two computer screens as quickly as he could when Jacobsén's wife had stormed in to the office. But she had literally torn him away from the keyboard and stared at Molly Wessman being subjected to the cowboy's rough treatment.

'What do you mean?' Fabian pulled a tissue from the box he'd found in one of the drawers and handed it to her.

'During the fifteen years Eric and I have been married, we've never come close to a functional love life, and we likely never will. We didn't even conceive Rutger naturally.' She trailed off and dabbed her eyes with the tissue.

Several minutes had gone by before she asked him to stop the video and explain who he was and what he was doing in her husband's study.

'Sure, we have a lot of other things. Money, friends, a life most people can only dream of. But just when you finally stop thinking about it and accept that things are what they are, you get this thrown in your face.' She nodded to the black screen.

'I understand this may be difficult to talk about. But as I mentioned, we're in the middle of a—'

'Fine, but what is he suspected of? Is he even a suspect?'

'The video you just saw wasn't an ordinary porn film.'

'No? But I don't understand? What—'

'The couple in it are in fact completely unaware they're being filmed by a hidden webcam.'

'Okay? And you're implying Eric put it there?'

Fabian nodded. 'And that particular woman died three days ago from poisoning.'

'Wait, hold on a moment. You don't think Eric might have killed—' Karolina clapped a hand to her mouth and shook her head. 'No, you're wrong. Eric would never. There must be some mistake. Are you listening to me? You've made a mistake. You've got him mixed up with someone else—'

'Do you recognize this?' Fabian held up a picture of Molly's tattoo.

Karolina looked at it like it was contagious, and her face went from red and puffy to ashen. 'Oh my God...'

'We found this on the murdered woman, and we suspect that—'

Karolina interrupted him by undoing her blouse with trembling hands and tears streaming down her face. Then she pulled it down to reveal her left shoulder, which bore a similar tattoo with a line penetrated by an arrow.

'Karolina.' Fabian tried to catch her eye. 'I understand that this must be very difficult for you. But I'm afraid I have to—'

'How can I help?' Karolina looked up and met his eyes. 'Just tell me how I can help you nail that bastard.'

'If you know where he is or how we can reach—' Fabian was interrupted by the door opening and Rutger entering, out of breath.

'Mum, we need a snack. We're super hungry.'

'You'll have to sort something out yourselves. There's yoghurt and crunchy, or sandwiches if you prefer.'

'Oh, come on. Can't you? We're in the middle of Guitar—'

'No, Mummy's busy. Now leave, so we can talk.'

'Why? I'm just going to spill and—'

'Rutger!' Karolina raised a warning finger. 'You know what Dad's told you. You're not even allowed in here.'

'Are you? And what about him! No one but Dad's allowed—'

Karolina grabbed his arm roughly. 'Out. Okay?' She stood up and pushed him towards the door.

'But—'

'No buts. You either make a snack or you don't. I don't care, so long as you stay out of here. Understood?' She closed the door behind him and turned to Fabian. 'I'm sorry.' She sat back down and tried to collect herself. 'Unfortunately, I have no idea where he is. He often stays out until the small hours.'

'Maybe you have a phone number for him? The one we have is for a phone he's left here.'

'I don't know anyone with more phones than Eric. I have three in my contact list, so you could try them, though I've always suspected there are at least a couple more.' She pulled out her phone, found her husband in her contacts and handed it to Fabian, who immediately forwarded the contact information to Molander.

'I'm sorry if my questions are uncomfortable, but—'

'Please, just ask instead of apologizing all the time. I promise I'll tell you what I know.'

'Okay.' Fabian nodded. 'You said you've never had a functional love life. But surely at first you must have. So what happened around the time it ended?'

Karolina answered with a smile. 'Right. That's how it's supposed to be. All you want to do is go at it, until reality catches up. But that's not quite how it was for Eric and me.' She shook her head. 'We didn't have sex. Not once. We tried a few times, of course, but he couldn't quite rise to the occasion, and what we managed definitely can't be defined as sex.'

'So it wasn't you who—'

'Quite the reverse. I wanted nothing more and couldn't work out what was wrong.'

'Did you talk about it?'

Karolina sighed. 'I tried to bring it up a few times, but he was evasive and said he didn't want to force it. At first, I actually thought it was kind of sweet that he wasn't like everyone else, just trying to get some as quickly as possible without a thought to how I felt. But then one day when I came home earlier than usual, I found him in front of the computer, taking care of himself. It turned out his hard drive was jam-packed with absolutely horrible things he'd bought or downloaded. We'd lived together for six months at that point, and I felt like he'd been cheating on me the entire time. I flew into a rage and pulled the computer out of the wall, cables and all, and threw it off the balcony. We lived on the third floor in Västra Berga, and I hate to think how it could've turned out if someone had happened to be walking by on the street.'

'And how did he react to that?'

'He had no choice but to confess and swear that he only loved me. But I put my foot down and forced him to choose between me and the porn.'

'And he agreed.'

'Well, that hard drive was beyond salvaging, and from what I gathered, he'd spent a fortune on those films. Either way, he started seeing a sex therapist in town. I never felt particularly comfortable about him. At the same time, though, I didn't want to be the problem so I did everything I could to help Eric.'

'And what could you do?'

'That's what I wondered. It was obviously Eric's addiction, not mine. But this sex therapist seemed to think I had an important role in the process.' She sighed and shook her head. 'It was torture. The idea was for us to make incremental progress. So he gave us homework, like for Eric to sit next to me in bed and watch me pleasure myself. I don't know how I could have agreed to that. But I did. I lay there, writhing and humiliating myself like some cheap tramp so he could get it up and want to come over to me. The problem was that he never did. Instead, he just sat there and watched and sorted himself out.'

Fabian handed her another tissue.

'I did almost everything he asked me to for over a year before I'd had enough and gave up.'

'Almost? What didn't you agree to do?'

Karolina looked him in the eyes. 'Is it relevant or are you just curious?'

'As I said, I fully understand if you feel uncomfortable. But what I'm looking for is a motive, and I believe it may be found in the turning points, in a pivotal moment that might have triggered him to go from watching porn to placing hidden webcams in other people's bedrooms.'

Karolina nodded. 'He wanted to watch me have sex with someone else. That's when I said no. He was angry with me, of course, and told me I was ruining his rehab programme. But that was my line in the sand.'

'And then what happened?'

'Nothing, really.' Karolina shrugged. 'In the end, I accepted that he just couldn't do it. I should of course have left him there and then, but instead, we decided to try to have a baby through insemination. Don't ask me why, but at the time it felt like a solution to our problems.'

'And when was this?'

'2001. Rutger was born a year later.'

That was the same year Jacobsén had quit his permanent job to start his own business. Was it Karolina's refusal to let him watch her that had triggered his decision? Was that what had made him start installing hidden webcams?

It sounded improbable. But for Jacobsén, with his background in the security industry and knowledge about the latest surveillance technology, it was definitely possible.

What he hadn't found was any logical connection to Columbus. What had made him go from watching to doing? 'So in all the years you've been together, you've never had sex?'

'We did, once. Though it was more akin to rape. It was after midnight. He was down here as usual, working late. I'm usually asleep by then, but I was in the middle of *The Girl with the Dragon Tattoo* and I couldn't put it down. It was several years after it first came out. I don't normally read crime novels. They're all the same. Anyway, it was much too late and I'd finally managed to tear myself away and turn the lights off when he came into the room.' She trailed off and swallowed hard. 'I didn't feel like talking, so I pretended to be asleep. That usually works out because I tend to fall asleep within minutes. But this particular night, he came and lay down right next to me, which he normally never does. It was as though it were the first time he'd touched me. Suddenly, his hands were everywhere, on my breasts and in my knickers. I just lay there and thought, finally, it's happening. He even had an erection. So I turned over and was about to kiss him when my cheek suddenly burned. It was dark and I didn't understand what was happening at first. Then he hit me a second time and hissed at me never to look at him ever again. Then he ordered me to get on all fours. But I just lay there in some kind of shock and didn't understand what was happening. So he grabbed my arm and almost yanked it out of the socket. I had no idea he was so strong, and suddenly there I was on all fours, feeling him penetrating me. But not where he was supposed to, so eventually I tore and started bleeding. I could feel it trickling down the insides of my thighs. I asked him to stop, but he just hissed at me to shut up. That I was a dirty bitch who should shut my mouth. That's exactly what he said, then he carried on until he was done.'

'That was two years ago?'

'Yes, almost exactly, actually. Just a few days before midsummer. How did you know?'

He could have told her the film in which Wessman received much the same treatment was also two years old and that it might have been her husband's inspiration. But it would have to wait. 'And the tattoo. You had that made after the incident?'

Karolina nodded. 'My birthday is the week after midsummer and I've always wanted a tattoo. I know it's not really my style, as Eric has never failed to point out whenever I've brought it up. But then he suddenly wanted to give me one. He'd designed it himself and told me the line symbolized me and his love for me was represented by the arrow. That I was number one, the first and most important thing in his life. I thought it was his way of apologizing. But that was before I became aware I was just the first in a long line of women.'

Fabian thanked her for her help and got to his feet. Almost all his questions had been answered. The one remaining unknown was what had made Jacobsén decide to commit murder.

72

'How are you getting on? Find anything?' Lilja said, trying to stretch in the cramped space at the back of Molander's van.

'That depends on what you mean by something,' Molander replied, studying the screens, which were filled with zoomed-in audio curves, equalizers and audio clips from the recorded conversation. 'I can't find any signs of there being a little girl present.'

'What? Are you telling me she's not there?'

'No, I'm telling you I can't hear any signs of her still being alive.'

'She might be unconscious or gagged,' Klippan said.

'Or just in another room,' Lilja added, and she dropped three lumps of sugar in her tepid coffee before stirring it and knocking it back.

'Let's hope so,' Molander said. 'Speaking of rooms, I think we can skip anything we'd label a "normal room", like hotel rooms, offices, shops and residences.'

'Why?'

Molander sighed. 'It's a bit difficult to explain to a novice such as yourself.'

'Maybe you could just tell us what you've heard?'

'I don't know about heard. It's more about what I haven't heard, or, to be more precise, what I can hear in the silence.

But I obviously have no idea how well-versed you are in the wondrous science of sound waves.'

'True, but I know you're desperate to draw things out for dramatic effect. Maybe you can hold off on that until some other time, though, since we're dealing with a six-year-old girl for whom every second probably feels like several hours in hell. So, I'd appreciate it if you—'

'The acoustics of the room,' Molander cut her off. 'Or rather, the so-called reverberation time – it's unusually long. Just listen to this.'

'*What, why? She's mine. The girl belongs to me.*'

'It sounds like he's in a basement.' Lilja could tell from the look on Klippan's face that he was asking himself the same question she was. How could they have missed that?

'Exactly. A basement or some other space with a stone or concrete floor and walls that bounce the sound back instead of absorbing it.'

'I'll redirect the teams to focus on basement areas.' Klippan pulled out his radio.

'Hold on,' Lilja said. 'What other spaces do we have? It can't just be basements?'

'I would say there's two obvious places,' Molander put in. 'The Maria Church and Kärnan. They both have hard walls and high ceilings.'

'But he can't be in the church, can he?' Klippan interjected. 'Don't people come and go there all the time?'

Molander shrugged. 'I haven't been in one since my mother took me to midnight mass. Maybe there are out-of-the-way spaces. Like up on the balcony or behind the organ?'

'Klippan to Team B, over.'

'*Team B here, over.*'

'What about Kärnan?' Lilja said. 'It's the same thing there, isn't it? A lot of tourists running up and down the stairs.'

'Not at this time of day.' Molander glanced at his watch. 'It's usually fairly quiet between three and five. The tourists are getting tired and prefer to have a sit-down at a café, and the rest of us mortals are rushing to get things done before we have to race home and pick up the children and make dinner.'

'I want you to abort the search of the hotels right now and focus on the Maria Church,' Klippan said. 'Is that clear? Over.'

'*It's clear.*'

'Sounds like you go there a lot,' Lilja said.

'A few times a year, certainly. At least. There's no better place to reflect on the events of the day than at the top of the tower, gazing out across Helsingborg, Denmark and the sound.'

'I haven't been there since sixth grade. But I remember there was a person at reception to let us in, and I honestly have a hard time seeing how he would get past—'

'As often as not, that reception desk's unmanned. I guess they're in the loo or checking their Facebook or something. What do I know? I've snuck in more than once. It's hardly on me to stand there and wait, just because they can't be bothered to do their job. Am I right? Or should I feel guilty?'

Lilja didn't have time to answer. She'd already leaped out of the van and was hurrying across the cobblestones towards the terraced stairs leading up to Kärnan. There was a lift in the mountain on her left. But she'd tried that once several years ago when she'd been on crutches after crashing her

Ducati. It had taken several minutes to arrive and once the doors finally opened, they'd had to wait for more passengers to come along before it began its slow climb.

So far, none of the search teams had been through Kärnan. The reason for that was that it was at the edge of the search area, and they had erroneously assumed it would be packed with tourists. But in hindsight, it was a simply flabbergasting way of prioritizing. It was on the direct path from the playground where the girl had disappeared, and if there were doors you could close in any of the rooms in the tower, they would in fact be perfect hiding spots.

When she reached the top of the terraced stairs, she had to stop to catch her breath before she could press on up the hill towards Kärnan, the entrance of which was, to make matters worse, several storeys up and of course, began with yet another steep flight of stairs.

The lobby itself was, as Molander had suggested, empty of tourists. But he'd been wrong about the reception desk. It was in fact manned by a young girl, who had headphones on and was transfixed by something on her phone.

'Excuse me,' she said on her way to the desk. 'You don't happen to have seen a man in his forties with a little girl, by any chance?' The girl sat motionless as though hypnotized by the phone in her hand. 'Hello, I'm talking to you!' The girl only looked up when Lilja leaned across the desk and waved her hand in front of the phone.

'One adult?'

'No, I'm not buying a ticket. I'm from the police, I'm looking for—'

'The first floor is free. If you want to go all the way to the top, it's fifty kronor.'

'For God's sake, I don't want a ticket!'

'I'm sorry, I didn't hear you.' The girl pulled out one of her earbuds.

'We're looking for a man of about forty who has a little girl with him. You wouldn't happen to have let someone like that in today?'

'Um… I don't really know… Or wait, yes, actually. A man and a little girl. Was he wearing a green top?'

Lilja hurried up the spiral stone staircase to the first floor, which was empty. As were the second and third. On the fourth floor, the door to the tower was closed, and when she tried it, it turned out to be locked as well.

It was a heavy wooden door, likely ancient and of significant cultural interest. But it couldn't be helped. She pulled her gun out of her shoulder holster and was aiming it at the lock when she heard the faint sound of a child crying, echoing down the stairwell behind her.

This time, she didn't run; she crept up the stairs as silently as possible. By the time she reached the top, she'd lost count of the number of floors she'd passed.

She could clearly hear the sound of a crying child through the crack in the door that stood slightly ajar, and before any more seconds of suffering could tick by, she threw open the door to the tower and aimed her gun at the man in the green top who was kneeling down, blowing on his son's arm in an attempt to console him.

73

The woman who stepped through the entrance doors and looked around before moving forward and taking a queueing number bore an undeniable resemblance to Dunja Hougaard. The hair, the clothes and that ghastly bag were just a few of the similarities. If she would just turn around and look up at the CCTV camera so he could see her face…

Cheap fucking Swedes, thinking they could get away with one lousy camera in a lobby of that size. The angle diagonally from above was nothing but a bad joke.

At least he could study her gait, though unfortunately it didn't match Dunja's at all. While she would somehow glide across the floor and suddenly appear in a different spot, this woman moved with unusually marked, almost militant steps.

She also looked taller than Dunja, who wasn't even five foot six. He backed up the tape and paused it when the woman passed the wall-mounted height strip. Despite wearing worn trainers, she reached well into the red field, which indicated a height of around five foot eleven.

Kim Sleizner felt a pang of disappointment, though he was far from giving up. It didn't matter how long he'd have to sit here and go through endless CCTV tapes, he wasn't going to stop until he found her.

His concern had been completely warranted. She hadn't taken a long vacation to lick her wounds. She hadn't moved because she wanted a bigger flat or a fresh start. No, the little piss cunt had deliberately gone off grid with one single goal in her sights.

Where it hurts the most, she'd written. *When he least expected it.*

She'd given him the finger, in writing, lured him straight into her trap and with a taunting laugh showed him she was in charge now.

The visit to her flat had been utterly humiliating, and it was the last time he was going to allow himself to underestimate her. From here on in, it was on.

Total war.

The first step was to find her, which had turned out to be easier said than done. The little bitch had been surprisingly smart, had made sure to cut all ties to her former life. But no one could vanish without a trace. Not even Dunja, short of being burned on the stake like the witch she was.

If anyone had the means to find her, it was him. His authority was going to come in handy, coupled with his extensive network and the hold he'd made sure to have on some of his contacts.

The questions he'd spent the greater part of the past twenty-four hours pondering were how she'd managed not to use any of her credit cards, where she was getting her money and, above all, how.

He'd found the answer to the first question at the Tax Agency. With the help of director Kai Mosedahl, he'd gained access to all her tax information. Since Kai was also a member of the Club, he had as much of an interest as the rest of the group in stopping her once and for all.

The police in Helsingør had paid her over five hundred thousand kronor in a lump sum. It was a shockingly large sum for a shitty provincial station. But, of course, it must have been that obese doughball Ib Sveistrup, who wasn't man enough to say no to a woman.

The money hadn't been deposited in her usual account with Danske Bank. It hadn't been paid into a Danish account at all, which explained why he hadn't discovered it sooner. Instead, the bank's head of security, his old colleague Ryan Frellesen, had been able to trace the money to an account in one of their Swedish branches on the other side of the sound in Malmö.

It had been considerably more difficult to get information out of them, but eventually he'd succeeded. It turned out she'd made one withdrawal. No more, no less. One withdrawal, of the entire amount, less than a week earlier.

That told him two important things.

First, she had help from the outside. Someone who wasn't just willing to lend her money, but who was also well-versed in going off grid. Her own skills were nowhere near up to what she was doing right now.

Secondly, she must have been recorded by the bank's CCTV cameras, which Frellesen had graciously provided a link to.

The withdrawal had taken place the Wednesday before at 12.33 at Danske Bank's branch on Neptunigatan in Malmö; with such an exact time, it shouldn't have been hard to find her. But apparently, it was.

Part of the explanation was that in order to take out such

a large sum in cash, you couldn't just stroll into a branch, take a ticket and wait for a free teller. You had to book an appointment several days in advance to give the bank a chance to prepare. The withdrawal itself wouldn't have taken place at the tills, either, but in one of the meeting rooms at the back; he hadn't managed to get a link to those cameras.

There was no information on when she'd entered the bank, so to be on the safe side he'd scrutinized the footage from the entrance camera for two full hours before until one hour after the withdrawal. He'd pressed pause several times, reversed and zoomed in to make sure he hadn't missed her. But his hours in front of the screen hadn't turned up shit.

She hadn't been let in through a staff entrance either, if the branch manager was to be believed. But maybe he wasn't the right person to talk to. Sure, there was a rule that said customers could under no circumstances use the staff entrance. But he hadn't personally served her, so in reality, he had no fucking—

He realized she could just as easily have been helped by someone unconnected with the bank. He sat back down. Of course that was how it'd been done.

He woke up his computer and pulled the time marker to fifteen minutes before the withdrawal. The surveillance footage started playing; he once again watched the customers pass in and out of the front doors. This time, it wasn't the women he studied, but the men. But none of them jumped out at him.

The time marker passed the time of the withdrawal; he decided to give it another half an hour before giving up. But he never got that far. Just six minutes later, he spotted a man with a backpack, leaving. He was short, didn't even reach the yellow field on the height indicator.

He recognized the man, an Indian, from twenty minutes earlier, when he'd entered the bank, without a backpack. Now he just needed to look for the backpack entering, which took him no more than a few minutes.

It was only when he paused the clip and zoomed in that he realized the woman carrying the backpack through the lobby really was Dunja. No wonder he'd missed her.

Her heavy boots, worn jeans and camouflage top had been enough to redirect his attention to all the other women. Her hair was shaved now, too; if not for the lipstick and large earrings, he would have taken her for a cancer victim.

He had his answers, but they were anything but uplifting. What he had somehow sensed and suspected all along had been confirmed, and then some. She not only had money, she was also being helped by some little cunt Indian, and unless the grainy image was misleading, she even looked fitter.

Even so, he felt excited. He'd managed to find her. Granted, only for a few seconds in CCTV footage. But he was on her trail now, and that was usually all that was needed.

74

It was finally happening. Finally, he could feel it growing again. Especially when he squeezed it. When he did that, he could even see the veins swell like fat, writhing worms around it. Another minute and he'd be ready.

Just like he'd hoped, the little girl had calmed down and stopped her silly attempts at freeing herself, not to mention that screaming that had almost driven him over the edge. The rag in her mouth had muffled it a bit, but not made it any less annoying. No wonder it had taken him so long to recover.

At home on the sofa, watching his films, it almost never took more than a few minutes. But then, this was real. The little girl wasn't on TV. She was lying right in front of him, staring wide-eyed. No wonder he was a bit nervous.

He was pulling out the tube of lubricant when his ears caught a distant sound, like a fire cracker. He turned around but couldn't see what it was. Maybe it was just those construction workers, still at it. That was probably it. He mustn't get nervous all over again. Mustn't think too much. He did that a lot, and it was never good. Never ever.

He tugged on it a few times and decided it was ready. It was now or never. He gently put his free hand on her. She flinched and started whimpering again behind the tape.

Goddamn whimpering. She was probably spoiled about always getting her way.

But she would like it soon enough. He was sure of it. After all, this was like a gift for her, too. In just a minute or two, she would be enjoying herself, just like him. And why wouldn't she? He took her virginity and in exchange, she took his. What could be more beautiful?

He lubed it up, wiped his hands clean of the gloop and grabbed her hips.

'Let go of her and get down on the ground with your arms and legs out!'

He turned towards the voice and saw a woman aiming a gun at him.

'I said let go of her and get down on the floor!'

How had she got there? How had she found him? He didn't understand. But it didn't matter. Nothing mattered. No one was going to disturb him now that they were about to have such a lovely time. Afterwards, when he was finished, he was going to give her a taste of his stabby knife.

Then he heard that bang again, a bit louder but still far away, almost as though it was coming from somewhere else entirely. As though maybe he hadn't heard it at all. It was only when he saw the blood seeping out of the wound in the side of his stomach that he realized he must've been shot. But it didn't hurt. He almost couldn't feel it, and he had no problem starting what they'd both been longing for for so long.

Finally… Finally he was enjoying his reward for waiting a whole lifetime. And how he enjoyed it. Not to mention the little girl. He could feel her wanting him. Wanting him and not being able to get enough.

Maybe there was another bang. He didn't really know. But he had another wound now that didn't hurt, even though he could see the blood pumping out of him, streaming down towards his crotch and making his scrotum all red and sticky.

But wait… Something wasn't right. Something was all wrong. He didn't understand. He wasn't even inside her. Was that why it had been so easy? Try as he might, he couldn't see it with all the blood. He couldn't even feel it.

And then there was that damn sound again. Why couldn't they just leave him alone? This was supposed to be his moment. He hadn't even had a chance to kill her. That's what the voices had told him. That it was the most important thing, after he was done.

He was supposed to use the water. That's what the voices had told him. He was supposed to dunk her in the water. But there was no time, not with that idiot in the room. Instead, it was going to have to be the hatchet lying next to her. He snatched it up and raised it in the air as the woman with the gun screamed. But he couldn't hear what she said, and though he didn't understand how it happened, the entire stone floor suddenly flipped over and hit him hard in the back of the head.

75

Lasagne was really more Sonja's dish than Fabian's. No one could make lasagne like her. He personally felt it required too many steps before it was finally in the oven, and then you were left with utter kitchen chaos. All the same, he'd decided to give it a go. Maybe the smell would find its way to the bedroom and cheer her up.

Having convinced Karolina Jacobsén that the best thing she could do was to take the two boys to her parents in Växjö, he'd put the house under surveillance in case Eric came back. Then he'd gone home, expecting Sonja to be up and about again and busy making some kind of dinner.

But as though nothing could change her state of mind, she'd still been in bed with the curtains closed. It was the second day in a row, and he was beginning to feel concerned that she was headed straight for a severe depression if nothing changed.

Theodor's closed door had, as usual, done little to keep his death music from reverberating through the entire house. When Fabian knocked and opened the door, he discovered a maelstrom of dirty underwear, pizza boxes with dried-up leftovers, stained sheets, drink cans, crisp and sweet bags, CDs and DVDs, *snus* tins and gaming controllers.

Theodor had been sitting in front of his screen in the middle of the mayhem, dressed in boxer shorts and a vest top, breaking uncountable traffic rules to get away from the howling police cars. He'd been struck by how big his son was. Not big as in grown-up but as in pudgy. He, who'd always been so thin they'd had to mix cream into his food. Now he was borderline overweight and so pale the spots shone like brake lights on his face.

But he hadn't said a word about any of it, had simply stepped inside and calmly opened the window. Then he'd turned the stereo down and asked Theodor to go and have a shower and then come down and help with dinner. But Theodor had been too engrossed in his escape from the police to respond.

He'd wanted nothing more than to turn off both the music and the computer and have a serious talk about how things couldn't go on like this. About how it was time for Theodor to face up to what he'd done, difficult as that may be. But he needed Sonja to back him up; as long as they weren't in agreement and she stayed shut up in their bedroom, his hands were tied.

He indulged in a glass of wine and decided to put on music for company instead. He went for The Orb's first album, a double disc from the early nineties with a title so long he'd never managed to learn it.

The sampled girl's voice in 'Little Fluffy Clouds' made him think of Matilda. She wasn't home, and that certainly didn't feel good, considering she'd only been discharged a few days ago. That neither Sonja nor Theodor seemed to have any idea where she might be did nothing to reassure him either.

But halfway through making dinner, just as he'd located the nutmeg in the jumble of old spice bags in the cupboard and started grating it into the béchamel, he thought he heard her voice. To make sure it wasn't part of The Orb's soaring audio collage, he turned the stereo down, and yes, that was Matilda he could hear in the basement.

He took the pan off the heat, hurried down the stairs and was met by a piece of red cloth blocking his path. In a way, he was surprised, though he should have known this is where she'd be. He was not, however, relieved.

On the other side of the red sheet, a handful of flickering candles cast twisting shadows of Matilda and her friend Esmaralda. When he took a step closer, he could see Matilda through a small gap in the improvised curtain, sitting across from Esmaralda with her back towards him.

She blocked most of his view, but it wasn't difficult to guess that they were sitting on either side of the Ouija board with their fingers on the pointer that was supposed to move across the row of letters to spell out words.

'I think she's ready,' Esmaralda said.

'Okay, let's do it,' Matilda said, clearing her throat. 'Greta,' she continued, now in a solemn voice that sounded several years older than her normal one. 'Exactly a month and a day ago, you claimed a member of my family was going to pass away. I came very close but survived. Now I need to know if you meant me and something went wrong or if it was my brother or one of my parents.'

The silence after she stopped speaking was so thick with the girls' expectations it was almost tangible. Or was it him? Did he actually believe the pointer would start moving and give them an answer? Was that why he didn't just rip down the curtain and ask them to stop that nonsense? He, who didn't believe in ghosts, spirits or whatever they were supposed to be.

'Why isn't she answering?' Matilda said, sounding like herself again.

'Maybe she doesn't want to?'

'What do you mean, doesn't want to? She can't just give us half the story and then clam up.'

'Of course she can. That's the whole point. They can do whatever they want. That's why you can never provoke them.'

'Esma, what are you doing? You can't take your hand away.'

'Are you really sure you want to do this?'

'Yes, I am. We've talked about this. You can't chicken out now.'

Esmaralda tilted her head; he caught a quick glimpse of her behind Matilda. 'Fine, one more try. But just one. Then I have to go home. Greta, are you in here with us?'

Fabian leaned forward but could only see a small section of the Ouija board.

'Look, at least she's still here,' Matilda said.

'Greta, do you feel like answering Matilda's question? If not, you can just say no.'

'Is someone in my family still going to die?'

After a few seconds of silent anticipation, Matilda turned fractionally to her left while moving her right arm in the same direction, and when he got up on tiptoe, he could see the pointer on the board underneath their fingertips.

'An A,' Matilda said. 'See. She does want to answer.'

'But who in your family has a name that starts with an A?'

'Mum… Her middle name's actually Antonia…'

He could tell Matilda was on the verge of falling apart, so he decided to step in and end the séance, but before he could act, he saw the pointer actually moving across the board.

'An L,' Matilda exclaimed. 'See?'

It looked like it was moving quickly.

'Then it can't be Mum.'

'And now another L,' Esmaralda said. 'Could it be someone else's middle name?'

'Not that starts with ALL. Something's not right. Greta, are you spelling out a name, or—'

'Wait, there's more,' Esmaralda cut in.

So quickly they seemed hard-pressed to keep up.

'YOU,' Matilda said. 'ALL YOU? What does she mean by that?'

He could hear the pointer was still zooming across the board and if the girls were to be believed, it was spelling out intelligible words.

'ALL YOU KNOW,' Matilda exclaimed. What does she mean, ALL YOU KNOW?'

'You have to calm down. You're just making her cross.'

'Greta, can you please just answer my question? Is someone in my family still going to die, or did you make a mistake?'

'Matilda, have you forgotten what happened last time? When you broke all the rules and—'

'But something's not right. She's not answering and I have to—'

'The only thing you have to do is listen to me! I'm leading this séance, not you! See, she's not done. Are you paying attention? An I. And an S. I'm guessing it's IS.'

'ALL YOU KNOW IS,' Matilda said and Fabian could see her shaking her head. 'I don't get it. Do you?'

Esmaralda shushed her. 'W, R, O, N and a G.'

'WRONG,' they said in unison. 'ALL YOU KNOW IS WRONG.'

They waited for the pointer to keep moving, but it didn't.

'Greta, if you're done, would you mind explaining what you mean?' Matilda said.

'Maybe we misunderstood last time. Maybe that's what she's trying to tell us.'

'What do you mean, misunderstood? There was nothing to misunderstand. I'm telling you, something's not right here. She said, I know she said, someone in my—'

'But did she? What if we just—'

'Esma, don't even. You know as well as I do what she said. Hello? Greta, are you still there? Are you still with us?'

They waited, but nothing happened. The pointer had stopped.

All you know is wrong.

Fabian repeated the words inwardly. The pointer had moved across the board. He'd seen it with his own eyes. Could it have been Esmaralda deliberately guiding it to try to reassure Matilda? To help her to put all the death and misery behind her? But if that was the case, why wouldn't she have spelled out *I was wrong*? Or simply *no one*.

All you know is wrong.

The explanation was, of course, that the pointer moved so easily across the board the girls were unaware that they were in fact the ones moving it.

All you know is wrong.

And this particular time, chance had made the letters form a full sentence that could possibly help to reassure Matilda.

All you know is...

He hadn't even noticed the sheet being pulled aside. Suddenly, Matilda was just standing there, pointing at him.

'I told you something was off.'

76

Lilja dropped her clothes on the floor, stepped into the shower, which had been on for a while to warm up, filled one hand with shower gel and started washing off her make-up under the hot jet. She was fully aware there were special make-up removal products, but she didn't keep things like that at home and, if she knew herself, she never would.

For the first time in her career, the newspapers had called her a hero following her arrest of Assar Skanås. She'd gone from being the left-wing extremist pointed out by Sievert Landertz to the protector of the city, the reason people felt safe letting their children play in parks again.

But hero and protector was the last thing she felt like. Her face was still tender where Hampus had struck her, and the hot water, coupled with her lack of sleep over the past few days, was helping tiredness triumph over anger. It was only quarter past eight, half eight at most. And yet she would have no problem falling asleep standing up in the shower.

She'd been running on fumes for the past few days, with Skanås evading them and making them look like fools. At least he was now in intensive care and would likely have a colostomy bag for the rest of his life and would never be able to get it up again, no matter how randy he felt.

She could have aimed for his shins, but she hadn't, even though that was exactly what she was going to claim in the impending investigation. It was hardly her fault he'd suddenly bent over just as she pulled the trigger. Guilty was the last thing she felt. Whatever she'd done to Skanås, it would never come close to the trauma Ester Landgren must have gone through. And what would have happened if she'd found them five minutes later didn't bear thinking about.

Tomorrow, when she was rested, she was going to take the day off and check some things off her personal to-do list. Like making sure the bank transferred half the money from her joint account with Hampus to her private savings account. They only had eleven thousand seven hundred and forty-three kronor, but what's right is right.

She was also going to have a look at that one-bed she'd found down on Carl Krook's Gata in town. It wasn't her favourite part of Helsingborg. But at least it was central, and the woman who'd answered when she called had sounded really nice and had even been willing to lower the asking price if she would consider signing a two-year contract. And given that it was available that Sunday, it could hardly get better.

Until then, she'd considered sleeping on a mattress in her office. That's what she usually did when she left Hampus. But this time, she'd decided not to disappear before the moving men came. This time, it was real, and once the penny dropped for Hampus, he'd be capable of anything. Like cutting up her clothes or selling or even burning her furniture.

As soon as he got back around five, she was going to grab the bull by the horns and tell him. Straight up, with no extraneous bickering, she would explain to him exactly what the rest of the week would look like. That he could sleep either on the sofa or wherever he pleased, so long as it wasn't in her bed. That they were going to have as little to do with each other as they could until she moved out, and that the kitchen was hers at breakfast, while he was free to use it for the rest of the day and night.

The problem was, he hadn't come back at five. He still wasn't home, which meant he was out trying to drown his guilty conscience at Pallas. In a way, avoiding the confrontation was nice; she certainly wasn't going to wait up until he came home all drunk and needy. Instead, she was going to catch up on sleep and make sure she was out of the house by the time he woke up.

Everything was ready. The letter in which she'd written everything she'd planned to tell him in big, clear letters, to make sure he couldn't miss any of it, even if he was still seeing double. All his clothes, which she'd removed from the bedroom and placed neatly in the armchair so he couldn't use them as an excuse to sneak in when he got back. The breakfast that was ready and waiting in the fridge and the thermos with scalding hot coffee.

To dot the final i, she turned on the floor lamp and aimed it at the letter. Then she went into the bedroom, crawled into bed and set the alarm on her phone for half five.

Hampus stepped through the front door twenty minutes later, but Lilja was already too asleep to notice anything other than her own dreams. Not even her phone on the bedside table managed to cut through the oblivion when, an hour later, it lit up and emitted the sound that meant she'd received a text message.

Soon, the little Jew cunt is going to be crying blood. Soon…

77

Fabian put on an oven glove and took the lasagne out. 'Matilda, could you go upstairs and let your mother and Theo know dinner's ready?'

'Mm…' said Matilda, who was still sulking about him listening in on their séance.

He'd tried to convince her Greta was probably completely indifferent to his presence. He, who didn't even believe in spirits. And he'd tried to persuade her that the words *All you know is wrong* was simply her way of telling them they'd misunderstood her words a month ago or that she'd been mistaken herself, and that there was nothing to worry about.

But she hadn't bought his arguments, and to be honest, he wasn't sure he did either. Somehow, you just couldn't get around the fact that the whole thing was very strange.

All you know is wrong.

His own explanation about it being a random string of letters didn't add up either. And if it wasn't that, what was it?

What's for dinner?

He read the text from Theo and replied *Lasagne* and added a small *Come on. It's going to be delicious. And nice :)*

'Matilda, go and let Mum know.'

'Oh my God, nag much? Calm down.'

'I'm completely calm, but the food's getting cold.'

I'll skip it, have a sandwich or whatever later.

The text was so typical of his son. A nonchalant shrug to signal just how little he cared.

No, Theo, you won't, he wrote as quickly as he could. *You're going to come down, and you're going to have dinner with the rest of your family. And you're going to do it now.*

'If it's that important, why don't you go yourself?' Matilda said.

Don't think so. PS: Might be a bit late for the whole authoritarian father bit.

Fabian left the kitchen without replying, climbed the stairs in a few steps and threw open Theodor's door. 'Who the fuck do you think you are?' he said as he entered the room, where Theo was sitting on the desk, smoking by the open window. 'And what have we said about smoking?' He snatched the cigarette out of his son's mouth and ground it out against the desktop.

'What have we said about knocking?' Theodor blew out the smoke as though he couldn't care less about Fabian being there.

'Don't you think I know what you're doing? Huh? Don't you think I can see right through you and your little play-acting now you have Mummy on your side?'

Theodor heaved a sigh.

'You seem to think you can do whatever you want. That the coast's clear because Mum's too tired to take this conflict. But this isn't working.'

'What do you mean, not working? What the fuck are you on about?'

'This! What the fuck did you think I was talking about?' Fabian spread his hands. 'Shutting yourself up in here, incapable of doing anything other than play video games, eat crisps and get fatter and fatter. Not even trying to hide the cigarette when you're caught smoking. The stench when you open the door and step into this pigsty. I'm talking about you, Theo! You and the self-pitying fucking martyr's act you're apparently going in for.'

'Right. Okay. You done?'

'No, I'm not. Far from it. And I want you to look at me when I'm talking to you.' He grabbed Theodor's chin and forced him to meet his eyes. 'There are limits, and you've crossed so many I've had enough.'

'Right, that's sad for you, I guess.'

'And you! Primarily you. Because from now on, you will face the consequences of your decisions.'

'What do you mean, my decisions?! The whole problem is I didn't have a choice!'

'You always have a choice. And you chose to pull up your hood and join them instead of coming to me.'

'To you?'

'Yes, to me! If you had done, we could have arrested them before they took another life.'

'Who the fuck are you trying to fool?' Theodor wrenched free of Fabian's grasp. 'As if I've ever been able to come to you for help.'

Fabian took a few deep breaths in an attempt to regain a modicum of composure. 'Maybe I've been naïve, but I've actually always felt you could come to me. And of course it hurts to be told I was wrong about that all this time. To be told how bad I've been at making you feel like I'm always there for you. But unlike you, at least I can accept that without feeling a need to blame everyone else. Those were my choices. If I could do it over, a lot of things would have been different, believe me. What I can control, though, are the choices I make now and in the future. And one of them is that I've decided to try to become a better dad who's there for you. Maybe it's too late. But better late than never. That's why I'm nagging you about family dinner. That's why I'm standing here now, even though you want nothing more than to throw me out of here and the stench is making me feel sick. I've also decided not to accept you sinking further and further into depression.'

'When you're depressed, you're depressed.' Theodor shrugged. 'You can't just choose for it to be over.'

'No, but you can choose to handle it the right way, instead of pretending like nothing's happening.'

'What do you mean, the right way? There's no right way in this fucking—'

'There is, actually, and it starts with the truth!'

Theodor was struggling with a growing lump in his throat. 'And then what? After I tell them?' he said in a voice so brittle it sounded like it was about to break. 'Then what happens? What happens to me?'

Fabian considered how to respond but never got the chance.

'Theo, no one here has the answers, no one can tell you exactly what's going to happen.'

Fabian turned around and saw Sonja in the doorway.

'What Dad's trying to tell you is that there are no alternatives.'

'But you said I didn't have to if I didn't want to. That it was up to me, if I—'

'Yes, I know I said that. But I've thought about this for almost two days, and I've realized Dad's right. Much as we might want to, we can't pretend nothing happened. It's going to haunt you until you face up to it, once and for all.'

For the first time since Fabian could remember, he and Sonja were standing united. He grabbed her hand and squeezed it in silent gratitude.

Theodor looked back and forth between them while he struggled with the lump in his throat. Silence fell. A silence that neither Fabian nor Sonja wanted to break by saying the wrong thing.

The thoughts Theodor was struggling with seemed to hurt so badly he could fall apart any second. But instead, he dried his eyes and nodded. 'Okay, then let's do that,' he said. 'We'll go tomorrow and have that dinner after I take a shower.'

Fabian wanted to hug his son and say something encouraging about how it was all going to work out, but he only managed a smile and a nod.

78

Exhausted as she was when she went to bed, Lilja had been convinced she'd be wide awake the moment Hampus stuck his key in the lock and opened the front door. Then she would lie awake, listening to every step he took outside her bedroom door.

Moving quietly wasn't his strong suit. Especially after a wet night at Pallas. On those nights, he was more like a badger that had just found its way into the bins.

But this time, she hadn't woken up. Maybe she'd been too tired after all. Or maybe he'd been so incredibly careful not to wake her he'd actually succeeded. In that case, it was on account of his guilty conscience, and if she knew him at all, there would be no trace of that left once he'd sobered up.

But... She was awake now. Wasn't she? Or was she in fact still asleep?

She reached for her phone on the bedside table to check the time but found she couldn't get to it; it was as though someone had pulled the table away from the bed. Or was it just that her arm wasn't moving? It was hard to say.

Either way, both her wrists and ankles hurt, and her mouth of all places. As though she were tied up, but she wasn't. At least, not as far as she could make out. And what was that smell? It was so overpowering she was starting to feel dizzy and was finding it increasingly difficult to focus her eyes.

That must have been what had woken her. What the fuck was he up to? She didn't understand and tried to get up but couldn't; it was as if something was holding her down.

Then she heard laughing. Or maybe it was more like snickering and whispering. And that hissing sound. Yes... What the fuck. Suddenly, she understood.

It was the smell of spray paint.

But why?

She tried again to sit up but only managed to lift her head a little. That was enough, however, to see that Hampus and two of his mates were busy spraying a giant swastika across one of the bedroom walls. She yelled at them to stop, but only indistinct mumbling came out.

One of the two other blokes turned around and pointed at her. 'Look, she's awake.'

Hampus turned around with a spray can in one hand and laughed so hard the *snus* under his lip slid down his teeth. 'Hey, babes! Daddy's home.' He nodded towards the swastika. 'Like it? Looks good, doesn't it? I figured, what the hell, might as well go all in, then we'll see how fast the house sells.'

'Hampus, where's the bog?' one of the others asked.

'Are you blind? Right there in the corner, obviously,' Hampus replied and resumed spraying red paint while his mate laughingly unzipped his trousers, walked over to a corner and started pissing so hard it spattered the walls.

Was he high or what was this? She tried to yell at them again to stop, but the only thing that came out of her mouth was saliva.

'I'm sorry, did I hear a squeak from over there?' Hampus turned to her again and put a hand behind his ear. 'Hm, I guess not. You're usually so good at talking back and spewing politically correct arguments until you get exactly what you want. But you're not so cocky now, are you? Not the big bad detective now. You know what? You're almost kind of cute, lying there, mumbling, wondering what the fuck's going on.' He stepped on to the bed and straddled her. 'You think you can get rid of me, just like that? That all you have to do is write some letter and then you're out? Let me tell you, it's not quite that easy. Because no matter how badly you want to fuck that Fabian Risk or whatever his name is—' He shook the spray can, threw off her duvet... '—you belong to me!'... and started spraying her pyjamas. First two red circles around each breast, then a dot in the middle of each one. 'Aren't you the one who's always refusing to wear make-up? Apart from when you've been taught a lesson, of course. Look how pretty she looks with a bit of paint.' Hampus kept spraying lower.

She tried to break free, but could only watch as he sprayed a belly button, a thinner waist and hips extending on to the bedcover.

'Blimey, you actually look pretty fit. Hey, come over here and have a look.' He drew a vagina between her legs.

One of the other men came up behind her head. 'Wow, she looks well up for it.' He leaned over her and squeezed her spray-painted breasts so hard it hurt.

Hampus tossed the spray can aside. 'Almost makes you want to have some real fun.' He grabbed her pyjama top and ripped it open; she could hear the buttons hit the floor.

She'd given up her attempts to scream and was instead

squeezing her eyes shut in the hope that the nightmare would end. It didn't. Instead, she felt him tear off her pyjama bottoms and stroke the inside of her thigh. This isn't happening, was the only thought she could manage.

Hampus had a dark side, she knew that, but this was something else. This just couldn't be true. But when she felt him pushing a finger into her, she realized hope was futile.

'She's waking up,' said a voice that sounded neither like Hampus nor either of the others, and she finally pieced it together. 'Should we give her another dose?'

She'd been dreaming. It wasn't Hampus and his mates. She was waking up now, only to realize that the reality she was in was, if possible, even worse.

'No, why?' said another voice. 'We're practically done.'

Even though she didn't really want to look, she opened her eyes, and it was in fact not Hampus straddling her, pulling out his finger to sniff it. It was Adolf Hitler, or someone wearing a Hitler mask. Someone with a beard and long hair who was dressed in a tattered denim waistcoat, showing the Terminator tattoo that reached all the way up his neck.

'What do you reckon?' said the other Hitler mask who was leaning over her, squeezing her breast with a hand that was missing a middle finger. 'Isn't it about time to pop this Jewish cunt's cherry?'

'Almost, but not quite,' said a third man outside her field of vision. 'We have to leave something to look forward to.'

'Be seeing you.' The man straddling her climbed off the bed, laughing all the while, and left with the others.

Lilja stayed where she was, not daring to do anything other than look around at the spray-painted swastikas on her walls.

79

While waiting for Theodor to come down after his shower, the lasagne went back in the oven and Fabian sat in the kitchen with Sonja and Matilda, chatting idly. Every once in a while, Sonja laughed at something Matilda said, and occasionally he tried to put on a smile, too. But he found it difficult; it mostly felt like an uncomfortable rictus.

In a way, he should be relieved. Sonja and he were finally on the same page and together they'd knocked some sense into Theodor. There was no doubt that going over to Helsingør and contacting the Danish prosecutor was the right thing to do. But his concern about what would happen after that was still there like a festering ulcer. Also, it had been almost fifteen minutes, and he didn't know anyone who showered as quickly as Theodor.

'I'm going to see how he's doing.' He stood up and left the table. 'Why don't you start?'

'No, let's wait until we're all here,' Sonja said, topping up her wineglass.

When he reached the upper landing, he walked up to the closed bathroom door and listened to the sound of running water coming from inside.

Was this in fact what had caused his concern? He hadn't considered it before, but even so he didn't feel surprised in the slightest. The shower was on, but the sound of it made the floor vanish from underneath him.

Was it his fault? Had he pushed too hard? Or had Theodor been right, was it too late? Unanswerable questions bombarded him while he dug a coin out of his pocket and with trembling hands managed to turn the lock and open the bathroom door. Maybe they should have taken Sonja's advice and pretended nothing had happened.

Freezing cold water that hadn't made it down the half-clogged drain and had instead overflowed and flooded the bathroom floor soaked his socks. But that was the least of his concerns as he stuck his head in the jet, turned the tap off and hurried over to the open window.

It was too long a drop to jump. Theodor had probably shimmied down the drainpipe right next to the window. Where he'd gone after that was, however, a question with virtually endless possible answers.

The door to the garden shed stood ajar, which suggested he'd taken his bike. Which in turn meant he'd already made it far enough that it would be hard to find him if he didn't want to be found. That insight drained his legs of strength and he had to lean against the washbasin not to lose his balance.

But this wasn't the time to fall apart. That was the last thing he could afford to do right now. With each minute that slipped through his fingers, his son got another third of a mile away. Grief and soul-searching would have to wait if he wanted to have any chance at all.

He hurried out of the bathroom and down the stairs. 'Theo's run away,' he called out to the others. 'You'll have to eat without me. I'll call when I know anything.' Sonja shouted something after him, but he didn't have time to hear what it was before he was out of the door and on his way across the street.

His hands were shaking so hard he had to use both to get the key into the ignition and turn it, still without any clue as to which direction to go.

Theodor had no friends he could just pedal over to without warning. Sadly, he only seemed to have made one good friend since they moved here. In other words, there was no point wasting time in their own neighbourhood or the area around the school.

Going south towards the city centre seemed the most obvious choice. But that assumed there was someone he could meet up with there. Otherwise, the train or ferries to Denmark could be his goal.

But fleeing the country cost money and required some kind of plan, and Theodor had neither. This wasn't a premeditated getaway. It was an emotional reaction. To the panic and fear of what awaited him in that courtroom. In fact, if there was one place in the world he wouldn't want to go to right now, it was probably Denmark.

Based on that reasoning, Fabian decided to go in the opposite direction, towards Pålsö, while he fought to suppress the thoughts that had been gnawing at him for the past few hours and were now threatening to overwhelm him.

He took a right on Johan Banérs Gata and then a left on to Romares Väg with Pålsjö Forest on his left.

He didn't even believe in the supernatural. That there were spirits on the other side with the ability to see the future, and that all you needed to communicate with them was a board with letters on it. For him, the future had always simply been the result of various chain reactions in which one consequence led to another.

Without any real thought as to why, he turned left on to Christer Boijes Väg at the roundabout and continued past the crematorium with its moat and into Pålsjö Forest, whose dense foliage effectively blacked out the bright summer night.

Even so, he found he couldn't dismiss Matilda's concern. It was real, there was no question. She'd clearly felt it a month ago but hadn't been able to tell them before being shot in the stomach and collapsing on the floor. When she woke up in the hospital after all those surgeries, it was the first thing she'd wanted to talk about.

If she had survived, who in the family was going to die?

The bike path ran alongside the road on the right, further into the trees, but he saw neither a bike light nor anything else to suggest he was on the right track.

Science, logic, common sense told him he should dismiss it. But much as he wanted to, he couldn't ignore the theme that had run through Theodor's whole life from his first school years all the way to the present.

Everything required to explain and understand was there, in hindsight. All the actions and consequences that over the years had colluded to paint him so far into a corner he could no longer see the way out.

Supernatural or not. What difference did it make?

If someone had asked Fabian, he wouldn't have been able to give a good explanation. There were no sound arguments or rational reasons for suddenly slamming the brakes so hard the tyres screeched, making a U-turn and going back a few hundred feet before turning right on to the gravel path and continuing straight into the forest. All he knew was that he'd taken a wrong turn but that he was now on the right path.

He drove down towards the Pålsjö Pavilion, a café that despite its impossible location in the middle of the woods was routinely filled to capacity with waffle-munching customers the moment the sun peeked out. He'd been there three times with Theodor and every time they'd had to wait for a table. Now it was empty and deserted. No customers. No staff. No Theodor.

And yet he didn't hesitate for a moment. It was as though he knew, despite there being no way of knowing.

Fifty yards later, he turned left, and after another few hundred yards he reached the pedestrian bridge crossing the train tracks.

It was as deserted as the café. The night had filled the cutting with so much mist the two tracks that ran past thirty feet below were impossible to see. He couldn't even see the other end of the bridge. Everything was shrouded; he only spotted Theodor's bike on the ground when he reached the middle of the bridge.

He'd found the place, but was he too late? While Theodor had cycled straight here along the extension of Pålsjögatan, he'd taken the long way round, circling half the forest.

'Theodor?' he shouted into the mist. 'Theodor, are you there?'

But the only reply was the echo of his own desperate voice, which subsided and grew increasingly diffuse and unclear the further away it retreated. It was as though he was listening to his own grief at the realization that his worst fears had become reality.

Something moved behind him. He turned around to see better, but with the dense mist all he could make out was a movement in the shadows. But there was something there. Something hovering in the air five or ten feet out from the bridge proper.

He walked up to the railing, which had been augmented with a tall fence whose top two feet angled outward to make it difficult for people who wanted to end things. That had clearly not deterred his son. Because there he was, or rather, there was his shadow.

It was only when he looked down and saw the metal wing jutting out above the tracks from the middle of the bridge that he started piecing it together. His son was perched at the tip of the wing, which didn't look strong enough to support a full-grown person. Clearly Theodor was light enough, however, despite his recent weight gain.

The mist cleared for a moment and Fabian could see him sitting there, dangling his feet, waiting for the next train.

'Theodor,' he said, trying hard not to let fear shade his voice. 'Theodor, sweetheart. Why don't you come here so we can talk about it instead?'

'There's nothing to talk about. Go home to your family and let me take care of this.'

'But you are my family. Hey… please, come here.'

'I'm a freak, that's what I am. A fucking freak.'

'No, Theo, you're not—' He was cut off by the sound he knew so well from his years in Stockholm. There, it was so ubiquitous he had eventually stopped registering it, except for when it had been so loud he'd had to cover his ears. Out here, the barely perceptible yet so very ominous whispering of the rails was enough to unnerve him completely.

'Please, come here!' He didn't know how far away the train was. It could be anything from minutes to seconds. 'Theo, I'm begging you!' he shouted. 'Come over here now, before it's too late!'

Theodor neither replied nor turned around. Instead, he just sat there, peering down into the mist, retreating further and further into himself.

Whether it was panic or a stubborn refusal to admit Greta was right in her prediction, it didn't matter. He had no choice. He couldn't just stand there and watch his son let go.

Climbing the fence wasn't too hard, though the outward angle was harder to negotiate than he'd thought.

'Theodor, please!' he called out as the rails stopped whispering and started screeching. 'This isn't what you want.' With one hand on the old wooden railing running outside the taller steel fence and one foot on the edge of the bridge, he cautiously placed his other foot as far out on the protruding metal wing as he could. 'You're not a quitter. You're a fighter. You hear me? A fucking fighter! You always have been.' He put as much of his weight on the outer foot as he dared. 'You're going to make it. I know you're going to make it!'

The creaking underneath him was drowned out by the howling rails. But he didn't need to hear it to know the metal wing was about to break under his weight.

'For fuck's sake, Theodor!' he bellowed, and his son finally turned around and held out his hand.

The next moment, the train came and everything happened so fast that in hindsight, Fabian could only recall a few disjointed flashes. Like that the train thundering past below never seemed to end. Or that the metal wing creaked again and suddenly tilted so severely Theodor had to hold on not to slide down it. That he screamed.

What, he would never remember. Just that he screamed out his terror and then felt Theodor's hand in his. He would never be able to explain how it got there, or how he managed to hold on to it even when the metal they were standing on disappeared. Nor would he be able to recount the sequence of events after that. All he knew was that eventually they were lying on the bridge with their arms around each other.

Too tired to speak.

To cry.

Think.

Maybe they fell asleep.

Maybe not.

80

FABIAN WAS SITTING IN the car with Theodor sleeping next to him when his phone shattered the silence, not for the first time but the third. Sonja again, of course. No wonder she was beside herself with worry. The problem was, he didn't know what to say to her. How he was ever going to be able to put what he and Theodor had just been through into words.

Maybe that was exactly what it was like for her with the events of a month ago. Maybe what her lover had put her through was beyond words, too. Regardless, he would never ask her about it again. Never ever.

But when his phone rang a fourth time, he had to pick up. 'Hi, Sonja,' he said softly, not to wake Theodor. 'I'm sorry I haven't called. But—'

'*Sonja?*' a woman on the other end cut in. '*Hmm... Beautiful name. Unfortunately, not mine.*'

'I'm sorry, who am I talking to?'

'*Sure, I could give you a name. I could give you several. Sadly, they won't be of any use since we weren't properly introduced when we met. But how about a clue? Hearts.*'

'Spades,' replied Fabian, who now recognized the voice of the woman from the swingers' club.

'*Nice one. Impressive, actually. Maybe you're not so dumb after all.*'

'I'm sorry, what do you want? It's half eleven at night and—'

'*Oh dearie me. I didn't realize you were in your jammies and off to dreamland. And there I was, thinking you lived a slightly more exciting life than that. Being an officer of the law and all.*'

'What's this about?'

'*Why don't we start by acknowledging that I've been a good citizen and asked around a bit on your behalf.*'

'Asked around about what?'

'*Maybe you're too tired and need your beauty sleep, I don't know. If not, you'd better mosey on over to Denmark, because rumour has it Columbus himself is planning to grace a private event in Snekkersten with his presence tonight.*'

81

The moment the door opened and Ingvar entered the bedroom, she closed her eyes. Until that point, she'd been lying on the outermost edge of the mattress, trying to sleep.

She'd grabbed one of the towels she kept in a box under the bed for when Ingvar wanted to have relations, folded it double and placed it over the clock radio to keep its blue digits from illuminating the room. She didn't need to see the time to know she'd lain awake for hours.

It had been over twenty-four hours since she'd spoken to Ingvar, and it had been the worst twenty-four hours of her life. Not even losing her father in that tragic accident at the summer house had made her feel this bad.

Suddenly, one puzzle piece after another had fallen into place. All the late nights he'd been gone and blamed work, even though there was no ongoing investigation. His yo-yoing mood. His fits of fury. Not to mention Hugo Elvin and all the intrusive and insinuating questions he'd asked whenever he got the chance. Questions she now acknowledged hadn't been the unfortunate by-products of too much alcohol.

She hadn't got food poisoning from that classic Berlin café. Ingvar had drugged her. Then he'd sedated her in their hotel room. Her own husband. She couldn't believe it, but it was the only logical explanation. It was the alibi he'd been after, not celebrating their anniversary. The same alibi his colleague Fabian had come around asking about in his investigation into the murder of Reidar's wife, Inga. An investigation that had been reopened without her husband's knowledge.

The whole thing had thrown open the door to a darkness so abysmally deep, she'd lingered in the kitchen, drawing out the cleaning process, for over an hour. That was where she usually felt safe. In the kitchen. It was her domain, unlike the bedroom, which for some reason had always belonged to him. Even though she was the one who spent the most time in it, reading and listening to the radio.

When Ingvar stepped over the bedroom threshold, she always hoped she'd be asleep enough for him to leave her alone. He mostly did, and over the years, she'd become better at pretending. But this time, it felt impossible to relax into that calm breathing, even though she was bone-weary after two sleepless nights.

She'd spent the day cleaning the house from top to bottom, even though it had only been three days since she last went over it. She'd washed and ironed the curtains in the living room, dusted her collection of crystal owls and reorganized the kitchen. It had been one pointless activity after another in a desperate bid to come up with a plan of action. Should she contact the police and have him arrested, or should she simply leave him and try to get as far away as possible?

The thing was, she had no idea what the police would do when they found she had no concrete proof, or where she could run without him finding her. As that dawned on her, fear had taken over. Fear of what he would do to her when he realized she knew. So she'd stood there, feather duster in hand, her pulse rattling like automatic rifle fire.

It hadn't slowed down yet. Was that why he was moving over towards her side and was starting to pull on the duvet she'd wrapped around her precisely so he couldn't get at her? Could he sense her galloping pulse?

'Hello? Are you awake?' He leaned in so close she could tell from the foetid smell of his breath he'd flossed his teeth, in itself a clear sign of what he was after.

She wanted to burst into tears and scream. But she couldn't. Not now. It would have to wait. Until this was over. The problem was, it would never be over. Whatever happened, no matter how things turned out, it was something she would have to live with for the rest of her life. Divorce, life-time imprisonment, name change. Nothing would turn back time.

'Gertie… Daddy's here.'

No matter how badly she wanted to, there was no way back to a time where she could walk around with a smile, pretending to be ignorant and claiming everything was coming up roses. Knowledge had opened up a chasm under her feet and since then, she'd kept on falling.

The thought of what he'd done to Inga Dahlberg filled her with absolute terror. Something that horrifying was unimaginable. And how long had this been going on? What kind of monster was it she'd shared her life with for almost forty years, who was now rubbing the tip of his nose against her right cheek?

'Gertie,' he whispered in her ear. 'Hello… are you there?'

She'd known for a long time that Ingvar was out of the ordinary. Ever since he'd asked her to his house on New Year's Eve and cooked lobster. He'd tried to impress her by placing the live lobsters upside-down, standing on their heads and claws, and pressing down with his finger on some point on their necks, claiming it hypnotized them. They had stood there in a row, motionless, until he plunged them, one after the other, into the boiling water.

She'd felt it was sheer cruelty, but he'd laughed and said it was a good thing she hadn't been with him in China when he tried Yin Yang Fish. A fried fish that, with the help of ice and a cold wet towel around its head, was kept alive during the cooking and served that way. One of the most delicious things he'd ever eaten, he'd said.

'Hello? Gertie?' he purred, and he sent one hand exploring down along her hip. 'You can't fool me. I can see you're awake.'

82

The surreal feeling was amplified by the banks of mist wafting in across the dark and deceptively placid waters of Öresund on Fabian's left and rows of opulent luxury villas striving to outshine each other on his right. As though it wasn't him behind the wheel, driving south along Strandvejen on the Danish Riviera.

But it was. Even though it had only been hours since he'd saved his son from jumping to his death, he was now on his way to some private party Columbus was rumoured to be attending.

Rumoured to be...

Apparently, that was all it took to make him feel like he had no choice and that everything hinged on him seizing the opportunity that had just revealed itself. It was as though nothing was up to him, just an accumulation of circumstances. As though there was, in fact, something to Matilda's assertion that everything was predestined.

In an attempt to clear his head, he rolled down his window; he was breathing in the cool night air when Tuvesson called.

'*Hi, how are you getting on?*'

'Okay. I think I'm here now,' he said as he passed an imposing white house with tall mullioned windows, arches and terraces and two guards at the bottom of the driveway. 'And you? Have you reached Sleizner yet?'

'That's actually why I'm calling. Surprisingly, he picked up on the first try. And believe it or not, he was pleasant and helpful to boot.'

'I suppose he doesn't want to make the same mistake as last time you were trying to reach him.' Fabian turned into a customer car park outside a closed supermarket and parked.

'Maybe. Either way, he's dispatching ten officers who should be there within half an hour.'

'Ten?'

'Yep, and if you need more, just call.'

'We run the risk of spooking him off if it's too many. That's the last thing we want.'

'Don't worry. They're going to keep their distance until you give the signal,' Tuvesson said, then she wished him luck and ended the call.

Just over three hours had passed since the woman from Club Spades had called to inform him about the party Columbus was allegedly attending. Granted, it was only a rumour, which was why the plan was to get in and verify it before calling in Sleizner and his SWAT team.

Once Theodor had finally woken up, they'd driven back home to Matilda and Sonja, who to Fabian's surprise hadn't asked a single question, just hugged them and told them she had tea with honey waiting.

After two large mugs, Theodor had started talking, trying to put into words how things had been for him. How the idea of taking his own life had been there on and off over the past few years but more so recently, growing stronger until everything felt completely meaningless. Like an endless uphill slog until it was finally over.

He'd explained how he'd sat there, on the edge, waiting

for the train to come, with nothing to lose. That it had all been about letting go at the right moment to make sure he didn't miss. But when his father – yes, he had in fact called him father – had come to save him, risking his own life in the process, everything had changed. Suddenly, he'd had everything to lose.

Sonja hadn't said a word the whole time, just nodded agreement from time to time and squeezed his and Theodor's hands harder and harder.

They were finally beginning to find their way back, Fabian thought as he got out of the car and doubled back on foot through the trees behind the houses. He could physically feel that recent events marked the start of something new. Something that, if all went well, might actually be really good.

The back of the garden consisted of a big lawn patrolled by a third security guard, who was scanning the area as though he were guarding an embassy. The luxury cars parked in a row along one side of the lawn were his in. Crouching behind them, he could get almost the whole way to the back of the house, where a short flight of steps led up to a door.

What remained was about thirty feet during which he'd have no semblance of cover. He looked over at the security guard, who was now standing still in the middle of the lawn. A flame sparked to life in the dark and was followed by a red dot, indicating that the man had stopped to light a cigarette.

The moment the glow of the cigarette disappeared, Fabian left his hiding place behind a Jaguar and dashed across the grass, praying the guard would keep his back turned long enough for him to reach the steps and the door at the top of them.

He did. Unfortunately, the door was locked, and he didn't even have time to get his lock pick out before the motion detector and the spotlight above the door bathed him in light.

'Hey! You!' the security guard shouted. Fabian could almost hear him putting out his cigarette and hurrying towards him across the lawn.

Options flickered through Fabian's mind like a spinning wheel of fortune, which eventually stopped on an attempt to try to reach the half-circle terrace above him. Without any idea what awaited him, he threw himself at the drainpipe.

'What the fuck. Hey!'

The metal had sharp edges and was practically impossible to hold on to, slippery as it was from the damp night air. But it didn't take Fabian long to get high enough to heave himself over the wooden railing and on to the damp terrace floor.

He could hear the security guard calling his colleagues on his radio, but instead of pausing to try to decipher his Danish, he crawled past some reclining chairs and over to the terrace door, which was ajar.

He entered a bedroom where a suggestive groove he recognized but couldn't place was streaming out of hidden speakers somewhere in the ceiling. Apart from that, the room was furnished with a sofa, a handful of armchairs and a dressing table, dominated by a large four-poster bed in the middle of the floor. It was impossible to say exactly how many people were in it. Fabian estimated about ten men and women, all naked and so entangled he couldn't tell which arms, legs, heads and genitals belonged to whom.

To avoid drawing unwanted attention, Fabian quickly pulled off his wet clothes and dumped them on the floor behind the sofa. Then he continued towards the bed where everyone was being sucked or penetrated, or climaxing. Like one great body that was too busy pleasuring itself to notice him.

Fabian, for his part, felt nothing. If anything, he was turned off by the moaning, sweaty bodies slapping against each other as though they were in the middle of a porno shoot where the cameras were off and the director had long since gone home.

He walked around the bed to study it from all angles, leaning in over the pile of naked skin, pierced genitals and spread legs. Once he was sure Eric Jacobsén wasn't there, he left the room.

In the hallway outside, the walls were lined with framed photographs of what looked like a completely normal Danish nuclear family with three blond children of different ages. Peder and Lykke Madsen were the names of the two adults residing at the address. Were they throwing the party or was Peder on a business trip somewhere sufficiently far away for Lykke to invite some friends over? And the children, where were they? Some posh boarding school on Jutland?

One of the doors opened and two women, whose slim bodies were out of proportion with their enormous breasts, came out together with a dark-skinned man, all three dripping from the shower he could still hear running.

Fabian entered the bathroom, made sure no one else was in there and grabbed a dressing gown he found folded on a shelf before pressing on.

A wide staircase led him down to a grand hall with built-in bookshelves overflowing with books. The hypnotic groove from the bedroom was playing here, too; his best guess was that it was something by The Future Sound of London. The lights were dimmed but bright enough to reveal that the room was filled with copulating silhouettes. In sofas and on chaises longues, on tables and chairs and the floor. Everywhere, people were fucking like there was no tomorrow, though some were also taking a break by the bar, sipping wine, making cocktails or just snorting a line or two.

He strolled around, trying to catch a glimpse of everyone without calling too much attention to himself. Jacobsén was nowhere to be found.

'What do we have here?' A woman came crawling towards him on the floor. Her curly red hair hung down over both her shoulders, making her vaguely reminiscent of a lion, prowling the savannah for its next prey.

'Hi. Look, sorry, I'm not interested.'

'Look alive, we have a Swede.' She smiled and dragged her tongue across his feet. 'Mm...'

'Excuse me, but I mean it.'

The woman got up and untied his dressing gown, which fell to the floor when she slipped it over his shoulders. 'Yes, I can see that. It really does look tired. So the question is what the two of you are doing here?'

'Columbus. He's apparently here. You haven't seen him, by any chance?'

'Maybe. Maybe not.' She got down on her knees, cupped her hand around his scrotum and started massaging it.

'Stop.' He pushed her hands away. 'Have you seen him and if so, where?'

'You don't ask for Columbus. He asks for you.'

Fabian was contemplating how to interpret her answer when he realized that, despite his resistance, she was about to close her lips around him. Not now, he thought, and was about to push her away when another woman came up behind him, grabbed his arms and started to kiss his neck. He'd never experienced anything like it. But not now, he couldn't. Not after everything that had happened. The moist mouth of the first one. The tongue of the other behind his ear. It didn't matter. That wasn't why he was there.

And yet, he was unable to resist and do what he ought to. Like a wretched animal, he was pulled ever further down towards his basest instincts and let go of one thought after another until none of them mattered any more.

Then he noticed the black downward arrow on the redhead's lower back. Suddenly, it was just there and just as suddenly, she stood up, wrapped his robe around her and left him standing there, blood pumping as though his body was refusing to accept that it was over.

He freed himself from the woman who stood pressed against his back and followed the redhead, who disappeared with a man through a door painted the same dark green as the wall. The door opened into a long corridor and he had to dash to reach the door at the far end before it closed completely behind them.

After hanging back for a minute, he pushed it open and continued down a flight of steps that led to a room with a tiled floor and a number of other doors, one of which was closing.

If not for the distinctive buzzing sound, he wouldn't have understood what he was looking at in the adjacent room as the crack in the door in front of him grew ever narrower. But the sound left him in no doubt. Inside, in what looked like a spa, Eric Jacobsén was leaning over a woman, halfway through tattooing his personal brand between her spread legs.

He hurried up to the door and opened it, only to be greeted by the man he'd seen enter with the redhead.

'What are you doing here?' The man shut the door behind him. 'There's nothing for you here. You should head back upstairs.'

'My name's Fabian Risk and I work for the Swedish police in Helsingborg.'

'The police?'

'I'm here to arrest Eric Jacobsén, who is suspected of murder and quite a few other things.'

'There's no Jacobsén here.'

'There is, in fact. But he also goes by the name Columbus, which might ring more of a bell.'

'Now, listen to me. Unless you want me to throw you out, you'll turn around and—'

'Maybe you didn't understand me. I'm—'

'I understood just fine!' The man started ushering Fabian towards the stairs. 'But until you can show me ID, you're nothing but a stupid Swede who's going to leave here as quickly as possible.'

'For Pete's sake, are you slow or something?' Fabian said, deciding not to hurry upstairs to fetch his clothes and ID.

'I'm a police officer!' The risk of Jacobsén slipping away was too great. Instead, he shoved the man in the chest with both hands, pushing him back into the anteroom.

The man, who was completely unprepared, tried to resist but didn't get a chance because Fabian managed to grab his lapels and pull his jacket up over his shoulders and all the way down to his elbows. Then he kicked the man's legs out from under him. He collapsed on the floor, and Fabian put a knee in his back while he tied the sleeves of his jacket together.

The man was writhing around like a wounded snake when Fabian flung open the door to the spa, where Jacobsén was now about to straddle the red-headed woman who was reclining in the jacuzzi, caressing his erection.

'Hi, Eric. Remember me? Or do you prefer Columbus?' Fabian said on his way in, as the woman who had just been tattooed got up and left the room.

'What are you doing here?' Jacobsén said, while the redhead carried on as though nothing was happening.

'Maybe the name Molly Wessman rings a bell? Or how about Vera Brahe or any of the other women you've been spying on?'

Jacobsén grabbed the woman's titian locks roughly and pushed her away. 'I think you'd better leave now.'

'But we—'

'Another time. Come on. Off with you.'

The woman sighed, climbed out of the jacuzzi and walked unhurriedly towards the door without casting Fabian so much as a glance. The door closed behind her and at the same time a fist hit him so hard in the stomach the air was knocked out of his lungs and he doubled over in pain.

When he could breathe again, Jacobsén was already on his way out. 'Stop,' Fabian shouted, then, braced against the pain, he rushed after Jacobsén and shoved him forward hard enough to make him smack his face against the door.

It was far from an elegant strategy, but the crunching sound of Jacobsén's nose and the blood dripping down on the white tiled floor indicated it had at least been effective.

He had absolutely no experience of fighting, but he knew instinctively he couldn't just stand around and wait for Jacobsén to recover, so with pain searing his chest with every heartbeat, he hooked his arm around Jacobsén's neck and pulled him backwards into the room.

Jacobsén, who was surprisingly strong, fought back and managed to get in quite a few hits, despite the awkward angle. Fabian endured blow after blow to his head before managing to force his opponent down on to the floor.

But in the end, lactic acid overwhelmed him and when Jacobsén managed to wrap his legs around him and roll them both over, he was at an undeniable disadvantage. The blow to his temple a moment later made everything go dark, and when he snapped back in a few seconds later, he couldn't understand where he was, until he saw Jacobsén's broken nose about a foot above him, blood dripping from it on to the surface of the water.

He tried to get out of the jacuzzi, but the hand around his throat forced him further down. At that point, fear sank its claws into him for real. Soon, he would start to suck water into his lungs. Was Jacobsén going to kill him? Until then, Fabian hadn't even considered that. Running was one thing. But killing a police officer?

On the other hand, there were no witnesses, and probably enough drugs floating around to make it look like an overdose. Besides, Jacobsén was there under a false name and had quite possibly prepared an alibi. But it would never be enough. His colleagues in Helsingborg would see through it and arrest him the moment he set foot in Sweden.

The lack of oxygen was making his lungs burn, and for the first time in his life, he could feel himself contemplate just giving up. He probably would have, too, had it not been for the round metal disc he could feel against his fingertips on the edge of the jacuzzi.

A gentle push on the perforated circle was enough to start the massage jets, which turned the water frothy with air bubbles. Having nothing to lose, he opened his mouth and sucked the air in.

It worked, though he breathed in quite a bit of water too, which made him cough and suck in even more water. Then the hand around his throat suddenly let go and disappeared.

A second later, Fabian resurfaced and saw Jacobsén on the floor with two SWAT officers on top of him.

'Wow!' Kim Sleizner exclaimed as he entered the room. 'Wowee wow-wow-wow! I have to say, it's not every day you see two men having such a good time together. That's what I call true love.' Sleizner smiled broadly and held out a hand to help Fabian out of the jacuzzi. 'I apologize for not waiting for your signal. I'm only human, and who doesn't want to go to a party like this one?' He winked and threw him a dry robe.

83

THE WOODEN EXTERIOR HAD clearly not been looked after properly for years. The ends of the boards were dry as a bone and absorbed the petrol like sponges. The wood was dry again within a minute, which meant it took four five-litre cans to drench the façade on all four sides. But that wasn't the problem. There were three more in the car if need be.

What she was running out of was time.

Having studied the farm from afar for an hour and a half, she knew the recent fires had resulted in increased security. Partly in the shape of two dogs, which were running around loose, partly in the shape of one and sometimes up to three security guards, who did a lap around the building every fifteen to twenty minutes.

The dogs had been surprisingly easy to deal with. They'd happily scarfed down a piece of meat laced with Propavan each and wouldn't be waking up until the fire department was wrapping up the salvage and overhaul. The security guards were a different story. They could come out at any moment and realize something was wrong.

The orange flame of her lighter caressed the petrol-soaked wood. But for some reason, the wall was refusing to burn.

At least, not as quickly as you might imagine it would after being doused with all that petrol.

She could hear the security guards coming out now, calling the dogs in the night. How long it would take them to find the dogs – and, by extension, her – was impossible to say.

It took two full minutes for the fire to start to spread. Slowly at first, then faster and faster like a quiet fuse along the underside of the façade and then off around the corners.

As the flames climbed higher along the walls, the security guards started screaming at the people inside the building. Less than a minute later, the whole barn was ablaze and the panic inside was a fact.

Apart from a few scantily dressed women, most of the people dashing out of the building were long-haired men with beards, tattoos and frayed denim waistcoats. Some of them were drunk and staggered through. Others threw themselves on the ground and rolled back and forth to put out the fire on their clothes. They were all completely unprepared for gunfire.

Lilja fired one shot and then another. One bullet ripped open the leg of the big man with the Terminator tattoo. The other shattered the kneecap of the man behind him. Both fell to the ground, screaming in pain. She didn't lower her weapon and walk up to them until people had stopped emerging from the inferno.

'Fucking Jew cunt,' the tattooed man hissed. 'You're dead, get it. So fucking dead.'

Lilja walked up to him, squatted down and studied his bleeding leg in silence. The blood-soaked trousers, the smaller entry wound on the front of his thigh and the bigger on the back.

'You think you know what we do to little police cunts like you,' he continued. 'But you have no idea. No fucking idea.'

She held his gaze without a word and stood up, let her empty magazine fall to the ground and pushed another one in. Then she turned to the others. 'You know my name and you know where I live. Some of you have been there, riding your motorbikes around on my lawn, and some of you have broken into my house and spray-painted my walls while I was asleep. It stops now!'

'What makes you think it will ever stop, fucking Jew freak?' the tattooed man growled. 'Your hell hasn't even started.'

'I don't know if the rest of you heard, but your little Terminator friend over here had a question. He wondered why you should leave me alone. And that's a fair question, especially since I just burned down your little clubhouse. But I happen to be convinced you're the arsonists behind some of this year's fires at various refugee centres!'

'You can't prove that,' someone shouted.

'That's true. We've had so much on our plate, we simply haven't had the time to check if the tyre tracks match any of yours. But you know what? As far as I'm concerned, it doesn't matter whether they match or not. I actually don't give a shit, since whatever happens, I'm going to make sure they match! And if not that, then something else. A fingerprint in the wrong place, or maybe one of these?' She bent down and pulled out a few of the tattooed man's long hairs and held them up. 'I'm holding in my hand enough evidence to send you down ten times over! Any further questions on that?'

The sirens and flashing blue lights of the fire department, who had received an alarm from an anonymous caller twenty minutes earlier, were approaching. Lilja turned back to her car, climbed in behind the wheel and drove off down the tree-lined road with adrenaline pumping through her veins. At the same time, the video she'd emailed to every news desk in the country, showing Landertz doing a Nazi salute, was already well on its way to going viral.

84

'IT'S NO BOTHER.' KIM Sleizner beamed as though trying to outshine the rising sun, which had already magicked away the mist over the sound. 'We'll just keep him here until one of you people come to pick him up. Deal?'

Fabian nodded. 'Absolutely. Tuvesson tells me a transport is already on its way.'

'Well, that's great, just terrific!' Sleizner said in his best Swedish. 'You just take him back to Sweden and help us keep Denmark clean. You're happy, we're happy. Terrific!' Sleizner laughed and held out his hand.

Fabian allowed himself a smile and shook his hand. 'And once again, thanks for all your help. I honestly don't know what would have happened if you hadn't turned up.'

'Don't mention it.' Sleizner shrugged and spread his free hand while still pumping Fabian's with the other. 'We do what we can to help one another, don't we?'

Fabian nodded and tried to let go of Sleizner's hand, but Sleizner held on tight and kept shaking.

'It would probably work out either way, I reckon. What is it they say? Love and quarrel go hand in hand.' Sleizner chuckled and shook Fabian's hand as though he was never going to let go.

'All right, then, it's about time for me to be on my way,'

Fabian said in his best Danish. 'As you say, we want to keep Denmark clean.'

They both laughed stiffly.

'Hey, now that I think about it, there was one other thing.'

'Yes?'

'Dunja Hougaard.' Sleizner stopped shaking Fabian's hand but still wouldn't let him have it back.

'Yes?'

'I may be wrong about this, but I had the impression the two of you liked each other?'

'Yes.' Fabian nodded. 'Dunja was, if I'm being honest, the only one who helped us out from your side; she was pivotal to solving that case a few years ago. Also, she saved my son's life. So, yes, that's correct.'

'Good. I figured as much. And as I'm sure you understand, there's a reason things turned out the way they did back then. But, hey, water under the bridge. I help you and you help me, and at this moment, I need her new address and phone number. Not a big deal. Just her address and phone number. Then I'll let you be on your way.' Sleizner chuckled again and resumed his hand-shaking.

'I'm sorry.'

Sleizner stiffened. 'Excuse me? I'm not sure I follow.'

'I'm sorry, but I don't have that information.' Fabian pulled his hand out of Sleizner's grasp. 'So I'm afraid I can't help you.' He shrugged to underscore his words, but felt like it had the opposite effect to what he'd intended.

'So you're standing here, telling me that you haven't heard from Dunja in the past month?'

Fabian thought about the cryptic email informing him of Theodor's involvement with the Smiley Gang, and how it must have come from Dunja. But even though Sleizner had just helped him arrest Jacobsén, he was the last person in the world he would ever trust, so he decided to shake his head.

'I'm sorry. I didn't even know she'd moved and changed her number.'

Sleizner stared Fabian right in the eye. 'I don't know why, but something tells me that can't be right.'

'I'm sorry, Kim, but it is. And I really do have to go.'

'I'll be properly cross if it turns out you're lying to me. Especially after everything I've done for you.'

'Hold on a minute. Are you accusing me of lying?'

'Of course not. I'm not accusing anyone. I'm just saying I'd be very cross. And believe me. The last thing you want is to cross me.'

85

SOMEHOW, EVERYTHING SEEMED NEW and different when he pulled out the old marble icosahedron and warmed it in his hand. At first, he hadn't been sure he was even worthy to take it out. It wasn't at all a given, and the situation he was currently in had been impossible to foresee.

But as ever, he'd been able to ask one of his six-sided dice, and it had given him unambiguous permission to take out the twenty-sided one to see if there would be a new mission and if so, when.

He released the dice, letting it fall through the air and land on the green felt. But as though it were having a hard time deciding which of its many sides to land on, it kept rolling for an unusually long time.

Every time so far, he'd dreaded rolling a one. The only number that could stop his little pastime. But today, he felt differently. He'd decided he would accept the outcome if he rolled a one. It's not that he was sated, but he definitely wasn't as ravenous as he had been.

It had been an extraordinary journey, offering both peaks and troughs, disappointments and pure, unadulterated euphoria. From time to time, he'd thought the dice was dead wrong, that it expected too many things at once, that it had made things unnecessarily complicated or that it had been both mean and unfair. But in hindsight, he could see it had in fact outperformed his wildest expectations and been right every single time.

A seven.

He exhaled. That was practically as good as it could get. The fun wasn't over yet. And he had a week before he was supposed to strike again.

He took out the box with the six-sided precision dice, picked one and did a pre-throw to determine the number of dice.

A three.

That meant using one dice, so he picked it back up and rolled again.

A two.

He walked over to the pinned-up map that was divided into a grid of twelve by twelve squares. Column two was a special column, full of contradictions. It started in the north with the idyllic village of Arild in northern Skåne and ended in its complete opposite in the southern part of Copenhagen, also called Amager. If chance happened to be in the right mood, his victim or victims might even be found at Kastrup International Airport.

He did another pre-roll.

A four.

The number of squares down would consequently be decided by two dice; he picked up an additional one.

A one and a six.

As though his pulse had already figured it out, he could hear it pick up both speed and force as he turned his eyes to the map and noted that the area the dice had chosen for his next mission was in the middle of Öresund, just north of the island of Ven.

86

Fabian pushed his fingers in under the skin of the chicken and gently separated it from the breast to create a pocket into which he could pour a splash of olive oil and throw a pinch of sea salt and freshly ground black pepper, which he then rubbed into the meat. Then he stabbed the chicken with the tip of the knife in a few select places and pushed the peeled and halved garlic cloves into the cuts.

It was Sunday, and he'd decided to pull out all the stops and make a roast chicken from his own recipe, which he'd made a big deal of keeping secret all these years. It was his signature dish and, to his mind, no one came close to making a better chicken.

Four days had passed since Eric Jacobsén's arrest in a luxury villa on the Danish side of the sound. Fabian had spent most of that time at home with his family, though he had, admittedly, been unable to completely let go of the Molly Wessman investigation, which, if all went to plan, should be concluded in the coming week.

Jacobsén had unreservedly confessed that he was the man behind both Columbus and the secret surveillance in eighty-seven flats all over north-west Skåne. He'd explained his actions by saying one thing led to another. From his pathological porn consumption to his wish to watch in real life to finally graduating to active participation.

He firmly denied, however, any involvement in Molly Wessman's murder, and when the attempted murder of Fabian in the jacuzzi was mentioned, he dismissed it as an act of panic and claimed there had never been any intention of actually killing him. An explanation unlikely to hold up in court.

What's more, Molander and his two assistants were far from done with the investigation of Jacobsén's home, and they were all convinced that if they only looked hard enough, they were sure to find part of Wessman's shorn fringe, traces of ricin extract or some other incriminating detail.

The murder of Lennart Andersson, on the other hand, remained unsolved. None of the clues and samples collected from ICA Maxi in Hyllinge had led anywhere, and the only person they'd managed to identify through fingerprinting was, ironically enough, Jacobsén, who'd taken his son shopping there the day before the murder.

Their hopes now rested with Klippan, who was busy combing through the CCTV footage from the week leading up to the murder and who had announced he was going to give a presentation at their next morning meeting.

With a bit of luck, they may be close to solving that, too. Either way, the doomsday headlines had been replaced with considerably more hopeful ones about how the residents of Helsingborg could finally feel safe again. They'd even been given personal praise, both from the National Police Commissioner and the Minister of Justice, for the intensive work that had led to the arrests of Jacobsén and Skanås.

Fabian was not at all prepared for the music that suddenly started blasting out of the speakers; even though he recognized the strings, the melody and the maracas in the background, he couldn't place it. He turned around to see Sonja enter from the living room.

'Remember this?' she said with a smile, and he nodded, even though he still didn't have the foggiest.

'It's Prefab Sprout's "Hey Manhattan", silly.' She poured two glasses of wine and sang along. 'Don't you remember how you always used to put this album on whenever I was feeling blue?'

Fabian nodded. He did remember now. The album was called *From Langley Park to Memphis*, and he'd found it a bit too poppy for his tastes when it first came out. But Sonja had loved it, and it had put her in a good mood whenever he played it. And in hindsight, he had to admit there wasn't a single bad track on it.

But that wasn't what he was thinking about now; he was wondering at the fact that it was the first time in years Sonja had turned on any music at all. Normally, he was the one who turned it on and she was the one who asked him to turn it down or, even better, turn it off altogether. Now, she'd turned it up to a pretty decent volume. When she also handed him a glass and raised her own in a toast, he felt the evening couldn't have started better.

Only a few days had passed since he'd saved Theodor from taking his own life, but the events above the tracks in Pålsjö Forest were already beginning to feel like an increasingly hazy memory from a different lifetime. It was as though they'd hit rock bottom and turned and were now finally starting to find their way back to some kind of peace and harmony.

They'd cooked together every night, played board games, watched films or just spent time together. Sonja had also found a therapist she wanted Theodor to meet the following week, even though he already looked like he was feeling much better.

Granted, he still spent large parts of every day in his room. But at least he'd given it a thorough clean and he'd gone back to reading books instead of just playing computer games. And right in the middle of dinner on Midsummer's Eve, he'd told them he was following the reporting on the trial of the four members of the Smiley Gang and had decided to head over to Helsingør after the weekend and tell the Danish prosecutor the truth.

Neither he nor Sonja had mentioned it. The decision had been entirely Theodor's own, and even though no one could say for sure what lay ahead, he seemed to have acknowledged that he had no other options.

'How about a music quiz tonight after the children go to bed?' Sonja smiled and walked towards him, glass in hand.

'You don't stand a chance.' He bent down towards her.

'Blimey, is this a bad time? We were wondering if you needed help with anything?'

They turned to Matilda, who had just come down from upstairs with Theodor.

'Of course it's not a bad time. Why would it be a bad time?' Sonja shrugged.

'Why's Dad's face all red?' Theodor said, making everyone burst into laughter.

'All right, I confess.' Fabian put his wineglass down. 'I was just about to kiss your beautiful mother, so your timing actually couldn't have been much worse. But since you're here now, there's potatoes to rinse and carrots and beetroot to peel. Have at it. I was going to make a salad.'

Theodor and Matilda nodded and went over to the fridge.

'Great, then I'll lay the table.' Sonja got out plates and cutlery, and within minutes, everyone was working away.

'Hey, are we doing something for the summer holiday?'

It was Matilda who had broached the subject, and when Fabian met Sonja's eyes, he could tell she was as dumbfounded as he was. They'd been in shut-down mode; neither one of them had had the energy to reflect on the fact that they were now in the middle of the summer holidays.

'I suppose we've given it some thought,' he said.

'We have?'

'Apparently not,' Theodor said, mixing chunks of beetroot in with the other root vegetables in an ovenproof dish.

'Esmaralda's parents have a boat. We should get one. It seems super cosy.'

'Boat?' For the first time in several days, Fabian thought about the two boat keys that had had him convinced Hugo Elvin owned a boat.

He wasn't so sure now. He had not only contacted the North Harbour in Helsingborg, which was the most logical marina for someone at Elvin's address, he'd also checked with all the other marinas along the coast, both north and south of Helsingborg, without finding anything under Elvin's or Molander's names.

'My family had a boat when I was a child,' Sonja said. 'Do you know how much work it is? We did nothing all autumn and spring but scrape and sand until we had frostbite on our hands.'

'But wasn't that, like, an old wooden thing?' Theodor said. 'We could buy a plastic boat.'

'Old wooden thing. Bite your tongue. That's my whole childhood you're insulting.'

On the other hand, there was nothing to say that Elvin, or Molander for that matter, had necessarily kept a boat under their own name. They might just as easily have borrowed it from someone else, which was why he'd spent a large part of that Thursday looking around the North Harbour.

'And just so you know, a fibreglass boat is a lot of work, too,' Sonja continued.

He'd found, among other things, three old Pettersson boats, any one of which could have belonged to Elvin. Sadly, neither of the keys were a fit. In them or any of the other boats he'd tested.

'You have to paint them and wax them and what not.' Sonja shook her head and put out napkins and cutlery.

He'd even tried punching in the four-number code from the larger of the keys as a passcode to the marina's boathouse, but had been rewarded with nothing but an angry red diode.

'But we can help.' Matilda turned to Theodor. 'We'd help, right?'

'Of course,' Theodor said with a nod.

'That's very sweet of you. But either way, it takes half a lifetime to get dock space at the marina. I remember, we had slip fifty-two and my dad was on the waiting list for the one next to ours, which was a few feet wider. But we never got it.'

How could he not have thought of that? Of course that was what the numbers 0388 on the key meant. It wasn't a passcode like he'd thought, it was a slip number, and given that there were four digits, it should be in one of the larger marinas, with more than a thousand slips.

'Fabian, would you mind backing me up here?' Sonja turned to him.

'Um, I'm sorry... But isn't Råå Marina pretty big? It is, right?'

'What's that supposed to mean?' Sonja looked from Fabian to the children, who looked no less surprised than she did, and back.

'Wow, Theo, hear that?' Matilda hugged her brother. 'He's on our side.'

If Elvin had had access to a boat, of course it would have been docked at Råå.

87

IRENE LILJA CARRIED THE last bin bag of clothes out of the bedroom and closed the door behind her. She'd been packing more or less all weekend. Box after box, of which at least half were going straight to the landfill. But it was worth it. She wasn't going to leave so much as a hairclip behind. When she was done, there'd be no sign she'd ever even set foot there.

As expected, Hampus had trailed her like a grovelling dog, tying himself in knots trying to make her change her mind. He'd tried everything from flowers every Friday to a trip to the Galapagos Islands. He'd even offered going to therapy and letting her choose which party he voted for in the next election.

But unlike all the previous times, she'd stood firm and ignored him. As expected, it hadn't taken him long to transition from anxiety to anger channelled into threats about how she'd never be free of him and how it made no difference that she refused to tell him where she was moving since he was going to find her anyway.

That was exactly why she'd told him she was moving out on Monday instead of right now when he was at Ring Knutstorp, drinking beer and watching cars drive round and round a bumpy track, adding to climate change.

The only question was when he was going to be home.

Any other Ring Knutstorp Sunday, he would have rushed out in the morning and not been back until dinner. Today, the opposite had been true. He'd dawdled, saying he wasn't feeling well, and almost cancelled even though he'd already paid for his ticket. He was clearly on to the fact that she was up to something, which was why she'd left the house before lunch, saying she had to wrap up the Moonif Ganem investigation.

In reality, Assar Skanås was still in intensive care with his gunshot wounds and couldn't be interviewed yet. Which wasn't much of an issue since Molander had found his fingerprints on the glass door of the washing machine, which meant the interviews, whenever they took place, would be more or less pro forma.

Anyway, Hampus could be home any minute, so she had to get out of the house and on her way to—

The hand on her shoulder made her stop dead.

'So this is where you're hiding out.'

The voice didn't match the person she'd assumed it belonged to; even though it only took her a fraction of a second, it felt like an eternity before she put it together.

'God, you scared me.' She turned to Klippan.

'I'm sorry, the door was open, so I—'

'Don't worry about it. Did you bring the trailer?'

'And my neighbour's van.'

'Perfect. You know, I just want to get out of here as quickly as possible.'

'Then we'd better get cracking. I suggest we start with the big stuff: sofas, beds, cabinets and so on. Unless you mind me being in charge of the loading, that is.'

Lilja laughed and shook her head. 'I trust you implicitly.'

'Great, *now* you tell me. Let's see how you feel about it when we're done. Let's start with the bed.' He turned to the bedroom door and was just about to open it when Lilja hurried over and blocked his way.

'Look, I was actually going to leave it. New life, new bed.'

'All right, any other cumbersome items in the bedroom that are coming with us? Wardrobe or chest of drawers?'

'No.' Lilja shook her head. 'Nothing. So there's no point going in.'

Klippan nodded, but seemed puzzled. 'All righty, then. Let's grab that sofa.'

Together, they carried the sofa through the hallway, out into the front garden and towards the driveway where Klippan had already unlatched the trailer so they could walk straight into the van.

'What happened to your lawn?' Klippan said as they walked back to the house. 'It looks awful.'

'Don't ask me. Hampus has some project to get rid of the moss. Come on, let's keep going.'

But Klippan stayed where he was, gazing out across the ruined lawn.

'Klippan, we don't have all day.' She'd managed to prevent him from entering the bedroom, but all she could do out here was hope he wouldn't notice the swastika behind the reclining chairs and wheelbarrow she'd brought out and strategically arranged to hide it. 'Please, Hampus could be back any minute.'

'I don't see any moss.'

'Right, I think it was dandelions, now you mention it.'

'I don't see any dandelions either.'

'Well, no, he got rid of them.' She sighed, hoping it was loud enough for Klippan to hear. 'That was the whole point. What does it have to do with my moving, anyway?'

Klippan turned around and looked her in the eyes. 'Irene. How are you really doing?'

'And what's that supposed to mean? Seriously, what's this in aid of?' She didn't have it in her. There was no time for this right now. 'Can't we just get the stuff out and—'

'You're not yourself,' Klippan cut in. 'You've been withdrawn and weird all week, and in the meetings you've stared at your phone the whole time. What's the matter?'

'Nothing's the matter! I have no earthly idea what you're talking about. Did you come here to help me carry things or to play therapist?'

'I came to help you, which is why I'm asking you what's wrong. I'm not allowed to go into your bedroom. Hampus can't even know you're moving out today, and now this.' Klippan walked towards the chairs. 'Whatever this is, it has nothing to do with moss or dandelions.'

'He hit me. Hampus hit me. Happy now?'

'What? What are you talking about?' Klippan stopped and turned to her. 'Are you serious? Hampus?'

Lilja nodded and wiped some of the make-up off her cheek. Klippan walked up to her and inspected the big bruise, which had turned every colour of the rainbow.

'Jesus Christ…' He hugged her. 'Aren't you going to report him?'

Lilja shook her head.

'Okay.' Klippan nodded as though to persuade himself. 'I assume you've thought it through. I guess we'd better get started before that prick comes back.' He turned around and started walking towards the house. 'Right, I keep forgetting to ask. Where are you moving to?'

'To a flat on Carl Krooks Gata in town. I came across it when I was looking for Assar Skanås. By the way, you wouldn't happen to know who P. Milwokh is, would you?'

'Milwokh?' Klippan stopped and turned to Lilja.

'Yes, my flat's right next door.'

'Did you say Milwokh?'

'Yes. Didn't I tell you I was ringing his door and he refused to open it?'

Klippan shook his head. 'Not that I recall.'

'Well, do you know who it is?'

Klippan pondered that. 'No. I thought the name sounded familiar for a second, but I probably just imagined it.'

88

Fabian turned off Västindiegatan and parked his car behind the Sailing Association's clubhouse in the Råå Marina. The summer night was dark and it had started to rain, just like on Midsummer's Eve. Tiny, wet droplets that never seemed to let up.

But despite the lousy weather, Fabian's heart was light when he opened his umbrella, locked the car and walked across the open, deserted car park in the direction of the dock with its row of pontoons, along which hundreds upon hundreds of boats jostled for space. The afternoon had been an unqualified success and when later in the evening he'd told Sonja he had to go, she'd promised to keep the bed warm until he returned.

When he reached the edge of the dock, he stopped and looked out across the marina, which though it was peak season had a kind of peacefulness to it, as though it were hibernating. There wasn't a soul in sight. Part of the explanation was, of course, that it was the middle of the night. Also, the weather was so bad all vacationing boat owners were probably huddled in double sleeping bags, shivering to stay warm.

It may have looked peaceful, but it was not quiet. On the contrary, there was a minor cacophony of noise: the whistling of the wind through shrouds and stays, halyards beating against masts and the lapping of the waves. Not to mention all the thousands of fenders being squeezed between the tightly packed hulls.

He pulled out the two blue keys he'd found in Elvin's drawer and checked the handwritten digits 0388 one last time.

He was sure they were boat keys; if the number did in fact designate a particular slip, the boat must be docked in a big marina, and Råå was the biggest by far near Helsingborg.

Luckily, Fabian didn't have to go out and check each of the approximately five-hundred-feet-long pontoons, because they were all labelled with exactly the information he needed.

The sign on the first one said *0087–0236*. He moved on to the next one, home to slips *0237–0402*, and continued out on to the long concrete jetty lined on either side with moored motor- and sailboats, both large and small. Most were facing the jetty, dark and abandoned by an unseasonably chilly summer. But here and there, an inviting glow could be seen through a window; a closer look revealed people inside, drinking wine and playing Yahtzee or watching films snuggled up in bed.

Further out on the pontoon, he passed a large Hallberg-Rassy, moored stern-to. It was a real beauty with a teak deck, aft cabin and a large, inviting cockpit with a table in the middle. The sturdy mast was so tall, it came equipped with double spreaders. Here too, the windows along the hull were bright, spreading a warm light across the water; Fabian had to admit there was something attractive about the whole picture.

The cabin hatch was opened by a man his own age, who climbed into the cockpit carrying a bottle of wine and two glasses, which he placed on the table under the canopy roof. He was followed by a woman of the same age, who was holding a lit hurricane lantern in one hand and a small speaker playing smoky old jazz in the other.

Maybe Matilda and Theodor were right. Maybe this was the thing for them. A sailboat. A shared project to help them find peace and harmony among the myriad cosy harbours of Öresund.

'Excuse me, did you want something or were you just looking?'

Fabian snapped out of his reverie and turned to the man in the cockpit. 'I'm sorry, I was actually on my way to my own boat. But I just had to stop and admire your beauty. She must be incredible on the open sea.'

'Sure, she can handle just about anything, though so far we've had nothing but smooth sailing all the way from Kalmar.'

'May I ask where you're headed?'

'Next stop is Humlebæk, straight shot across the sound to the Danish side. As soon as the weather improves, that is. Then a night leg to Göteborg; after that, all we know is we're sailing around the world,' the man said with a smile, as a boy of about ten stuck his head out of the cabin. 'We sold our house and took two years' leave from work. For starters – we'll see if we ever go back.' The man laughed and filled the wineglasses.

'Vincent, I thought you were asleep,' the woman said, hugging the boy.

'I want to sleep with you tonight.'

'But why, when you have your own room and everything?'

'What if there's a monster? I'd be all alone in the back.'

'Vincent, there's no such thing as monsters, you know that.'

'Yeah, but still. Please…'

'Of course you can, sweetheart. Right, Frank?'

'I thought we'd talked about this. But all right, on one condition. That you and I check to make sure there are no monsters in the aft cabin before we hit the hay. And I'm talking a thorough search.'

The woman let out a laugh and winked at her husband before walking their son back down into the boat.

'So, what kind of boat do you have?'

'Um, it's just down here, slip 388, and it really doesn't hold a candle to—'

'388?' the man broke in, frowning. 'But that's right here.'

He nodded to the slip next to his, which was empty.

Fabian went over and confirmed the small sign said *0388*.

So the slip was unoccupied. In fact, it was the only vacant slip on either side of the pontoon.

'I'm sorry, but this is our fourth day here, and it's been empty the whole time,' the man continued.

Had he got it wrong? Was it a different marina, or was the number something other than a slip? Had Molander already been here, covering his tracks?

'That's just bloody outrageous. Nothing's safe any more.'

'Good luck on your trip.' Fabian turned back towards the dock.

'I hope you have good insurance,' the man called out after him.

Back on dry land, Fabian gazed out across the deserted marina again, but saw nothing but cars parked neatly in the dedicated parking bays. He hurried over to the northern end, which opened on to the harbour inlet proper.

Immediately to his right was a gravel area full of empty cradles. But not a single boat. He did spot one, however, on the other side of the river, next to the old harbour museum. He couldn't be sure, of course, but it definitely was a weather-beaten old Pettersson boat in a cradle, and if there was one kind of boat he could imagine Elvin owning, it was an old wooden one.

Ten minutes later, he'd driven all the way around via Kattegattsgatan and Rååvägen and parked on the other side of the river next to the boat, which, for obvious reasons, assuming it was Elvin's, hadn't been launched this year.

An electric cable dangled down the side of the hull and continued in behind the museum building; all that remained of the protective tarpaulin was a few tattered patches, flapping in the wind. Underneath the cradle, Fabian found a ladder, which he leaned against the boat's transom.

Once he reached the cockpit, which contained a fair amount of sand and seaweed, he pulled out the key again and pushed it into the lock. It got stuck halfway, but he'd thought ahead and brought lubricant; a couple of attempts later, he was able to unlock and open the hatch.

The sight that greeted him was exactly what he'd hoped for. The narrow cabin, where you had to stoop not to hit your head on the ceiling, reminded him of his own study in the basement.

There wasn't just a computer, there was also a number of external hard drives, marked either *Molander's PC – Home* or *Molander's PC – Work*, followed by a date. The obligatory whiteboard was filled with Elvin's notes and ideas and pictures he hadn't seen before. In fact, it looked like enough material to keep him busy for days, if not weeks.

The contents of Elvin's desk drawer were clearly just the tip of the iceberg. This had been Elvin's real office. This was where he'd been able to work undisturbed, safely away from Molander.

He flicked a switch on the wall to the right of the hatch, and several small lights around the cabin came on. He spotted a folder marked *Berlin* in a small bookcase.

He opened it; the first thing he saw was a copy of the framed photograph from the traditional Berlin café, showing Gertrud and Molander sitting together with two cups of coffee and a half-eaten strudel on the table in front of them. The date stamp at the bottom was circled in red, but the wristwatch of the man at the next table wasn't, which indicated Elvin hadn't discovered the twelve-and-a-half-hour time lapse.

He did, however, have a printout of the two boarding passes. They had likely been digitally downloaded to Molander's home computer and been part of the contents Elvin had copied to his external hard drive.

SAS Boarding Pass
Mr Ingvar Molander – Fast Track Available
Flight Date Time From To Seat Boarding
SK1673 24 Aug 13:30 Berlin Copenhagen 14F 13:10
2007 TXL CPH

easyJet Boarding Pass
Mr Ingvar Molander
Flight Date Time From To Seat Boarding

EZY8627 24 Aug 19:05 Copenhagen Berlin Free seating 18:45 2007 CPH TXL

It was the puzzle piece he'd been looking for. It was all he needed to break Molander's alibi. That must have been what Molander had realized. It must have been why he killed Elvin. Finally, he had enough to inform Tuvesson.

Fabian pulled out his phone to call her. It rang and rang and rang again before he was redirected to her voicemail. Instead of leaving a message, he hung up and called back. It was late and hardly surprising if she was asleep. But this couldn't wait, so he called a third time.

'*Yes, hello?*'

'Hi, Astrid, it's—'

'*Hello! Who is this?*' she slurred.

'Hi, it's Fabian. I'm sorry to be calling so late.'

'*I said who the fuck is this?*'

'It's Fabian. Fabian Risk.'

'*Risk? Bloody hell, why can't you ever leave me alone? What the fuck do you want now, you goddamn—*'

'Nothing, I accidentally dialled the wrong number. I'm sorry. See you tomorrow.' He ended the call and could only remark to himself it was lucky he hadn't confided in her sooner. This might be her first relapse. But there would be more, many more.

He folded up the printout of the boarding passes, slipped it into his inside pocket and started poking around. He flipped through a stack of pictures he hadn't seen before, and looked through a shoebox containing a number of crystal owls like the ones Gertrud collected and a precision drill with a number of different sander attachments and drill bits.

He picked up one of the owls and realized it wasn't glass at all but plastic, with a round, flat battery in the base. He tried to find an explanation but was forced to give up.

Instead, he sat down in front of the computer and turned it on. It didn't ask for a password. Elvin had obviously felt certain Molander would never find this place.

There was a programme open on the screen, which reminded Fabian of the sound-processing software Molander used. There were various rectangles with sound waves on a timeline; he clicked on one of them.

Monotone noise streamed out of the computer's speakers; it took him a while to identify it as the sound of a vacuum cleaner. But why record a vacuum cleaner? The most recent recording was from Tuesday 19 June at 11.26 a.m. Which meant Elvin hadn't recorded it himself; it had to be automated.

It looked like there were two recordings from the day before. One at some point in the morning and the other later that night. It was only when he checked the exact time stamp in the top left corner of the rectangle that he realized it was the same time he'd paid a visit to Gertrud.

He clicked it and heard his own voice.

'*This won't take long.*'

'*Isn't he a sweetheart?*'

'*I'm sorry, who?*'

'*Reidar, who else? The man you were talking to yesterday. Water?*'

'*No, thank you, I'm good.*'

Had Elvin installed a hidden microphone in one of the owls? Was that why he had a collection here?

It was far too technical for Fabian to understand exactly

how it worked. That should have been true of Elvin as well. He was, if anything, even worse at technology than Fabian. The only explanation was that he'd somehow used Molander's know-how against him.

He clicked the second recording from the same day, and got Molander's voice.

'*Fondue. Can't remember the last time we had that. What are we celebrating?*'

'*Nothing at all.*' Gertrud could be heard replying. '*No need to panic.*'

'*That's a relief. I was worried there for a second. I thought I'd forgotten our anniversary or something.*'

'*No, I was just cleaning the kitchen cupboards and I found our—*'

Suddenly, the playback stopped and the time marker, which had turned red, jumped to the present.

Fabian was instinctively reaching for the mouse to move the marker back to the conversation he'd been listening to when he realized it was recording something new.

'*Hold on a minute. What did you talk about?*' Molander was saying. '*Gertrud, I said wait!*'

'*Ingvar, you're scaring me.*'

'*I want to know what you talked about!*'

'*I'm going to have to ask you to calm down.*'

'*I am calm! I just need to—*'

'*No, you're not! And besides, it's late. We'll have to discuss this some other time, because I'm going to bed in the guest room. And I would appreciate it if you would respect my privacy.*'

'*I'll give you all the privacy you want, as soon as you tell me what in God's name Fabian Risk was doing here!*'

ACKNOWLEDGEMENTS

Writing a book is like crossing an ocean. It's just you, the water and the horizon, no matter which way you look. Or at least, that is how it can feel sometimes. The truth is, without help and guidance, I would not have made it very far before the water inevitably entered my lungs and I sunk helplessly to the ocean floor.

My wife Mi has always been there, lifeboat in tow, to cheer me on, read drafts and give feedback – invaluable feedback that eventually helped me reach the shore and feel the ground beneath my feet again. Thank you.

My two eldest, Kasper and Filippa, have supported me when the waves seemed perilously high and the story was impossible to finish. Thank you for always listening and telling me exactly what I needed to hear.

My two youngest, Sander and Noomi. Thank you for existing and for reminding me that there are other things to live for besides work and the next book. Without you, I would be hopelessly old in every way.

My editor, Andreas. This is our fourth book together, and it becomes more enjoyable with every one. Without you I would never dare pursue what is interesting, rather than what is safe. Thank you for that and for access to your thoughts and ideas.

Julia, time flies and soon it will have been two years. I would never have reached the millionth reader in the thirty-something countries in which my books have been published if it hadn't been for you. Adam, Sara and Hannah at Forum. Concentrated excellence. Thank you for everything you do and more.

King of Sales. I cannot claim that these books would not exist without you, but they would never have reached such a wide audience as they do now. You have been there since my debut, *Victim Without a Face*, and made sure that my Sveavägen-based publishing house have given these books their all.

Lastly, I want to thank Johanna Björkman and Thomas Vedel Larsen for their expertise.